C000053535

THE LAST RESORT

T. J. EMERSON

Boldwood

First published in Great Britain in 2024 by Boldwood Books Ltd.

Copyright © T.J. Emerson, 2024

Cover Design by Head Design Ltd

Cover Photography: Shutterstock

The moral right of T.J. Emerson to be identified as the author of this work has been asserted in accordance with the Copyright, Designs and Patents Act 1988.

This book is a work of fiction and, except in the case of historical fact, any resemblance to actual persons, living or dead, is purely coincidental.

Every effort has been made to obtain the necessary permissions with reference to copyright material, both illustrative and quoted. We apologise for any omissions in this respect and will be pleased to make the appropriate acknowledgements in any future edition.

A CIP catalogue record for this book is available from the British Library.

Paperback ISBN 978-1-80549-032-6

Large Print ISBN 978-1-80549-028-9

Hardback ISBN 978-1-80549-027-2

Ebook ISBN 978-1-80549-025-8

Kindle ISBN 978-1-80549-026-5

Audio CD ISBN 978-1-80549-033-3

MP3 CD ISBN 978-1-80549-030-2

Digital audio download ISBN 978-1-80549-024-1

Boldwood Books Ltd
23 Bowerdean Street
London SW6 3TN
www.boldwoodbooks.com

PROLOGUE
CYPRUS

October 2008

The day Sofia will never forget is a beautiful autumn one. It is early afternoon, and she is sitting at the desk in her small bedroom looking out of the window, mesmerised by the gold and crimson leaves of the cedar trees and by the tall pines, evergreen. By the Troodos Mountains, their green summer pelts now russet brown.

Open on her desk is *Algebra for Beginners*. The tattered textbook, published in 1981, contains the exercises she is supposed to be doing for her maths homework. She closes it and opens *The Encyclopaedia of Greek Myths* instead. Charles, the benefactor of the Pure Heart community, gave her this book last week for her twelfth birthday. She is currently reading the chapter about the Underworld. A dark and scary land of the dead, where people seem to disappear and other people go and rescue them.

She glances at the door that connects her room to her mother's. This building was once a hotel and she and Eva have adjoining bedrooms. Eva is still asleep. On the days when her depression is at its worst, she can sleep all day. As if, Sofia thinks, Eva is lost in her own dark Underworld.

If only Sofia could rescue her. She is trying. Everyone at Pure Heart is trying, especially Quinn. When Sofia was younger, she thought Quinn was a witch. The potions, the chanting that sounded like magic spells, the black cat that followed her everywhere. Eva says Quinn is a powerful healer. Eva says only Quinn can cure her.

Sofia, who loves Quinn with all her heart, is sure this is true. Over the summer it seemed as though Quinn's magic was working. Her mother was happier. Less erratic than usual. Recently the deep depression has returned, and Sofia can't stop doubt creeping in. Doubt is bad. Quinn has told her many times that for a miracle to happen, everyone must believe in it.

The door between the adjoining rooms opens and Eva appears.

'You're up,' Sofia says.

Eva smiles. 'I am up.'

Her mother is awake and smiling and Sofia's heart floods with joy. Eva is wearing a long white dress with thin straps and gold Grecian sandals. She looks like one of the goddesses on the front of *The Encyclopaedia of Greek Myths.*

'You look beautiful.' Sofia wishes she looked like her mother, but while Eva is tall and blonde, Sofia is short for her age and plump. Her thick, dark hair reaches down to her shoulders. Her father, who died when she was two years old, was Italian so she probably inherited her colouring from him. She and Eva do share the same dark eyes, and Eva says she didn't grow tall until she was fourteen so there's still hope.

'*You* are beautiful.' Eva strolls over to the desk and kisses the top of Sofia's head. '*You*, Sofia Belova, are the most beautiful girl in the whole world.'

Eva doesn't speak Russian any more, but her English is still heavily accented and lends all her statements an air of conviction.

'I am going for a walk,' Eva says. 'Is good for me.'

'Shall I come?' Sofia asks, delighted her mother is having one of her good days and keen to enjoy it with her.

'No.' Eva ruffles her hair. 'You must do homework.'

'I am.'

'I think maybe you are reading your new book.'

'Charles says the classics are the only education a person needs.'

Eva laughs. 'Crazy man.'

Eva sits on Sofia's narrow bed and tightens the delicate straps of her sandals.

'We're having *moussaka* tonight,' Sofia says, knowing the dish is one of Eva's favourites. She hopes Eva will eat a proper meal. She is so thin these days. Bony and brittle. Surviving on tiny mouthfuls of food like a baby bird.

'It will be delicious,' Eva says.

'And the new people will be at dinner. You can meet them.' Sofia describes the three newcomers. Two Swedish women and a man from Wales. Pure Heart now has seventeen members. The most ever. Sofia is still the only child. She's always enjoyed being the centre of attention, but recently she's been longing for some friends her own age.

Eva stands up. 'I go now.'

'Shouldn't you put a coat or a jumper on?' Sofia asks. 'You'll be cold.'

'I will be fine.'

'Okay,' Sofia says, used to her mother's eccentric dress sense. 'See you later.'

Eva blows her a kiss. 'See you later.'

In the future, Sofia will replay this moment over and over. *See you later.* So casual, her mother's last words to her. No hint of what was coming. That kiss floating invisible towards her. How she will wish she could have caught it and put it in a jar and kept it forever.

PART I

PART I

1

HOLLY

2019

What happened at Pure Heart last year was a tragedy. I have yet to process it fully. I'm not sure I ever will. The terrible events that took place that night were sensationalised in newspapers and reported on television. The truth lost amidst clickbait headlines. Sometimes it's hard to remember exactly what occurred.

When I think about it now, I have to remind myself that we, the members of the Pure Heart community, believed in miracles. In the late 1990s, after the founding members met in Ibiza, we decided we wanted to make a life for ourselves outside of mainstream society, an alternative existence filled with peace, love and harmony. A new millennium was approaching and, ready to abandon Ibiza and its hedonism, we asked the universe to provide us with the perfect place to live out our dream.

At the start of that new millennium, we came to Cyprus, and the universe gave us exactly what we were looking for.

It's hard to describe the joy we felt when we first saw our new home. A former hotel on the northern foothills of the Troodos Mountains, surrounded by forests of cedar and pine. In the 1950s and 1960s, the hotel was popular with wealthy Cypriots and tourists seeking relief from the intense heat and humidity of the coast in summer. Business thrived for decades until the area fell out of fashion.

As well as respite from the fierce summers, the hotel also offered its guests privacy. A narrow, winding access road led from a slightly larger road that in turn led to the main road through the mountains. One way in, one way out.

The two-storey building had three connecting wings that enclosed a large courtyard. It gave the illusion of rustic simplicity – wooden roof, whitewashed stone walls, ceilings crossed with thick oak beams and wide flagstone corridors made colourful by large Turkish rugs. A simplicity that suited us and our minimalist philosophy. It also had flamboyant touches we couldn't resist keeping. The faux Ancient Greek statues that kept watch from the hotel's landings and stood guard in the courtyard. Gods and goddesses with stunted arms and blank eyes. The swimming pool shaped like a heart. The gaudy mural of the Furies – the three Greek goddesses of revenge – that kept watch over the courtyard from the central wing of the building.

That first day there, we all sensed the potential of the place. Fifteen bedrooms, a large industrial kitchen, spacious communal areas and plenty of terraced land where we could grow fruit and vegetables, as well as herbs that would nourish and heal.

We stood in the hotel courtyard, looking out across the hills. In the distance we could see the deep blue water of Morphou Bay in the Turkish Republic of Northern Cyprus. The steep limestone mountains that rose behind the hotel cut us off from the rest of southern Cyprus. Cut us off in a way that filled me with peace and relief. That was the moment I shed any doubts I had about abandoning the safe, conventional life my parents had planned for me.

At twenty-three years old, I knew I'd found my sanctuary. The others did too. Here we could create a life most people only dream of. We'd never have to waste our time doing jobs we hated to make money we didn't have time to enjoy. We were going to be free.

Yes, we at Pure Heart believed in miracles, and, over the years, wonders small and large filled our lives. We thought the universe was benevolent and had only our best interests at heart. Even when a hard lesson or a tough loss came our way, we saw it as a chance to learn and grow.

That is why, when we were facing the greatest challenge in the history of our community, we knew the unexpected email that arrived from Sofia was the answer to our prayers. We knew another miracle had occurred.

We didn't know Sofia coming back into our lives would change us forever.

We didn't know one of us was going to die.

2

QUINN

2018

On Friday June 29th, the day of Sofia's arrival, Quinn – the founder of Pure Heart – leaps out of bed at 5 a.m. She has already been awake for two hours, her small, agile body motionless in her narrow single bed, her green eyes staring out into the darkness.

It is almost time.

Despite the special day ahead, Quinn observes her usual morning routine. Still dressed in her orange cotton pyjamas, she makes her bed, methodically tucking the white sheet beneath the mattress, folding the thin, orange blanket on top of it and thumping her one hard pillow back into shape. Her bedroom contains her bed, a bedside table and a chest of drawers. The furniture is made of heavy dark wood, just like the shutters on her window. The exposed stone walls are painted white. Not all the rooms in the former hotel are as basic as hers, but she prefers simplicity. She arrived at Pure Heart with a small rucksack of possessions and, apart from books and basic clothing, has acquired little else in her eighteen years here. She sees herself as living a monkish existence.

Her hair makes her look like a monk. Seven years ago, when it turned from raven black to silver, she shaved it close to her head and has kept the low-maintenance style ever since.

As she leans over the sink in her small en-suite bathroom and startles her face with cold water, she wonders what changes Sofia will see in her – apart from the hair of course. After patting her face dry with a hand towel, she takes a rare look at herself in the mirror. Sofia is twenty-two now and she is fifty-nine, and she wonders how different she will look to the younger woman. People often say she doesn't look her age and, even though she resists attachment to anything superficial, she knows by society's standards she is considered attractive. Still, she can't help being mildly repulsed by the deep lines around her eyes and the horizontal grooves across her forehead. Then she reminds herself these lines are evidence of a life well lived and of wisdom.

Still dressed in her pyjamas, she moves through to the living area adjoining her bedroom, another tranquil, sparsely furnished space. A worn armchair and a low coffee table with a kettle, a mug and a glass jar of mountain tea on it. A pine desk by the window. A bookcase along one wall, crammed with books on spirituality, healing and the religious traditions of the world. Quinn believes all the great spiritual traditions have something to offer and, over the years, she has created her own eclectic programme of transformation. After all, as she often tells the others at Pure Heart, they should never believe in dogma.

Sitting on the armchair is Aphrodite, Quinn's most loyal cat. Strong and sleek and black with emerald green eyes. She is seven years old and is the self-appointed queen of the other twenty or so stray cats that have made their home at Pure Heart. When Quinn enters the room, Aphrodite slips down from the chair and curls herself around Quinn's small, neat feet. Purrs in response to Quinn's gentle stroking.

'Time to go out?' Quinn asks.

The cat slinks over to the door and waits until Quinn releases her for her morning prowl of the premises.

After closing the door, Quinn unrolls her yoga mat in the centre of the room and sits on it, cross-legged. Eyes closed against the dawn light creeping through the window, she meditates. Transcendental Meditation, a technique she learned decades ago from the Maharishi himself in an

opulent hotel in Switzerland. After meditation comes thirty minutes of
Ashtanga yoga. A practice she took up while living in an ashram in Kerala
in Southern India. A week from now, Quinn will turn sixty, but as she
moves through a series of sun salutations, she feels fitter than she did in
her twenties. A little wear and tear, knees that twinge with arthritis in the
colder months, but she believes her energy, her soul essence, has never
been so pure.

After yoga, she sits at her desk, puts on her reading glasses and writes
in her daily gratitude journal.

Grateful to still be here in this beautiful place.
Grateful for all the joy in my heart.
Grateful our little Sofia is coming back to us.

The words blur as she stares at them. Her prescription for glasses is a
year out of date but she can't afford a visit to the optician.

She closes the journal and makes herself a mug of mountain tea. The
sideritis plant grows plentifully on the hillsides nearby and Quinn picks it
herself and dries the flowers and leaves to create the tea. So many health
benefits. Everyone at Pure Heart loves it. Shunning the comfort of her
armchair, she sits again on her yoga mat. It is almost quarter past six. In
just over six hours Sofia will be here. At least that's what she said in the
email she sent two days ago. Quinn hasn't heard from her since. She
doesn't have a phone number for Sofia, even though she made sure to pass
on the community's landline number. How will Sofia get here? Will she
hire a car? Quinn doesn't like the thought of the young woman navigating
the winding mountain roads. What if something happens to her?

She glances across at the bookcase, at the framed photograph of
Charles she keeps there. Their beloved benefactor, whose money made
the dream of Pure Heart a reality. In March, Charles died in his sleep, aged
eighty-three, and Quinn found herself blindsided as the dire state of his
finances emerged.

When she told the others they only had enough money to keep Pure
Heart going for a few months, she assured them they'd find a way to

survive. The universe had sent them what seemed like an impossible challenge, but, if they kept the faith, they would find a way.

After her rousing speech, she looked around at the remaining five members of the Pure Heart community and saw the fear and doubt on their faces. For one terrible moment, she thought they might leave. For the first time she felt uncertain of their love for their community.

Then she realised that despite everything she'd done to help them heal and evolve over the years, they didn't possess her strength or her wisdom. How could they? As founder of the community, it was up to her to show them the path through the darkness. Not that Quinn has ever aspired to leadership. No. Never in her life has she sought that kind of status, yet over and over she finds herself in charge.

She promised them if they shared her belief, the rest would follow. She led them in the sacred rituals that held them together as a community. They danced together, they exorcised their impurities in the sweat lodge, they sat in a circle and chanted. They did all they could to access their higher selves, to connect to the source of all things and to create the abundance they needed.

When, last month at a community meeting, she read out to the others the email that had arrived from Sofia, so unexpected and miraculous and yet, in some ways, so inevitable, she watched their doubt and fear transform into wonder. Abundance had manifested, in a way they could never have imagined. Quinn knew without doubt that each of them loved Pure Heart as much as ever. Each of them loved her.

Questions were, however, unavoidable.

Are you sure that's a good idea, Quinn?

Like all strong leaders, she provided reassurances. She didn't tell them about the dread that pulsed through her when she first opened Sofia's email. How did Sofia even get the email address? Pure Heart didn't have a website or any online presence. As she read Sofia's words, Quinn remembered the terrible day she was taken from them. The stern, middle-aged woman sent by Sofia's grandparents to collect her, bundling the sobbing, hysterical child into the back of a sleek Mercedes with blacked-out windows.

Other memories surfaced too. Harder ones she has not yet fully come to terms with.

She puts her tea aside and gets up from her yoga mat. 'The past does not exist,' she says. 'The past does not exist.'

This mantra is one of the community's founding beliefs. One they all share.

She is nervous about the day ahead. So much still to do and everyone is relying on her to make this visit a success. She won't fail them. She will do everything she can to ensure Pure Heart and its vision survive.

On the bottom shelf of the bookcase is a pack of Tarot cards wrapped in a piece of purple tie-dye cotton. She needs a sign from a higher power to help her this morning. She picks up the bundle of cards, carries it over to her desk and unfolds the tie-dye fabric with reverence. The Tarot cards have shiny silver backs, and their familiar weight comforts her as she shuffles them. She lays them out across the desk in a long fan and, with her eyes closed, she lets her right hand hover over the spread before diving in with thumb and forefinger to pluck out a card.

When she opens her eyes and turns the card over, she finds a skeleton in a jaunty hat looking up at her. A skeleton with a wide, toothless grin splitting its skull. A skeleton that represents death.

3

HOLLY

2019

The media coverage of that violent August night often misrepresented us. Pure Heart was not a cult. We were an intentional community, all of us sharing a common purpose, but each of us free to follow our own spiritual path. Some of us believed we were a soul family, destined to reincarnate together over and over, and share our lives so we could learn the lessons necessary for our souls to evolve.

Whatever our personal beliefs, each of us abided by the community's seven founding principles. We painted them above the front entrance of the building.

The past does not exist.
Our thoughts create our reality.
The good of the community comes before individual desires.
We believe in miracles.
To live in the light, we must embrace the darkness.
Our souls are not for sale.

One Cypriot newspaper accused us of being ignorant expats exploiting the island's cheap property prices and low living costs. Nothing could be further from the truth. We knew we lived in a land still divided by conflict. In his youth, Charles spent many summers at his aunt's villa in Famagusta. He was there when the invasion happened in the summer of 1974 and had to flee the approaching Turkish army. Some newspaper reports depicted him as a debauched heroin addict with ties to the British aristocracy, but, thanks to Quinn, Charles kicked his destructive drug habit decades before his death. The reports of his aristocratic connections were true.

He'd always intended to return to Cyprus and give something back to the island he loved so much. We wanted to create a utopia within this complex country. To project peace and positivity into our surroundings. To live a life untainted by the corruption of the capitalist world and its war machine.

When we started Pure Heart, everyone contributed what they could, but compared to Charles we had little to give. He didn't care. What was money between family, he often said? He transferred his considerable fortune into the hands of Evimería Assets, a wealth management company based in Limassol, and then used the interest from his investments to keep Pure Heart going and to pay each of us a small monthly income. He told us the bulk of his money remained untouched. After his death, when his financial adviser, Michalis, paid us a visit, we discovered this was not the case.

To be honest, money had been sparse in the year leading up to his death, and we were already living on a tight budget. The winter was a cold, miserable one and there were times we went hungry. Charles told us he had a temporary cash-flow issue and that as soon as a few of his larger investments matured, everything would be fine. When he died, we discovered that as well as losing everything in bad investments, he'd remortgaged the Pure Heart property. Only a miracle could save our beloved home from repossession.

When I heard Sofia wanted to come and stay with us for a month, I was overjoyed. I'd loved her like she was my own. We all did. I knew it might be difficult for her to return to the place where Eva died, but Pure Heart was her home. In her email, she told us her grandparents were now dead, and she claimed she was feeling lost. Before taking up her duties as heiress to her family's business empire, she wanted to retreat from the world, to be in a safe space where she could find herself again and heal. How could we refuse her?

When she first offered to pay for her stay with us, we refused. Even though she offered a generous sum of money, we said no. Sofia insisted she wanted to give something back to the people who helped raise her and to the place where she'd shared so many happy times with her mother.

We would have welcomed Sofia whether she had money or not, but, after a unanimous vote, we agreed to accept her kind gesture. After all, sometimes giving makes people feel good. Sofia paying for her stay in exchange for our help would also make her more invested in her own well-being and recovery.

All we wanted to do was make her feel better.

4

Insight Investigators: Background Report

Andreas Constantinou: Born March 18th 1956 to Nikoleta Constantinou and Stephanos Constantinou. He was born and raised in the small town of Lefka (now Lefke) in what is now the Turkish Republic of Northern Cyprus. His father died in a terrorist bomb attack on a café in Nicosia in 1973. Like many Greek Cypriots, Andreas and his mother fled south when the Turkish army invaded in 1974 and settled in Kakopetria, a village in the Troodos Mountains thirteen miles away from Pure Heart. (This is the closest village to the community and it's where the members go for basic supplies etc.)

Andreas worked at the Pure Heart property when it was still a hotel. After the community moved in, they kept him on as a handyman. He lived in Kakopetria but did have a room at the community so he could stay over when necessary.

He often drank in the bars and cafés of Kakopetria and, like many, was still bitter about the invasion and the violence that preceded it. Not only did he lose his father, but his elder brother, Giorgos, stayed in the north to fight when the Turkish army invaded and went missing, like thousands of Cypriots on both sides of the conflict.

Andreas was often in touch with the Committee on Missing Persons, who do incredible work finding the remains of those who went missing in the conflict. It seems he always hoped his brother's body would be discovered, but this never happened. I think it's fair to describe him as a man with a lot of sorrow and anger in his heart.

5

QUINN

2018

A few minutes before 7 a.m., Quinn rushes from her room and skips down
the first set of wooden stairs to the first-floor landing, leaving in her wake
the scent of the home-made rose oil she applied to her neck and wrists
after showering. She hums to herself, unable to stop smiling. The Death
card might have scared a novice. She's often seen people react with terror
at the skeleton's morbid grin. All for nothing. Quinn knows that the card,
rarely, if ever, signifies actual death. No, the skeleton represents both a
symbolic death and a rebirth and she can't think of a more appropriate
symbol for today. Sofia's visit is the start of a new phase for Pure Heart –
she can feel it. Their recent troubles will die away and abundance will
bloom.

The wood beneath her bare feet is warm. Quinn only wears shoes in
winter. The rest of the year she prefers to connect directly to the ground,
earthing herself and using her feet as her ancient ancestors would have
done.

The silver bangles on her arms jangle like percussion as she moves.
Silver pendulum earrings sway in her ears. Her best ceremonial jewellery,
haggled for with an elderly tribal woman in the hills of northern Thailand

when Quinn was in her twenties. The orange silk dress she wears, with its wide sleeves and wrap-around design, came from the same tribe. She hasn't worn it for a long time, but this is no ordinary day.

On the first-floor landing, the sound of a vehicle coming towards the building from the winding access road makes her stop, heart trembling. What if this is Sofia? What if she's come early? No one else is up yet. Nothing is ready.

She exhales, relieved to see a black Toyota Hilux rumbling into the small car park at the front of the building. She forgot she'd asked Andreas to come in early today to help with the last-minute preparations. He parks between the grimy white Hilux and the battered Toyota Cressida that belong to Pure Heart.

'*Kalimera*,' she calls, as his wiry body springs down from the driver's seat. At sixty-two, he is the only one in the community older than her.

'*Kalimera*,' he replies with a wave, tilting his weathered face up to the window. He is dressed in his usual outfit of jeans and a black T-shirt with a heavy checked shirt over the top, despite the warm day that lies ahead.

'Beautiful weather,' she says in Greek. He nods and fires off a lengthy reply, also in Greek, a language which, despite all her years in Cyprus, Quinn still struggles to understand. She does pick up the name Sofia.

'You must be looking forward to seeing Sofia again,' Quinn says, reverting to English. She hopes the visit won't dredge up painful memories of Eva for him. Like everyone at Pure Heart, he found it impossible not to fall under her spell. His grief for her was dark, intense and, at times, unsettling. 'It's been such a long time,' she adds.

'Not so long.' He hauls his toolbox out of the back of the Hilux.

Quinn supposes ten years is nothing to Andreas. Decades of waiting for news of his missing brother has probably warped his perception of time.

'How's Nikoleta?' she asks. 'Is she settling in okay?'

Even from this distance, she catches the pained expression that flits across Andreas' face.

'She is good.' He smooths back his tousled silver hair, as if worried his mother might appear and reprimand him for his scruffy appearance.

Almost a year ago, Andreas had to put his eighty-nine-year-old mother into a care home in Limassol after her dementia became too much for him to handle.

'It is hard,' he says.

'Don't feel guilty, Andreas. You're an amazing son to her.' The care home he's found for Nikoleta sounds like a good one. One of his cousins, a lawyer in Nicosia, is helping to cover the costs.

After a brief discussion of the work Quinn wants completed before Sofia's arrival, Andreas makes his way to the gate at the side of the house and the passageway that leads directly into the courtyard. Even when the community had more members, many of them skilled with their hands, they still needed Andreas' practical expertise and local knowledge. Quinn sometimes wonders if he stays on at Pure Heart because he likes the community's commitment to forgetting the past. He, like many people on both sides of this divided island, has plenty he would rather forget.

Quinn has been urging him to give up drinking for years, with varying degrees of success. After he had a mild heart attack in his mid-fifties, she thought he might finally see the importance of a healthy lifestyle but, apart from doing the occasional session in the sweat lodge, he resists most of her efforts to change him. More than once he's described her spiritual beliefs as *pellares* – rubbish – but she knows he has superstitions of his own. She's seen the evil eye hanging from a hook above his bed. A blue glass pendant with a dark pupil at its centre. *Mati* to the Greeks, *nazar* to the Turks, it is said to ward off evil spirits. As far as Quinn knows, Andreas hasn't had a drink since Christmas. No evil spirits for six months.

As she closes the window, Quinn is briefly unsettled by the question of how she will pay for all the extra work Andreas has done recently. The money Sofia sent as a payment for her visit has gone. Quinn spent most of it on a few months of extortionate mortgage payments. After Charles died, Michalis the financial adviser did try and explain everything to her, but Quinn, who always left business decisions to Charles, can't get her head around it. All she knows is that the company Charles borrowed money from now owns their mortgage and is charging vast interest on top of the monthly payments. It would be easy to be angry with Charles, but Quinn loved him too much for that. She has had the occasional moment of frustration; she's only human.

She shakes her head, trying to shake the worry away with it. The universe will provide. All she, all they, have to do is believe. Look at the abundance they've already received. The Death card has made her certain there is even more to come.

Onwards. So much still to do. She can hear banging sounds coming from the kitchen downstairs. She must see what everyone is up to. She did go through the drill for today at the community meeting last night, but she wants to make sure they stick to the plan.

Before she can hurry down the next flight of stairs, a fluttering sensation in her belly stops her. She stands still and listens to what her body is trying to tell her. She's learned the hard way that intuition starts in the gut.

Mel. Something to do with Mel. She turns and walks along the corridor to Mel's room, unable to dampen a surge of irritation. This morning? Really? Doesn't she have enough to deal with? She sighs. When people need you, they need you. Her gifts, unasked for, are both a blessing and a curse. Still, she must honour them. She is only a channel. A humble messenger.

She knocks on Mel's door. 'Mel,' she says, 'are you okay?'

6

QUINN

2018

'Come in.' Mel's voice, tremulous.

Inside the room, Quinn finds the community's newest member on her burgundy yoga mat in a burgundy T-shirt and yoga trousers, her sturdy legs crossed. Her face is blotchy and the skin beneath her glacial, pale blue eyes is puffy and raw.

'Are you okay?' Quinn asks.

Mel nods. 'I had a nightmare.'

'I had a feeling something was wrong.' Quinn kneels opposite her on the mat. 'Tell me everything.'

Mel stares at her. 'Is that a new dress?'

'New to you,' Quinn says, remembering Mel has only been with them for eight months.

'You've got your ceremonial jewellery on.'

'Well, today is a special occasion.'

Mel lowers her eyes. 'Of course.'

Mel's shoulder-length black hair, currently tucked behind her ears, is shiny with grease. Quinn knows one of the joys of living at Pure Heart is not having to make an effort with your appearance unless you choose to, but she hopes Mel will at least shower and change into something clean before Sofia arrives.

'You look lovely,' Mel says, eyes still downcast.

'Tell me about the dream.'

'Nightmare.'

'Yes. Tell me.' Quinn can't help feeling guilty. She's been so busy preparing for Sofia's visit she cancelled Mel's weekly intuitive healing session yesterday.

'There was a man,' Mel says. 'His hands were around my throat. I couldn't breathe. I thought I was going to die.'

'That's awful.' Quinn opens her arms. Mel edges closer and leans into the hug, letting out a stifled sob. Quinn allows the distressed woman to rest against her chest. Even though she is now celibate, she believes nourishing, platonic touch is vital and feels Mel needs it more than most. Mel has always apologised for her shyness, and Quinn still senses resistance in her body. A result of the trauma she has suffered.

'It was so real,' Mel says.

'Your past is behind you now.' Quinn rubs Mel's back. 'Your relationship with your ex was abusive and dangerous, but you got out. You were strong.'

'I don't always feel strong.'

'Let's do some breathing together.'

Mel nods but doesn't move. The weight of her head reminds Quinn of Blake, her last lover. After sex, he liked to rest his head on her chest while she stroked his dark dreadlocks. He was fifteen years younger than her, but the age gap didn't matter to them. Blake said they were kindred souls and souls were ageless. Quinn can't believe nine years have passed since he left Pure Heart.

Mel's sigh brings her back to the present. Her heart rate quickens at the thought of all the jobs she must get done before lunchtime.

'Some alternate nostril breathing will help,' she says.

Mel finally lifts her head and the two women sit cross-legged on the mat, facing each other. Mel closes her eyes and they breathe together, in through one nostril and out through the other. A yogic breathing exercise designed to calm the mind.

Quinn breathes with her eyes open. She notices the burgundy robe hanging on the back of Mel's door. The colour of Tibetan Buddhism. Does Mel only wear one colour now? It's a while since she's been in Mel's room, but she can see how much it resembles her own. Folded on the neatly made bed is a burgundy blanket. The walls are bare and on Mel's bedside table sits a pack of playing cards. Mel enjoys playing Patience and Solitaire. She claims to find the cards soothing. Quinn is pleased to see the bookshelf next to the window is crammed with self-help manuals and books on spirituality.

She smiles. It's an honour to be a role model for Mel. A joy to pass her wisdom on to a spiritual beginner. Mel is such a different woman from the one who arrived at Pure Heart. She is less tormented. More open to experiencing joy.

After a few moments, Quinn brings the breathing practice to a close. When Mel opens her eyes, Quinn can see she is calmer, more focused. More of her best self.

Mel smiles. 'The power of breath work still amazes me.'

Quinn nods. 'Such a beautiful practice. So transformative.'

'When I was on the force, I'd never have done anything even remotely alternative.'

'I'm sure the police would be better for it.' Quinn still finds it hard to believe that this shy, gentle woman was once a police officer. Mel did twelve years in the London Met and ended up as a detective inspector working Organised Crime. She finally resigned, after being diagnosed with post-traumatic stress disorder. She told Quinn she has seen terrible things. The very worst of humanity.

From the moment they met, Quinn knew Mel was destined to be part of the Pure Heart family. She often thinks back to their chance encounter at a café in Kakopetria. On her way back from the supermarket one morning, Quinn stopped in the village for a cup of tea and ended up sharing the only free table in the café with a stranger. An Englishwoman wearing sunglasses, even though they were sitting inside and it was October. They started talking and when Mel removed her glasses, revealing bruises around her eyes and cheekbones, it didn't take long for Quinn to get her to open up.

Mel explained she was in Cyprus for a holiday after leaving an abusive relationship. She'd just resigned from the police and didn't know what to do with her life or where to go. Quinn invited her to stay at Pure Heart for a few nights and Mel has been here ever since.

'You must be tired?' Mel says.

'Tired. Why?' Quinn is fizzing with energy. Every cell buzzing.

'I heard you get up in the night to go to the bathroom. Did you have a bad night's sleep?'

Quinn casts her eyes up to the ceiling. Her bedroom and en-suite are directly above. The uneven wooden floors in all the bedrooms do little to soak up the noise. Mel must hear her moving about all the time. 'I've got a lot on my mind,' she says.

'What time is Sofia arriving?'

'Twelve-thirty. In time for lunch. Well, that's what we arranged last week. I haven't heard from her since, but—'

'You haven't heard from her?' Mel frowns. 'She should let you know if—'

'She'll be here.' Quinn uncrosses her legs and gets to her knees.

'I just... I wouldn't like you to be disappointed.'

The day after Sofia's initial email arrived, Quinn found Mel in the office, using the community's one shared laptop to search online for information about the Belov family. Mel apologised for investigating but said the policewoman in her couldn't resist.

Quinn often wonders if Mel, with all her training and experience, can tell when a person is withholding information.

'What was she like as a child?' Mel asks.

'Smart.' Quinn smiles. 'Smart and funny and such a wild imagination. Always making up stories.'

'It must have been amazing for Sofia to grow up here.' Mel's voice is wistful. 'I'd be a totally different person if I'd grown up in a place like this.'

'She did love it here.' Quinn strokes her silver scalp. 'I hope she still does.'

'I don't want things to change,' Mel blurts out, as if confessing. 'What we have here is so special.'

'Resisting change is very human.' Quinn rests her small, dry hands on

Mel's face. 'But how can we grow if we aren't forced out of our comfort zone?'

Mel sighs. 'I know you're right.'

'I'm sure your dream was just—'

'My nightmare.'

'I'm sure the nightmare was just you processing the new situation.'

'There's a lot to process.'

Quinn knows she must be patient with Mel. The trauma she experienced during her relationship and her career means she likes to feel in control at all times. 'I know we've had some tough challenges recently,' she says, 'but I really think Sofia's visit is a sign things are going to change.' Her knees creak faintly as she stands. 'We all made this happen, you know. Miracles like this are only possible when everyone believes.' She smiles down at Mel. 'Everyone.'

Mel gives her a half-smile in return. 'I know.'

Instinct tells Quinn there is a part of Mel still hidden. A secret self she hesitates to share, despite all the good work they've been doing together.

Not to worry. Quinn is sure that with time Mel will open up like a beautiful flower. With time she will reveal her true self.

7

QUINN

2018

Quinn steps out of Mel's room and closes the door behind her. Her hands sweep around the top of her head as she cleanses her aura. She is sensitive to the moods of others and must be careful not to absorb them.

As she sets off along the flagstone corridor, two white kittens appear at her heels. 'Hello, Apollo; hello, Artemis,' she says. The kittens follow her downstairs to the ground floor, chasing one another and tumbling over themselves. Before coming to Cyprus, Quinn never considered herself a cat person, but the island has a bigger feline population than a human one. According to legend, cats were first brought to Cyprus from Egypt and Palestine in the fourth century by Saint Helena, the mother of Constantine the Great. The cats were her solution to the venomous snakes that were threatening parts of the island. Now Cyprus is overrun by cats, not snakes.

As well as her connection to the cats of Pure Heart, Quinn also loves her hens. She's keen to get out and feed them, but first she needs to check on progress in the kitchen. Not that she needs to worry about the catering. Joe will be on top of everything. Normally on a Friday he drives to the east coast of the island and visits the refugee camp where he set up a kitchen a few years ago. He loves his voluntary work but was happy to change his plans to accommodate Sofia.

Joe is nowhere in sight when she enters the kitchen. What if he's forgotten about today and set off for the camp as usual? The comforting scent of freshly baked bread soothes her anxiety. Two sourdough loaves sit cooling on one of the kitchen's stainless-steel workstations. Joe has obviously been up for some time, getting ahead of schedule. The dark, cloying scent of coffee also permeates the air. Quinn glances at the large espresso pot on the industrial hob. Most of the community members have converted to her mountain tea now, but not everyone has her discipline. She hasn't touched coffee for thirty years, even though she found caffeine the hardest drug of all to give up.

'Joe?' she says, as the kittens tug at the hem of her dress. She picks a handful of red grapes from the fruit bowl beside the cooling bread and pops one into her mouth.

The kitchen, once used to feed a busy hotel of guests, still has two stainless-steel workstations, each with an oven and a large hob and grill. There is a tall, wide fridge and a deep chest freezer. All the equipment is old and prone to the occasional breakdown but they can't afford to replace any of it.

This room is where the community gathers, especially in the cold mountain winters. At the other end of the long space is a pine dining table that seats up to fourteen. Behind that, two saggy sofas flank the wood-burning stove. By the side of the stove, in a large basket, two cats are curled up together, napping. Odysseus, a ball of ginger and white fluff and Hera, her grey fur balding, are two of the community's oldest cats.

The kitchen is a homely, quirky room and Quinn loves it. Plants everywhere, as well as abandoned pairs of thongs and slippers. Open shelves are stacked with mismatched crockery and glasses, some of which belonged to the former hotel. Framed photographs hang on the exposed stone walls. Images dating back to the beginning of Pure Heart. In recent days, they have reinstated the photographs of Eva they took down after her death. Quinn finds herself glancing away from the pictures now, still unable to look Eva in the eye.

The kittens abandon her dress for the cat basket beside the fire, poking at the older cats with their paws until they are batted away.

'Apollo, Artemis,' Quinn says, 'respect your elders.'

The kittens stop and look up at her, their deep blue eyes brimming with mischief. Mischief they turn on each other, leaving the seniors in peace.

'Hey.'

Startled, Quinn turns to see Joe's tall, bulky figure entering the door that leads from the side of the kitchen into the larder and utility room. In one hand he wields a large knife.

'Good morning,' he says. He hasn't lived in his native Scotland for decades now, but his gentle Perthshire accent is undiminished.

'Hi,' Quinn says.

'Can't find the sharpener anywhere.' Joe holds up the knife, as if inviting Quinn to inspect it. 'We could do with new knives to be honest, but this'll do for now.'

Quinn opens her arms wide and, after putting the knife down, Joe enfolds her in a tight bear hug.

'Big day,' he says.

'Huge.'

'Holly and I hardly slept. How about you?'

'Like the dead,' Quinn says, glossing over the hours she spent staring at the ceiling. Joe's fleshy waist sags over her narrow forearms. Has he put on more weight? Quinn has always practised moderation in all things, but has given up on Joe following her example. He's always been the main cook at Pure Heart, even when it had more members.

When they part, Joe pats his stomach, as if reading Quinn's thoughts. 'I'm probably twice the size I was when Sofia last saw me.'

'And you had hair.'

'Harsh.' Joe chuckles. 'Harsh but true.' He is forty-five now, but his hair abandoned him in his thirties. Since then, he's opted for a shaved head and a big, bushy beard streaked with blond, ginger and grey.

They run through the menu again. Lunch, which Quinn wants to serve at 1 p.m., will be a Greek salad made with the fresh feta Joe picked up from a farm near Kakopetria.

'I'll make flatbreads to go with that,' Joe says. 'We'll have the sour-dough tonight.'

For dinner, Joe will roast two locally sourced quails. Sofia, Quinn told him, is no longer a vegetarian, but Joe will also make a vegetarian moussaka for those who are. Later, he will pick apricots from their orchard and make an apricot and walnut cake. There will be Cypriot wine for those who drink alcohol and his home-made ginger kombucha for those who don't.

It's clear Joe is delighted to have a larger food budget again. He has done a brilliant job of feeding them on their meagre funds – plenty of stews and casseroles with Holly's vegetables and the most basic super-market products – but even Quinn with her modest tastes was beginning to find their diet dull.

'Does Sofia drink?' Joe says. 'I have to keep reminding myself she's not a kid any more.'

'She might choose to abstain. I got the impression she's coming here to make some big life changes.' Quinn thinks of the first email Sofia sent her.

I know inheriting such great wealth is a privilege and I should be living my best life, but I feel overwhelmed. I'm too young to be in charge of everything. I feel out of control. I need perspective.

'I'm sure she'll be happy to eat as we usually do. After today.'

'Aye, we need to make today special,' says Joe. 'Give her a proper welcome.'

He points to the five large aubergines on the chopping board on his workstation. 'I'm making *melitzanosalata*.'

'Sofia's favourite dip.'

'She used to eat it by the spoonful.'

'She'll love it.'

'Are you talking about Sofia?' Holly, Joe's wife, bustles into the kitchen. 'What will she love?'

'*Melitzanosalata*,' says Joe.

'Oh yes, she'll love that.' Holly's mass of mousy brown curls skims Quinn's face as she kisses her cheek. 'I hardly slept at all. Too excited.'

'So I hear,' Quinn says as Holly pulls her in for a tight squeeze. Holly, firm and fit from all the gardening she does, is so different from the frail creature Quinn met all those years ago in Ibiza. A young woman broken by the trauma of her teenage years. A young woman Quinn put back together.

'I feel great, though. Really great.' Holly's dark blue eyes are bright and alert, despite the lack of sleep. She hums as she fills the community's large metal kettle, puts it on the hob and lights the gas beneath it. Holly is often dishonest about her feelings. Crying in Quinn's arms one moment, putting on an impenetrable show of cheeriness to the others the next. Today, Holly's happiness seems genuine, but Quinn detects a dizzy energy lurking beneath it. The community's financial situation has been tough for everyone, but Holly has been especially anxious at the thought of Pure Heart failing. Sofia's arrival has given her a vital injection of hope.

Holly drops a handful of Quinn's mountain tea into a teapot and returns to Joe's side. She wraps her arms around him, and he kisses the top of her head. Quinn notes their almost identical outfits of baggy yoga pants, loose T-shirts and Birkenstock clogs. A sweet couple and perfect together, despite their different backgrounds.

'Sofia used to love helping Joe out in the kitchen,' Holly says.

Quinn smiles. 'She did.' She can see Sofia clearly, sitting on a stool at the workstation, her small, plump hands gripping a mixing spoon, her round face dusted with flour. One afternoon, when Sofia was six years old, Quinn found her at the workstation pressing a heart-shaped cookie cutter into a sheet of rolled dough.

'I'm making heart biscuits for everyone,' Sofia said. 'To show you all I love you.'

'Are they pure hearts?' Quinn said.

'They're chocolate chip ones.' Sofia smiled. 'The best hearts of all.'

The wheezing kettle brings Quinn back to the present. Holly releases Joe and hurries over to the hob. 'I hope Sofia's grandparents treated her well,' she says.

'I'm sure they gave her the best of everything,' says Quinn.

Holly lifts the whistling kettle off the hob and pours water into the teapot. 'The day she left, I promised her she could come back and visit. I knew it was a lie.'

'You were only trying to make her feel better,' Joe says.

'Her life must have been so different to the one she had here,' Holly slots the lid onto the teapot. 'Eva would have wanted her to stay with us.'

'And now she will be,' Quinn says. 'For a month at least.'

Or maybe more. Who knows? She doesn't want to put any limits on this miracle. Sofia might want to stay for good.

'We'll make sure she's happy here,' Holly says.

'Aye,' Joe says. 'We will.'

When Holly offers Quinn tea, she refuses. So much to do; she has to get on. 'Are you still happy to set the table up outside?' she asks Holly. Today they will eat lunch in the courtyard, underneath the white canvas sails that shelter them from the sun in the summer months.

'Of course.' Holly pours tea for her and Joe into two mismatched china cups.

'Would you mind letting Mel help you?' Quinn asks. 'I think she's finding all the upheaval stressful.'

'Well, she has had you to herself for a while,' Holly says.

A sharp scratch on her left ankle makes Quinn gasp. She looks down to see one of the kittens sparring with the hem of her dress.

'Mel asked me some questions last night,' Joe says. 'About Eva.'

Quinn swoops down and picks up her attacker. The kitten calms immediately when she strokes its spine. 'What did you tell her?'

'Not much.' Joe picks up his knife. 'Gossiping about Eva would dishonour her memory.'

'I agree,' Quinn says. The community has told Mel the basic details of Eva's suicide and the events that followed, and, up until now, Mel has been sensitive enough not to press them for more information. 'We need to remember Mel's new here. We've had our ups and downs over the years but—'

'God, yes,' Holly says.

'But we've always come through them,' continues Quinn. 'We can't expect Mel to have our insight.'

'Living in a community's not always easy.' Joe applies his knife to the nearest aubergine and slices it into two halves. 'Sometimes tough decisions have to be made.'

'We can't always agree on everything,' Holly says. 'Conflict is inevitable.'

'And healthy,' Quinn says. Joe and Holly have been with her from the start of Pure Heart. Reliable and trustworthy, they've helped her overcome all the challenges of the past eighteen years. 'But in the end, the needs of the community come first.'

Another slice of aubergine succumbs to Joe's blade. 'That's what it takes to survive,' he says.

'We will survive?' Holly asks Quinn. 'Won't we?'

'Of course.' Quinn doesn't want to admit there were times, after Charles died, when she feared she might lose what mattered most. Her dream. Their dream.

'This visit is the abundance we prayed for,' Holly says. 'Isn't it?'

'It is,' Quinn says. 'I know it.'

'We're totally with you,' Holly says. 'We'll do anything to keep this place going.'

'This is our home,' Joe adds. 'Why would we want to be anywhere else?'

'We don't want to leave here.' Tears glisten in Holly's eyes. 'Ever.'

8

Insight Investigators: Background Report

Joseph Craig Muirhead (known as Joe): Born December 31st 1973 to Mary Muirhead. Father unnamed on birth certificate. Raised in Crieff, Perthshire. Mary Muirhead worked as a dinner lady at Crieff High School. She remained unmarried and had no other children. Now deceased.

Joseph did his Cookery and Hospitality training at what was then Telford College in Edinburgh. He worked as a chef in various restaurants in Edinburgh and Glasgow before taking a job in Ibiza.

Holly Wingfield: Born April 13th 1975. Daughter of Peter and Alice Wingfield. Father was a high-ranking civil servant in the Home Office. Mother a housewife. One older brother, Daniel, who is a corporate lawyer. Holly studied History and Politics at Cambridge University and graduated with first-class honours.

She appears to have little contact with her family or with her former life in the UK. I tracked down a woman called Lisa Rennick, a former friend of Holly's. They studied together at Cambridge and, according to Lisa, Holly's father secured her a junior administrative position at the

Foreign Office after she graduated. A job Holly was supposed to start after returning from a holiday in Ibiza with Lisa and a few other girls.

Holly never returned from Ibiza. The last time Lisa spoke to her, just before the move to Cyprus, Holly hinted at a rift in the family. Lisa didn't know what had caused it, but it sounds as if Holly and her family were estranged.

9

HOLLY

2019

Money and murder. Typical of the media to fixate on those elements of the story. Salacious headlines in the seedy sidebars of online newspapers and magazines. Most journalists fixated on the details of Sofia's money. As if she had no identity outside of her wealth. And when media reports emerged about Eva killing herself at Pure Heart ten years previously, it made the tragedies of our past and present look even more sinister.

None of us choose the family we're born into. If we could, I wouldn't have picked mine. Same for Sofia. She was born into a family her mother tried hard to escape. Ivan Belov, Sofia's grandfather, made his first fortune on the black market in Moscow, selling desirable consumer goods to a population deprived of them by the communist regime. A successful gangster was how Eva described him. In 1991, when the Soviet Union collapsed, Ivan was in the perfect position to profit from President Yeltsin's disorganised and corrupt privatisation scheme. He gained large stakes in mining and oil companies and stashed his profits in foreign bank accounts, later diversifying into a range of different businesses.

He was amongst the first wave of wealthy Russians who sent their children to expensive boarding schools in Europe. Eva, the family's only surviving child, arrived at Priory Ladies College in Richmond, London, in 1995, aged sixteen, and proceeded to behave in a very unladylike fashion, sneaking out of school to rave in the capital's nightclubs and warehouses. At seventeen she found herself pregnant to Luca, a DJ from Rome, and married him without her parents' permission. After her older brother Mikhail's death in a car accident a few years previously, she was supposed to step up and become the heir to Ivan's business empire, but she wanted nothing to do with it. She always said her parents' wealth was blood money, plundered at the expense of ordinary Russians. When Sofia was born, she and Luca moved to Ibiza.

When Luca died of a ketamine overdose during an especially hedonistic weekend, her parents expected Eva and Sofia to come home to them, but by then Eva had met Quinn who offered her a room in Charles' villa near Ibiza Town.

This was around the time Joe and I first met Quinn. Six months earlier, I'd arrived in Ibiza with some university friends to celebrate our recent graduation. We went for lunch one day in a trendy restaurant in San Antonio where Joe was a sous chef. When he came to check we were enjoying our food, he and I got chatting. Love at first sight, even though I'd never believed such a thing existed. I didn't realise I was looking for a way out of my life until I met him.

When my friends flew home, I stayed in Ibiza with Joe. My parents begged me to come home and focus on my career, but Joe's unconditional love made me realise how conditional theirs was. Living with a chef soon exposed my strange eating habits – a remnant of the anorexia I struggled with in my teens. When, aged thirteen, I first began losing weight, my parents put my 'faddy eating' down to vanity. As time went on, they claimed my 'issues' stemmed from my perfectionism, a personality trait that would later drive me to academic success. They didn't want to accept the real reason behind my eating disorder. They never have.

In those early days in Ibiza, Joe and I partied hard, but he didn't know I had demons to outrun. We existed in a limbo of drugs and dancing but in every comedown, I found the past waiting for me. Then, one afternoon in San Antonio, stoned, we accidentally wandered into a Spiritual Restructuring workshop Quinn was holding in the back room of a popular café. That was the start of the journey that would bring us to Pure Heart.

Eight years later, when Eva died, her family claimed her body and her daughter. Ivan had just acquired a Golden Visa for the UK, and he took Sofia to live in a townhouse in Belgravia. We never saw her again.

After she left, Joe and I considered trying for a baby. We'd discussed it before, but I'd never felt ready. The following year we almost went ahead with it, but when we reflected on the state of our world, we decided it was kinder not to bring a child into such precarious circumstances.

I did search for Sofia online sometimes, hoping for a mention of her or a photograph, but the Belov family did a good job of protecting her identity. I did come across Ivan Belov's obituary – *a successful businessman... a generous philanthropist*. Much was made of the family's charitable foundation and all the good work it had accomplished.

Most people believe money will liberate them, but Eva said her wealth was a prison. We didn't want to think of sweet, gentle Sofia trapped by her tainted inheritance. We wanted to set her free.

10

ZOE

2018

Gratitude and Prayers Journal: Friday 29th June, 7.45 a.m.

Grateful for the sun and the blue sky. (Why am I saying that? Every morning is sun and blue sky at this time of year!)

Grateful my face yoga routine is showing results.

Grateful that, finally, something IS ACTUALLY HAPPENING AROUND HERE!!!!

Zoe sits at the round, wrought-iron table in the middle of the orchard, a cheap notebook in front of her, a Mont Blanc fountain pen in her left hand. The table, positioned between two apricot trees, is her favourite spot to sit in the mornings. Her lilac silk kimono is cool against her naked body. The sparse, yellow grass tickles the bare soles of her feet. On her lap sits Aphrodite, sleek and black, her warm body vibrating with a satisfied purr. Of all the cats that belong to the community, she is Zoe's favourite.

She puts down her pen and picks up the mug of strong black coffee she made in the kitchen before coming outside. Joe and Holly were already in there, beavering away. Joe whizzing things up in his blender, Holly up to her elbows in the sink. They were frosty when she first greeted them, Holly muttering something about her shirking last night's washing up even though her name was on the rota. And then Joe reminded her how much there is to do before Sofia arrives. As if she needs reminding. Firstly, she is thirty-seven years old; she's not the wild teenager they first met all those years ago in Ibiza. Secondly, as a former entertainer who started her career in theatre and television as a child, she has punctuality and discipline in her bones.

All she has to do before lunchtime is a final tidy-up of the guest suite in the east wing of the house. Put some fresh flowers in a vase, plump up the cushions. Hardly a drama.

And yet, fizzing deep within her is a sensation she can't quite identify. Excitement? Nerves? What should she wear for Sofia's arrival? She can't remember when she could last afford to buy new clothes. Here, where she sees the same people every day, she can just about bear her shabby collection of cotton dresses, yoga pants and tops. She'll have to wear one of the outfits packed away in a suitcase beneath her bed. Something reserved for special occasions.

A memory hustles into her mind. She is fifteen and shopping on Carnaby Street with the stylist assigned by her record company. They are laden with bags and giddy on cocktails she is far too young to be drinking, but she is Zoe Tempest and it's the week before the release of *Straight to the Stars*, her debut album. It will be a huge hit. Entering the UK album charts at number five. She was living the dream, unaware how brief it would turn out to be.

What will Sofia think of her now? As a child, she insisted on listening to *Straight to the Stars* and made Zoe teach her the dance routines for all the hit singles. She badgered Zoe constantly for stories of her pop star past. Zoe smiles, thinking of those innocent times. With Sofia, she could remember the good parts of her success. She could remember fans coming up to her in the street and asking for autographs. She could forget other, less pleasant occasions when strangers would accost her in the street and call her all sorts of names.

With her free hand, she gathers her long, red hair and smooths it over her shoulder. No trips to celebrity hairdressers in Soho these days. No trips to any hairdresser. She dyes her hair with henna and lets Holly trim the ends when they need it. Later, even though her hair is perfectly clean, she will ignore the strict community rules about water wastage and wash it anyway. She makes plenty of other sacrifices for the environment. She'd love to have her hair cut into a bob, but Carl, her husband, insists he prefers it long.

Only a few days ago he caught her in their bathroom pulling out a rogue grey hair. He laughed at her distress and pointed to his own mop of thinning silver hair. She told him that was different. He was fifty-nine. He was ancient. He laughed and said he was relieved she was finally catching up with him.

'I don't want to catch up with him,' she tells Aphrodite. The cat yawns in response, exposing her neat white teeth. 'Anyway, I can't. When I'm fifty-nine, he'll be eighty-one.'

Saying those words aloud makes her uneasy. She doesn't want to imagine either of them being so old.

She savours another sip of coffee. Quinn has advised her many times to switch to mountain tea, but Zoe refuses to give up all her highs.

As the caffeine seeps into her system, she gazes at the land spread out before her. Since the community arrived here, they've all worked hard on the terraced land. Above her is the courtyard, the swimming pool and the former hotel building they now call home. The level Zoe sits on now is an orchard of apricot, apple, cherry and lemon trees. On the next terrace down are the flower beds, Quinn's herb garden and a long polytunnel where they grow as many of their own vegetables as they can. Behind the polytunnel is the hen coop. The terrace below that one houses the yurt, where they hold their community meetings and practise yoga and conduct the rituals that bind them together. Next to the yurt is the olive grove where they built their sweat lodge. After their first few years here, they bought up acres of the forest and scrubland that borders their bottom terrace, giving them more space and privacy.

A movement on the terrace below catches her eye. It is Mel, a vision in burgundy, wandering along with a wicker basket over one arm. She must be off to collect some vegetables for Joe. Sure enough, Mel disappears into the polytunnel.

When Mel first arrived at Pure Heart, Zoe hoped they'd hit it off. She was longing for someone new to hang out with, but Mel, so quiet and earnest and committed to her spiritual development, always holds herself at a distance. Apart from with Quinn. Mel is all over Quinn at every opportunity. Zoe tells herself not to be harsh; Mel is still struggling with a lot of stuff. She remembers what it's like to be chosen by Quinn. To feel special. To be truly seen and heard for the first time in your life.

Her gaze drifts beyond the bottom terrace, to the distant trees. A shudder passes through her when she glimpses white stone amongst the pines and cedars. One of the walls of the abandoned monastery that sits on their land. Monastery makes it sound grand, but the small, dilapidated building is more like a rural church.

She averts her eyes. She hasn't ventured inside the place for years. Holly and Joe go down there sometimes to lay flowers in Eva's memory, but everyone else avoids it.

Especially Andreas. On her way to the orchard earlier, Zoe found him kneeling by the side of the pool. He explained the pool's dodgy filter valve had finally broken. For months now, the water in the pool has been cloudy and keeps draining away, forcing them to top it up using a hosepipe. Andreas can no longer patch the valve up, and they can't afford to have it replaced. The pump is also threatening to fail. How will any of them, especially Sofia, survive the summer without a pool?

When Zoe asked Andreas how he was feeling about Sofia's visit, he puffed out his cheeks and let the air escape in a low whistle. *I think it is, like you say here, it is a lot.* His unrequited love for Eva was no secret in the community. He adored her, and Eva, to her credit, treated him with kindness and respect. They were good friends.

Zoe wonders what Sofia looks like now. She imagines her curvy and creamy skinned with wavy dark hair hanging down to her waist.

Aphrodite stirs on Zoe's lap and slips to the ground, her green eyes scanning the terrace below. Seconds later, Quinn appears. She must have finished feeding the hens. What outfit is that she's wearing? Zoe hasn't seen her so dressed up for a long time.

Aphrodite slinks away. No doubt her favourite cat will join the feline throng that usually follows Quinn around all day. She can see Zeus and

Eros, two brown and black tabbies, trailing Quinn as she disappears into the polytunnel.

Zoe fights back a surge of irritation. She hasn't forgiven Quinn for rejecting her proposal to turn Pure Heart into a spiritual retreat. When Quinn first told them all about their money issues, Zoe suggested they turn the community into a business and take in paying guests. The idea seemed like an obvious answer to their precarious financial position, but Quinn wouldn't hear of it. She insisted they would never monetise themselves and their lifestyle for insincere spiritual tourists. Nor would they ever exploit vulnerable people for money. The community voted on the matter, but only Carl backed Zoe's suggestion.

Zoe gets it. She isn't beyond sneaking into the office and looking up the global spiritual community on Instagram or YouTube, and she can see where Quinn is coming from. The Internet is flooded with self-proclaimed tantric goddesses posing in bikinis while urging their followers to reject the male gaze and embrace their inner beauty. Yogis strike impossible poses beneath the setting sun, glowing 'priestesses' meditate on mountain tops and share videos of themselves dancing ecstatically on their YouTube channels.

Zoe knows most of these supposedly enlightened beings are charlatans. She also knows this is how the modern world works and she can't help thinking she'd make a great Instagram shot right now, with the front of her kimono gaping open, her hair loose, a mug cupped in her hands.

The perfect morning spot for writing in my gratitude journal. #blessed

She imagines herself welcoming guests to Pure Heart and sharing the spiritual insights and practices she's picked up over the years. It would be fun to have more people around the place again. Bring it back to life.

This place has so much potential. *She* has so much potential.

Ever since they met, Quinn has been telling Zoe to step into her own power but whenever she tries – like with the suggestion about the retreat – Quinn stops her doing so.

Guilt niggles at her. She feels bad for criticising Quinn. Their leader has genuine intentions, unlike most of the online fakes Zoe can't help envying. Where would she be if Quinn hadn't found her in Ibiza all those years ago? She was such a mess. There was a time she did everything Quinn asked of her. A time she could only survive by doing so.

She tells herself she needs to keep an open mind. What if Quinn's right and Sofia's visit is the miracle they hoped and prayed for? She needs to keep believing. They've all learned the hard way that when one person stops believing, terrible things happen.

11

ZOE

2018

Just as Zoe is finishing her coffee, she hears the crackle of dry grass underfoot and turns to see Carl ambling towards her, dressed in loose black yoga pants and his favourite Smiths T-shirt, the one with the album cover of *The Queen is Dead* on the front. She smiles and snaps her notebook shut.

'Hello, beloved,' he says. He stops behind her chair and slides his arms around her. On the inside of his right arm is a black ink tattoo of a lotus flower. Identical to the one on the inside of Zoe's right arm. 'You were up early.' He stoops to kiss her neck. 'I missed you.'

She caresses his cheek. 'Didn't sleep much.'

As she lay awake beneath the thin cotton sheet that covered them both, she could tell he was only pretending to sleep. Nerves oozed from him, mingling with hers, the overhead fan spreading their joint anxiety around the room with each creaky rotation.

'Big day ahead,' Carl says in his cultured, confident voice. He releases her and sits in the chair opposite. Wipes his forehead. His hair sticks up on end and his T-shirt clings to his chest. Even in this dishevelled state he is undeniably sexy. #silverfox

'You're all sweaty,' she says. 'Been dancing?'

'Yup.'

Carl clings rigidly to a morning routine, but the content of it changes all the time. In the winter, he likes to plunge into the cold swimming pool. Some days he likes to meditate for an hour but just now he's going through another obsessive phase of dancing in the morning. Playing tunes from his nineties clubbing glory days, over and over, on an old iPod. He does it to stay one step ahead of himself. To tame the twin beasts of anxiety and depression.

'It feels like I need to be really grounded in my body just now,' Carl says.

Zoe doesn't feel at all grounded. The prospect of Sofia coming to Pure Heart has knocked her off balance, and part of her is enjoying the sensation.

The table tilts as Carl rests his elbows on it. 'I had the weirdest dream.' He describes how in the dream he returned to his childhood home only to find the ceilings leaking in every room and the floors melting beneath his feet. 'Really strange.'

Zoe used to love the chats they had upon waking. Sleepy, intimate discussions about their dreams and what they might mean and whether they should work harder on healing their childhood wounds and releasing their inherited ancestral pain. These days, she often wakes with a fierce longing to be alone.

'What you writing?' he asks, nodding at her notebook.

'Just doing my journal.'

'Cool.' Carl interlaces his fingers and cracks his knuckles. This was his warm-up gesture when he still wrote. When Zoe first met him, he was still Carl Fowles, critically acclaimed author with an award-winning debut novel to his name. His glory, like hers, was short-lived. A shared trauma they bonded over. One that binds them still.

'Have you seen Quinn this morning?' he says.

'She's in the polytunnel. With Mel.'

'Ah yes. I saw Mel earlier with her little basket. Skipping along.'

Zoe smiles. 'Mel doesn't skip.'

'All in red... well, burgundy. Skipping along like a slightly butch Little Red Riding Hood.'

'That's mean.'

'Bet they're having sex down there right now. Doing unspeakable things with Holly's prize courgettes.'

'Carl.' Zoe shakes her head. 'You're dreadful.'

He sighs. 'I know.'

'Quinn is on one of her missions to help Mel. That's all.' Zoe has wondered if Mel's devotion to Quinn is more than just spiritual, but even if it is, Quinn is celibate now. 'She told me she didn't want another lover after Blake.'

'Mel would be a big improvement on that Aussie tosser,' Carl says. 'I hated that guy.'

'We all did.' Zoe tried to make allowances for Blake's troubled past. At seven years old he was taken from his alcoholic single mother in Sydney and placed in a series of foster homes before running away to Melbourne when he was sixteen. Then came the drugs and the spells in psychiatric care. 'Quinn loved him, though.'

'Suppose someone had to.'

Zoe suspects Blake's abrupt departure from Pure Heart hurt Quinn more deeply than she ever admitted.

A bird lands on Zoe's notebook. Black back and tail. White chest and head. It pecks at the notebook's yellow cover before flitting away.

'A Cyprus wheatear,' says Carl.

Zoe isn't sure if his recent interest in birds signals a deeper connection to nature or the approach of old age.

Carl clears his throat. 'It'll all work out,' he says. 'If Quinn says Sofia's visit is what we need then we should trust her.'

Zoe nods. 'I guess so.'

'I keep picturing Sofia as a kid. I can't believe she's twenty-two now.'

Zoe suspects he's thinking about Pippa, his daughter, who turned twenty-two last month.

'I suppose Sofia will want to talk about Eva?' Carl says.

Zoe's stomach twists into a knot. 'We haven't really talked about Eva for ten years.'

'Well then.' Carl cracks his knuckles again. 'I guess it will be healing for all of us.'

'Maybe.'

Carl scrapes back his chair, drops to his knees in front of her and rests his hands on her thighs. 'Everything will be fine.'

She remembers how she trusted him when they first met. She liked his maturity and wisdom. She liked feeling protected. Since Charles' death exposed the community's financial vulnerability, she's sensed a neediness in her husband. Sometimes, if he wakes to find her side of the bed empty, he gets anxious. As if she might have left him in the night. As if she might decide there are other lives she could be living and other men she could live them with.

He rests his head on her lap. His warm breath penetrates the flimsy fabric of her kimono. Hot pulses of arousal between her legs make her shift in her seat. His lips find her through the fabric, making her moan. When she tries to loosen the kimono's belt, he looks up and smiles.

'Breathe with me.' He rests back on his heels and places a warm hand on her chest. Her hand mirrors his and they gaze into each other's eyes. One of the many tantric rituals they use to deepen their intimacy. Carl has deep brown eyes, framed by long dark lashes.

'The sexiest eyes in literature,' she says, quoting an article once written about him in *The Face* magazine.

'The cutest pixie in pop,' he says, quoting *Smash Hits*.

Pixie. She was never sure if that was a compliment or not. She was never a conventional-looking pop star. Wide mouth and full lips. Dimpled cheeks. Hazel eyes that were, according to one tabloid newspaper, 'disturbingly large.'

She tries to focus on Carl's lauded eyes, but his noisy breathing distracts her. It jars with the gentle birdsong surrounding them.

'It's so beautiful to connect with you like this,' he says.

She nods, suppressing a wave of frustration. She doesn't want him to connect with her. She wants him to fuck her. Here and now, while whispering filthy words in her ear, the way he used to when they first got together. She tells herself not to be ungrateful. This man considers her body to be sacred. He worships her. He is her audience of one and she is the star performer.

There was a time, in the early days of the community, when they occasionally invited someone to join them in bed. Men and women. Carl said it felt right not to be selfish with their love and Zoe agreed. She knew he got off on watching her with someone else and it turned her on to please him that way.

As she remembers this, her hand moves from his chest to the waistband of his yoga pants. His eyes narrow. He takes her hand and lifts it to his lips.

'Let's revisit this later,' he says. 'When we're both more present.'

She forces a smile. 'Can't wait.'

His knees creak as he gets to his feet. A noise that fills her with tenderness and irritation.

'I'm off to shower,' he says. 'No doubt Quinn's got some jobs lined up for me.'

'No doubt.'

The sun is already gathering warmth, but, as Zoe watches Carl walk away, she shivers. Cold, unwelcome thoughts intrude. What if Quinn is wrong? What if they can't find a way to save Pure Heart? Where would she and Carl end up? What would they do? She'd have to get an actual job. Something real and poorly paid and beneath her. Even if she qualified as a yoga teacher or a therapist of some kind, she'd have to compete with the thousands of others out there.

She pictures herself and Carl living in a poky flat in some nowhere town in the UK, Carl working way past pension age in some degrading job. Would he even qualify for a pension?

She picks up her pen, opens her notebook and adds a new line to her journal.

Please let us keep Pure Heart. Whatever it takes.

12

Insight Investigators: Background Report

Zoe Louise Aldridge (stage name: Zoe Tempest): Born May 3rd 1981 in Chelmsford, Essex, to Faye and Simon Aldridge. It's no secret that Faye was a pushy showbiz mother. Zoe made her first TV appearance in an advert for Pampers nappies. She attended the prestigious Italia Conti Academy of Theatre Arts and starred in a number of West End musicals and had bit parts in various TV shows. Got scouted by a record company when she was fifteen and became Zoe Tempest, pop star. One hit album and then it all went wrong. Second album flopped after she was hung out to dry by the press for having an affair with Leon McGregor, the married lead singer of rock band The Desert. It all kicked off when they were caught joining the mile-high club on a first-class flight from London to New York.

Faye and Simon divorced shortly after that. Simon remarried and now lives in New Zealand with his new family. Faye was notorious for spending Zoe's earnings on herself – mostly on bottles of Kristal champagne and nights in five-star hotels with the man who is now Zoe's stepfather. A class act. Even sold a story to the tabloids about her shame at Zoe's affair. According to a friend of Faye's, she and Zoe only speak a couple of times a year. If that.

Carl Fowles: Born April 16th 1959 to Kevin and Jane Fowles in Bedford. Mother now deceased and father in residential care. Has an older sister, Jean who still lives in Bedford and manages Kevin's care. To hear Carl Fowles speak you'd think he was born into money and educated at an exclusive private school but Kevin worked in a car factory and Jane was a care worker. Carl, who was apparently bright from a young age, went to a local comprehensive school and then on to Cambridge University, where he adopted his current accent to hide his working-class roots.

He hit the big time in his mid-twenties when his first novel, *The Dispossessed*, won a number of literary prizes and was made into a TV series. He married Savannah Richardson and had a daughter, Pippa. Had it all but he blew it. Heavy drinking, nasty coke habit, string of affairs. His second novel bombed, and he fell out with his agent and his publisher. Savannah divorced him and took what little money he had left. (She has since remarried, and Carl and his daughter have zero contact.) In his last ever interview, Carl declared he was moving to Ibiza to work on his magnum opus. He said he would win the Booker within the next five years.

As far as I can tell he hasn't published a word since.

13

HOLLY

2019

How happy we were the day of Sofia's arrival. By noon, we were all ready to greet her. The long trestle table in the courtyard was set with our best plates – vintage Cypriot pottery, hand-painted with pink and red poppies. Our finest crystal goblets were on display, along with our silver cutlery. The beautiful lunch Joe had prepared was in the fridge ready to bring out when she arrived. We were going to present it on our ceramic Turkish serving dishes – decorated in the classical blue and white Iznik tradition.

The cats, sensing an occasion, had gathered in the courtyard. The small brown sparrows we shared our lives with alighted on the table, hoping for crumbs.

We'd all dressed up for the occasion. Quinn in her orange dress and Carl in long black linen shorts and a black collarless linen shirt. Zoe in a floaty white sundress, her hair pinned up. Joe in khaki cargo pants and a bright Hawaiian shirt I bought him years ago from a shop in Nicosia. Mel matched burgundy linen trousers with a burgundy T-shirt. Even Andreas had showered and put on a white shirt with his jeans. I had on my old paisley kaftan. Cool and comfortable.

It was already twenty-eight degrees. Cloudless sky and brilliant sunshine. The mountains don't suffer the extreme temperatures and humidity of coastal and inland Cyprus, but we couldn't escape the summer entirely. Over the coming weeks, the temperature would steadily climb, trapping us in a cocoon of heat.

I'm not saying the weather's an excuse for what happened, but it is easy to get confused in the heat. Harder to think straight.

As I sat there, looking at our beautiful home, I wondered what Sofia would make of it now. Andreas had applied a fresh coat of white paint to the exterior of the building. The mural of the Furies looked even more faded in comparison, but you could still make out the three old crones with their snake hair and demonic expressions.

By 12.30 p.m. we were buzzing with excitement. We sat at the table, listening out for the sound of a car engine navigating the long access road to Pure Heart. We assumed Sofia had hired a car. It was strange to think of her being old enough to drive. By 1 p.m., we wondered if she was lost. Pure Heart wasn't easy to find; that was one of its attractions.

Half an hour later, we couldn't help being anxious. We nibbled on bread and olives, not wanting to spoil Joe's lovely lunch. The cats were restless. They brushed against our legs beneath the table and chased one another around the terracotta Grecian urns that decorated the courtyard.

Every now and then, Joe lifted my hand to his lips and kissed it. He's always so good at reassuring me. On one occasion, I saw Quinn staring at us, a pained expression on her face and I wondered if she was thinking about Blake. He was always touching and kissing her in public. Often explicitly so. I remembered walking through the orchard one day and stumbling across the pair of them having sex. Quinn had her face and body pressed against the trunk of an apple tree and didn't see me, but Blake did. He smiled at me as he pushed himself deep inside her. I hurried away, but later he found me alone in the kitchen.

'Sorry about earlier,' I said, embarrassed.

He shrugged. 'No worries. It really turned me on you watching me like that.'

At 1.30 p.m., Quinn went to the office and checked our email account in case Sofia had tried to contact her. We had a landline and answering machine in the study, but none of us owned a mobile. We wanted to protect ourselves from modern technology as much as possible, and our area had random mobile coverage. Strong in some parts of the house and grounds, non-existent in others.

At 2.30 p.m., we held hands and sent our energy out into the universe to guide Sofia to us.

Come home, Sofia, we whispered in unison. *Come home.*

Mel was the first to hear a vehicle approaching. The trained police officer in her coming to the fore. We looked at one another and smiled. All we'd prayed for had come true. A new chapter of the Pure Heart story was about to begin.

14

QUINN

2018

Quinn steps out of the former hotel's main entrance and into the car park, Aphrodite cradled in her arms. The others follow. She hears the rumble of a car engine, but the vehicle is still out of sight.

To Quinn's right, almost uncomfortably close, stands Mel. On Quinn's left are Joe and Holly and beside them are Zoe and Carl. A semi-circular welcoming committee. Andreas is lurking near the front door, flicking the ash from his cigarette into one of the terracotta pots that line the front of the building.

'Two cars,' Mel says, her elbow brushing against Quinn's.

'What?' says Quinn.

Mel frowns. 'There are two cars coming, not one.'

Quinn attunes herself to the approaching noise but can't tell if Mel is right or if the hyper-vigilant policewoman part of her is imagining things.

'Look,' Holly says, breathless with excitement. 'Look.'

Heading towards them down the narrow access road are two black Land Rovers, dust billowing in their wake.

'Did Sofia say anything about bringing someone with her?' Zoe asks.

'No.' Quinn holds Aphrodite's warm body close to her chest.

'Security,' Mel says. 'She's brought security with her.'

'Why would she do that?' Carl asks.

Before anyone can answer, the Land Rovers squeal to a halt in the car park. Driving each vehicle is a man in a white shirt, black waistcoat and dark sunglasses.

'Yup,' says Mel. 'Bodyguards.'

'They look like chauffeurs,' Quinn says.

Mel shakes her head. 'Trust me.'

Bodyguards? Quinn is sure the men are just escorting Sofia. It's not as if Sofia needs protection. Not from anyone at Pure Heart. She bends down and puts Aphrodite on the ground, but the cat crouches by her ankles.

The waistcoated men leap out of the vehicles in synchronised fashion. Mel edges closer to Quinn, as if to shield her, which makes Quinn smile. She doesn't need protecting. Not from their little Sofia.

The vehicles have tinted windows. No way of seeing which car Sofia is in.

Holly gasps. 'It's like a member of royalty's arrived.'

'Or a drug dealer,' Mel says. 'They always have tinted windows.'

Quinn sizes the men up. The older of the two is short and compact, his blond hair clipped close. The younger man – tall, bulky and bald – looks brutish and intimidating.

'They're armed,' Mel whispers.

Quinn spots a bulge beneath the right side of the men's waistcoats. Are they really carrying guns? The grinning skeleton on the Tarot card flashes through her mind.

In another display of synchronicity, both men open a back door of each vehicle. Mel clenches her fists. Quinn wonders if the men are triggering bad memories of her time in the police.

'Relax,' she tells Mel. 'It's only Sofia.'

The big guy reaches inside his Land Rover and pulls out an extravagant bouquet of flowers. Birds of paradise, canna lilies, giant sprays of green foliage.

Like everyone else, Quinn turns her eyes to the other vehicle. The short guy holds out his arm. A slender hand, fingers decorated with sparkling rings, meets it. Then comes one long, toned leg, followed by another.

Aphrodite hisses.

Quinn stares at the young woman standing before her. She is at least six feet tall, even in her flat, Grecian sandals. A white maxi dress hangs from her slender, long-limbed body. Her skin is bronzed and flawless. Oversized sunglasses shield her eyes. Her platinum blonde hair, dark at the roots, reaches past her shoulders in feathery layers. Hair that frames a narrow face with sharp cheekbones.

A face so familiar it shocks Quinn to her core.

'Eva?' she says.

'Oh, Quinny.' The woman laughs. 'I do look like her, don't I?'

Quinn's heartbeat tumbles over itself. She glances around her. Joe, Holly, Zoe and Carl are all staring at the visitor, their faces ghost white. Is hers as pale? Mel's eyes are fixed on the smaller bodyguard, a muscle twitching in the side of her face.

'It's me,' the woman says. 'It's Sofia.'

'You do,' Quinn says. 'You do look like her.'

'Little Sofia?' says Carl. 'Wow.'

'Oh, my God,' chorus Zoe and Holly.

'No way,' Joe mutters.

There she is. Sofia. Standing before them, in the same spot where she disappeared from their lives a decade ago.

Quinn is aware of Andreas' footsteps behind her. The sharp, woody scent of his tobacco. 'So beautiful,' he says. 'Just like your mother.'

Sofia removes her huge sunglasses, revealing thick eyebrows hovering over eyes so dark they are almost black. Eva's eyes.

Sofia stares at the house. Her lips move but no sound emerges.

Quinn also finds herself struggling to speak. Only when she feels the eyes of her community upon her, expecting her to take charge, does she summon some words. 'Welcome home,' she says, 'we're so happy to have you here.' When she opens her arms and steps in to hug Sofia, the larger bodyguard intercepts with the bouquet of flowers. 'Oh.' Quinn takes the bouquet, feeling like an overwhelmed minor royal on a walkabout. The heady scent of the flowers is overpowering. 'These are... my God, they're so beautiful. You didn't have to—'

She breaks off as Sofia bends down and kisses her on both cheeks.

'It's lovely to be here,' Sofia says. She has a polished, upper-class English accent. Hers is the clear, confident voice of someone who has attended the very best schools. Someone who mixes in privileged circles. 'So lovely.'

The thin gold chains around her neck catch the sunlight. As do her diamond drop earrings and the large diamond ring on the middle finger of her right hand. Quinn suspects this display of wealth is merely armour. Sofia will soon realise she doesn't need to hide behind anything at Pure Heart. Everyone here is interested in her soul. Not her money.

'Look at you, Quinn,' Sofia says. 'Don't you look well?'

Quinn smiles. 'That's kind, but—'

'Sixty next week. I can hardly believe it.'

'You remembered my birthday?'

'Of course. I haven't forgotten anything about my time here.' Sofia looks around at the others. 'I hope we're having a birthday party?'

'This is Pure Heart,' Carl says. 'We know how to party.'

'Wonderful.' Sofia graces them with a smile, exposing flawless dentistry. 'I've so many fun ideas for it.'

Holly rushes over to Sofia and enfolds her in a tight hug. 'Thank you for coming,' she says, her voice thick with feeling.

Zoe dives in next. After embracing Sofia, she compliments her on her dress.

'It's Max Mara,' Sofia says.

'I thought so,' gushes Zoe. 'It's divine.'

Divine. Quinn rolls her eyes. Honestly. She watches them all, the bouquet of flowers heavy in her arms. After Zoe comes Carl, who holds Sofia a little too long in her opinion. Then Joe, who looks overcome with emotion, like a father greeting a long-lost child.

When Andreas finally steps forward to kiss Sofia on both cheeks, Quinn finds their reunion quiet and touching. As if no time has passed at all. As if they saw each other only yesterday.

'Dear Charles,' Sofia says, glancing around the car park. 'Even though

Quinn told me he's dead, I keep thinking he's about to appear.'

'He thought the world of you,' Quinn says.

Sofia smiles. 'You must all miss him so much?'

'So much,' Zoe says.

'If only we could speak to him one more time,' Carl says. 'I've got so many questions for him.'

'We think about him every day,' says Holly.

Joe nods. 'It's impossible to forget him.'

'Where's Blake?' Sofia asks.

Heat crawls across Quinn's chest. 'He left.'

'A long time ago,' Holly adds.

'Oh.' Sofia tilts her head to one side. 'That's a shame.'

Quinn waves the sympathy aside. 'This is Mel,' she says, keen to change the subject, 'the newest member of the Pure Heart family.'

Mel cuts off a potential hug by offering her hand, which Sofia clasps in a formal handshake.

'Sofia Belova,' their guest says, 'I can't wait for us to get to know one another.'

Mel murmurs something indistinct. Her eyes are trained on the body-guards, as if she expects them to pounce at any moment.

Quinn waits, expectant, wondering if it's her turn for an embrace, but Sofia walks past her and stares up at the Pure Heart building. Quinn pushes aside a momentary feeling of hurt. Sofia must be overwhelmed right now. No need to rush anything. The two of them will have plenty of time together.

'I've never stopped thinking about this place.' Sofia's tone is suddenly serious. 'About all of you.'

The silence that follows is broken by a loud thud as a huge suitcase lands on the driveway.

'I am sorry,' says the smaller of the bodyguards. Is that a hint of menace in his accented English? Quinn brushes her fear away. She must be picking up Mel's paranoid energy. The larger man hauls two more iden-tical cases from the boot of the same vehicle.

'I'm dreadful at packing light.' Sofia lets out a high, brittle laugh. 'There's even more I'm afraid.'

'Are those Louis Vuitton?' asks Zoe, admiring the cases.

'Of course,' says Sofia. 'A little crass I know but the quality *is* exceptional.'

'Exquisite craftsmanship,' Zoe says, then glances around her, a guilty expression on her face.

Quinn calculates all her worldly possessions would struggle to fill just one of those cases. Sofia will soon remember how liberating it is to live without so many things. Owning too much can weigh a person down.

'Well, we want you to feel right at home,' Quinn says. When the big guy asks where to take the luggage, she shakes her head. 'Don't worry. We've got this.'

'It is not a worry,' he replies, his accent even thicker than his colleague's.

'No, it's fine,' Quinn says. 'Thanks for dropping her off, but you're free to go now. We'll take it from here.'

Both men look at Sofia.

'My bodyguards have to stay with me the whole time,' she says.

'Oh.' Quinn's forehead creases with confusion. 'You didn't mention them.'

'I must have.'

'You didn't,' Mel says. 'We would have remembered that.'

'It's a pain, but these days I'm considered a kidnap risk.' Sofia points to the smaller man. 'This is Dmitri.' Dmitri stops what he is doing to spare them a brief nod. The larger man, still unloading cases from the boot of the second Land Rover, doesn't bother looking at them at all when Sofia introduces him as Grigor. 'They'll need a room each. Is that okay?'

Quinn hesitates, trying to catch up with this turn of events. She didn't factor in the presence of bodyguards. She mistakenly assumed that with her grandparents gone, Sofia would be a free agent, able to make her own choices. Never mind. The men will soon see how much everyone at Pure Heart loves Sofia. How safe she is here. After a while, the two of them will probably leave.

Mel eyes Sofia with suspicion. Quinn knows she must be doubting the young woman's fragility. Sofia's imperious tone doesn't give the impression of someone on the verge of a nervous breakdown. Quinn knows her behaviour is a facade. A persona to hide the frightened, insecure girl inside.

'Quinn?' Sofia says. 'Is that okay?' She turns to her bodyguards. 'Quinn's in charge here. We must all remember that.'

'No, no, no.' Quinn recovers her composure. 'We're a democracy here. I may have founded this place, but we're all about equality.'

'We vote on everything,' Holly says.

'Quick vote,' Joe says. 'All in favour of our extra guests.'

Joe, Holly, Carl and Zoe raise their hands. When Quinn raises hers, Mel follows with a sigh.

'Well, that was easy,' Quinn says. 'We'll open up two extra rooms for Grigor and Dmitri.'

Dmitri speaks to Sofia in Russian. She replies in the same language.

'They'll check out the hotel and decide which rooms they need,' she says to Quinn.

'No problem at all,' Quinn says. 'We'll have it all sorted by tonight.'

'And I'm in my old rooms?' Sofia asks. 'The ones I shared with my mother.'

'You are,' Zoe says, 'I got them ready for you this morning.'

Sofia smiles. 'How sweet.'

'Maybe we should eat while your luggage gets carried up?' Joe suggests. 'I've made Greek salad and—'

'Sorry, Joe, but I stopped in Kakopetria and had lunch there,' Sofia says.

'Oh, right.' Disappointment flashes across Joe's face.

'I went to that restaurant Eva used to take me to. The one where the old guy sits outside all day roasting chickens on a spit. I made a total pig of myself.' Sofia pats her stomach, which is so flat it looks like she never eats at all. 'I should save some room for dinner.'

'Aye, good plan,' says Joe. 'I've made some of your favourites.'

Grigor asks Sofia something in Russian.

'This pair could do with feeding,' she says. 'If there's enough?'

Joe nods. 'Aye, sure.'

Quinn steps forward and links an arm through Sofia's. 'There's plenty for everyone at Pure Heart,' she says.

15

HOLLY

We didn't need to lead Sofia into the house. She knew exactly where she was going. With her long white dress, golden sandals and flowing blonde hair, she looked like a Greek goddess, and we followed like dazed worshippers as she stepped through the front door and into the hallway.

She stood still for a moment, taking it all in. She said everything was just as she remembered. When she turned and headed for the wooden staircase, we followed her up it.

In the corridor outside the rooms she once shared with Eva, she hesitated. Quinn opened the door and ushered her into the living room we'd created for her. It was once her bedroom and, as we followed her inside, her gaze roamed hungrily around the small space, as if she expected to find her mother there.

The bodyguards appeared, red-faced and sweating and dragging hefty luggage behind them. Sofia ordered them around in Russian. She was clearly used to being in charge.

None of that fazed us. Despite her entourage and her expensive clothes and jewellery, we could still see the girl she once was. Although, I must admit her resemblance to her mother was unsettling.

After the bodyguards left us alone again, Sofia explored the adjoining room. It was once Eva's bedroom but now she would sleep there. What she found on the bedside table made her gasp. *The Encyclopaedia of Greek Myths.*

'I meant to take this with me when I left,' she said, 'but it all happened in such a rush.'

After checking out the bedroom, she returned to the living room and rushed over to the small oak desk by the window where she used to sit and do her homework. I remembered sitting with her there, reading to her from a dated textbook about World War One.

'Why does history matter?' she'd asked me.

I'd stroked her thick dark hair. 'It helps us understand who we are.'

Now her body tensed as she looked out of the window, and I wondered if she could see the monastery through the trees. Was she picturing her mother hanging from one of the wooden rafters inside it? The lifeless body swinging back and forth?

We told her she could move rooms if she wanted to. Away from that view. She shook her head. She told us it was good to remember.

At that moment the room appeared to go dark, despite the sunlight outside. I thought it was the memory of Eva's death casting shadows. I didn't know the darkness was an omen of what was to come.

16

ZOE

2018

Is Sofia the miracle they hoped and prayed for? Or is her return to Pure Heart a bad idea? Four hours after Sofia's arrival, Zoe isn't sure. With her rubber-gloved hands deep in the kitchen sink, tending to a stack of dirty plates with an eco-friendly coconut scourer, Zoe replays the image of Sofia emerging from the Land Rover. The shock like a punch to her stomach. For a moment she thought it was Eva come back from the dead. Ridiculous. Zoe believes in many things – auras, chakras, the healing power of crystals for example – but she knows the departed don't rise from their graves.

Now it's nearly 6 p.m. and she's in the kitchen with Carl, Holly and Joe, clearing up the remains of the lunch Joe put out earlier for the bodyguards. Now Joe is busy stuffing two pale, plucked quails with rosemary and thyme.

When Carl appears behind her and slides his hands around her waist, she jumps.

'I'll dry.' He kisses her neck before yanking a grubby tea towel from the hook beneath the draining board.

'Thanks,' she says. After they left Sofia to settle into her accommodation, Quinn announced she needed to go and meditate. There was, she said, a lot to mull over. Everyone drifted away to their rooms, claiming to need a rest after all the excitement. As if they didn't want to admit how much they had to discuss. In their own room, she and Carl held each other for a long time in a silent embrace, and she wondered if he was thinking of Eva. How beautiful she was.

'Do you think she's sleeping?' Holly asks in hushed tones, as if Sofia might hear her.

'Maybe.' Joe drizzles oil over the skin of the birds.

Carl shakes the suds off a large serving bowl. 'I imagine she's still unpacking,' he says wryly.

Zoe has never seen so many Louis Vuitton cases. She remembers her stylist kitting her out with a Louis Vuitton clutch bag for her first and only Brit Awards. A wrap of cocaine tucked in the zipped pocket inside. After she didn't win the Rising Star award she was nominated for, she sneaked away to the toilets and snorted the whole lot with her publicist.

'She'll sleep well here,' Holly says. 'It's so peaceful.'

The window above the sink is open. Through the mesh fly screen Zoe hears only cicadas and birdsong. Peaceful indeed, but Zoe feels anything but. She can sense Sofia's presence in the building. A presence both alien and familiar. The others sense it too; she can tell. A strange tension grips them all. As if the kitchen is a stage set and they're waiting for the curtain to rise on the next act of a play so they can burst into action and say their lines.

Zoe has changed her costume for the evening. Loose black yoga pants and a cropped grey T-shirt. She's still wearing the make-up she put on for Sofia's arrival and her eyelashes feel stiff and claggy.

She tackles another plate with the scourer and hands it to Carl. She loathes washing up. Until two months ago they still had a functional dishwasher, but it packed up on them and added one more daily chore to the never-ending list. She glances at the wall beside the sink, where a printed, laminated sign warns her not to waste water. Other, similar signs are pinned up all over the kitchen.

Please recycle all tins and cardboard. Follow the colour codes for the
chopping boards. DO NOT switch the oven off at the red switch on the
wall!!!!!

Zoe bets Sofia has a sleek, modern kitchen in her home as well as staff
to run it for her. Sofia is a woman who gives orders. She wouldn't let laminated signs boss her around.

'Honestly.' Holly scrapes the remains of a Greek salad from a large
serving dish into a small bowl. 'Those bodyguards ate almost everything.'

'I've seen starving refugees at the camp eat less,' Joe says.

'We'll have our hands full looking after our guests,' Holly says. 'Won't
we, love?'

'Aye.' Joe tosses herbs over the oily skins of the quails. 'We will.'

'It'll be like the old days.' Carl gives the dripping plate in his hand a
vigorous rub with the tea towel.

The old days. Zoe remembers the noisy happy chaos of mealtimes.
Does Sofia's visit herald a return to those times?

'Do you think she remembers leaving us?' Holly says.

Silence apart from the splash of Zoe's hands in the greasy water, the
squeak of Carl's tea towel against the plate, the creak of the oven door as
Joe opens it.

'Who knows?' The roasting dish packed with quails clatters as Joe
shoves it into the oven. 'There's a lot she might want to forget.'

'We should have stopped her grandparents from taking her,' Holly
says.

Joe slams the oven door shut. 'There's a lot we should have done.'

The kitchen door opens. Everyone turns in anticipation, but it's only
Mel. She strides into the room, face flushed, dark islands of sweat on her
burgundy T-shirt. She has dirt streaks on her burgundy shorts and dust on
her black trainers.

'I went for a run up the mountain path to the viewpoint,' she says. 'Had
to clear my head.' She glances around the kitchen. 'Anything happened
here?'

Zoe isn't the only one in the room to straighten up and pull her shoulders back. Earlier, she could tell Mel was dying to interrogate them all about Sofia's arrival.

'Where's Andreas?' Mel asks.

'He left a while ago,' Holly says.

Concern clouds Mel's features. 'I thought he'd stay the night,' she says, as if Andreas is the only responsible adult amongst them and they won't make it through to dawn without him.

'He's gone to visit his mum,' Joe explains.

Mel sighs. 'I went to Quinn's room. Her Do Not Disturb sign is up so she must still be meditating. Although I'm not sure how much peace she'll get with that bullet-catcher in the next room.'

'Bullet-catcher?' Zoe says.

'A nickname we police used to give bodyguards,' Mel says.

'He did seem determined to have that room,' says Carl.

'It's a perfect strategic location.' Mel sounds as if she's in a police briefing. 'Right next to the fire exit that leads to an outside set of stairs. Easy for someone to break into the building. Or break out of it.'

'It's all very James Bond,' Holly says.

Mel frowns. 'Hardly.' She marches over to the fridge, opens it and takes out a jug of chilled water. 'Poor Quinn. I'm sure she needs all the rest she can get just now.'

Poor Quinn? Zoe glances at Carl who rolls his eyes.

'Aren't any of you worried about these men being here?' Mel picks up a glass tumbler from a shelf. 'They're armed. Or does that not bother you?'

'Look.' Joe wipes his hands on his apron. 'None of us are in favour of guns, but these guys are just doing their job.'

'I doubt they're expecting to shoot any of us,' Carl says. 'This must be a cushy number for them.'

Zoe wonders if Mel came up against armed men when she was in the police. She never talks about the specific cause of her post-traumatic stress disorder. Or maybe having men like Sofia's bodyguards around reminds Mel of her ex-boyfriend. It's hard to imagine Mel helpless at the hands of an abuser, but Zoe knows how easy it is to become a victim.

Mel pours herself a glass of water and gulps it back. 'Weird they didn't travel with a driver. Safety wise. It's like Sofia doesn't want anyone knowing she's here.'

'That's maybe the point if she's a kidnap risk?' Joe says.

'Maybe.' Mel wipes her mouth. 'They've probably done background checks on all of us.'

Joe shrugs. 'We don't have anything to hide.'

'I'm not so sure,' Carl says. 'The reviews for my second novel were atrocious.' His laughter sounds hollow to Zoe.

'Not as bad as the ones for my second album,' she says.

'Poor baby.' Carl leans in and kisses her. 'Fuck the lot of them.'

Her laughter is more hollow than his. She doesn't like the thought of people trawling through the lurid tabloid headlines that prompted her self-imposed exile from the UK. *Pop Pixie in mile-high tryst with married rocker. Zoe Tempest's stormy affair shocks fans. Leon McGregor's wife stands by her man.*

Shame flushes her cheeks. She snaps off her rubber gloves and tosses them on the draining board. Mel has stopped by one of the framed photographs of Eva they put up on the wall. Eva sitting poolside with her feet in the water. Capturing the camera's curious gaze with her own enigmatic one.

Mel scrutinises the picture, as if it's a clue pinned up on a crime scene evidence board. 'Sofia looked really shaken up when she saw the monastery,' she says. 'She's still not over what happened.'

'Sofia was the one who found Eva's body,' Zoe says. She was here, in the kitchen that day, and she will never forget the screams that carried across the courtyard into the house. Piercing, feral screams that chilled Zoe to the bone before she even knew what had happened.

Carl slides an arm around her shoulder. She sags against him.

'I see.' Mel leans against the workstation. 'Traumatic for her, at that age. It's shocking at any age. The first dead body I saw in the Met was a suicide. Guy in his fifties. Overdose.' She shakes her head. 'I'll never forget it.'

'Poor Sofia,' Holly says. 'Losing your mother at such a young age is tragic.'

Mel nods. 'I was only five when my dad died, so I can't really remember him. Sofia had time to get to know Eva. That must be so much worse.'

Zoe has only heard Mel mention her dead father once before. She's not sure now is the time to bring him up again.

'There's no hierarchy of suffering, Mel,' Holly says, repeating one of Quinn's favourite quotes. 'Everything you feel is totally valid.'

'What if she's inherited Eva's... vulnerabilities?' Mel says. 'If she has, is it really a good idea for her to be here? I mean she—'

The kitchen door opens, stopping her mid-flow. Dmitri enters the room and shuts the door behind him. He is still wearing his smart trousers, white shirt and black waistcoat. His cold, grey eyes sweep the room. When they settle on Zoe, heat surges across her chest. She eases herself out of Carl's embrace.

'Good evening,' he says.

'Evening,' Zoe replies, as the others offer similar greetings. She wonders how old Dmitri is. Mid-forties maybe? The lines on his impassive face hint at a hard life but his compact body is lithe and trim. He is, she decides, quite attractive. She sees the bulge beneath the right-hand side of his waistcoat. Good of him to hide his weapon. He must know he doesn't need to intimidate them in any way.

Mel retreats to the dining table, pulls out a chair and sits down. One of the white kittens, Zoe can't tell if it's Apollo or Artemis, darts out from under the table and circles Dmitri a few times before stopping to look up at him with pleading eyes. Dmitri stares back and, with a wounded squeak, the kitten scurries back beneath the table.

'Can we get you something?' Carl asks him. 'Coffee? A snack?'

The bodyguard shakes his head. 'Sofia will not join you for dinner. She must rest.'

'Oh.' Joe glances at the oven, where the skins of the quails are already blistering in heat. 'No worries. We can have the big welcome meal tomorrow.'

'Yes, she must rest,' Holly says. 'Rest is very important.'

'She sends apologies,' Dmitri says.

'We could put a tray of something together,' says Joe. 'If she's hungry.'

'Maybe later.' Dmitri checks his watch. 'First she will rest, then she will take a bath.'

Zoe helped to prepare the room next to Sofia's quarters for Dmitri. She wonders if sorting out meals isn't the only menial task he performs. She imagines him running Sofia's bath for her. Turning down her bed covers at night.

'We don't have baths here,' Mel says.

Dmitri stares at her. 'There is a bath. In the bathroom. I have seen it.'

'I mean we don't use the baths,' Mel explains. 'It's a waste of water.'

'I do not understand.' Dmitri looks at the rest of them, quizzical.

'It doesn't matter,' Zoe says. 'I'm sure Sofia needs a bath after her journey.'

'Only the best for our guest,' Carl says.

Only the best for such a generous guest, thinks Zoe. Mel needs to remember that.

Dmitri nods, turns and exits the room.

* * *

They wait a few moments in silence. Mel gets up and checks the corridor outside is empty. Zoe sighs. Does she really think Dmitri will be listening in on them?

'We can have the quails cold tomorrow,' Joe says.

'Perfect,' Holly says. 'They'll still be delicious.'

'I have a bad feeling about all this,' Mel says.

'Got a hunch have you, Detective?' Carl's tone is gently teasing.

'We shouldn't have let Sofia pay for her stay,' Mel says.

'She insisted,' Zoe reminds her.

'Being in debt to these people is a bad idea,' Mel says. 'Where do you think Sofia's money comes from? There's no way her grandfather was legit.'

'Not originally,' Carl says. 'Eva was very upfront about that.'

'That's why she wanted to raise Sofia here,' Joe adds.

'When I worked Organised Crime, I came up against the Russian mafia all the time.' Mel grimaces. 'They're hardcore.'

'Well, you made a mistake coming to Cyprus then,' Carl says. 'Andreas is always banging on about the Russian mafia taking over his island.'

'He's got a point,' Mel says. 'Some of the mafia guys I failed to put away ended up retiring over here.'

'Sofia's two generations away from all that,' Zoe says. 'We accepted money from an old friend, not a gangster.'

'There's a fine line,' Mel says. 'Once you cross it you can never get back.'

'Sofia's one of us,' Holly insists. 'She's part of the Pure Heart family.'

'Aye, exactly,' says Joe. 'Maybe you've still got some limiting financial beliefs you need to work on, Mel?'

'Who doesn't?' adds Carl. 'We all have blocks about abundance.'

Zoe doesn't like what Mel is implying. As if they're the kind of people who would put money before ethics. 'Quinn says this visit was destined to happen. Don't you believe her?'

'Of course, I believe Quinn.' Mel looks flustered now. 'I'm just saying we—'

'We'd never do anything that wasn't in alignment with our integrity,' Zoe says. Another of Quinn's favourite sayings. Perfect for this moment.

'Hey, I know,' Carl says, 'let's kidnap Sofia ourselves. Get a huge ransom and live happily ever after.'

Zoe smiles at the joke, as does Joe. Holly lets out a nervous giggle.

'That's not funny,' Mel says. 'Not funny at all.'

17

Insight Investigators: Background Report

Rachel Jane Wilde (known as Quinn): Born 6th July 1958 to Amanda and Jonathon Wilde. (Both parents now deceased.) Until the age of four, she was raised in Warwick, where her father was Director of Estates at Warwick University. Not long after Rachel's first birthday, her mother took her to live in a commune in Islington run by a guy from Dublin called Tom Quinn. (Seems Rachel renamed herself in his memory as soon as she legally could.) Tom Quinn was a dubious character. Claimed he had special healing powers and often told followers he was the second coming of Christ. He died in 2008 in Dublin.

When Rachel was thirteen, Tom Quinn was arrested and charged with tax evasion and the commune fell apart. Amanda went back to her husband in Warwick. Rachel had trouble settling back into 'normal' life. When she was expelled from school at sixteen, she left home and moved into a squat in Brixton.

After that there's little official trace of her, but I did manage to track down some former Pure Heart members who've been willing to talk.

18

QUINN

2018

The morning after Sofia's arrival, Quinn wakes at 6.30 a.m. She sits up in bed, disorientated. Six-thirty? She never sleeps in this late. The sound of coughing from the room next door sparks off a rush of irritation. Her new neighbour is the reason for her disrupted routine. His snoring woke her in the middle of the night. Deep, rattling snores that penetrated the thick wall between them.

Grigor, it turns out, does not only snore. He also coughs and passes wind and talks to himself in Russian. Quinn wasn't overjoyed at the big man moving in next door to her, but Mel told her yesterday that, in her opinion, Dmitri was the more dangerous of the bodyguards. She said she'd met men like him on both sides of the law.

Not that Quinn is intimidated by her unexpected guests. Not at all. They're just an unhelpful connection to the life Sofia needs a break from.

Yesterday she tried to approach Sofia's room, barefoot and silent as always, but Dmitri appeared before she even got close. When she explained she wanted to check in on her guest, Dmitri gave her a smile that didn't reach his steely eyes and told her Sofia was sleeping.

Imagine having those men with you all the time. It seems to Quinn that Sofia's money has so much fear attached to it. Her wealth is a dark, negative energy she needs to free herself from.

Still, Quinn is pleased Sofia is resting. It's a sign their visitor is succumbing to the healing energy of the community. It will take time for her to decompress and process the enormity of her return to Pure Heart. Quinn knows what it feels like to be torn away from the place and the people you love. When she and her mother left the commune in Islington to return to their stuffy suburban life in Warwick, Quinn was distraught.

Next door, Grigor unleashes a ferocious fart. Yesterday, before taking to her bed, Sofia promised Quinn no one would even notice the bodyguards were there. A promise Quinn is finding hard to believe. It sounds to her like Grigor might have a digestive disorder of some kind. He looks fit but she imagines his job involves long, irregular hours and high stress levels. She might give him some mountain tea to try, and she could even show him a few yogic breathing exercises to relieve his snoring.

She swings her legs out of bed and stands up. The spiritual path is full of obstacles, big and small, and it's important not to sweat the small stuff. She still has time for a short meditation and yoga practice this morning and then she'll feed her beloved hens before getting on with the day. She's bound to see Sofia today at some point. Then the two of them will talk properly, and Quinn can work out the best way to progress. There is so much the girl needs to shed to find peace again. To connect with true joy.

Quinn is determined to do everything in her power to help her.

19

QUINN

2018

After feeding her hens, Quinn makes her way to the terrace below, Aphrodite trailing behind her. The sky is blue and cloudless, the sun already heating up. First, she checks on the sweat lodge, a low, dome-shaped structure made up of thick blankets attached to a willow framework. The community built it together. She intends to include a sweat lodge ceremony as part of her birthday celebrations. It hasn't been used for a while, so she pins back the pink blankets that cover the entrance to let in some air. After a quick inspection of the lodge's musty interior, she makes a mental note to stock up on sage leaves for the ceremony.

Then she proceeds to the clearing next to the sweat lodge, where she will continue digging her own grave. Beneath the shade of a tall cedar tree, is a hole six feet long and three feet wide. Quinn chose the position herself, knowing that on the night of her birthday, a full moon will shine down on the clearing.

It is a beautiful spot. Fringed by a sprawling carpet of smooth oregano in bloom, the green leaves releasing a rich, herby scent, the pinkish-purple flowers adding a burst of colour. Behind the oregano, sit thick clusters of prickly burnet bushes. Charles' memorial plaque is just beyond the clearing, beneath a towering pine. After he died, Quinn discovered that despite his dire financial situation, he'd already paid for his body to be flown back to the UK and buried in his family plot in Norfolk.

This was a shock, but she tried to understand. Charles always said he wanted his ashes scattered at Pure Heart but, for religious reasons, cremation has until recently been illegal in Cyprus. Even though it's now legal, there is still no crematorium on the island. When Quinn found out Charles had arranged for his body to go back to England, she assumed he would be cremated and have the necessary permission for his ashes to return to Pure Heart. Still, he did leave them the memorial plaque along with instructions of where to put it so they would always remember him.

'Not long now,' she calls out to him. 'In six days, I'll be sixty years old.'

Her grave must be finished by then. Joe and Carl have done most of the hard work, digging deep into the rocky soil, but Quinn wants to finish the process herself.

As she picks up the spade that leans against the trunk of the cedar, she spots a short-toed treecreeper tapping its way up the tree with its long, curved beak. She bids it good morning before lowering herself into the ground. Aphrodite flops down at the graveside and watches as Quinn starts to dig. The simple activity – the downward thrust of her spade, the scooping of dirt to heave over the side – turns into a form of contemplation. She needs to still her busy mind. So much to think about. So many possibilities.

Yesterday, after taking time to meditate on the day's unexpected events, Quinn once more pulled a lone card from her Tarot pack. Her fingers tingled as she turned it over.

Death.

Of course, it was. The grinning skeleton.

She couldn't have asked for a clearer message from the universe. Sofia was the miracle they'd prayed for. Sofia had returned to Pure Heart to kill off her old self and emerge reborn and, by helping her, the community would be reborn too.

She trusted the message. Felt the truth of it in her bones.

When she shared her insights with the others over supper last night, she was happy to find they agreed with her. Holly and Joe were delighted to have Sofia back and Zoe and Carl said they would, of course, do all they could to help Sofia evolve into a happier, healthier human being. Mel was quiet and withdrawn, but she nodded her assent to Quinn's interpretation of events. It gave Quinn a lot of joy to see her family united. All of them putting Sofia's wellbeing first.

A rustling in the nearby bushes makes her pause. Snakes do inhabit the area. Quinn has seen both a black whip snake and once, in a beam of torchlight, the nocturnal European cat snake. According to Andreas, the droughts of recent years have forced the snakes out of hiding in search of water. He even claims he saw a blunt-nosed viper in the forest a few miles from Pure Heart, but Andreas is fond of a tall story and Quinn isn't sure she believes him.

She returns to her digging, the soil beneath her bare feet dry and dusty and jagged with stones. Her thoughts turn to her upcoming party. Her rebirthing ceremony will be the climax of the celebrations that will begin five days from now, on the evening before her birthday. First, they will graze on a light supper in the courtyard. Afterwards, she will conduct a healing sound bath in the yurt, and they will enjoy some Buddhist chanting together. Then they will dance until midnight, united and ecstatic.

At midnight, bathed in moonlight, Quinn will lead the way to her open grave. She will undress, lower herself into the hole and lie on her back, her arms crossed over her chest while the others cover her with olive branches. She will lie beneath the symbolic soil and ask the universal spirit to guide her as she begins the next phase of her life.

After she emerges reborn from her grave, they will finish up with a sweat lodge ceremony so she can release any remaining toxicity from her body.

Quinn stops digging, leans on the handle of her spade and looks down at the distant trees. A shallow breath catches in her throat as she spots the white walls of the monastery. She thinks of Eva's body, lifeless on the monastery floor after they cut her down from the rafters.

The crackling of footsteps on dry grass makes her twist round. Approaching the grave, the morning sun at her back, is a shimmering figure dressed in white. Eva? Of course not, but the resemblance leaves Quinn momentarily breathless.

'Morning,' Sofia says, drawing closer. The morning light bounces off her Grecian sandals and her gold bracelets and earrings.

'Hi,' Quinn manages eventually. 'Good to see you.' She must proceed carefully, casually. These first few days with Sofia are so important. 'Did you sleep well?' Sofia looks fresh-faced, but Quinn can see she's wearing make-up. Sofia will soon realise she doesn't need to hide behind a mask here. At Pure Heart they care about who she is on the inside.

'I slept amazingly,' Sofia says.

'That's good.' During the night, Quinn thought of Sofia, lying in the bed she once shared with her mother. Would she sense Eva's presence there? After Eva's death, Quinn feared her spirit would hang around Pure Heart. Not to haunt them. No, there was no cause for that, but Quinn worried Eva might not want to leave. In the weeks after the tragedy, she wafted burning sage all over the house and the terraces. She and the others prayed and chanted and did all they could to send Eva's unhappy soul to a peaceful place.

'I wanted to swim before breakfast,' Sofia says. 'What's up with the pool?'

'The filtration system's broken,' Quinn says. 'We've been trying to fix it but...' She trails off as Dmitri comes into view. She should have known he'd be nearby. He addresses Sofia in Russian, his voice low and even. As he speaks, he adjusts his black suit jacket. Quinn assumes he and Grigor have to stick to their formal dress code, whatever the weather.

'What's he saying?' asks Quinn.

'He's slightly concerned to find you digging a grave.' Sofia giggles before replying to Dmitri in Russian. Her explanation leaves him looking perplexed.

'I guess our customs may seem strange to you, Dmitri,' Quinn says, 'but sixty's a big milestone, you know? Makes sense to honour it.'

'Tell me about the party?' Sofia says. 'What do you have planned?'

When Quinn fills her in on the night's itinerary, Sofia claps her hands. 'Dancing. I love dancing.' She turns to her bodyguard. 'In his younger days, Dmitri here was a regular on the Moscow techno scene.'

'Oh, we don't do that kind of dancing,' Quinn says. 'We dance purely to express ourselves and to connect with Spirit.'

She explains they will drink cacao beforehand to help them connect with their heart chakras.

'Cacao?' Dmitri frowns. 'You drink hot chocolate?'

'No,' Quinn says. 'Cacao is not the same as cocoa. It's chocolate in its purest, rawest form. It's an ancient medicine used in rituals. You make it into a hot drink and add spices and it—'

'So is basically hot chocolate?' Dmitri says. 'No?'

'We drink it during a special ceremony,' Quinn says. 'It's very sacred.'

Dmitri speaks to Sofia in Russian. She laughs.

'He says he's sure it will be a night to remember,' she says.

'We'll do our best,' says Quinn.

Sofia peers into the grave. 'My mother's in a mausoleum.'

'Sorry?'

'A mausoleum in a North London graveyard. It's so gaudy. She would have hated it.'

Quinn flinches as something sharp digs into the ball of her right foot. She lifts her foot up and sees the jagged tip of a stone sticking up from the earth.

'I knew coming here would be a good idea.' Sofia smiles. 'I feel different after just one night.'

'That's wonderful.' All Quinn wants is for Sofia to be her very best self. For ten years the girl has been indoctrinated by her grandparents.

'I feel freer somehow,' Sofia says. 'Maybe it's being away from all my stuffy advisers. Grey men in grey suits telling me what to do all the time.'

Quinn smiles. 'You are free.' Here, Sofia can do as she pleases with her money. Spend it on whatever she likes.

She bends down to pick up the jagged black stone that has left a red mark on her foot. When she straightens up, Dmitri is beside the grave, his grey eyes fixed on her.

'You will have to dig a little deeper than that,' he says. 'If you want them to give you a proper burial.'

She holds his gaze for a moment, uncertain whether to laugh.

A loud buzzing noise distracts her. Shielding her eyes against the early sun, Quinn glances around, trying to locate the source of the noise.

She jumps as a small black object zips towards the grave through the musky air and hovers over her. Four metallic limbs are attached to its small, neat body.

'It's just a drone,' Sofia says. 'The guys use them for routine surveillance.'

Quinn glares up at it and then rearranges her features into a smile. Is Grigor looking at her right now?

'They don't approve of technology here,' Sofia tells Dmitri. 'They try to live without it as much as they can.'

Quinn is mesmerised by the whining, inquisitive drone. She watches it until it darts away, back in the direction of the house.

'It's a drag, all this, I know,' Sofia says. 'But the team have a job to do.'

'Of course,' Quinn says. 'Whatever you need to feel safe.'

20

HOLLY

2019

The security measures happened fast. The day after Sofia's arrival, a firm from Limassol turned up to install a new gate at the top of the driveway. It required a code to open it. We were informed the code would change daily and that Grigor or Dmitri would provide it on request.

The same firm installed security cameras inside and outside the building, as well as an alarm system. The engineers pointed out that our poor Internet connection and mobile coverage could compromise some of the systems but were instructed to do the best job they could with the resources available. We were informed the alarm would be turned on at midnight and switched off at five-thirty in the morning. To leave the property during these hours we'd need to ask for the alarm to be deactivated.

Although these intrusive measures did clash with the Pure Heart ethos of trusting in the best of humankind rather than fearing the worst, we understood Sofia's need for safety. She was apologetic and promised all the equipment would be removed when she left. We told her not to worry about that. No need for her to be talking about leaving.

She paid for everything, of course. The Sunday after she arrived, over dinner, she announced she wanted to get the swimming pool fixed as a birthday gift for Quinn. We tried to refuse, but she told us money exists to be shared and enjoyed. She told us that, amongst her other duties, she would be taking over as head of her grandfather's charitable foundation. She was excited about supporting worthy causes but said the responsibility of her wealth sometimes made her feel lonely.

We told her she wasn't alone any more. She had us now.

The next day, the first Monday in July, another set of workmen appeared. They cleaned the pool and installed a new filter valve and a new pump. It was so good to be able to swim again. It sounds silly but it was like the heart-shaped pool was our heart and now it was beating again. It filled us with a sense of joy and hope.

As well as the security arrangements, having guests meant we needed to go food shopping more than usual. To make life easier for us, Sofia insisted Joe place his food orders over the phone with the supermarket in Kakopetria and the various local suppliers we used so that Grigor or Dmitri could drive and collect what we wanted. No need for us to be running around after her, she said.

The day of the party drew closer. Sofia was more excited about it than anyone. When she wasn't sunning herself by the pool and reading her book of Greek myths, she insisted on helping with the arrangements. We all agreed it was good for her to have something positive to focus on. Even though we didn't intend to start her healing programme until after the party, there was no doubt she was already benefiting from her return to Pure Heart. We did worry she might want to visit the monastery, but her party planning distracted her from morbid journeys into the past.

The days leading up to the party were busy but happy ones. All of us shared a renewed sense of connection and purpose. Sofia helped Joe and I with the food preparation. She said menial chores were fun for her. At home she had a chef and never had the chance to get her hands dirty.

She kept hinting she had more surprises in store for Quinn's birthday. On the day of the party, when a van arrived to deliver two crates of champagne, we thought that might be it.

I told her to stop spoiling us. No more surprises.

She said she couldn't promise that.

In the afternoon, we all retired to our rooms for a siesta and to prepare for the celebrations. At 7 p.m., dressed in appropriate loose clothing, we made our way to the courtyard for supper. The warm air carried the soothing scents of jasmine and lavender. We were happy and hopeful. It seemed as though everything we had prayed for was finally coming to pass.

We would soon realise we should have been careful what we wished for.

21

QUINN

2018

It is just gone 8 p.m. Sunset is almost over, and, in the upper reaches of the indigo sky, the first stars are revealing themselves. The full moon is a pale disc, waiting for darkness to fall so it can show off its full light. A gentle breeze caresses the back of Quinn's neck, most welcome after the heat of the day. Even this early in July, the temperatures are climbing, hinting at hotter days to come.

She sits at the head of the trestle table in the courtyard, clothed once more in her orange wrap-around dress. She can't remember the last time she was this happy. Her Pure Heart family is here to celebrate this important life transition with her. She couldn't ask for more. Beneath the table, Aphrodite's warm body is curled around her toes. The feline members of the community are here to honour her too – some lying beneath the table, others sprawled beside the pool, the younger ones chasing each other around the terracotta pots and eyeless statues.

She looks around the table, drinking in the sight of her fellow spiritual warriors. Their chatter and laughter echoes around the courtyard. The church candles flickering on the table give them all a golden glow. On her right is Carl, smart in black cotton yoga pants and a black silk shirt. Holly, beside him, looks charming in a floral skirt and pink vest top, although she still has soil beneath her fingernails. She spends so much time gardening, the soil has become a permanent fixture. Next to her is Zoe, elegant in a flowing black silk skirt and a black halter-neck top. On Quinn's immediate left is Mel, her simple burgundy tunic and trousers a calm block of colour. Next to Mel sits Joe, garish in another of his Hawaiian shirts.

Sofia sits beside him, regal in a white maxi dress, a statement gold necklace imprisoning her slender neck. Diamonds sparkle in her ears and on her fingers. Now and then she looks up from whatever conversation she's engaged in and gives Quinn a smile that fills her with ecstatic happiness. How amazing it is to see Sofia settling back into Pure Heart again. Everything is going just as Quinn hoped.

Even the bodyguards seem to be relaxing a little. Dmitri is sitting over by the firepit. If he thought Sofia was in any danger, he'd surely be hovering nearby. Grigor is nowhere to be seen. Sofia said he was taking care of something for her. She was vague about what that something might be. Another of her surprises?

Quinn's gaze settles on the Pure Heart building. The workmen Sofia has brought in over the past few days have fitted discreet solar lights to the front of the central wing, including a trio of uplights beneath the mural of the Furies. The faces of the three vengeful hags loom out of the wall, their all-seeing eyes looking down at the gathering.

To escape their inspection, Quinn turns her attention to the dark bulk of the mountains rearing up behind the property. At dawn tomorrow, after she's finished in the sweat lodge, she will take a solo hike up to the viewpoint and watch her first sunrise as a sixty-year-old woman. It will be the perfect end to a perfect birthday.

The only imperfection so far is Andreas. Where is he? Quinn knows he won't take part in the dancing or any of her rebirth rituals, but, when she saw him this morning, he did say he'd join them for this part of the celebrations. Perhaps he went to Limassol to visit his mother and got stuck in traffic? If he turns up, he can take the seat at the opposite end of the table. Sofia insisted on leaving it free for him.

'Quinn?' Carl offers her a platter of crudités. Slices of home-grown cucumber, courgette and carrot. She thanks him and helps herself to a small handful.

'They're amazing with this.' Carl points to the bowl of baba ganoush dip in front of her.

Quinn dunks a carrot stick into the baba ganoush and nibbles at it. The food Joe has prepared is perfect for the occasion. A selection of raw vegetables and salads. Plates of soft, ripe figs and bowls of toasted almonds. Anything too heavy would interfere with the cacao ceremony later. She has been fasting all day, determined to stay as pure as she can for her rebirth ceremony.

The others, with the exception of Mel, are tucking in to the food. Quinn doesn't expect them to have her level of self-control, but she is surprised to see Joe and Holly sipping on crystal flutes of the Dom Perignon Sofia ordered in for the occasion. Perhaps they don't want to make Sofia feel uncomfortable by letting her drink alone. Sofia has a bottle of champagne in an ice bucket beside her and is topping up her glass at regular intervals.

'Are you okay?' Mel whispers in her left ear.

'I'm great,' Quinn says. 'Couldn't be better.' Mel is a vortex of nervous energy. Quinn almost wishes she'd have a glass of champagne to relax. It might stop her eyeing Sofia with suspicion and glancing back to check on Dmitri. Quinn has fielded numerous questions from her about all the new security measures. She hopes whatever fears their new guests have sparked in Mel will soon fade. She hopes Mel will let herself go a bit tonight. Use the dancing to shake off her suspicions and inhibitions.

It's also possible Mel just wants tonight to be perfect. Quinn touches the wide bracelet on her left wrist, a new one amongst the old. Two bands of silver entwined together. A gift from Mel, even though Quinn told everyone not to waste money on birthday presents. Mel visited her room earlier to give it to her and, after Quinn pulled off the recycled brown paper wrapping, Mel fastened the trinket around her wrist with trembling fingers. Tears shone in her eyes when she told Quinn how grateful she was for the last eight months. How she'd changed in ways she never thought possible. When they embraced, Quinn felt Mel's heart hammering against her ribcage.

Quinn's fingers move from the bracelet to the silver chain and heart-shaped pendant around her neck. The necklace was a gift from Blake. On the pendant, an inscription in Greek.

Αγνή καρδιά

It means Pure Heart. Blake had an identical necklace made for himself. A romantic gesture Quinn loved him for. Wearing his gift makes her feel connected to him. She is, to this day, grateful for the time they shared. Their souls will always be bonded, even if their paths never cross again.

'As long as you're having a good time,' Mel says.

Quinn smiles. 'I am.'

She congratulates herself for selecting such brilliant kindred spirits to share her vision with. She hasn't always made the right choices in the past. Some of the people she brought to Pure Heart discovered they weren't cut out for this way of life or couldn't support her ideas for the community, but she's learned over the years that she can't please everybody.

A vision of Blake appears in the empty chair at the head of the table. His black dreadlocks, his alert brown eyes. Skinny, scarred arms poking out of his black T-shirt.

She shuts her eyes, and when she opens them, Blake is gone. She reminds herself she is about to turn sixty. An exciting new phase of her life is about to begin. Her grave awaits, deep and welcoming, the pale outline of the full moon is already visible in the evening sky. Sixty years old. She can hardly believe it.

The others continue to eat, but Quinn feels so full of love she doesn't need another bite. Her family are sustenance enough. Looking around her, it's hard to imagine these happy people were once troubled souls who'd turned to her for guidance. Quinn knows she can't take credit for every aspect of their healing, but she feels privileged to have been part of their journey. Having Sofia here makes her feel Eva would want the community to celebrate everything it has achieved. She remembers when they first moved into Pure Heart. Eva took her by the hand and together they ran like giddy children through the house. In and out of every room and along the wide corridors.

'Promise me we'll live here forever,' Eva said to her.

Yes, Eva would want Pure Heart to continue.

The clear, ting ting ting of silver against crystal. Zoe tapping her fork against her goblet of kombucha. Applause and wolf whistles and fists banging on the table.

'Order, you rabble.' Zoe's voice rings out above the din. When the noise settles down, her gaze sweeps along the table and settles on Quinn. 'Now I know you said you didn't want any birthdays presents but—'

'I don't.' Quinn laughs. 'Honestly, you lot.'

'But we couldn't let this occasion go unmarked,' Zoe says. 'So we would like to give you the gift of our sincere thanks.'

More applause and banging of fists.

'Unaccustomed as I am to public performance of any kind,' Zoe says with a coy smile, 'I've agreed to try and convey our gratitude to you.'

Quinn places a hand over her heart and smiles at Zoe. They might wind each other up sometimes, as all family members do, but Quinn knows she is blessed to have such a strong female ally.

A quiet, respectful atmosphere settles over the table.

'All of us here owe you so much,' Zoe continues. 'You believed in us, and you made us believe in ourselves. You show us over and over that, if we keep the faith, if we believe, we can produce miracles.'

Quinn knows Zoe is referring to their most recent miracle. Sofia sitting here tonight. All the promise her presence brings.

'Sixty is just the beginning for you,' Zoe says. 'We know this new phase of your life will bring you even more wisdom and insight. We know you'll continue to dedicate yourself to us and to this beautiful sanctuary where we are all safe and loved and cherished.' She raises her glass. 'A sanctuary we want to stay in forever.'

'Well put, my darling girl,' Carl says. They all raise their glinting glasses.

Quinn clears her throat. Time for her to speak now. She has prepared a speech, of course. Not that tonight is all about her. Not at all. It's about all of them. Celebrating what they've made together.

Before she can get to her feet, Sofia rises, glass of champagne in hand.

'Thanks, Zoe,' she says. 'That was beautiful.' She glances around the table. 'I hope it's okay if I say a few words?'

'Knock yourself out,' Joe says.

'Speech,' cackles Holly.

Quinn responds with a sage nod, as if granting permission. Dmitri leaves his post at the firepit and stands behind Sofia's chair.

'I know if my mother were here,' Sofia says, 'she would have something to say to you, Quinn.'

Quinn, looking at Sofia's dark eyes and sharp cheekbones feels as if this could be Eva in front of her. A resurrection.

'Her belief in you was absolute,' Sofia says, 'and in Pure Heart. Eva loved this place.' She takes a sip of champagne. 'Now, when a little bird told me about the difficult spot Charles left you in when he died and how he—'

'What little bird?' Quinn's voice sounds strange and high-pitched in her ears. She glances around the table. The others look as surprised as she sounds.

A sparrow lands on the rim of Quinn's plate and looks up at her, as if admitting its guilt.

'Doesn't matter.' Sofia waves her glass in the air as if banishing the question. 'The point is, when I heard you were broke—'

'We had some cash-flow issues,' Quinn says, shooing the bird away, 'but we're managing to—'

'I wanted to help,' Sofia says. 'That's why I'm here.'

'Oh,' Quinn says. 'Well, that's kind, but—'

'I have an offer for you,' Sofia says, 'and I know you'll be open to it. After hearing Zoe's speech, I'm even more certain you'll do anything you can to keep Pure Heart going.'

'We do love this place,' Holly says.

'Of course, you do.' Sofia smiles. 'Which is why I'd like to offer you three million euros.'

Stunned silence around the table. Zoe breaks it first with a peal of laughter.

'Sofia,' she says, 'that's... oh my God.'

'Seriously?' says Joe.

Sofia shrugs. 'I can afford it. You'll all be set for life. You can carry on living here, cut off from the rest of the world. Just like you did when Charles was alive.'

'Whoa,' Carl says. 'This is... this is mind-blowing.'

'It's too good to be true,' Mel says to Quinn in a low voice.

Quinn ignores her. The wondrous expressions on the faces of the others reflect what she knows in her heart. This is the abundance they prayed for, although even she never imagined such benevolence from the universe as this.

'Sofia,' she says, trying not to appear too keen, 'that is such a beautiful thought. But we can't accept such a generous gift.'

'Don't worry,' Sofia says. 'It's not a gift.'

'Oh,' says Quinn, confused.

'No, it's not a gift.' Sofia's dark eyes glitter. 'I want something in return.'

'What?' Quinn asks, her heart pounding. 'What do you want?'

'Justice,' Sofia says. 'I want justice.'

22

QUINN

2018

Everyone is staring at Sofia. In the background, the pool gurgles. The birds high in the nearby trees call out to each other. One of the candles at the centre of the table flickers and dies.

'Justice for what?' Mel asks.

Sofia sips her champagne. 'For my mother's murder.'

'What?' Quinn looks at the others. They sit in stunned silence. 'Sofia, your mother took her own life.'

'That's the official story,' Sofia says.

'Darling girl,' Holly says, 'we... we all saw her.'

'We cut her down,' Joe says. 'Me and Carl.'

'I know,' Sofia says. 'I was there.'

Quinn glances at Dmitri. He is still standing behind Sofia's chair, his expression unreadable. If he's surprised by what Sofia is saying he isn't showing it. Is this an unrehearsed outburst or was it planned?

'My mother hanged herself,' Sofia says, 'but she wasn't responsible for her death.' She plucks a grape from the bunch in front of her. 'You are, Quinn.' She puts the grape between her teeth and bites down on the purple skin. 'You killed her.'

Quinn's solar plexus throbs, as if Sofia has punched her there. 'You know how depressed Eva was in those last few weeks,' she says. 'She went to a very dark place.'

'It was so hard to watch,' Holly says. 'I thought she was getting better.'

'She seemed to be.' Zoe glances at the others. 'Didn't she?'

A chorus of agreement.

'The thing is, Mel,' Sofia says.

'Mel wasn't with us then,' Quinn says. 'Don't involve her in this.'

Beneath the table, Mel lays a hand on Quinn's jiggling thigh. Quinn takes a deep breath, tries to settle herself.

'She's an outsider,' Sofia says, 'who better to judge you?'

'I'm not an outsider.' Mel removes her hand from Quinn's thigh. 'I'm one of them.'

'You were part of the establishment once,' Sofia says. 'A dedicated upholder of law and order. I'll be interested to know what you make of what you hear tonight.'

'Sofia,' Holly pleads, 'sweetheart. Being back here must be hard but—'

'About six months before my mother killed herself, she had a serious breakdown,' Sofia says, still addressing Mel. 'The worst I'd ever seen. She was up and down all the time – I was used to that – but this was next-level depression.'

'Poor Eva.' Zoe sighs. 'She wasn't herself at all.'

'She was seriously fucking low,' says Carl.

'And Quinn,' Sofia says, the obscene diamond on her right hand flashing in the candlelight, 'Quinn thought she could cure my mother all by herself.'

Quinn searches for the right words. Sofia is clearly upset. How best to help her? Her inner voice, the one that guides her in all situations tells her to be honest. 'Eva didn't want traditional treatment. You know that.'

'She hated doctors,' Holly says.

'And medicine,' Joe adds. 'She even refused to take paracetamol.'

'Ironic really,' Carl says, 'considering all the coke and ecstasy she took back in the day.' He flinches as Zoe elbows him. 'Sorry, but you know what I mean.'

Quinn feels unmoored. This isn't the night she had planned. What on earth is happening? Aphrodite jumps onto her lap. The cat's warm, solid presence grounds her. 'I've never claimed to be able to cure anyone of anything,' she says, 'but I can help people to heal themselves.'

She recalls Eva slipping into her room one night, tears streaming down her face.

'I want to cure this depression holistically,' Eva said, climbing into bed beside her in search of a cuddle. 'Will you help me?'

Quinn shares this memory with everyone now. 'I told her I'd do anything to help her. I said I believed she could make herself better.'

'We all believed she could,' Zoe says.

'I remember,' Sofia says. 'You all helped. Joe, by cooking her all the right foods. Zoe with the tantra exercises for self-love. Carl with the dancing, Holly with the gardening and Quinn with her "intuitive healing".' Sofia puts air quotation marks around her last phrase.

'Most importantly we all believed,' Quinn says. 'We knew that if we all committed to Eva's healing journey, every single one of us, she would get better.' Aphrodite launches into an approving purr. 'You believed it too, Sofia. Your belief was the most important of all.'

'Isn't that cruel, Mel?' Sofia says. 'Making a twelve-year-old girl think she has power over her mother's state of mind. Making a child think the universe is listening to her, ready to do her bidding.'

'It sounds like you were angry with your mother's choices,' Mel says to Sofia.

'And that's okay,' Quinn says. 'That's understandable.'

'I'm angry with you.' Sofia jabs a finger in Quinn's direction. 'This is about you.'

'You were a child,' Quinn says. 'Eva and I wanted to protect you.' She can't bear to see Sofia tormented by the past like this. 'Memory is tricky. There's a lot you were too young to remember properly.'

'You're right.' Sofia drains the last of her champagne. 'I was only twelve years old. There's a lot I didn't understand or remember correctly.' She smiles. 'But I know someone who does.'

23

ZOE

2018

Zoe's pulse thunders in her ears. Despite the drop in temperature that comes with darkness, sweat beads on her upper lip. What is Sofia talking about? Who knew the truth about Eva?

Beneath the table, Carl squeezes her thigh. She can't tell if he's trying to reassure her or relieve his own tension.

'Who?' Quinn asks Sofia. 'Who are you talking about?'

Andreas appears in the doorway of the house. Zoe wonders what on earth he will make of all this. As he weaves his way across the courtyard, Grigor following close behind, Zoe frowns. Why is he so unsteady on his feet?

'Welcome, Andreas,' Sofia says, when their handyman reaches them. Grigor, who clutches a blue cardboard folder in one hand, pulls out the chair at the head of the table and stands behind it. Andreas sinks into the chair, his left hand knocking over a crystal goblet. He reaches out and, just in time, stops it falling to the floor.

'Has he been drinking?' Carl whispers.

Andreas' lined face is as inscrutable as ever but the dark pouches of skin beneath his eyes and his mournful expression make Zoe's stomach lurch. Sober or not, he's in a bad way.

'Who is this someone?' Mel asks, her alert body angled towards Quinn as if protecting her. 'Are you saying you have evidence?'

Sofia nods towards Andreas. He looks around the table with his haunted eyes. 'Sorry.' He plucks the champagne from the ice bucket and fills his crystal goblet to the brim. 'For this, I will need a drink.'

* * *

'Andreas,' Quinn says. 'Whatever's going on here, whatever you've done, alcohol is not the answer.'

'I have been drinking again for some time,' he confesses.

Zoe watches as half of Andreas' champagne disappears in one swallow. Carl tenses beside her. She suspects he's imagining how cold and crisp and decadent the Dom Perignon must taste. She could do with a glass of it herself. Unlike Carl, she is capable of drinking in moderation, but she abstains to make him feel better.

'Tell them what you know about my mother,' Sofia says.

Andreas sighs. 'I knew Eva had been to see a doctor.'

'A doctor?' Zoe says, confused.

'A psychiatrist,' Sofia says. 'His name is Doctor Petrides, and he ran a private clinic in Nicosia before he retired.'

'You?' Mel asks Andreas. 'How did you know?'

The nearby cats draw closer to the table, as if eager to hear more.

'One day, Eva asked if I would drive her to Nicosia,' Andreas says. 'She said she wanted to buy a birthday gift for Sofia. A surprise.'

Eva's inability to drive used to irritate Zoe. After spending most of her life being chauffeured around, Eva expected everyone at Pure Heart to take her wherever she needed to go.

'I was happy to drive her,' Andreas says. 'I liked to help her.'

'You loved her, didn't you?' Sofia says.

He shrugs. 'This is no secret. She did not love me, but she was my friend. For me, this was enough.'

At the other end of the table, Quinn inhales, slow and deep.

'What happened in Nicosia?' Sofia asks.

'After we park the truck, Eva said she will do shopping. We agreed to meet after a couple of hours. When she walked away, I followed her.'

'Why?' Sofia asks.

'I was worried for her,' Andreas says. 'For many days she was staying in her bed. Not eating. I did not want something bad to happen to her.'

Zoe glances around the table. Two tight lines have appeared between Holly's eyebrows. Joe is staring at Andreas, his face filled with uncertainty. Mel's intense blue eyes are flicking from person to person, as if anticipating a sudden, threatening move from somewhere. Only Quinn appears serene, as she listens to the story that is unfolding. Zoe keeps expecting her to interrupt, but instead she's behaving like a defendant on trial. Forced to sit through the evidence before she can give her side of the story.

Andreas knocks back the rest of his champagne. 'I follow her to this doctor's clinic. This Petrides. She was inside a long time. When she came out and saw me standing there, she did not even ask why I had followed her. She was crying. She said she needed a drink but instead I took her to a café and ordered us both a coffee. That's when she told me everything.'

'Why did she tell you?' Mel asks.

'She trusted me,' Andreas says.

'Grigor,' Sofia says. The big man steps forward and opens the cardboard folder. He walks around the table and places a printed document in front of each of them. Zoe counts six sheets of paper stapled together. She reads the title at the top of the first page. *Dr Tony Petrides: Written Statement.*

She feels like a member of a jury. The written statement takes up two of the pages and the rest look like photocopies of the doctor's records, including notes on Eva dated 2008.

'Whoever this guy is,' Mel says, 'he's breaking doctor-patient confidentiality.'

'Heads up, Detective,' Sofia says, 'the usual rules don't apply in this game.'

Zoe scans the first page of the doctor's statement. 'He says here he diagnosed her with bipolar disorder.'

'Bipolar?' Joe shakes his head. 'We never... she never said anything to us.'

The others echo similar expressions of surprise. Quinn stays silent, her eyes fixed straight ahead.

'I guess it's sort of obvious,' Carl says. 'She could be manic sometimes.'

'And then she would crash,' Zoe adds in a low voice.

'She sometimes said she felt like two different people,' Holly says.

'In the café she told me she did not want this diagnosis, this label,' Andreas says. 'But also she knows she must get help. She wants to be better for Sofia.'

'How could she trust someone who diagnosed her after one appointment?' Quinn says. 'What if he got it wrong?'

'Bipolar is often misdiagnosed,' Sofia says. 'A lot of doctors miss it and say the patient is only depressed.'

Zoe skims through the notes of the doctor's first session with Eva. *I recommended a course of antipsychotics and antidepressants.* 'He prescribed her drugs?'

Andreas nods. 'She showed me this prescription. When she said she is going to take it, I said, yes. Good idea.'

'I can't get my head round Eva taking medication,' Joe says.

'She was scared,' Andreas says. 'She thinks maybe her parents come and take her and lock her away in some hospital. Or they take Sofia from her.'

'When was this?' Mel asks.

'September,' Andreas says. 'Ten weeks before she died.'

Zoe loops back in her memory to that autumn. To the relief she and everyone else felt when Eva appeared happier. More balanced.

'She did seem better,' Holly says. 'Do you remember?'

Joe nods. 'She ate a wee bit more. I remember that.'

'Why didn't she tell us about the medication?' Zoe says.

'She was ashamed,' Sofia explains. 'She wanted your methods to succeed. She didn't want to let Pure Heart down.'

Zoe remembers how they congratulated themselves on Eva's apparent recovery. On their strength of belief and their healing powers. All the time the drugs were in her system, balancing her out. Rewiring her brain.

'When her drugs were running out, she asks me to take her back to the doctor,' Andreas says. 'He gave her another prescription.'

'So what went wrong?' Mel asks.

'Eva told Quinn about the doctor and the medication,' Andreas says. 'This is when everything is going wrong.'

Zoe stares at their leader. 'You knew?'

'Yes.' Quinn holds Aphrodite to her chest. 'Not straight away, but I worked it out.'

Carl glares at her. 'You knew and you didn't say anything?'

Quinn sighs, as if impatient with them. 'Eva begged me not to tell any of you.'

Zoe is filled with a mixture of dread and curiosity. She wants to hear Quinn's testimony and she doesn't. The same feeling she used to get watching horror films as a kid.

'I thought something was wrong and I confronted her about it,' Quinn says. 'I could tell she wasn't herself. She was vibrating at a much lower frequency than usual.'

'See?' Sofia turns to Dmitri. 'This is the kind of bullshit I was telling you about.'

Dmitri nods, but his expression remains neutral.

Zoe recalls thinking something similar about Eva. She may even have said something to Carl about it. *Is it me or is Eva on one of her downers again?*

'You all know doctors diagnose people with conditions like bipolar so they can prescribe the drugs the big pharmaceutical companies sell them.' Quinn's voice rings with righteousness.

'Big pharma is a conspiracy,' Carl says, 'no doubt about that.'

'Exactly,' replies Quinn. 'Eva wanted to stop taking the drugs. She hated the side effects. She realised she'd made a mistake, and she asked me to help her.'

'No,' Sofia says. 'You told her she'd made a mistake. Isn't that right, Andreas?'

Andreas reaches again for the champagne bottle, but before he can get to it, Grigor steps in, takes the bottle and pours him another glass.

'One morning I found Eva in the monastery,' Andreas says, 'maybe three weeks before she died. She was upset.' He glugs back some champagne, as if trying to dissolve the memory. 'I ask her what is happening, and, in the end, she says Quinn wants her to stop taking the medication.'

'What was your response?' Sofia's face is a hard mask. Zoe senses she knows this story so well it is almost no longer painful for her. Or she has managed somehow to disassociate from it.

'I tell her, no,' Andreas says. 'I tell her, stay on the medication. Only stop if the doctor helps you to stop. Otherwise, bad side effects.'

'What did my mother say?' Sofia asks.

'She would not listen.' Andreas rubs his forehead. 'I offer to take her back to the doctor; she would not go.'

'Why didn't you tell us any of this?' Zoe asks. All the years she's spent feeling guilty. Wondering if there was something she could have done to prevent Eva's death.

Andreas leans forward in his chair, his eyes ablaze. 'Eva made me promise not to. She said Quinn was healing her... they were doing special work together. She said if everyone knew about this diagnosis and about the medication it would interfere with the prayers she was sending to the universe.' He lets out a cynical laugh. 'The fucking universe. She thinks... she says to me I could kill her with my doubt.'

'You could have told someone,' Mel says.

'Every day since Eva died, I think this,' Andreas says. 'I should have said something.' He shakes his head. 'I loved her. I did not want her to be angry with me. And... maybe some crazy part of me was scared I could kill her if I didn't believe.'

'You weren't crazy,' Sofia says. 'You were brainwashed, just like me. Quinn was always telling me any negative thoughts could hurt my mother.'

Zoe knuckles are white around her glass of kombucha. It's all too much. She can't take everything in.

'How can we trust this doctor's evidence?' Mel asks. 'Did you intimidate it out of him, Sofia, or did you make a generous contribution to his pension fund?'

'Dr Petrides is not lying,' Quinn says. 'He's given an accurate representation of facts, but that's not the same as the truth.'

'Andreas asked me one day if I had a contact number for my grandparents,' Sofia says. 'I've always remembered that. He wouldn't tell me why.'

'I wanted to tell them,' Andreas explains. 'I thought maybe they would help.'

'Weren't you drinking at that time?' Quinn asks. 'You'd been sober for a while but you started again.'

Andreas hangs his head. 'This is true.'

'It's okay,' Sofia says. 'I don't blame you.'

'You should,' he says.

Sofia rises from her chair, champagne glass in hand, and stands by Andreas' side, her hand on his shoulder. 'The night before I left this place, Andreas came to find me in my room. He was very drunk. He told me I deserved to know the truth about my mother's death. He said Quinn was to blame, but before he could say more, he passed out on the floor.'

'I remember that,' Joe says. 'I had to come and move him.'

'I was twelve years old,' Sofia says, 'and I'd just lost my mother. Everything about that night was a blur. Years later, when I was searching for answers about what happened, I remembered Andreas and what he said and, almost a year ago, I came back to Cyprus and spoke to him.'

'I told her everything I remembered,' Andreas says. 'Everything I have been carrying for so many years. History can poison you. I know this. Everyone on this island knows this. Sofia told me she needs to know the truth so she can be free. What else could I do? She is all this time thinking her mother abandoned her, but I know in my heart that stopping the drugs made Eva sick. She would not have left her daughter otherwise. I had to help her.'

'And is she helping you?' Mel says. 'Let me guess. She's paying for your mother's care home?'

Andreas looks down at the table.

'I was happy to help an old friend,' Sofia says.

'What else?' Mel asks Andreas. 'Got somewhere to go after tonight? Has she got you a new job, a new home? You can't expect to stay here now?'

'This is about truth,' Andreas insists. 'If we can be honest here, tonight, Sofia can get on with her life. We owe this to Eva.'

'Oh, come on,' Mel says.

'Please, Quinn,' Andreas cries, 'if you can admit the truth and apologise, this will all be over.' He looks up at Sofia. 'This is right? This is what you said? Quinn must confess and apologise.'

'I'm not sure Quinn is the apologising sort,' Sofia says.

'You don't understand,' says Quinn. 'Eva's situation was very complex.'

'No, I think it was simple.' Sofia's gold necklace glitters in the candlelight. She looks beautiful and deadly. 'Quinn was so deluded about her own healing powers that she persuaded my sick, vulnerable mother to ignore the advice of a highly qualified psychiatrist. As a result, my mother killed herself.'

'Eva chose her own healing path,' Quinn says. 'I offered to walk beside her, nothing more.'

'She died because you wanted to protect your beliefs,' Sofia says. 'Your beliefs and this community were more important than my mother's life.'

'No,' Quinn objects, 'this is not who you are, Sofia. This hatred. This anger. Eva would be heartbroken to see you like this.'

'My mother deserves justice.' Sofia savours another sip of champagne. 'And I'm going to buy it for her.'

'Buy it?' Zoe asks.

'Three million euros. That's my offer to you.' A cold smile haunts Sofia's lips. 'And in return I want you, the members of the Pure Heart community, to kill Quinn.'

24

HOLLY

2019

Someone laughed. I can't remember who. Sofia's proposal was so bizarre. Surreal, almost. No one spoke. We were trapped in the moment.

Suspended.

Sofia caught us unawares. We were all feeling emotional after Zoe's speech. Full of love for Pure Heart. So when Sofia first offered us the three million euros, it seemed like the miracle we'd prayed for was really happening. I'd never felt so much joy and wonder in all my life.

Eventually, we found our voice. We asked Sofia if she was joking. When she asked us once again to kill Quinn, we told her we couldn't possibly take her money.

Poor Andreas. He was shocked by Sofia's offer. Any suspicions we had of his involvement in this part of the plan soon evaporated. He pleaded with Sofia to see sense. He thought she only wanted to discover the truth about Eva. He thought justice meant shaming Quinn in front of everyone.

We tried to reason with Sofia. We told her Eva would never approve of what she was doing. She told us we should take a vote on the matter. Wasn't that the Pure Heart way?

'All in favour of rejecting this offer,' we said.

Unanimous. Every hand immediately raised.

She laughed and told us we would change our minds. Even though we had yet to process the night's revelations, we knew no one amongst us was capable of cold-blooded murder. She said she was here for another month. Plenty of time for us to think about it.

We told her the offer was ridiculous. We assured her we wouldn't change our minds.

'Everyone has a price,' she said. 'You're about to find out yours.'

PART II

PART II

25

Insight Investigators: Background Report

Rachel Jane Wilde (Quinn): The information I gathered from former Pure Heart members presents a complex picture of Quinn. I spoke to two women and one man. I won't go into details about them and their reasons for leaving. Suffice to say at Pure Heart it was either Quinn's way or the highway.

What did become clear from speaking to those who knew her, is that Quinn, who calls herself an intuitive healer, has no formal qualifications or training. She told people she didn't need to study healing because she'd lived it. Her childhood experiences at the commune had, so she claimed, introduced her to her healing powers and after her time at the squat in Brixton, she lived in a van on a travellers' site near Glastonbury. There she mixed with alternative, spiritual types and experimented with different holistic therapies. She claims she then travelled all over the world, learning different healing methods from indigenous teachers in South America and South-East Asia.

While the former community members were often disparaging about Quinn and resentful of the authority she wielded at Pure Heart, they admitted she did possess extraordinary insight and healing gifts. One woman I spoke to claimed Quinn had cured her chronic back pain and eczema. The other said Quinn had cured her alcoholism and that she still doesn't drink to this day. The man I spoke to told me Quinn healed his depression. All of them said there were times she made them believe in miracles.

26

QUINN

2018

The morning after Sofia's offer, Quinn slips out of her room at 5.30 a.m., Aphrodite at her heels. She is dressed in orange leggings and an orange hooded top and a small backpack hangs from her shoulders. She pads barefoot along the cool flagstones, silent and stealthy, but before she can reach the stairs, the door to Grigor's room opens.

'You are going somewhere?' he says. Even at this hour of the morning, he is smart in his uniform, his waistcoat buttoned over his solid bulk.

'For a hike up the mountain trail.' Quinn's birthday celebrations didn't exactly go to plan, but she is determined to salvage this part of them. Besides, she needs to think. Get some perspective.

'Without shoes?' Grigor looks down at her feet.

'Yes.'

'How far?'

'I'll be back for breakfast.'

He hesitates, as if considering something, and Quinn wonders if he is about to stop her going.

'I'm not running away,' she says. 'There's nothing for me to run from.'

He must know that. He saw her community refuse Sofia's disturbing offer.

'It is dangerous,' he says, 'walking alone.'

'I always walk alone.'

He asks her to describe the route she will take. 'In case anything happens. You might have accident.'

'I'll be fine,' she says but does as he asks. When he seems satisfied, she turns and hurries towards the stairs.

'Be careful out there,' he says.

* * *

Quinn exits the Pure Heart car park and sets off at a brisk pace up the driveway, inhaling lungfuls of cool, fresh air. She glances back but there is no one behind her. As she crept out of the front door, she half-expected to hear Mel call her name. Last night, as Quinn lay awake, her tense body fidgeting in her narrow bed, she heard the toilet flushing in Mel's bathroom and felt comforted by the knowledge Mel wasn't sleeping either. Not that she was scared. There was nothing to be scared of, although at one point in the night she thought of the unlocked door to her room. Not that she would ever lock it. No need.

The full moon is still visible in the approaching dawn. A wash of pale yellow coats the lower regions of the sky. Jays squawk over the reedy, high-pitched songs of the coal tit and the Cyprus wheatear. A yellow gecko scuttles across the driveway in front of her and disappears into a bush.

Aphrodite trots dutifully beside her but when the driveway meets the road, they part ways, the cat slinking away into the nearby burnet bushes.

Quinn crosses the road. It connects traffic to a larger mountain road three miles away and is never that busy. A bus to Kakopetria drives this way twice a day during the week.

On the other side of the road, she meets the start of the forest and makes her way between the trunks of towering pines and slender cypresses. Before long, her feet find a familiar path. She stops, shrugs off her backpack and takes out a pair of black, barefoot trainers. She used to walk this whole route without shoes but tough as her feet are, even she can't clamber over rocks like she used to.

Once her shoes are on, she sets off up the trail that leads to her favourite mountain viewpoint. Only a dim dawn light filters through the tree canopy, but it's enough to guide her.

One foot in front of the other. Picking her way over tangled tree roots and fallen branches. Somewhere in the distance an owl releases what might be the last of its nocturnal calls.

Did Sofia really offer money in return for her death? Now, with the sun about to claim the day, the proposal seems crazy. When Sofia suggested they vote on the matter, Mel's hand shot up immediately. The others were slower to react, but Quinn doesn't blame them. They were all so stunned. Unable to process what was happening.

After losing the vote, Sofia retired to her room. Quinn suggested they all do the same, promising they'd discuss the matter as a community in the morning. She wanted to get away from everyone as soon as she could. Sofia's words had wounded her deeply and she needed to rest and to think. Mel insisted on escorting her back to her room. Before going inside, Quinn laid a hand on Mel's arm and was relieved when she didn't pull away. She promised to explain everything properly soon and was reassured when Mel said her police career taught her there are always two sides to every story.

Forest sounds swell around her. Creaking branches and rustling leaves. She thinks of the secrets these trees could tell. In the 1950s, these mountains provided hideouts for EOKA, a rebel group of Greek Cypriots whose desire for unification with mainland Greece brought them into conflict with the British forces stationed on the island. Andreas knew some of these men. He drank coffee with them in the cafés of Kakopetria and listened to their stories.

Andreas. He really did seem blindsided by Sofia's offer, and he did vote with the community to reject it. Last night, before she headed to her room, he reassured her once again he'd had no idea what Sofia was planning. He was slurring his words by then and, as she watched him swallow champagne like it was water, she couldn't help a rush of compassion for him. The healer in her hated to see him succumbing to his demons.

Still, she can't help feeling betrayed. After everything she's done for him over the years. Yet she also understands his desire to help his mother and to honour Eva's memory.

How could he imply she didn't have Eva's best interests at heart? All Quinn remembers is how hard she tried to make Eva better. She thinks of all the times she brought Eva on this very walk, knowing exercise was one of the best cures for depression. Eva would talk on these excursions and Quinn would listen. She absorbed all of Eva's fears and negativity. One morning as they walked, Eva turned to her and said, 'All this I say is only between me and you. Promise me you will never tell anyone the things I say to you.'

'I promise,' Quinn said. 'Never.' True to her word she never did share Eva's ramblings with anyone. Not even with Blake, and there were many days she could have done with her lover's support. No, her work as a healer is sacred to her. She carried Eva's pain alone; unaware Eva was also confiding in Andreas. Quinn suppresses a rush of anger for the dead woman. Eva was sick. She can't be held responsible.

After a while the trees thin out and the path leads her onto open, rocky ground. A canyon, with towering walls of limestone rears up on either side of her. As she navigates rocky boulders and piles of scree, she wonders why she didn't spot any warning signs of Andreas' conspiracy. Surely, she should have detected some subtle change in his aura?

Stones and fragments of rock shower down from above. She dodges the downpour, almost losing her footing. Once steady again, she glances up and sees a mountain goat glaring down at her, dirt clinging to its shaggy brown hide, the tip of its right horn missing. It snorts before trotting away, the tight clip of its hooves echoing around the rocks.

Quinn picks her way out of the canyon and joins a trail that leads her through scrubby bushes. Tension drains from her shoulders as the viewpoint approaches. This is her happy place. Here she will be able to think.

When she reaches her destination, a cool wind whips around her shoulders. She opens her bag, takes out a burnt-orange pashmina and wraps it around herself. The sun is cresting golden over the hills to her east, infusing the sky with a pinkish tint. The viewpoint is at the crest of a craggy limestone pinnacle. Far below it is a deep ravine, still in shadow.

Tourists and hikers rarely visit this spot and Mel is the only community member to come here regularly. There are no signs warning people to stay away from the edge. To beware of the dizzying drop below.

As Quinn recovers from the exertion of the walk, she takes in the panoramic view. To the north, not fully visible yet, is the sea and beyond it, the coastline of Turkey. To the east, more forest and mountain peaks. Looking back in the direction she has climbed she can see the Pure Heart property. Her own rebel hideout. She has a partial view of the driveway, car park and front of the building. From this angle, the courtyard is obscured but she can see the terraces below it.

She spots a small object flying over the terraces. The drone, out on its morning patrol. Circling and dipping.

She sighs. This dawn walk was supposed to christen a new phase of her life. She didn't expect to greet the day with a crisis on her hands.

Looking down at the hotel, she wonders if Sofia is sleeping. Did her well-executed plan bring her any peace and satisfaction, or will she keep pursuing this unjustified revenge?

An image of the Death card floats into her mind. The skeleton grinning up at her. Did she interpret the Tarot card the wrong way? What if it did signal actual physical death?

She thinks of her freshly dug grave beneath the cedar tree and shivers. It isn't the empty grave that scares her. It's the memory of Dmitri standing beside it, looking down at her. *You will have to dig a little deeper than that. If you want them to give you a proper burial.*

What Sofia doesn't realise is that broken people cannot always be fixed. Not in this lifetime anyway. If Quinn was guilty of anything back then, it was not being specific enough with her healing mantra. *Please let Eva be free of her terrible illness.* Over and over, she addressed those words to Spirit, but she never expected Eva to find release in the way she did. Since then, Quinn has been very careful how she phrases her prayers. Humans often underestimate their power to manifest their reality.

Should she ask Sofia to leave? Would that work out best for all of them? Then she remembers Sofia has paid to stay here. A generous sum of money Quinn can't repay because she's already spent it. She groans. The universe does send some difficult challenges at times.

'What do you want me to do?' she asks the wind.

An object soaring swiftly up from the ravine catches her eye. At first, she thinks it's the drone, come to spy on her, but then she realises it is a bird. Not just any bird. An eagle.

She gasps as the magnificent creature soars into the air above her. Sunlight catches the white underside of its body and the dark markings on its wings. A Bonelli's eagle, native to Cyprus and, judging by the size of it, a female. The females are always larger than the males.

It is a sign. To Native Americans, the eagle is the Great Spirit. In Greek mythology the bird is the embodiment of Zeus. It is a connection to the angelic realm, a messenger from a higher source.

Quinn watches the bird circling above her, buoyed by the air currents. It has come to tell her to soar high above the drama and discord down below. Suddenly it all becomes clear to her. She knows what to do. 'Thank you, Great Spirit,' she says to the eagle, but it is already flying away, scanning the mountainous terrain below for prey.

27

QUINN

2018

When Quinn enters the kitchen, she finds Joe, Holly, Zoe, Carl and Mel sitting at the table, nursing mugs of tea and coffee, the remains of breakfast spread out before them. Their conversation ceases. They stare at her.

'We were just discussing the best way to kill you,' Carl says.

Zoe slaps his arm. 'That's not funny.'

'We weren't doing that.' Holly's eyes are ringed with dark hollows.

'Not at all,' says Joe.

'This isn't a joking matter,' Mel says.

'What else are we supposed to do?' Carl scratches the greying stubble on his chin. 'This situation's crazy.'

In the spiky silence that follows, Quinn hesitates, suddenly unsure what to do with herself. Then she remembers the eagle and takes her usual seat at the head of the table. Aphrodite, who has followed her into the kitchen, slinks away and jumps onto the threadbare arm of one of the sofas. There she sits, tail curled around her feet, observing them all like some kind of referee.

'I came to your room to find you,' Mel says. 'I thought you'd run away.'

'Why would I do that?' Quinn asks.

'I was worried,' Mel says, 'then Grigor told me where you were.'

Quinn gives her a reassuring smile. 'I couldn't sleep so I went for a hike.' She appreciates Mel's concern. Shows she's keeping an open mind about the events of last night. 'Where's Andreas?'

'Sleeping off his hangover?' Holly suggests. 'He must have had a bottle of champagne to himself.'

'He deserves to feel terrible,' Mel says.

'I can't believe he knew all that about Eva and didn't tell us,' Zoe says.

'He was honouring his promise to her,' Quinn says. 'As I was.'

'You can understand why we're all a bit shocked,' Carl says.

'Shocked I honoured Eva's confidentiality when she came to me for help?' Quinn replies. 'What kind of healer would I be if I shared everyone's secrets?'

Holly clears her throat. 'True.'

Quinn thinks of the many times the people around this table have come to her for guidance. How she has helped each of them piece their broken souls back together. They didn't question her methods then.

'Surely the rest of you must have noticed changes in Eva?' Mel asks. 'She was on those meds for a while. Didn't you realise?'

'Don't judge us,' Carl says. 'You weren't here. You don't know.'

Mel shrugs. 'I'm just saying.'

'Eva was desperate to get off that medication,' Quinn says. 'She asked me not to let her crack. No matter what she said.'

'She could be very persuasive,' Joe says.

'Stubborn,' Zoe adds.

'She put a lot onto you, asking you to keep her secrets,' Mel says. 'That can't have been easy?'

'It was hard.' A dark tangle of grief shifts from Quinn's chest into her throat. 'I just wanted to make her well. I really believed I could.' A solitary tear trickles down one cheek. 'I never thought she'd kill herself. I've had to live with that failure every day.'

'We've all made mistakes,' Mel says. 'Can anyone here say otherwise?'

A synchronised shaking of heads.

'Why didn't you tell us everything after she died?' Zoe asks.

'What was the point?' Quinn sighs. 'She was gone, and she wouldn't have wanted you to think badly of her. She was ashamed of taking the medication. She felt she'd let herself down.'

'We wouldn't have seen it like that,' Holly says.

'I know,' Quinn says, 'but she'd made up her mind.'

'You could have acted differently,' Zoe says. 'But I think we all understand why you did what you did.'

Synchronised nods.

We? Quinn wipes her lone tear away. Is Zoe speaking for everyone now?

'Question is what to do next?' Mel says, exuding quiet authority. 'Sofia's unhinged in my opinion. Let's give her the money back and tell her to leave.'

'The money's gone,' Quinn says.

'Already?' says Joe.

Quinn stiffens. 'The mortgage payments are huge. You have no idea.' None of them do. None of them know how much she has sacrificed so they can live their best lives.

'Sofia's fixated on revenge,' Mel says. 'It's not safe to have her here.'

'She doesn't want to hurt me,' Quinn says. 'Not really.'

Zoe's eyebrows shoot up. 'It did sound that way.'

'If she really wanted me dead, I'd be gone already,' Quinn says. 'She could have sent someone to kill me. Or got Dmitri or Grigor to do it.'

'Fair point,' Joe admits.

'I know what to do,' Quinn says. 'It came to me, up on the mountain.'

'What did?' Holly says.

'Sofia is consumed by grief, not revenge. She needs our help.' Quinn can see the unresolved trauma lurking beneath the girl's bravado. 'She doesn't want to kill me, she wants to kill her pain. Her grief.'

'She was pretty clear about wanting you dead,' Mel says.

'She's a hurt little girl who wants her mother,' Quinn says. 'She needs to be healed.'

This is what Quinn realised up on the mountain and she also realised this situation is a new challenge from the universe. She must use all her knowledge and skills so she can become the wise elderwoman she was always destined to be.

'How exactly are we going to heal her?' Carl asks.

'Let her stay,' Quinn says. 'Let Pure Heart work its magic on her. In time, she'll let go of the darkness in her soul.'

'I don't think that's a good idea,' says Mel.

'Why not?' Quinn looks at her fellow community members. 'No one here has any intention of hurting me. Do you?'

An emphatic chorus. *No. Of course not. We would never hurt you.*

The Tarot card did signal a rebirth but not just hers. Sofia must also be reborn.

'It does make sense for Sofia to stay,' Zoe says.

When Quinn suggests they vote on it, everyone apart from Mel puts up a hand.

'I think you're underestimating the situation,' Mel says.

Quinn seeks out Mel's cool blue eyes and finds them pleading with her. 'This is a journey we need to undertake together,' she says, ignoring Mel's silent plea. 'Eva died here, in our community, and only we can clear that karma.'

Holly nods. 'I agree.'

'Me too,' says Joe.

'You're not thinking this through clearly,' Mel says.

'Five votes to one,' announces Zoe. 'That means it's decided. Sofia stays.'

28

HOLLY

2019

Our second vote in twenty-four hours was unanimous. Looking back, I often wonder if letting Sofia stay was the right choice, but it made sense to us at the time. She needed our help. What else could we have done? We had no idea then of the consequences our decision would bring.

When Sofia finally got out of bed at lunchtime that day, we made it clear we had no intention of accepting her offer. We told her we thought she should stay on with us so she could heal from the past and move on with her life.

She laughed. 'You do amuse me,' she said.

We pointed out unresolved trauma is a very serious matter. She told us if we really wanted to resolve her trauma, we should kill Quinn.

We told her that would never happen.

She told us she would wait and see.

29

ZOE

2018

Four days after Sofia's offer, Zoe is lying by the pool on one of the new sunbeds Sofia had delivered the previous day. Frames of gleaming teak and soft cream, cushions. Solid and luxurious.

It is late morning, and the other members of the community are hard at work gardening, cooking and doing laundry. Zoe feels momentarily guilty for her laziness but reminds herself she is here to speak to Sofia, who has established a routine of coming straight from her bed to eat breakfast by the pool and sunbathe. Quinn suggested that as the youngest Pure Heart member, Zoe should try and rekindle the special bond she once shared with the young Sofia.

Since the community asked Sofia to stay at Pure Heart so they could heal her, the two sides have skirted around each other. A buffer zone between them like the militarised one that divides the south of Cyprus from the north. Sofia spends her time either by the pool or in her room and her meals are taken up to her by one of the bodyguards. Zoe wonders if she's regretting what happened at Quinn's party and can see now how ludicrous her offer is.

Zoe's sunbed is tilted towards the house, giving her a clear view of

Grigor as he exits the building, clutching an ice bucket. As he gets closer, Zoe sees the gold foil top of a champagne bottle peeking out of a mountain of ice.

'Sofia's on her way down then?' she says.

Grigor nods and places the ice bucket on the teak table between Zoe's sunbed and the next. Then he turns and strides back towards the house.

Zoe adjusts her bikini. Her retro, fifties-style two-piece is five years old and the cheap black polyester is bobbled and losing its elasticity. Her pink cat's eye sunglasses came from a cheap tourist shop in Limassol, as did her grey bucket hat.

As she rearranges her breasts inside her bikini top, the black, four-legged drone zips overhead before returning and hovering above the pool, looking directly at her. Dmitri must be operating it this morning, while Grigor waits on Sofia. She stares at the inquisitive machine. Heat flushes her chest. The sensation of being exposed is not unpleasant.

She glances up at her bedroom window. The shutters are still half-closed. What is Carl up to? He's on garden duty today but she still hasn't seen him leave the house.

The drone zips away again, its metallic buzz fading as it heads down to the lower terraces. Dmitri must be well paid for protecting Sofia, but he also seems deeply loyal to her. Imagine having a man like that to help you with whatever bizarre scheme you come up with. A resourceful man. Tough and more than a little dangerous.

She closes her eyes and disappears into the warm, kaleidoscopic world behind her eyelids. The tops of her arms and chest are already stinging from the heat.

Minutes drift by. She's surprised to find herself humming the chorus of 'Dance With Me, Baby', her biggest hit single. A week at number one. After her career fell apart, she grew to hate the song. Now she is ashamed of it.

A splashing sound drags her back to the present. She opens her eyes to see Andreas kneeling by the side of the pool, arms elbow-deep in the water. Since Quinn's party he has chosen to stay in his room here, rather than go back to his place in Kakopetria. It jars, seeing him go about his work as usual, as if nothing has changed. As if he hadn't betrayed Quinn and made a tricky situation so much worse. Quinn has her faults, but she's been good to him over the years. They all have. He seems remorseful about it. Remorse he's trying to cover up by drinking on a daily basis, even though they've all advised him to stop.

'*Skatá*,' Andreas says.

The Greek word for shit is one of the only curse words Zoe knows in that language. 'What's wrong?' she says. 'I thought the pool had been fixed?'

'There is... there is blockage.' He pulls at something beneath the surface. 'I have it.' When he lifts his arms from the water, he has the body of a dead bird clutched in one hand.

Zoe recoils as Andreas drops the bird onto the flagstones beside him. A jay. Even she recognises the pinkish-brown plumage, black tail and the vivid blue panel of feathers on its wings. 'How did that get in there?'

'I don't know.' He shakes water from his hands before wiping them on his jeans. His expression darkens as he looks towards the house. 'She is here.'

* * *

Zoe watches Sofia sashay across the courtyard, a white beach dress skimming her thighs, gold thongs slapping against the flagstones. In one hand she carries a white straw sunhat with the biggest brim Zoe has ever seen. Over one shoulder she has a Louis Vuitton beach bag. Cream and grey check with beige leather handles.

'Isn't it an amazing morning?' Sofia drops her bag to the ground and tosses her hat onto the sunbed next to Zoe's. Zoe clocks the scarf tied around the band of the hat. Cream silk and patterned with the interlocking Cs of the Coco Chanel symbol in black and gold.

'That scarf's gorgeous,' she says.

Sofia glances down at it. 'Oh that. I've got loads of them.' She turns to Andreas. 'Is that dead?' she asks, tipping her head at the jay.

'It was stuck in the pool filter,' Zoe says.

'In Greek mythology, a dead bird is an omen of renewal and transformation. It can herald the start of a new generation.' Sofia smiles at Zoe.

'Quite fitting, don't you think?' She unknots the scarf from her hat and waves it at Andreas. 'Wrap the poor thing in this.'

Andreas hesitates, but, having nothing else suitable with him, he scoops up the bird in one hand, walks over to Sofia and takes the scarf. Crouching on the ground, he smooths the scarf out flat and lays the bird's body on top of it.

Zoe peers down at the colourful corpse and tries to see it through the eyes of Greek mythology. The death of one thing making way for the life of another. There is, she has to admit, a certain beauty to it.

Andreas wraps the designer scarf around the bird's body, making a shroud of it. Even from this distance, Zoe detects a whiff of alcohol fumes seeping through his skin.

'You should bury it,' Sofia says when he stands up, the shrouded creature in his palms.

'I will.' His dark eyes search Sofia's face. 'You are feeling better today?'

'I'm not ill, Andreas,' she says. 'And I haven't changed my mind about Quinn, if that's what you're asking?'

'Your mother had a good heart,' he says, 'and I think so do you.'

'I might look like my mother,' Sofia says, 'but I don't think I inherited her heart. Or maybe life has changed the heart I was born with.'

Andreas presses the dead bird close to his chest. 'You're a good person,' he says. 'My own heart tells me this.'

* * *

A few moments after Andreas leaves them, Grigor appears, holding a tray aloft in one hand.

'Breakfast.' Sofia applauds when Grigor places the tray on the end of her sunbed. Zoe glances at the bottle of Dom Perignon chilling in the bucket beside her. The delicious drops of condensation beading on its neck. Quinn will surely have words to say about Sofia drinking in the daytime.

'Tell Joe this looks amazing.' Sofia appraises the spread he's prepared for her. Chopped apricots on Greek yoghurt, topped with swirls of local honey. A slab of sourdough topped with crumbled feta, avocado and plump, ripe tomato.

'I will tell him.' Grigor pours Sofia a glass of champagne before pushing the bottle deep into the bucket with an icy crunch.

'Can you get an extra glass for Zoe?' Sofia asks him.

'I'm fine,' Zoe says. 'Not for me.'

'Do you want something else instead?' Sofia asks, as if they are sitting by the pool of a five-star hotel and there is a menu to choose from. It makes Zoe want to laugh. It also makes her want to take advantage of the moment.

'Actually,' she says, 'I'd love a black coffee. If that's okay, Grigor?'

He nods and turns away. If he begrudges having to act as butler as well as bodyguard, he doesn't show it.

Sofia pulls her sundress over her head to reveal an extravagant, bronze-coloured bikini. High-leg bottoms, tiny triangles of material over her small breasts and straps that criss-cross her taut abdomen. 'Balenciaga,' she says when she sees Zoe admiring it. 'Gorgeous, isn't it?'

'Totally.' Zoe sees her own ill-fitting swimwear reflected in Sofia's over-sized sunglasses. Her cheeks grow hot with embarrassment instead of sunlight.

Sofia settles herself on the sunbed and takes a sip of champagne. Zoe sneaks a look at their guest's perfectly proportioned figure. So like her mother's. A memory of Eva naked flits into her mind. She wonders if Sofia also has a mole on her left breast, just below the nipple.

'You must get dreadfully bored here?' Sofia says.

'No,' Zoe says, defensive. 'There's always so much to do. Especially now we—'

'Don't you go anywhere? Do anything?'

'Sure. We go for day trips or out for dinner. We go to art galleries and music festivals in the cities.' Zoe is lying. It's a long time since they could afford to do any of those things.

'You must be thrilled I've come back to entertain you.' Sofia swaps her crystal goblet for the bowl of thick, creamy yoghurt.

'I wouldn't call what you're doing entertainment.'

'It's keeping me amused.'

'You are just winding Quinn up?' Zoe says. 'Messing with her head?'

'I'm too busy to take time out of my life just to mess with someone's head.' Sofia swallows a mouthful of yogurt and heaps her spoon with chopped apricots. 'I had to beg my advisers to let me come to Cyprus. My godfather, Egor, who's also my lawyer, backed me in the end. He knows I need a break before taking on my duties.'

'Did he know what you planned to do here?'

'God, no. Although he is a man who believes money can buy anything.'

Zoe watches Sofia polish off the bowl of yoghurt. Does she really think the Pure Heart members will kill one of their own? If so, Zoe finds that very offensive. 'Our souls are not for sale,' she says but the words sound prissy and hollow.

'Whatever.' Sofia puts the empty bowl aside. 'Quinn killed my mother and she will be punished for it.'

Does Sofia really think it's that simple? Even Zoe, who was surprised at the extent of Quinn's dishonesty, can't condemn her entirely. If she really believed she was helping Eva, can she be held responsible for Eva's actions? 'Quinn tried her best,' she says. 'We all did.'

'Don't worry, Zoe. You're not the one on trial here.'

Something about the long, cool look Sofia gives her makes Zoe feel she could have been. She feels a sudden rush of relief, as if given a reprieve.

Sofia pushes her tray away, Joe's lovingly prepared breakfast unfinished. 'Okay,' she says, 'why don't we forget the past for a bit? Isn't that the Pure Heart way? Let's just hang out. You and me.'

'Okay,' Zoe says. 'I can do that.' This is what Quinn wants her to do, isn't it? Get close to Sofia. Make her feel comfortable. When Quinn assigned her the task, in front of everyone, Zoe couldn't help feeling special. Chosen.

Grigor returns with a mug of coffee for her and one of Joe's homemade chocolate chip cookies.

'Wow,' Zoe says. 'Thanks for doing that.'

Surprise flits across Grigor's face before he backs away and takes a seat under the canvas sails. Zoe wonders if Sofia is ever truly alone. Does she find her security as claustrophobic as Zoe sometimes finds life at Pure Heart?

'How did you know about the bird and Greek mythology?' she asks, ashamed at her own ignorance of the subject. After all these years in Cyprus she should know more.

'Charles started me off with that book of Greek myths.' Sofia puts on her sunhat and her face retreats into shadow. 'I never stopped being interested. I did Classics at A level and really wanted to study it at Oxford, but my grandfather insisted I do economics and management.'

'You went to Oxford?' Surprise raises the pitch of Zoe's voice.

'Yes. I got a first.' Sofia smiles. 'Brains and beauty. Sickening, isn't it?'

She says it with a roll of her eyes. Zoe laughs. Sofia isn't without humour. That's surely a good sign?

Sofia yawns. 'I really can't get over how quiet it is. This place used to be so full of life. Do you remember?'

'I do.'

'What happened to Blake?' Sofia says. 'Did he and Quinn fall out?'

'Not that I know of.' Zoe picks up her coffee. Takes a sip.

'He just left without telling her?'

'Yup. Not even a note.'

'I never liked him.' Sofia stretches her arms overhead. Glances down at her lean, tanned stomach. 'He gave me the creeps.'

Zoe turns on her side to face Sofia. 'So,' she says, 'how about you? Do you have a boyfriend?' She wants to know what kind of life Sofia has waiting for her back in England. Any emotional ties that might interfere with her plans for revenge.

Sofia shrugs. 'There's a few guys. No one serious.' She smiles. 'You and Carl are still the hottest couple ever.'

'I don't know about that.'

'Even as a child I could tell he adored you.' Sofia's manicured nails trace a pattern across her stomach. 'Kids can be very observant.'

Could they? Zoe wonders what Sofia did observe back then.

'I used to hear you having sex all the time,' Sofia says. 'Like, if I was down here or sometimes even in the house.'

'God. Sorry.'

'Don't apologise. You always sounded like you were having fun. Eva used to say a good sex life was a true blessing.'

'It's certainly nothing to be ashamed of.'

'You never thought about having kids?'

'No. We're happy being child-free.'

'Good call.'

'It suits us.' In the past, Zoe used to wonder if maternal urges would overwhelm her at some point, but they never have, and Carl was always clear he didn't want any more kids. He never mentions Pippa now, but Zoe knows, in his quieter moments, he regrets not being the father he should have been.

'Do you still sing?'

'Not really,' Zoe says, struggling to keep up with the change in mood and topic. 'Only in the shower.'

'That's a shame.' Sofia hums a tune Zoe recognises instantly. The same song she had in her head earlier.

'No.' She groans. 'Don't.'

'I loved that song. When I was a kid it was exciting for me to have a pop star as my friend.'

'Yeah, well, I haven't been a pop star for a long time and I prefer shamanic chanting these days.'

'I bet that's not as catchy.'

'It's not as embarrassing.' She thinks of how desperately she wanted to forget her pop star persona when she first went to Ibiza. How she longed to be cool. To be respected. Then she met Quinn and her entourage. Ex-ravers and travellers. True dropouts. When these people accepted her as one of their own, she felt credible for the first time ever.

'You should be proud of your past,' Sofia says. 'How many people can say they've had a number-one single?'

'That sort of success is meaningless,' she says. 'The music world is so shallow.'

'I agree.' Sofia props herself on one elbow and faces her. 'I'm just saying you deserve to shine whatever world you're in.'

Zoe imagines an Instagram post of herself lying by the pool in a bikini like Sofia's.

#ShiningMyUniqueLight #Pure Heart Spiritual Retreat

'Morning.'

Mel strolls towards them from the direction of the terraces. Little Red Riding Hood in her burgundy shorts and T-shirt with her wicker basket over one arm.

'Good morning, Detective Inspector,' Sofia says. 'Out on patrol?'

'Isn't that what your guys do?' Mel stops next to the sunbeds, her expression disapproving as she takes in the champagne and the discarded breakfast. The lazy decadence of the scene.

Zoe feels a prickle of unease.

'Do you believe in justice?' Sofia asks Mel.

Mel's pale blue eyes settle on her. 'Justice is complicated.'

'I don't agree.' Sofia sits up. 'You're still in the honeymoon phase with Quinn, but it won't last. She'll hurt you one day.'

'I doubt that.'

'She's not who you think she is.'

'I think I know her pretty well.'

'Sometimes people surprise you, Detective Inspector. Sometimes appearances really are deceptive.'

Mel's stare turns icy. 'I'll take my chances.'

'I'm not sure Quinn's a safe bet,' Sofia says.

A loaded silence swells between the two of them.

'We'll see,' Mel says eventually. 'We'll see.'

30

ZOE

2018

An hour later, when Zoe returns to the rooms she shares with Carl, she finds him sitting at the desk in their tiny living room. Blue smoke curls into the air and escapes through the open window in front of him. He doesn't usually smoke inside. Something about the image is familiar. Him at his desk, cigarette in hand.

'Are you writing?' she says.

He turns to her, his face glowing with an energy she hasn't seen for a long time.

'Just journaling,' he says. 'So much has been going on I wanted to make sense of it.'

When Quinn was helping Carl fight his addictions, she advised him to stop writing for a while. She said his writing was serving his ego when it should be the other way around. Only when he'd mastered his ego should he return to the page. Over time, Carl became so absorbed in working on his ego that he lost the desire to write a new novel.

He stubs out the cigarette on the windowsill. 'Sorry. Won't smoke in here again.'

'That's okay.' Zoe wanders over to the desk. He closes his notebook and slides an arm around her waist. Peering through the half-open window, she can see the pool and the sunbeds where she and Sofia were lying all morning. 'Were you watching us?'

'No.' He smiles. 'Maybe a little.'

'You were supposed to be gardening.'

'I got carried away with the writing.' He kisses her stomach through the long black T-shirt that covers her damp bikini. 'What you got there?' he asks, tapping the large book tucked under her right arm.

She hands it to him. 'Sofia said I could have it.' On the way back from the pool, Sofia invited Zoe to her room and insisted on giving her *The Encyclopaedia of Greek Myths*.

Carl opens the book where Sofia has turned down the page. It is a chapter dedicated to the Furies.

'What's their story?' Zoe says. 'They get revenge for people?'

'Something like that.'

She cranes her neck and peers out of the window at the mural of the Furies. 'I've never really looked at that image before.'

'I've always thought them a dark decor choice.'

'Maybe whoever owned this place before us had a warped sense of humour.'

Carl closes the book and puts it on his desk. 'They're the perfect backdrop for our current drama.'

A cold tingle spreads up Zoe's spine. She can sense the three crones watching her. Watching all of them.

Holly and Joe appear in the courtyard below on their way back to the house. Holly's high-pitched chatter floats up to her. Was Carl listening to her and Sofia?

'It looked like it was going well with our visitor?' he says, his thumb massaging her hip bone.

Zoe strokes his hair. 'She's still in there somewhere. Little Sofia.' Is she? Zoe isn't sure. Sofia has an old and bitter spirit for someone so young. Yet despite her unhinged offer, Sofia is not unwell like her mother. She seems balanced. In control of herself.

In control of everyone.

'She's going to join us for dinner tonight,' Zoe says.

Carl smiles. 'That's a start.'

Zoe does feel she made a breakthrough today. Quinn will be pleased with her.

'Eva would be gutted to see Sofia corrupted by money and power like this,' Carl says. 'That's why she wanted nothing to do with her parents.'

He lifts his head and presses his lips against her right breast. Nuzzles her through her T-shirt. She looks at the crown of his head. The patch of pink scalp beneath his thinning hair makes her feel sad.

'She looked just like Eva lying by that pool today,' he says. 'It's freaky.'

Did Carl think about Eva's naked body, just like she had? Did he sit here remembering the nights Eva would come to their room and join them in bed? Zoe glances at his journal. Is that what he was writing about?

She reaches up to her hair and unties the other gift Sofia insisted on giving her. A Chanel silk scarf. A black background this time, patterned with the Chanel logo in cream and gold.

'From Sofia?' Carl says when she shows it to him.

Zoe nods. 'She said she'd be offended if I refused.'

'You don't want to offend her.'

'That's what I thought. I won't wear it.'

'It's only a scarf.'

'Exactly.' Zoe winds the glossy material around her hand. 'It's only a scarf.'

31

QUINN

2018

When Quinn reaches the gate of the hen enclosure, she unlocks it, shuts it behind her and locks it again.

'Won't be long,' she says to Aphrodite, who sits on the other side of the high mesh fence that protects the hens from predators.

When Quinn opens the door of the coop, all five of Pure Heart's hens stream out into the lukewarm morning, their fussy clucking bringing joy to her heart. She has always loved this part of her day and now she appreciates it more than ever. She needs time to collect herself. She remembers Tom Quinn warning her how difficult it was to be a leader. He was right.

Quinn unseals the lid of the large plastic tub where they keep the pellets of chicken feed. The hens crowd round her as she scoops the dry brown pellets into one of the metal bowls stacked on the ground. 'Patience, beautiful ones,' she says to them. 'Patience.' These Brahma chickens are her favourite breed. They are hardy birds and pretty too. Thick white feathers on their bodies and legs. Black necks and tail tips and red faces.

She fills the bowl and puts it down. With a flurry of flapping wings and squawks, the pushiest of the hens fill their beaks. Quinn puts another full bowl down for the other birds. Then she steps inside the musty coop, brushing away a cobweb that clings to her face.

The coop is made of pine. Nesting boxes and roosting perches line the walls. Matted straw covers the floor. A mesh screen protects the open window and mesh fills the ventilation gaps between the walls and the roof. She checks the nesting boxes and finds ten eggs, which she puts in one of the wicker baskets hanging by the door. As a kid, Sofia loved omelettes. Quinn will ask Joe to make her one this morning.

They've reached a turning point with Sofia – Quinn is sure of it. Last night she ate dinner with them. She was already seated at one end of the long table when Quinn entered the kitchen. Eva's old seat.

'I see they haven't killed you yet?' Sofia said and Quinn laughed, to show she knew Sofia was joking. The atmosphere over dinner was a bit strained, despite Joe's delicious vegetable moussaka, but Quinn knows she must be patient.

At least the evening ended on a positive note. Sofia is going to join them for today's Community Bonding session. A regular event where the Pure Heart members gather to enjoy activities and to express their authentic thoughts and feelings. Quinn will lead a gentle yoga class and then conduct a sound bath with her Tibetan singing bowls. It will be a beautiful day. A chance for Sofia to connect with everyone on a profound level and to feel the true wisdom of her soul. Quinn is sure a solid display of Pure Heart unity will make Sofia realise that no one here could ever do what she is asking of them.

* * *

On her way back to the house, Quinn finds Mel waiting in the courtyard.

'Thought we could go to breakfast together,' Mel says, getting up from her seat by the firepit. Sweet but unnecessary, thinks Quinn, the way Mel keeps shadowing her everywhere, as if she needs a bodyguard.

'Did you sleep well?' Quinn asks.

'I had that nightmare again.' Mel glances up at Sofia's window. 'Do you really think she's starting to come round?'

'I think she's ready to start her healing journey. Zoe spending time with her yesterday seems to have helped.'

A sullen shadow crosses Mel's face. 'I'm not sure watching Sofia drink champagne in the morning counts as helping her.'

Quinn smiles. 'Let's see how today goes.' Is Mel jealous at Zoe being singled out for such an important role? Difficult emotions are all part of the spiritual journey and Mel will have to deal with hers. Sofia's wellbeing is Quinn's main priority just now.

'Don't get me wrong,' Mel says, 'I do understand why Sofia's so messed up.'

Quinn's smile falters. 'Well, yes. She's been through a lot.'

'Tough to lose your mum at that age.' Mel's cool blue eyes gaze into Quinn's. 'But I also know we can do something with the best of intentions, and it can go wrong.'

'It's good you can see both sides of things.' Quinn lays a hand on Mel's arm. 'I think that's why we have such a special connection.'

Mel's cheeks flush. 'Thank you.'

'I hope you feel that connection too. I hope you trust me.'

'I... I really care for you,' Mel says, in a low, shy voice. 'A lot.'

Quinn is delighted to hear Mel expressing her emotions so clearly. Such sharing would have been impossible when she first came to Pure Heart.

'We all care for each other here.' Quinn squeezes her arm. 'That's why we'll get through this. Together.'

* * *

When Quinn enters the kitchen, Mel and Aphrodite in her wake, she finds Joe and Holly at one of the worktops, each wielding a large stainless-steel knife with a gleaming blade. They freeze, mid-conversation, knives held aloft.

'Good morning,' Quinn says.

'Hi.' Holly slides her knife reverently into the wooden knife block in front of her.

'Morning.' Joe does the same.

'Are those new?' Mel pushes past Quinn and heads over to the worktop. She examines the knife block with suspicion. 'And what about this?' She turns her attention to the worktop behind her where a shiny coffee machine sits. A glinting chrome beast more suited to a coffee shop than a home.

'It all got delivered this morning,' Joe says.

'It's from Sofia,' Holly adds. 'Obviously.'

'This food processor too?' Mel lifts an unopened box from behind the coffee machine.

Joe nods. 'She said it would help with the extra catering.' He turns to Quinn. 'We can send it back, if you prefer?'

Quinn looks at Joe's broad, earnest face. He's been in need of new kitchen equipment for ages, and catering for their guests is a lot of extra work. Surely Sofia's generous gesture shows she is thinking of others? Of the good of the community?

'I don't think we should keep it,' Mel says.

'I agree,' comes a voice from behind them. They turn to see Andreas hauling himself up from one of the saggy sofas at the far end of the room. He comes towards them, swaying slightly, smoothing down his rumpled T-shirt. His hair is tousled, his face creased with sleep.

'Did you sleep down here?' Quinn asks.

'I fall asleep on the couch. Big deal.' He stands in front of her, hands in the pockets of his jeans. Quinn recoils as the alcohol fumes on his breath hit her.

'Andreas, the drinking must stop,' she says. 'I recommend a long session in the sweat lodge. Start getting the toxins out of your body.'

'I saw you with a bottle of whisky last night,' Mel says. 'Who gave you that?'

'Please.' He raises his hands. 'No lectures.' He wanders over to the sink, fills himself a mug of water and gulps it back. 'You must give everything back. All of it.'

'Coming from the man who's having his mother's care home bills paid,' says Holly.

'This is what I am meaning.' Andreas wipes his mouth. 'Temptation is very dangerous thing.'

'Maybe you're the person we need to worry about,' Mel says. 'Is Sofia's latest offer tempting to you as well?'

'No.' Andreas slams his mug down on the draining board. 'I would never hurt Quinn.'

'You're getting paranoid, mate,' Joe says. 'It's the drink.'

'This is not paranoia.' Andreas rubs his forehead. 'We are living like in a prison. I cannot drive out of here without security code. They are controlling everything.'

'You're in no state to go anywhere,' Holly says. 'You're not fit to drive.'

'Okay.' Quinn takes a deep breath. 'That's enough.' She must soar high like an eagle, soar above the drama and petty disputes. 'We don't want to offend Sofia by refusing her kind gesture, so we'll keep the equipment. I'm sure Joe will make good use of it.'

'Andreas is right,' Mel says. 'Even if he is still drunk.'

'I don't think a few kitchen implements will tempt Joe to murder me,' Quinn says.

Joe laughs. 'Don't be too sure. I'd do away with anyone for a bread machine.'

Quinn and Holly join in the laughter. Mel crosses her arms over her chest.

'One day this will not be funny for you,' Andreas says. 'Not funny at all.'

32

QUINN

2018

Late morning. Quinn sits on a yoga mat at the centre of the yurt's wooden floor. Six other mats surround her in a circle. On them, cross-legged, sit Mel, Joe, Holly, Zoe, Carl and Sofia. Dmitri sits on a wooden chair by the yurt's door, surveying them with an amused expression.

Sunlight filters through the canvas roof. The dense scent of sandalwood incense fills the air, masking the yurt's mustiness. An electric fan at the far end of the circular space whirs merrily from side to side, attempting to cool them.

Quinn springs to her feet. 'Let's come to standing at the top of our mats.' The others get up, accompanied by sighs and the snap and crack of stiff joints. She leads them through two sets of sun salutations then instructs them to do three more at their own pace. As they do so, she wanders amongst them, adjusting their postures, whispering advice. Her year as a yogi's assistant at an ashram in Kerala taught her most of what she knows. The rest she learned from books. She is a great believer in self-taught knowledge.

Sofia's inverted body is clad in matching white yoga pants and a crop vest. Designer no doubt. Before they started the class, Sofia was raving about her private yoga instructor back in London, but, as Quinn appraises her downward dog, she thinks the expensive lessons might be a rip-off. She is about to pull Sofia's hips up and back when she spots Dmitri glaring at her and decides against it.

'Move in time with your own breath,' she tells Zoe, who is on the mat beside Sofia's and clearly trying to keep up with the younger woman. 'Go at your own speed.'

Carl is moving with more vigour and focus than Quinn has seen for a long time. Even Joe is making an effort to stretch his stiff knees, and Holly's arms are flowing with an uncharacteristic grace. Mel's asanas are strong and controlled. Sofia's presence has given them all a new purpose and energy.

She returns to the centre of the circle, but her eyes travel back to Sofia. She thinks of Eva, here in this yurt, practising yoga with her at dawn. Quinn was sure their rigorous practice was bringing peace and balance to Eva's troubled mind.

After the sun salutations are complete, Quinn leads the group through a standing sequence. Triangle, side-angle, half-moon. 'Now into warrior two,' she says.

Soon the others are facing her, front knee bent, their front arm pointing towards her, hands outstretched. Their warrior energy flows in her direction. Their fierce warrior expressions make her feel suddenly hemmed in. She sees Sofia's knowing smile and thinks of the grinning skeleton on the Tarot card.

'Let's come down onto our mats,' she says. She is about to instruct them to lie down in Shavasana, corpse posture, but the words stick in her throat. Why not try something else for a change? They finish the session cross-legged with their hands in prayer position.

'Namaste,' Quinn says, and they echo the word back to her. 'Now, I know how much we all appreciate a sound bath, so I've brought my singing bowls and I thought—'

'Let's do trust games,' Sofia says.

'Trust games?' says Quinn.

'You know what I mean.' Sofia beams at her. 'We used to do them all the time.'

'Yes, you loved that sort of thing,' Holly says.

'Let's do the one where everyone catches you.' Sofia rushes to the back of the yurt, behind the wood-burning stove, to the area where they keep various bits of equipment. 'Wow.' She drags out a small wooden chest. 'I can't believe this is still here.' She flings open the chest and, after a quick search, pulls out a black silk blindfold. The kind they sometimes wear when dancing to help them shed all inhibition.

'I'll go first,' Sofia says. She fetches one of the wooden chairs stacked behind the chest and drags it into the centre of the yurt. Quinn snatches up her yoga mat and steps aside.

'Slow down,' Carl says. 'Let us get into position.'

Dmitri springs to his feet and calls out what is clearly a warning in Russian, but Sofia ignores him and climbs onto the chair.

'Everyone in a circle, arms crossed,' bellows Joe.

Sofia wraps the blindfold around her eyes and knots it at the back of her head.

'Grip each other's hands,' Holly says.

Sofia flings up her arms and lets out a reckless whoop.

'Wait,' Zoe says, 'we're not ready.'

Ignoring the warning, Sofia launches herself backwards from the chair. Quinn winces as Joe's strong hands drag her and the rest of the circle over to the left, just in time to catch Sofia.

'See?' Sofia applauds them. 'I knew you'd catch me.'

'Lower her to the ground,' Quinn says. 'Slowly.'

Together they bring Sofia safely to the floor.

'See, Dmitri,' Sofia says, still blindfolded. 'These people have my back.' She giggles. 'Literally.'

Dmitri, a look of relief on his face, returns to his chair.

Quinn places her hands lightly on the crown of Sofia's head. 'Let's finish by giving you healing energy. Pure Heart energy.' The others nod. Each person places their hands on a different part of Sofia's body. Mel, left with Sofia's feet, touches them gingerly.

Sofia sighs. 'Nice.'

They sit in silence. Quinn closes her eyes and visualises a shimmering violet light passing from her hands into Sofia. She is sure the girl must be able to feel their love for her.

After a couple of minutes, Sofia rips off her blindfold. 'Who's next?'

Zoe goes first, throwing herself into the air with even more abandon than Sofia. Joe goes next and, although his bulk is a challenge, the net doesn't break and they lower him to the floor gently. Then comes Carl, who crosses his arms over his chest before he falls.

'Don't bloody drop me,' Holly says before she lets her body drop, plank-stiff into their waiting arms.

Mel has a focused expression on her face throughout. Quinn can imagine her taking part in police drills, working as part of a team. Taking each exercise seriously. When it's time for Mel to climb up on the chair, her focused expression turns dubious.

'I'm not wearing that,' she says when Holly tries to hand her the blindfold.

'It's part of it,' Zoe says.

'Didn't you do trust games in the Met?' Carl asks.

'Funnily enough, no.' Mel gives Quinn a worried look. Quinn wonders if being blindfolded reminds Mel of some difficult moment in the past. One she'd rather forget.

'It's okay.' Sofia places a reassuring hand on Mel's shoulder. 'Just close your eyes. That will be enough.'

Mel gives her a grateful smile before stepping up onto the chair. When the time comes for her to fall, she does so silently. When the community catches her, a joyous smile spreads across her face. 'Thanks everyone,' she says. 'That means a lot to me.'

As soon as Mel is on her feet, all eyes turn to Quinn.

'Your go,' Sofia says to her.

'Yes,' Dmitri says from his sentry post. 'Your turn, Quinn.'

'Of course,' she says. Any opportunity to experience the complete trust they all have in one another. She is surprised to find her legs trembling as she steps onto the chair. Her fingers fumble as she ties the blindfold.

'Ready when you are,' Sofia says.

Quinn hesitates. She imagines the group silently edging away, leaving only hard wooden floorboards to break her fall.

'We're here,' Mel says. 'We've got you.'

Mel's calm voice reassures her. She arches her back and lets herself drop, a gasp trapped in her throat. A moment of freefall and then... into the arms of her beloved community who lower her to the floor with what feels like reverence.

Hands cover her body from head to toe.

'Your turn for some healing energy,' Joe says.

'Your heart's beating like crazy,' Sofia says, and Quinn realises the hands on her chest are Sofia's. 'Let's all send our love and energy there. Help calm her down.'

The pressure on Quinn's chest increases as everyone moves their hands there. She feels like she has a tight band of metal around her ribcage.

A voice begins to chant. Zoe. A repetitive Buddhist healing mantra Quinn taught her years ago. The others join in, low and dissonant.

The noise builds, as does the pressure in Quinn's chest. She tries not to focus on it. She should concentrate on receiving all this beautiful love into her body. She must release her fear and negativity.

Shallow breaths are all she can take. Panic builds inside her. Her body wants to struggle, but she holds herself still.

'And release,' comes a voice somewhere above her. Holly? Mel? She is too disorientated to tell.

Air rushes into her lungs as the hands lift from her chest. She remains still, composing herself, waiting for a moment to pass before she slowly removes her blindfold.

The first thing she sees is Eva looking down at her, an ambiguous smile on her face. No. Not Eva. Of course not. It's Sofia.

Quinn sits up and the others scuttle back to their yoga mats.

'Amazing,' she says. 'That was... that was very powerful.'

They bow their heads in unison.

'Namaste,' they say.

33

QUINN

2018

Quinn crosses the courtyard in the dawn light, the flagstones cool beneath her bare feet, Aphrodite trotting behind her. She glances at the windows of the other community members' bedrooms and finds their shutters still closed. She did check the kitchen before coming outside and was relieved to find the couch empty. Hopefully Andreas had a long and sober sleep after yesterday's drama.

When she and the others returned to the house after the bonding session, they found Andreas and Grigor arguing in the kitchen. Andreas wanted to drive to Kakopetria, but Grigor refused to give him the security code for the gate. A responsible move as Andreas had been drinking again. Eventually, Quinn persuaded him to back down. Still fuming, he went to bed and slept until late afternoon. After that, he took her advice and did a long stint in the sweat lodge before returning to bed.

She wants him to recover from this relapse, but that will only happen if he's willing to do the work. He has to want to be healed. She sometimes thinks his difficult past – the invasion, his father's death and his brother's disappearance – hasn't left him enough strength to conquer his demons.

As she passes the pool, her spine tingles, as if warning her she is being watched. She turns around but finds only the Furies staring down at her from the central wing of the building. She turns her back on them.

As she makes her way down to the chicken coop, she remembers last night's dinner with satisfaction. Not just for Joe's excellent *yemista* – roast peppers and tomatoes stuffed with rice and spices – but because Sofia ate with them again and, after the bonding day, the atmosphere at the table was much less strained. Quinn picked up a strong community spirit amongst them all. A shared sense of purpose. Even Dmitri and Grigor appear to be mellowing. Quinn made Grigor a mug of mountain tea yesterday and explained its many health benefits to him. He looked bemused but drank it and afterwards thanked her. Last night, she caught Dmitri leafing through a book on stoicism in the office. He put it down as soon as she came into the room and returned to his numerous laptop screens.

Sofia even suggested they all drive out to the wild and secluded Lara Beach this afternoon for a swim. A place she remembers going to with her mother.

Before Quinn reaches the enclosure, she hears her beloved hens screeching and squawking. They can't be that hungry.

Aphrodite takes up her usual position outside the fence as Quinn enters the enclosure and locks the gate behind her. When she opens the door to the coop, the hens barge past her, wings flapping, and run in giddy circles around the enclosure.

'It's okay,' she says, 'Mama's here.'

She picks up the empty metal bowls from the dusty earth and fills them from the tub of feed pellets. She has to rattle the bowls for several minutes before the hens settle enough to eat from them.

She wonders if her birds are picking up the shifts in energy taking place at Pure Heart. Change is always unsettling.

Humming to herself, she enters the coop. As she is checking the nesting boxes for eggs, the sound of rustling straw distracts her. She stands still. Listens.

There it is again. She hopes they don't have mice.

She glances around her bare feet, looking for mouse droppings. As she peers into the far corner of the coop, the straw lifts and ripples. Unable to see clearly, she moves closer.

The straw scatters. At first, she thinks she is looking at a pile of rope. Only as it uncurls and a narrow, reptilian head appears does she realise she's looking at a snake.

She freezes. The snake rises up and is, for a few seconds, suspended. Adrenalin makes Quinn's vision pin-sharp. She sees the dark, circular markings on the snake's light brown, scaly skin. She sees a forked tongue flicking in and out.

She tries to move, but her body has shut down. She thinks of the Medusa, the Gorgon from Greek myth with snakes for hair whose victims turn to stone if they look into her eyes.

The snake opens the pale pink cavern of its mouth, exposing sharp white fangs.

She screams and the sound startles her into action. She stumbles backwards. In the confusion she loses sight of the snake but then something rough and dry slides over her bare toes and two sharp fangs sink into her skin.

34

QUINN

2018

Quinn is limping up to the house with the help of the broom from the hen enclosure, when she sees Mel hurrying towards her, a burgundy figure made blurry by the tears in her eyes. She blinks them away. It's only pain, she tells herself. Deep breaths. Mind over matter.

'What's wrong?' Mel sprints across the distance between them. 'What the fuck happened?'

'Snake. In the hen coop.' Quinn is trembling. She is in shock, she reminds herself. A normal, healthy reaction to threat.

'Jesus. What kind?'

'I don't know. Big.'

Mel examines Quinn's right foot, which hovers just above the ground. Her ankle is already swelling up. The fang marks the snake gifted her are red and vivid.

'Let's get you inside,' Mel says. She puts an arm around Quinn's waist and instructs Quinn to put an arm around her shoulder. Quinn drops the broom and lets Mel haul her up towards the orchard.

Aphrodite trails them, stopping every now and then to look behind her.

'It's okay,' Quinn says, breathless. 'It might not have been a viper.' Saying that makes her feel better, but she has no idea what kind of snake it was.

'The bite looks nasty to me,' Mel says. 'Let me take your weight.'

As they lumber up the steps that lead from the orchard, Grigor's stocky figure appears, blocking their way.

'What is happening?' he says.

'As if you care.' Mel tightens her grip on Quinn's waist. 'I need to get her inside.'

'Let me help,' Grigor says.

'We don't need your help,' Mel says, but Grigor ignores her and sweeps Quinn up off the ground. 'Fine.' Mel releases her grip.

'Thank you,' Quinn says, her small body encircled by Grigor's sturdy arms.

'Have you ever seen a snake in the coop before?' Mel asks.

'No.' Quinn is starting to feel dizzy now. 'Let's not make a big deal of this.' Dizzy and nauseous. What if there is venom circulating in her bloodstream already? She tells herself people get bitten by snakes every year in Cyprus but no one has died from a bite for decades. This fact fails to reassure her.

When they reach the courtyard, Quinn sees Zoe at her bedroom window. She manages a weak wave before Grigor whisks her into the building.

Upon entering the kitchen, the smell of coffee overpowers her. Holly is fussing around the new coffee maker, which hisses and gurgles as she holds a stainless-steel jug beneath the steam wand.

'Oh my God,' she says, when she sees Quinn.

'What happened?' Joe, a mound of chopped apricots and apple in front of him on the workstation, puts down his knife and wipes his hands on his apron.

'Snake,' Quinn says. 'Bit me.'

Grigor lowers her onto one of the sofas and scares away the kittens that try to jump onto her lap.

'I'll take it from here,' Mel says.

Grigor shrugs before backing away.

'Thank you, Grigor,' Quinn says as he disappears out of the door.

Mel pulls over a footstool and instructs Quinn to place her injured foot on it. Quinn can see her police training come to the fore. Mel is calm and focused. Happy to take charge.

'We'll get this sorted,' Mel tells her. 'We'll get you to a hospital.'

'I'll fetch Andreas,' Holly says. 'He knows about stuff like this.'

Joe appears, a mug in his hand. 'Tea for you. With honey.'

Quinn accepts the tea with thanks and shaking hands, although for the first time in years she has a craving for the hit of a strong black coffee to alleviate the shock. It's because of the smell. Since they got that machine, she can smell coffee everywhere.

Zoe bursts into the kitchen, her hair piled on top of her head, her silk kimono hiding very little. 'What's going on?' When Mel explains she gasps. 'Fuck. What kind of snake? Was it venomous?'

'We don't know,' Mel says.

'Let's not panic,' says Quinn, although her foot and ankle are swelling as she watches. The skin around the puncture wound is puffy and tinged with blue.

'Carl's down at the yurt, writing,' Zoe says. 'Should I go and get him?'

'Snake bite expert, is he?' Mel says.

Zoe tosses her hair over one shoulder. 'No need to be snippy. We're all concerned.'

'Writing?' Quinn says. 'He's started writing again?'

Holly enters the kitchen, followed by Andreas. His jeans and grey T-shirt are crumpled as though he has slept in them. Despite the dark hollows beneath his eyes, he looks alert.

'I knew something bad would be happening,' he says to Quinn.

'It was an unfortunate encounter with Mother Nature,' Quinn says. 'Nothing more.'

Andreas orders Mel out of the way and kneels to take her place. 'Tell me about this snake. What colour? What did it look like?'

'Light brown colour. Markings on its skin.'

'The markings, they are like rectangles or circles?' he asks.

She conjures the image of the snake rising from the floor. Those still, endless seconds when she stared at it.

'Circles.'

'Not rectangles?' Andreas says. 'You are sure?'

'Yes.'

'Okay. Is good. Viper has rectangles.' He peers at the puncture wound. When he prods the area around the wound with his thumb, the hot stab of pain makes bile rise up Quinn's throat.

'A viper can leave fangs in the wound,' he says, 'but I feel no fangs.'

'That's good,' Mel says, 'isn't it?'

'Maybe a coin snake, I think,' Andreas says. 'Still very nasty. Sore.'

A seething band of pain grips Quinn's ankle. 'Yes, I'm aware of that.'

'We must take you to the hospital,' Andreas says.

'I'll drive,' Mel says. 'We'll take the Toyota.'

Quinn feels faint at the thought of being in a hospital. Such sterile, soulless places. 'If it's not venomous, I can fix the wound myself,' she says. 'I've got herbal tinctures to clean it and I'll do some Reiki healing to bring the swelling down.'

'You need to get the wound cleaned properly,' Joe says.

'Absolutely,' Holly insists.

'They'll have to give you a tetanus shot,' adds Mel.

'It's all good.' Sofia sweeps into the kitchen in a black silk dressing gown, her hair stylishly tousled. 'We've arranged for a doctor to come out.'

Mel stiffens. 'What?'

'A private doctor from Nicosia,' Sofia says blithely, as if that should be obvious. 'My team always does their research before I travel.'

Dmitri appears in the doorway and talks Russian at Sofia in his low monotone. Quinn shrinks back into the sofa as he looks at her. Is that a smirk forming on his face? She takes a sip of tea. She needs to hold herself together.

'The doctor won't be long,' Sofia says.

'She needs proper treatment,' Mel says. 'Injections, bandaging and—'

'I'm sure this guy can manage all that,' Sofia says airily.

'Are you trying to stop us taking her to the hospital?' Mel says.

Sofia rolls her eyes. 'I'm trying to save Quinn a long, uncomfortable car journey.'

'She is scared we will tell someone what is going on,' Andreas says.

'Nothing's going on,' says Quinn.

'Sofia's just trying to help,' Zoe says.

'Thanks, Sofia,' says Holly. 'It's very kind of you.'

Andreas shakes his head. 'You people.'

'Andreas, mate,' Joe says. 'How about I make you a coffee?'

'Someone put the snake in there.' Andreas points at Dmitri. 'You. Did you do this?'

'Me?' Dmitri frowns. 'If I wanted to kill Quinn, I would not use a snake. Or at least I would use a venomous one. No?'

Quinn's stomach roils. She feels faint and vulnerable. No one would do this to her on purpose. Would they?

'Andreas,' Mel says, 'I share your reservations about Sofia's presence here, but even I think this was an accident.'

Quinn manages a weak smile. Of course, this was an accident. Even Mel thinks so. All this suspicion is the real danger in this situation. 'Enough of these crazy theories,' she says. 'If I started thinking like you, Andreas, I'd realise you're the one who knows all about the wildlife round here. You'd know where to find a snake.'

Andreas pales. 'I would never—'

'Or maybe it was Carl?' Quinn says. 'He was down near the chicken coop this morning.' She laughs. 'See – crazy talk.'

She does feel very dizzy. Is she about to be sick?

Andreas crouches beside her. His dark, sad eyes look deep into hers. 'They are going to hurt you,' he says. 'This is how it begins.'

35

HOLLY

2019

The doctor hired by Sofia arrived at Pure Heart an hour after being summoned. He must have dropped what he was doing at the time to come and help Quinn, and we were grateful for it.

He couldn't have been more attentive. He cleaned and bandaged the wound, gave her a tetanus shot and took blood samples for testing. Only as a precaution, he said. In his opinion, Quinn had nothing to worry about. Her foot would be sore and swollen for a while and she would perhaps feel unwell for the next forty-eight hours but, apart from that, she would recover easily.

He offered to send a nurse to stay with Quinn for the next twenty-four hours, but we said we wanted to look after her ourselves.

After the doctor departed, some of us ventured down to the chicken coop. We found the hens outside in the enclosure, huddled together. We were hesitant to go inside the coop but figured the snake would have been more terrified of the encounter with Quinn than she was. With rakes and spades, we searched amongst the straw on the floor and made tentative inspections of the nesting boxes.

We found no sign of the snake, but a closer examination of the coop showed gaps in the mesh that blocked the gap between the roof and the walls. Gaps a snake could easily get in. We set about repairs immediately.

As we worked, we discussed how lucky we were that none of us had experienced a snake attack during our time here. It was only a matter of time, we said. Over the years, I'd often told Quinn walking barefoot outdoors was dangerous. She didn't listen. The same way she didn't listen when I said I'd seen her having sex with Blake in the orchard.

'Afterwards, he told me being watched had turned him on,' I said. 'That made me really uncomfortable.'

Quinn smiled. 'Blake doesn't have any filters. I love that about him.'

'I'm not the only person who thinks he's out of order sometimes.'

Quinn sighed. 'Holly, we both know you have a tendency to let your past trauma cloud your judgement. Try to remember that.'

Her words hurt me, although there was some truth in them.

'We're all damaged souls,' Quinn said. 'That's why we must have compassion.'

Blake was broken, not damaged, but I knew Quinn wouldn't want to hear that.

'When I first met him, I felt this instant sense of recognition,' Quinn said. 'I knew we'd met in a previous life and were destined to love each other in this one.'

Quinn often spoke of the intense spiritual connection between her and Blake, but it was clear to me and everyone else she was consumed by lust. Not that I dared say so then. Maybe it would have been better for her if I had.

36

ZOE

2018

Two days after Quinn's accident, Zoe is lounging on a sunbed by the pool, hoping Sofia will get up soon and join her. It's 10 a.m. and although the air is fresh and laced with the invigorating aroma of pine trees, the sun is already fierce. She's yet to take off the white linen shirt that covers her bikini and the tops of her thighs.

In her lap is *The Encyclopaedia of Greek Myths*. She's reading about Python, the giant serpent who guarded the sacred site of Delphi until Apollo killed him and also about the Hydra, the nine-headed water snake slain by Herakles.

Since Quinn's encounter with the snake, Zoe has been on the lookout for them but has seen nothing. She knows how rare it was for Quinn to come across one like that, but the thought of it still creeps her out.

Last night in bed, she and Carl mocked Andreas' paranoia. His wild theories.

'The Mystery of the Killer Snake,' Carl said. 'A dark and disturbing thriller.'

'A gripping tale of revenge,' Zoe said. 'You should definitely write it.'

They laughed at the absurdity of the situation, but when Zoe woke this morning she found Carl already at his desk, head down over his notebook, pen nib scratching against paper.

She removes her sunglasses and looks up at the Furies, squinting to better appreciate the snakes writhing around their heads. She's already read the chapter on these three scary dames. It seems that when they thought vengeance was justified, they would pursue the guilty party relentlessly. They never gave up until the balance of justice was restored.

Quinn's living room window is open. Zoe wonders if she'll come downstairs later or if she'll finally obey the doctor's advice and rest her foot for a while. Yesterday, she lightly sprained her already injured ankle while moving around her room when she wasn't supposed to be.

Zoe bets Mel is up there now, fussing over her. No surprise that Mel volunteered to nurse Quinn. Thanks to the sprain, she's managed to stretch out her duties.

Last night, after Zoe and Carl had finished laughing about Andreas, he joked Mel and Quinn might be indulging in some kinky patient-nurse role play. Zoe pretended to retch.

'Do you remember the role plays we did when I first met you?' she said, when they'd stopped laughing. 'Teacher and student, client and whore. That was fun.' His response, a tiny flicker of his eyes, was almost imperceptible but she caught it. What she said had repulsed him.

'How about this?' He pulled back the sheet to reveal her naked body. 'You be a goddess and I'll go down on you and worship your second chakra.'

'Hey there.' A voice pulls her back to the present.

Zoe turns her head towards the terraces and sees Sofia approaching, Dmitri in tow. Her cheeks flame. She touches her hair, smooths it over one shoulder. 'Hi,' she says. Sofia is wearing a pair of grey, mid-thigh shorts and a tight white T-shirt. Walking boots encase her elegant feet. Brand new, by the look of them. Her vast hat shields her face from the sun.

'We've been down to the monastery,' Sofia says.

'Oh.' Zoe's eyes flick to Dmitri. As usual, his face gives nothing away. 'Did you go inside?'

Sofia shakes her head. 'I couldn't. It was... it was too hard.'

'You should stay away from there,' Dmitri says. He looks at Zoe. 'I am right, no?'

'Eva wouldn't want you to upset yourself,' Zoe says.

Dmitri rewards her with an approving nod.

Sofia glances down at the woods. 'I can hardly see it from up here, but just knowing it's there freaks me out.'

'We will ignore it,' Dmitri says.

Zoe wonders what a bodyguard-client role play would be like? The thrill of boundaries crossed, some sort of threat or danger to be protected from. She glances at Dmitri, who has retreated and stands with his hands in his pockets. Would he treat her like a goddess, or would he take what he wanted from her? Would he be the one demanding worship?

'Good to see you're enjoying the myths,' Sofia says.

'Oh.' Zoe remembers the open book in her lap. 'Yes.'

Sofia looks at the picture of Apollo slaying Python at Delphi. 'The Ancient Greeks did love their snakes.'

'Some of these stories are pretty dark,' Zoe says.

'The snake symbolises good as well as evil,' Sofia says. 'Life and death, creation and destruction.' She smiles. 'It's also a powerful symbol of rebirth and regeneration. Just like that dead bird.'

A tremor shoots up Zoe's spine. First the bird and now the snake. Quinn would say such symbols were a message from the universe.

'Right,' Sofia says, 'I'll leave you to your stories.'

'Aren't you coming for a swim?'

'I've calls to make. Future business to attend to.' She looks up at Quinn's window. 'The future doesn't just happen, Zoe. You have to make it happen.'

37

ZOE

2018

After Sofia returns indoors, Zoe gets up from her sunbed. Holly is in the garden this morning and she wants to talk to her alone. See where her head is at. Since Sofia arrived it's been almost impossible to have a proper chat with her fellow community members.

'Hello, you,' Holly says when Zoe finds her outside the polytunnel, tending to the vegetable beds.

'Thought you might need some help,' Zoe says.

Holly, dressed in loose cotton trousers and a baggy grey T-shirt, is standing on one of the raised vegetable beds in battered hiking boots, gripping a spade with grubby hands. Her nails are black with earth, as always.

'I'm digging the beds over for the winter veg,' she says. 'I've got some new compost to mix in with the soil.'

Soil is an obsession for Holly. She loves to nourish and care for it. Every year she seems newly amazed at what it can produce. Out here, along with the three raised vegetable beds, is Quinn's herb garden, the contents of which infuse the air around them with a heady blend of scents. Mint and thyme, basil and rosemary, cilantro and lemon verbena. Herbs for cooking with and for Quinn to use in her tinctures.

'Hi there.' Joe appears from the mouth of the polytunnel, dragging a sack of compost behind him. 'Got tired of quaffing champagne by the pool, did you?' His twinkling eyes confirm he's only teasing.

'Cheeky fucker,' Zoe says. 'Aren't you at the refugee camp today?'

Joe drops the compost next to the vegetable bed. 'Thought I'd take a break from there for a while.' He wipes his hands on his beige cargo shorts. 'With everything going on here—'

'He's so busy in the kitchen,' Holly says. 'I don't want him overdoing it.'

'What would I do without you to look out for me?' Joe says.

'Right back at you.' Holly beckons him closer. They share a gentle, lingering kiss.

Zoe smiles. Look at the two of them. Still so into each other after all these years. One of those rare relationships where everything just works. Their happiness with each other makes them solid, somehow. They're good people and Zoe has always been grateful for their presence in her life.

Holly breaks away from the kiss and returns to her work, pushing the tip of the spade deep into the soil.

'I've just seen Sofia,' Zoe says. 'She was on her way back from the monastery.'

The spade falls from Holly's grasp. 'Oops,' she says. 'Clumsy.' She picks up the spade with one hand, wipes her forehead with the other. 'How was she? What did she say?'

'She didn't go inside. I think it's hard for her, knowing it's there.'

'It is hard. And it is always there.' The veins in Holly's forearms bulge as she grips the spade with both hands again. 'Poor Sofia.'

'Maybe she's trying to face the past head on?' Joe says.

'Sometimes the past is better off buried.' Holly glances at the spade in her hands. 'And other gardening-based metaphors.'

Zoe feels a rush of affection for the warm, messy woman in front of her. Holly has more reason than most to bury her past. Raped by an uncle when she was thirteen years old. An act of abuse that changed the course of her life forever.

'I can't believe Sofia's been here two weeks already,' Holly says. 'I'm sure she's getting better. Don't you think?'

'Aye, she's settling in now,' Joe says. 'You're doing great with her, Zoe. The two of you have a really nice bond.'

'Oh.' Zoe allows herself a flush of pride. 'Thanks.'

'And she hasn't mentioned... she hasn't said anything about the money again,' Holly says. 'I'm sure she just wanted to make a point about Quinn.'

'Oh, totally,' agrees Zoe.

'I mean, there are difficult memories here for her but also good ones,' Joe says.

Zoe nods. 'That's right.'

'The other day,' Holly says, 'when we were down here picking vegetables for dinner, she offered to pay for a new irrigation system to be fitted. Isn't that generous?'

'Very,' Zoe says. Their current system consists of the rusting old water tank behind the polytunnel, and the network of unreliable pipes connected to it. A new system would allow Holly to grow double what she does now. She could even start trading with local businesses again. Get a stall at the farmers' market in Nicosia.

Pure Heart stall at the farmers' market. Look at our beautiful produce. #homegrownfood #organiclife #slowfood #farmersmarkets

'I refused,' Holly says. 'It didn't seem right.'

'I'm sure she just wanted to help,' Zoe says.

'She did buy us a load of premium-quality compost,' Joe says, as if making a confession. 'And some new gardening equipment.'

Zoe clears her throat. 'The other day she gave me a Chanel scarf. I didn't want to seem rude, so I took it.'

'Quite right,' Joe says.

'I won't wear it though.'

Holly laughs. 'It's only a scarf.' Her face falls. 'Here comes Mel.'

Zoe turns and sees Mel striding towards them, arms clasped behind her back. The detective inspector out on patrol in her burgundy uniform.

'Hi, Mel,' Joe says. 'How's the patient?'

'Better.' Mel's eyes scan the vegetable beds and the herb garden and settle on the sack of compost. 'I've just changed her dressing and the foot's not as swollen.'

'That's great.' Zoe recalls how, in the early days of Pure Heart, she was the one who followed Quinn around. Always keen to help and to learn from her.

'I did some Reiki on the wound.' A shyness creeps into Mel's voice. 'I've only just learned so I'm probably not that good but—'

'I bet you are,' Holly says. 'I bet you're a natural.'

Mel waves the compliment away. 'I doubt that, but it feels good to help.'

'When Quinn first told us about you, she said she'd met a special soul,' Zoe says.

'A kindred spirit,' adds Holly.

'That's nice to hear.' Mel's features soften. 'It's good to look after her for a change. After all she's done for me.'

'It's hard to see her looking vulnerable,' Holly says.

'Not that she's vulnerable,' Joe adds.

'Unwell,' Holly says. 'We're not used to Quinn being unwell.'

Zoe can't remember Quinn ever having anything more serious than a cold. When she first saw Quinn lying on the sofa after the snake attack, pale and shaking, she found the sight unnerving. Quinn looked diminished somehow. More human.

'I've always thought Quinn would live to be a hundred,' Holly says.

'Why wouldn't she?' Mel asks.

'She'll outlive us all,' Zoe says. A sobering thought. She can't imagine Quinn giving up control of Pure Heart at any age.

'Are you off to feed the hens?' Joe asks.

Mel nods. 'Then I'm going to clean out the coop and put some fresh straw down.'

'You're very brave,' Holly says. 'I wouldn't go in there alone.'

Mel shrugs. 'I've been in scarier situations.'

'Need a hand?' Joe says.

'No, I'm good.' Mel's cold blue eyes narrow. 'Andreas looked hungover again this morning. How long do you think this bender will last?'

'Hard to tell,' Joe replies. 'I'm sure he'll pull out of it.'

'Maybe,' Mel says. 'Let's hope Sofia and her plans don't drive him right over the edge.'

* * *

'She makes me nervous,' Holly admits once Mel is out of sight. 'I end up saying silly things.'

'It's just her way,' Joe says. 'She was trained to see the worst in people.'

'At least she didn't buy into Andreas' crazy ideas about Snakegate,' Zoe says.

Joe nods. 'That's something.'

As if any of them would have put the snake there, thinks Zoe. There would be far simpler ways to kill Quinn. She thinks of the trust game they played in the yurt. Quinn blindfolded on the floor, their hands on her chest. It would have been easy to press harder. To keep on pressing.

'I'm worried about Andreas,' Holly says.

'His behaviour is worrying,' says Joe.

Zoe figures Andreas won't rock the boat. Not with Sofia paying for his mother's care bills. He could have voiced his suspicions to the doctor the other day, but he said nothing. 'Well,' she says, 'we'll all have to keep an eye on him, won't we?'

Holly looks around at the gardens she's put years of work into. 'The thought of having to leave this place.'

Joe reaches for his wife's hand and gives it a reassuring squeeze. 'It won't come to that.'

'Quinn told us everything would be okay,' Zoe says. 'She said Sofia is the miracle we prayed for and she's always right. Isn't she?'

Joe and Holly nod in unison.

'She may have made a mistake with Eva,' Zoe continues, 'but she's still the leader of this community and we believe in her. Don't we?'

'Absolutely.' Holly's knuckles are white around the handle of the spade.

'One hundred per cent,' says Joe.

38

Insight Investigators: Background Report

Melanie Harris (known as Mel): Born January 8th 1980, in Chelmsford to Bill and Elizabeth Harris. Bill Harris, a train driver, died of a heart attack when Mel was five years old. Elizabeth married Mike Piercy and had a son, Christopher. As you'll see further on in this report, Mel and her family are no longer what you'd call close.

Mel left school at eighteen. After two years of temp work in London, she applied for the London Metropolitan Police, successfully completed her initial training and became a uniformed PC.

That's when her story starts to get interesting.

39

QUINN

2018

Quinn sits in the back of the Land Rover as it makes swift progress along the busy A6. Grigor is silent at the wheel, eyes hidden behind his sunglasses. Next to her sits Mel, freshly showered and smart in a burgundy linen shirt with matching culottes.

'Sitting in the back of cars always makes me queasy,' Mel says. 'How far away is this restaurant?'

'About another thirty minutes.' After an hour in the back of the Land Rover, negotiating the winding road down from the mountains, Quinn is feeling nauseous herself. She should have brought some crystallised ginger to suck on.

When Sofia announced this morning that she was taking the whole community out for dinner, Quinn wasn't sure if the outing was a good idea but now, despite the car sickness, she is glad to be away from Pure Heart. She needs a change of scene. Five days have passed since the snake attack and she's feeling cooped up. Impatient to get moving again. Thanks to the crutches Sofia bought her – currently resting against the back seat – she can get about, but she's keen for her injury to heal fully. She looks down at her feet, encased in unfamiliar orange Crocs – also a gift from Sofia. A perfect match for all her clothes, including her trusty orange dress, which she's wearing again tonight. She's grateful for Sofia's thoughtfulness, but she hates her new shoes. She feels noisy and clumsy in them, like a cat forced to wear a bell so everyone knows where it is at all times.

'Wow,' Mel says, as they round a headland of scrubby, terraced land. 'Beautiful.'

There, spread out before them, is the sapphire-blue gleam of the Mediterranean. It is almost 7 p.m. In an hour they should get a magnificent sunset. This western side of the island is one of Quinn's favourite areas. She takes a deep breath, the sea view lifting a weight off her chest she didn't even realise was there.

When Mel glances out of the rear window, Quinn does the same. The other Land Rover is still behind them, with Dmitri and Zoe in the front and Sofia and Holly in the back. Quinn notes how relaxed Zoe looks in the luxury vehicle. Maybe it reminds her of the days she was once driven around like someone important. When they got into their Land Rover, Mel quizzed Grigor on its safety features. He was proud to point out the bullet-proof windows and reinforced doors.

Bringing up the rear of the convoy is the community's Toyota Cressida with Carl at the wheel, Joe beside him and Andreas in the back. Andreas, already drunk and surly, refused to travel in either of the Land Rovers. Quinn thought he should stay behind, but Sofia insisted he accompany them.

Perhaps Sofia was right. Good for them all to get off site. Trying to bring Sofia into the light is proving challenging. Quinn feels drained. Someone with less faith than her might feel shaken by recent events, but she has stayed strong.

'Don't be anxious.' Mel gives her hand a comforting squeeze. 'I'll be with you all night.'

'I'm fine.' Quinn returns the squeeze. 'Absolutely fine.' She releases her grip, but Mel holds on a fraction longer before letting go.

Absolutely fine, she thinks, turning her attention to the sparkling sea. Even when she woke last night, her blood pounding in her ears and

Aphrodite not in her usual place at the foot of her bed, she remained calm. She longed to go outside and sit in the courtyard to listen to the cicadas and feel the cool mountain air on her skin, but she didn't want to risk setting off the alarm system.

No, she didn't want to do that.

40

QUINN

2018

Dionysus by the Sea sits on the rocky limestone shoreline of Peyia, close to the famous sea caves. The nearby shallows are a translucent aqua, the sky already tainted with the first blood-orange fingers of sunset. The restaurant is small and exclusive, and Sofia appears to have booked out half of it. Their table, the furthest from the restaurant, sits on wooden decking close to the water. A faint sea breeze stirs the white canvas umbrellas overhead. Citronella candles flicker at the centre of the table, attempting to keep away the mosquitos that are more prevalent in this area.

From her side of the table, Quinn has a clear view of one of the main attractions of this popular viewpoint. The shipwreck of a merchant vessel that ran aground on the rocks here over a decade ago and remains tilted on one side. Ugly and magnificent.

'What happened there?' Mel asks her, swatting away a mosquito. As soon as they arrived at the table, Mel slid into the seat beside her. A shadow Quinn can't shake.

'It's called the *Edro the Third*,' Quinn says. 'It was on its way to Rhodes when strong winds blew it onto the rocks.'

'All the crew were rescued,' Joe says from his seat on the other side of Mel. 'The British Army stepped in I think.'

At the other end of the table, Andreas mutters something in Greek. A criticism of his island's former rulers, Quinn suspects.

She is seated at the end of the table furthest from the restaurant, her crutches on the ground beside her. Mel is on her right, with Joe next to her and Holly beside him. Sofia sits at the far head of the table, with Andreas on her right. Maybe it's good she's keeping an eye on him, Quinn thinks. Next to Andreas is Zoe and Carl sits next to his wife. Quinn feels out on a limb at the end of the table. The seat no one wants to have when out for a group meal.

Dmitri has stationed himself on a chair nearby. Grigor stands some distance away, closer to the other outside tables. When they passed these tables on the way to their own, Quinn was sure she heard someone speaking Russian.

There are no menus for them to look at. When they arrived, Sofia announced she'd arranged for the chef to cook them a banquet with tasters of all their best dishes. She said everyone she knew who'd been to Cyprus raved about this restaurant.

First, a young, handsome Cypriot waiter brings them jugs of iced water. He is tall, with sculpted stubble covering his strong jaw and he flirts with Sofia as he guides her through the drinks menu. Sofia, shimmering in a gold, halter-neck pantsuit, flirts back, looking up at him from beneath her eyelashes.

'What's your name?' she asks him.

'Pavlos,' he replies.

'Well, Pavlos, we'll have two bottles of Dom Perignon to start,' she says. 'Zoe, you'll join me in a glass, won't you?'

Zoe looks to Carl for approval, which he grants with a grudging nod. 'Oh, go on,' she says, 'seeing as it's a special occasion.'

'Count us in.' Holly kisses Joe on the cheek.

'And can you make your best non-alcoholic cocktail for all my sober friends,' Sofia says.

'Water's fine for me,' says Quinn.

'Me too,' says Mel. 'Just water.'

'A bottle of Cypriot whisky,' Andreas says to Pavlos.

'I don't think that's a good idea,' Quinn says.

The waiter looks at Sofia. She shrugs. 'If that's what he wants.'

'We have Lion Spirit, sir,' the waiter says.

Andreas nods. 'Good Cypriot whisky.'

Everyone looks down at the table, waiting for the moment to pass.

'Look at the sunset,' Zoe says finally. 'Isn't it gorgeous?'

Pale pink streaks high in the sky. Lower down the blood-orange fingers are melting into a blazing orange sheet. Above their heads, tiny fairy lights attached to the frame of the umbrella blink on. The lights in the restaurant gardens do the same, signalling the transition into a different phase of the evening.

When the drinks arrive and everyone has a full glass, Sofia leads them in a toast.

'To friendship,' she says, 'and to new beginnings.'

Quinn's heart softens at these words. She was right about Sofia needing a rebirth. The Pure Heart magic is beginning to work. Each night since Sofia's arrival, Quinn has sent her long-distance healing. Powerful energy work that is beginning to show results.

Platters of food arrive. So much to choose from. A variety of salads – Greek, salmon and wakame, and prawn and avocado. Quinn's eyes are drawn to crispy fried squid, garlic butter prawns and halloumi the waiter assures them is artisanal. Aromatic flatbreads with an overwhelming number of dips. How will they ever get through it all?

'These are just the starters,' Sofia says. 'We'll be trying all the mains as well.'

A clatter of cutlery and appreciative gasps as everyone helps themselves to the food. Quinn, who didn't even think she was hungry, finds herself wowed by the salmon and wakame salad. The flavours of chives, sesame seeds, lime and wasabi explode on her tongue.

'This is insanely good,' Joe says, unable to stop himself speaking with his mouth full. 'I've got to know what's in this feta dip.'

'We'll get the chef to come out and speak to us,' Sofia says.

Even Mel is tucking into a full plate. 'This is incredible,' she says.

Quinn looks around at everyone enjoying food together. What a beautiful sight.

Everyone apart from Andreas. He is knocking back another whisky, the bread and dips on his plate untouched. He stares at each of them in turn, a look of despair on his face. Suddenly Quinn sees themselves through his eyes. Greedy people seduced by their senses. Gorging themselves at someone else's expense. She shakes the image away, determined not to let Andreas' negativity spoil the evening.

Still, when the next wave of food comes – platters of fragrant falafel, slow-cooked shoulder of lamb and grilled whole chicken – Quinn finds herself racked with nausea. She shouldn't have let that doctor give her a tetanus shot. It's having a toxic effect on her finely tuned system.

Mel pushes her chair back and stands up. 'Just going to the bathroom. Won't be long.'

Quinn nods and turns her gaze to the sea and the glowing red embers of sunset. Darkness gathers around the table. The citronella candles spill pools of light onto the white tablecloth. When Quinn drags her attention away from the sunset, she sees an elderly couple at one of the other tables have ambushed Mel on her way back from the bathroom. The man and woman pose, cheeks pressed together as Mel takes a picture of them with a mobile phone. When she hands the phone back to the elderly man and tries to walk away, he traps her in conversation.

'This is the best meal I've had for ages.' Zoe dabs her mouth with a napkin. 'No offence, Joe.'

'None taken,' he says.

Holly rests her head on his shoulder. 'You're still our number one.'

Joe and Holly's display of closeness makes Quinn think of Blake. One afternoon they came to Peyia and swam in the sea caves. Afterwards, as they dried off on the hot rocks, he laid his head on her chest.

'I'm so different when I'm with you,' he said. 'You have this incredible healing effect on me.'

She wonders what he's doing now. Who he's with. All of a sudden, she feels old and tired and washed up, like the shipwreck silhouetted against the evening sky.

Andreas grabs his half-empty bottle of whisky and staggers along the
table to sit beside Quinn.

'Hello, old friend,' he says.

'Hello,' Quinn replies, distracted by the sight of Mel and the elderly
man approaching the table. Behind them is a tall, rangy man with a shock
of bleached white hair. A bodyguard, Quinn assumes, from the look of his
smart black suit and threatening demeanour. When Grigor stops the trio a
few metres away from the table and talks to the other bodyguard, Mel slips
away and hurries back to Quinn.

'Sorry,' she says.

'Who is he?' Quinn asks.

'Some old Russian guy who says he recognised Sofia. He claims he
knew her grandfather.' She looks at Andreas. 'You're in my seat.'

He points to the other end of the table. 'Take mine.'

'Quinn?' Mel says.

'I'm fine,' Quinn tells her. 'Honestly.'

As Mel picks up her plate and stalks off to claim Andreas' empty seat,
Grigor approaches Sofia and whispers in her ear. When she nods in
response, he beckons the elderly man and his bodyguard over to the table.
As the older man gets closer, Quinn sees he has the red, bulging nose and
ruddy cheeks of a hardened drinker. He is smartly dressed in pink trousers
and a white linen shirt, but his white, shoulder-length hair is slicked back
with gel and he has a coarseness about him.

Sofia stands and shakes his hand. The man addresses her in Russian in
a booming voice. Sofia nods before sitting down again.

'This is Roman Timchenko,' she announces to the table. 'He says he
knew my grandfather.'

Roman surveys the table, as if noticing Quinn and the others for the
first time.

'These are my friends,' Sofia says. 'I'm staying with them for a while.'

'Very nice,' Roman says. 'Cyprus is a beautiful place.'

Sofia's face shows no sign of anxiety. If she is perturbed by her two
worlds colliding, she isn't letting it show.

'Ivan and I knew each other in Moscow,' Roman says. 'Long, long time
ago.'

Sofia smiles. 'So you were a gangster too?'

Roman laughs. 'Everyone is gangster then. But most of us, we are not as successful as Ivan. Not businessman like him.'

'He did well for himself,' Sofia says.

'But now I cannot complain,' Roman says. 'For years I live in London. Is a shitty place. Then I retire and my wife and I live in Limassol a few years now. Is a good life on this island.' He examines Sofia's face. 'You look like your grandfather, but do you have his killer instinct?'

An uncomfortable silence settles on the table. Sofia reaches for her champagne. 'I think so,' she says, 'but only time will tell.'

Roman laughs again. As Sofia resumes her conversation with him in Russian, relieved chatter breaks out amongst everyone else. Joe and Holly discuss the varieties of local cheeses on the table. Carl and Zoe feed each other mouthfuls of succulent lamb.

Andreas glowers at the invading Russian. 'These people,' he snarls, shooting Timchenko a dark look. 'Russian mafia taking over my island.'

'Retired Russian mafia,' Quinn jokes, trying to lighten his mood. She resists the temptation to remind Andreas that Russian money is paying for his mother's exclusive care home. Andreas was only doing what any good son would do. More men should love their mothers that way.

'They will kill you,' he says, his voice low and threatening.

'The old Russian couple?' Quinn smiles. 'It's okay, I think I can take them.'

'It is not funny.' Still clutching his whisky, Andreas slides off his seat and kneels on the ground beside her. 'These people,' he says, gesturing around the table. 'They will kill you.'

'You're drunk,' Quinn says.

Andreas props his whisky between his knees and produces a delicate silver bracelet from the pocket of his jeans. 'You need this.' He shows her the evil eye charm dangling from it. 'You need protection.'

'Andreas, I don't—'

He cuts off her protest by grabbing her right wrist and fastening the bracelet around it. 'There,' he says. 'I fear it is not enough, but it is something.'

'Andreas.' Quinn takes his worn, lined face in her hands. 'No one will kill me.'

Tears swell in his eyes. 'Yes, they will.'

'Look how attentive Sofia's been since my accident. Getting the doctor out, getting me the crutches.'

'She wants to keep you alive for her big finale.'

'You're being ridiculous.'

'Sofia is right. Everyone has a price.'

'What's that, Andreas?' Sofia enquires from the other end of the table. Quinn looks up to see Timchenko has gone, leaving their party alone again.

'I am telling the truth.' Andreas grabs his whisky and, with the aid of the table, hauls himself to his feet. 'I tell her you will kill her. All of you.'

'Come on, pal,' Joe says. 'Take a seat and I'll order you a coffee.'

Andreas waves the whisky bottle in the air. 'I know this. In my heart. You will kill her and you will take the money.'

Sofia looks on, an amused expression on her face. Dmitri rises from his chair.

'I know this because I would do it,' Andreas says. 'When you decide to kill her, I will agree.'

'You're drunk,' Quinn says. 'You don't mean any of this.'

'Skatá,' Andreas says as the bottle slips from his hand and hits the decking with a sharp crack. When he picks it up, Quinn sees the bottle's neck is broken.

'Sit down, Andreas,' Mel says.

'Arrest them for murder, Detective Mel.' Andreas sways precariously, the jagged neck of the bottle glinting as it catches the candlelight. 'Arrest them all.' He laughs. 'Arrest yourself.'

'That's enough,' Carl says.

'Please stop,' begs Zoe.

'We shouldn't have let him drink like that,' Holly says.

Pavlos comes over to investigate the noise. Before he can reach the table, Grigor steps out and touches his shoulder. Shakes his head at him.

'Pavlos,' Andreas says. 'My friend.' He rattles out a stream of Greek, which Quinn doesn't understand but, from the way Andreas is pointing at her and then Sofia, she is sure he is telling Pavlos some twisted version of recent events.

Pavlos leans towards Grigor, listening as the big man whispers something to him. Eventually he smiles and turns back towards the restaurant.

'Hey,' Andreas says. 'You need to help us.'

Quinn reaches out and touches his hand, but he shakes her off and bolts, chasing after the waiter. Dmitri springs into action but Mel jumps up from her seat and gets there first. She blocks Andreas with her body and grabs his wrist, forcing him to release the bottle with a yelp of pain. He shoves her aside and keeps running but when he meets Grigor, his bullish strength falters and Grigor soon has him in a headlock.

'Enough,' Grigor says. 'Enough.'

41

HOLLY

2019

The scene at the restaurant was ugly. No doubt about it. Poor Andreas. That's what happens when a troubled, paranoid man drinks a bottle of whisky.

When Grigor grabbed him, it was as if the full effect of all the alcohol in his system kicked in. He struggled for a few moments, and then his eyes rolled back in his head and he blacked out.

Despite my efforts to come to terms with my past, I couldn't help my reaction to the violence unfolding before me. Fight, flight or freeze. Our three physiological reactions to any real or perceived threat. When my Uncle Mike first raped me, I froze. Lay beneath him like a corpse and let him do whatever he wanted. That night in Dionysus by the Sea, I sat frozen in my seat, my heart racing.

We managed to get Andreas out of the restaurant and into the back of one of the Land Rovers. We apologised to the restaurant managers and the waiters. Sofia left them a very generous tip.

Up until then it was an amazing evening. Great food, great views, great conversation. The unexpected visit from the old Russian man, which turned out to be something I should have paid more attention to. When

Sofia made her toast to new beginnings, I really thought we were headed for a fresh start. I was too busy enjoying myself to notice how much Andreas was drinking.

What happened when we got home was as distressing as the scene in the restaurant. When Joe and Grigor hauled Andreas out of the back seat of the Land Rover, the fresh mountain air jolted him awake. He shouted at us again. Threatened to go to the police in the morning and tell them about Sofia's offer.

'Sorry, Sofia,' he said. 'I cannot let you do this.'

Then he vomited all over Grigor's polished black shoes. After that he passed out again and Grigor and Joe took him to his room. The rest of us followed and watched as Grigor put Andreas on his bed in the recovery position and placed a bucket on the floor nearby in case he needed it. We all agreed he needed to sleep it off.

In hindsight, I can see we should have stayed with him, but as the saying goes, hindsight is always twenty-twenty.

42

QUINN

2018

Aphrodite is sprawled on her side at the foot of the bed, deep in sleep and twitching with dreams. Quinn, wide awake, watches her cat with envy. It is almost 5.30 a.m., and she hasn't slept all night. How could she, after what happened at the restaurant?

Sunrise isn't far away. Light creeps in through Quinn's open window, along with the smell of pine and jasmine.

Her right foot throbs. Two hot, distinct points of pain where the snake's fangs entered her. If pain is, as she believes, the body's way of trying to communicate, what is her body trying to tell her?

The bracelet Andreas gave her is still fastened around her wrist. The evil eye looks up at her, glassy and blue. *You need protection.*

She can't shake the image of him in the restaurant, charging after the waiter with the broken bottle in his hand. Brave of Mel to intervene like that. She must have dealt with plenty of drunk people during her police career. Quinn feels lucky to have someone so multi-skilled in the Pure Heart family. Someone so loyal.

Part of her is dreading the coming day. What if Andreas still wants to go to the police and tell them about Sofia's offer? Hopefully he was too drunk last night to remember what he said.

She needs to stay positive. Last night's excesses might have purged Andreas of his paranoia. He might have hit the rock bottom of his current drinking spree and come to his senses. Tom Quinn believed the honest expression of difficult feelings to be fundamental to wellbeing. Members of the Islington commune took self-expression very seriously. The sound of sex saturated the townhouse day and night. Vicious arguments and furious debate heated the unheated rooms. Screams ricocheted off the damp walls. Tom was a great champion of scream therapy.

A banging noise startles her. Seconds later, she hears movement in Grigor's room as the big man hauls himself out of his bed, the mattress springs sighing. She recognises Dmitri's voice and then comes a low, urgent discussion in Russian.

Aphrodite opens one eye and stretches as Quinn gets out of bed and shuffles her way into her living room, where she shoves her feet into the unyielding Crocs and grabs one of the crutches to lean on.

When she taps on Grigor's door, Dmitri answers. Even at this time of day he is immaculate in his suit trousers, shirt and waistcoat.

'What's going on?' she asks.

In the background, Grigor is buttoning up his shirt.

'Andreas is gone,' says Dmitri.

'Are you sure?' Quinn asks. 'What do you—'

'There is problem with Wi-Fi,' Grigor says. 'The alarm is not working.'

'Maybe he went out hours ago,' Dmitri says.

Quinn's foot throbs. 'Do you think he's gone to talk to the police?'

Dmitri sighs. 'I don't know. All the cars are still here and the gate is still closed.'

Grigor interjects in Russian.

'Yes, he could have walked up to the road,' Dmitri says.

'I will drive up to the road.' Grigor picks up a holster from the bed and slips it over one shoulder. A black pistol peeks out of it. Quinn shudders. She tells herself Grigor is contractually obliged to wear it. The gun is part of his uniform, just like the waistcoat he is buttoning over it.

'What's going on?'

Quinn turns to see Mel bounding up the stairs.

'It's Andreas,' Quinn explains, 'he's missing.'

As she and Mel follow the bodyguards down the stairs, Quinn fills Mel in on what the men have told her. With each step, she forces herself to put more weight on her foot. By the time they reach the ground floor, she hardly needs her crutch at all, despite the discomfort.

Grigor heads out of the front door to the car park.

'I will tell Sofia,' Dmitri says, before hurrying away.

'What shall we do?' Mel asks. 'Should I get the others?'

'Not yet,' Quinn says. 'I need some air.'

They head out to the courtyard. Quinn inhales the clean mountain air. A crescent moon hangs in the dawn sky, sharp as a scimitar. Some of the cats are on the prowl, slight figures darting behind statues.

'Will Andreas go to the police?' Mel asks.

'I hope not. He'll only be wasting their time.'

'Maybe it would be best if he does. For all of us.'

'Why? To say what? No one here is going to take Sofia up on her offer.' A sharp cry from the heavens. Quinn looks up and sees a large bird of prey circling. Watching them with its clear vision.

When she looks down again, she spots something she didn't see when they first stepped out into the courtyard. A wisp of smoke rising up from the olive grove below.

'It's okay,' she says, a smile spreading across her face. 'I know where he is.'

43

QUINN

2018

As soon as Quinn lifts the blankets at the entrance to the sweat lodge, a tangle of smells greets her. Burnt sage, the sharp tang of alcohol, a sour hint of body odour and another, herby smell she can't immediately identify.

'Andreas?' she says. 'It's only me.'

How her heart lifted when she saw the smoke. Andreas wasn't on his way to the police station. He was purifying himself. Sobering up. He'd soon be back to his old self and they could talk rationally about recent events.

When she steps inside the sweat lodge, an unfamiliar scent assaults her. Meaty. Fleshy. It travels down her throat and sticks there, making her want to gag.

Mel enters the sweat lodge, forcing Quinn deeper inside. As Quinn's eyes adjust to the gloom, she sees the outline of a slumped figure.

'Andreas?' Her voice is croaky and strained. Her heart batters against her ribs.

Mel pushes past her. 'Prop open the door. Get some light in here.'

Quinn does as instructed. The dim light that floods in illuminates a terrible scene. Andreas, naked, face down in the lodge's pile of hot volcanic stones.

She retches, the meaty scent rising up in her throat. She watches as Mel grabs Andreas' shoulders and pulls him upright.

'Andreas.' Mel shakes him. 'Andreas.'

One side of his face is charred. His eyes are wide open. Vacant. Quinn doesn't need police training to see he's already dead.

Mel lays him on the ground, tilts his head back and puts two fingers in his mouth to search for obstructions.

'It's too late,' Quinn says.

'We have to try.' Mel puts her hands on Andreas' chest and pumps hard. Quinn retches again as Mel proceeds to pinch Andreas' nose and put her lips against his half-melted ones. The image of the grinning skeleton swims before Quinn's eyes in the pale dawn light. Was the Tarot card trying to warn her Andreas would die?

The sound of Mel's desperate exhalations is deafening. Quinn thinks of her recent pleas to Andreas to visit the sweat lodge.

After a while, Mel sits back on her heels, wipes her mouth with the back of her hand and spits onto the dusty ground. 'He's gone.'

'No.' Quinn, shocked into action by the finality of Mel's words, lays her hands on Andreas' chest. She pictures violet-coloured energy pouring through her palms and entering his heart. She visualises his heart jumping into action again, beating hard beneath her hands.

She is shaking. No, Mel is shaking her.

'Quinn,' Mel says. 'It's over. He's gone.'

Quinn folds over. Presses her forehead against the earth.

'We should get out of here,' Mel says. 'We've disturbed the scene enough already.'

'What scene?' Quinn already knows what happened. Andreas must have woken up earlier, still drunk and confused. Full of remorse for his behaviour at the restaurant, he decided to get sober again and came to the sweat lodge to detox. Either he passed out on the stones and died of shock or had a heart attack and fell onto the stones after that. 'I should burn some sage to help Andreas' soul find its way to the next world.'

'Quinn.' Mel grabs her arm. 'We need to call the police.'

* * *

Quinn allows Mel to lead her back to the house. Aphrodite follows behind, gathering other cats to her as they cross the courtyard. Quinn has a sudden urge to jump into the pool and cleanse herself of the stench of burnt flesh.

Dmitri and Sofia are waiting for them by the door. Sofia in transparent white pyjamas, a shimmering gold pashmina wrapped around her shoulders.

'We've found him,' Mel says.

Sofia brushes her hair back from her face. 'That's a relief.'

'He's dead,' Quinn says.

As Mel explains what they discovered in the sweat lodge, Sofia, her face expressionless, pulls her pashmina tighter around her.

Dmitri sighs. 'This is sad news.'

'We have to call the police,' Mel says.

Sofia and Dmitri exchange glances.

'That's what you do in the case of a sudden death,' Mel says, an ominous tension radiating from her.

Sudden death. Quinn can't process those words.

'Don't you want to consult the others first?' Sofia asks.

'This is non-negotiable,' Mel says.

'Fine.' Sofia glances at Dmitri. 'We'll sort it.'

Mel shakes her head. 'I'll go to the office, and I'll call them.'

Sofia shrugs. 'Be my guest.'

'Last time I checked,' Mel says, 'you were the guest.'

44

Insight Investigators: Background Report

Melanie Harris (Mel): Mel passed out of police training school as the top student in her intake, and it didn't take her long to rise through the ranks. She always wanted to specialise in Serious and Organised Crime (SOCU) and that's where she ended up, dealing with the most serious criminals and helping to take them off the streets. Making her bosses happy and disrupting London's criminal networks.

Until she resigned from the force in September 2017. Official reason – post-traumatic stress disorder. Thanks to my contacts, I've been able to dig deeper into the unofficial reasons and, trust me, I was surprised by what I found.

45

QUINN

2018

Andreas is dead. Quinn still can't believe it. Half an hour ago, a police car arrived, shortly followed by an ambulance. Now two policemen and a team of paramedics are down at the sweat lodge, doing whatever it is they do. Mel wanted to accompany them to ensure they were following correct procedures but the officer in charge, Detective Louca, told her to stay at the house.

Quinn recognised the tall, sombre-looking detective immediately. He came to Pure Heart ten years ago, on the day Eva died. She recalls him handling the traumatic event calmly and efficiently.

Now the community members are in the kitchen, waiting for the police to report back to them. Quinn sits at the head of the long table, Aphrodite on her lap. Joe, Holly, Zoe and Carl are at the table too, sipping on flat whites and cappuccinos. The coffee machine hisses in the background, a constant presence. Quinn, a mug of mountain tea in front of her, swallows down a violent craving for an espresso.

Mel paces around the kitchen, shooting dark glances at Grigor who is leaning against one of the worktops, arms folded across his chest. Sofia has

retired to her room. According to Dmitri, who has disappeared somewhere, she is overcome with emotion and needs to gather herself.

'What a horrible way to die.' Zoe clutches the gaping folds of her
kimono. 'I can't get the image of it out of my head.'

'Dial down the melodrama,' Mel says. 'You didn't even see him.'

'Well,' says Carl, 'thanks to your thorough description of the scene,
we've all got a pretty good idea.'

Quinn, who sees Andreas' burnt, disfigured face every time she closes
her eyes, thinks they have no idea. No idea at all.

'Do you think he had another heart attack?' Holly asks.

'Wouldn't be surprised.' Joe rubs the space between his wife's shoulder
blades. 'Or he maybe passed out drunk on the stones.'

'It was a terrible accident,' Grigor says.

Mel stops pacing and glares at him. 'It would be easy for someone to
make it look like an accident.'

'Mel,' Quinn says. 'Please.'

Mel keeps her eyes on Grigor. 'Someone could easily have overpow-
ered him and smothered him.'

'No,' Quinn says. 'That's not possible.'

'What about your surveillance cameras?' Mel asks Grigor. 'Have you
checked the footage to see who was up and about last night?'

Grigor shakes his head. 'Last night, the cameras failed.'

A short, bitter laugh from Mel. 'That's convenient.'

'The Wi-Fi cable was cut,' Grigor says. 'Everything affected. Cameras.
The alarm. Andreas must have done this.'

'Obviously,' Mel says. 'I mean, last night he looked totally capable of
carrying out sabotage.'

'It's my fault,' Quinn says.

'No.' Holly's reassurance is emphatic. 'No.'

'Of course not,' says Zoe, less convincingly.

Quinn rubs her eyes. 'I practically ordered him to use the sweat lodge.'

A bleeping sound from Grigor. He checks his phone and leaves the
room immediately.

'Where's he going?' asks Mel. 'And where's Dmitri? I bet he's with that

Louca now, offering a nice cash payment in return for not asking difficult questions.'

'Stop being so cynical,' Carl says.

'Stuff like that happens all the time. Trust me.' Mel joins them at the table, slipping into the seat beside Quinn. 'We need to tell the police everything.'

'What do you mean by *everything*?' Joe says.

'All of it.' Mel leans back in her chair. 'Sofia's offer.'

'We can't do that,' Zoe says. 'We'd sound crazy.'

'This whole business has gone far enough,' Mel says. 'Don't you agree, Quinn?'

Quinn presses her fingers to her temples. Hard to think clearly. Hard to get Andreas and his melted lips out of her head.

'We're making breakthroughs with Sofia,' Zoe says. 'I can see changes in her already.'

'Me too,' Holly agrees. 'This news about Andreas is bound to remind her of the day we found Eva. I'm worried it could be a setback for her.'

'What if it wasn't an accident?' Mel says.

'No one here would kill Andreas,' Quinn replies. She doesn't like the picture Mel is painting of this community. Pure Heart is a family. They love one another.

'Maybe not.' Mel lowers her voice. 'But what about Sofia? She could easily have made one of the bodyguards do it to stop Andreas speaking to the police.'

'Mel.' Quinn looks directly into her cool blue eyes. 'I'm so disappointed to hear you talking like this. After all the work we've done together. I really thought you'd left this negative way of looking at humanity behind.'

The blotches of shame that appear on Mel's cheeks almost match her burgundy T-shirt. 'I have... I'm... I'm different now.'

'Maybe you killed him, if it's so easy,' Carl says.

'Don't be ridiculous,' Mel snaps.

'I agree, it's a ridiculous theory,' Carl says, 'but so are yours.'

'You have to trust us,' Zoe says. 'This is how Pure Heart works. All of us believing. All of us aligned towards a common goal.'

Quinn is comforted by the words of her community. The people she loves. The people who love her.

'You all heard Andreas in the restaurant last night,' Mel says. 'He was warning us how easy it is to give in to temptation. He was being honest about his darkest impulses.'

'It was the drink talking,' Quinn says. 'He'd never have hurt me.'

Mel's face twists with frustration. 'I'm not so sure.'

'He was projecting his troubled conscience onto everyone else,' Quinn says.

'Exactly,' agrees Zoe. 'He was judging us by his own standards.'

Mel groans. 'You don't know that for sure.'

'I loved Andreas,' Holly says.

'Aye,' says Joe, 'me too. Loved the guy.'

'We all did,' Carl says, 'but he betrayed Quinn and he took money from Sofia.'

Tears shine in Zoe's eyes. 'Maybe he wasn't who we thought he was. Maybe we never really knew him.'

Quinn refuses to believe such things of Andreas. He was one of them. 'We can't mention any of this to the police. I won't have his name tarnished.'

'Look,' Mel says, 'I really think—'

'No.' Quinn raises both palms as if to ward Mel off. 'You're not to speak of it. Any of you.'

The kitchen door opens. Detective Louca steps into the room. Despite the early hour, the underarms of his pale blue shirt are stained with sweat. He looks shaken, thinks Quinn. Understandably so, considering what he's just seen in the sweat lodge.

Dmitri follows the detective into the room. The two men exchange a look.

'Well?' Quinn says.

Louca turns to her, a stern expression on his face. 'The paramedics and my colleague are still at the scene. We will know more soon.'

'Do you know how the accident happened?' Zoe asks.

'The accident?' The inspector's dark eyes assess each of them in turn. 'I must ask you some questions now.'

'Of course,' Joe says. 'Can I offer you a coffee?'

The inspector's appraising gaze falls on the gleaming coffee machine. Quinn is embarrassed by the obscene size and obvious expense of it.

'No,' Louca says. 'Thank you.'

Quinn glances at Mel. Is she going to say something about Sofia's offer, or will she follow the will of the community?

The detective seats himself at the other end of the table to Quinn. 'This first.' From his shirt pocket he pulls a plastic evidence bag containing a handful of charred olive leaves. 'He was burning these.'

'Olive leaves,' Holly says.

Of course, Quinn thinks. The smell she picked up in the sweat lodge but couldn't identify.

'Correct, olive leaves,' the inspector says. 'You know why we burn these here?'

'For the evil eye,' Quinn says.

'Yes, for the *mati*.' The policeman looks at them. 'You burn the leaves in the bowl, pass them—'

'Three times around your head in a clockwise direction,' Quinn says. 'It keeps away negative energy.'

'Why would he do this?' the inspector asks. 'What was he trying to protect himself from? What energy was he trying to keep away?'

'Maybe his own,' Mel says. 'Maybe he was frightened of his own darkness.'

Louca turns his level gaze on Mel. 'Tell me about this darkness.'

'Andreas had been drinking recently,' Quinn says. 'Heavily.'

'He tried to quit a few times in the past,' Carl says. 'Never managed it.'

Louca nods. 'We knew Andreas at the station. Many times he is sleeping in a cell with us after we find him in the streets of Kakopetria.'

'It's my fault,' Quinn says. 'I said he should spend some time in the sweat lodge. To get the alcohol out of his system.'

'Not when he was drunk,' Zoe says. 'You didn't mean for him to do that.' As she turns towards the inspector, her loose kimono reveals the dip of her cleavage. 'Quinn was trying to help him.'

'She's an amazing healer,' Holly says. 'The best.'

Quinn gives them both a grateful smile.

'What was happening in Andreas' life?' the inspector asks. 'Did he have problems? Money or maybe health? Any stressful events?'

Before anyone can speak, the kitchen door opens again and Sofia sweeps in, dressed in a plain black T-shirt and black leggings. As if already in mourning.

'Sorry to keep you waiting,' she says, although Quinn wasn't aware they were waiting for her. 'I needed time to pull myself together.' She dabs her eyes with a black lace handkerchief. 'Poor Andreas. I still can't believe it.'

'None of us can,' Zoe says.

The inspector gets up and offers Sofia his seat, even though there are others vacant at the table. She folds her limber body into it with a dramatic sigh.

'Thank you,' she says.

He takes the seat beside her. 'You don't remember me?'

'Sorry,' Sofia says, 'I don't—'

'You were so young then.' Louca leans back in his chair and appraises her. 'You are very like your mother,' he says. 'Such a sad day.'

Sofia's dark eyes fill with tears. Quinn glimpses for a moment the traumatised child who found her dead mother in the monastery.

'I am sorry,' Louca says. 'I do not wish to upset you.'

'It's fine.' Sofia dabs her eyes again. 'I remember you now. You were very kind to me that day. Thank you.'

'And now you are back here?' he says.

'I wanted to visit the place I grew up in. To see the people who cared so much for me and my mother.'

'This tragedy today,' Louca says, 'I hope it does not bring back bad memories?'

'Such a sad way for Andreas to die,' Sofia says. 'A silly accident.'

The detective nods. 'Two tragedies here. Very sad.'

'I'd like to tell his mother myself,' Sofia says. 'I'm close to her and I'd like her to hear it from me.'

'That can be arranged,' Louca says.

'And of course, I'll continue to help her in any way I can,' Sofia adds. 'Andreas was always loyal to me, and I like to reward loyalty.'

Louca hesitates. 'That's very decent of you.'

'I think everyone here knows that.' Sofia's bright, white smile fails to reach her dark, shifting eyes. 'I always stick to my promises. When I make an offer, I never, ever go back on my word.'

46

HOLLY

2019

Some of the media reports about the events at Pure Heart also discussed Andreas. Once journalists discovered there'd been a death in our community only a few weeks before our night of bloodshed, they did some digging.

They didn't find the scandal or intrigue they were hoping for. Only a police report confirming Andreas had died of natural causes – a heart attack – and that his death was not being treated as suspicious.

Not that I needed the police to tell me his death was accidental. None of us had a motive for killing him. Our certainty about this united us as we tried, in those first terrible days after his death, to come to terms with what had happened. We knew Andreas would never have spoken to the police. Doing so might have made Sofia look bad, and Andreas wouldn't do that to Eva's daughter. In retrospect, we could see he was still obsessed with Eva. Still consumed by grief for her loss and guilt at his perceived part in it. We hoped, without his obsession fuelling hers, Sofia might finally let go of the past.

There's no doubt that for Sofia, the incident brought back painful memories of her mother's death. She never expressed regret for asking

Andreas to speak out against Quinn, but I'm sure she felt it. I hoped his death would be a turning point for her. True to her promise, she broke the news of Andreas' death to his mother. Nikoleta's dementia prevented her from fully registering the loss of her son. A blessing I suppose.

The following week passed in a grief-stricken blur. Dmitri organised for engineers to come and repair the Wi-Fi connection and fix the alarm system. As soon as the police verdict on the death was confirmed, we dismantled the sweat lodge. None of us wanted to sit inside it ever again.

Ten days after his death, Andreas was buried in a Greek Orthodox cemetery in Kakopetria by his maternal aunt and several of his cousins. We've always opposed organised religion, so instead of attending the burial we held our own memorial for him. We planted an olive tree on the site of the banished sweat lodge and, sitting in a circle around it, shared our memories of him.

Doing this gave us some kind of closure. Quinn said we'd see him again in another lifetime when our soul family was reunited.

After the memorial, Sofia announced she would extend her stay at Pure Heart for a month. To give us more time to consider her offer, she said. We knew that was just bravado. Deep down she wasn't ready to leave us. Deep down, she knew Pure Heart was where she belonged.

PART III

PART III

47

ZOE

2018

Gratitude and Prayers Journal: Wednesday 1st August, 9 a.m.

Zoe sits at the table in the orchard, flanked by apricot trees. On the table lies her open notebook and a cheap black biro. She closes the notebook. Since Andreas died just over two weeks ago, she tries and fails every morning to write. She doesn't want to commit her darkest thoughts and feelings to paper.

Carl was furiously scribbling away at his desk when she left their room. When his biro ran out a few days ago, she lent him her Mont Blanc fountain pen. He claims his thoughts flow much better when he writes with it. She doubts he'll give it back.

The straps of her black cotton sundress have fallen onto her tanned upper arms. She slips them back into place and picks up her mug of flat white. How nice it is not to have to drive miles for a decent coffee.

The warm air around her is laced with the scent of overripe fruit. The temperatures have been steadily rising since Andreas left them. Often, when August is as hot as this one promises to be, dramatic thunderstorms visit the mountains.

A purring sound fills the air. Soft fur brushes against her bare calves. 'Hello, you,' she says, when Aphrodite leaps onto her lap. A rare visit. The loyal black cat rarely leaves Quinn's side these days.

Zoe strokes the underside of Aphrodite's chin. More to soothe herself than to pleasure the cat.

The day of Andreas' death left her with a strange fizzing in her blood, her pulse thundering in her ears. These sensations haven't left her. She's finding it hard to get to sleep and, when she does drop off, she wakes startled in the early morning hours. Carl is the same and his recent feverish writing sprees aren't helping. He hasn't told her what he's working on yet, but she can sense it growing inside him, as if he's a pregnant woman.

Sometimes at night she thinks of Andreas in the sweat lodge, the skin of his weathered face sticking to the hot stones. Lying in bed, she wonders if he fell onto the hot rocks after he lost consciousness or did he have to endure fiery, searing pain before he died? She even lets herself imagine, just for a moment, how easy it would have been to suffocate him in his drunken state and place his dead body over the smouldering stones.

Not that she would have. Not that any of them would have.

She also, when sleep eludes her, thinks about him in the restaurant, waving the broken bottle in the air, ranting at them all. No one at Pure Heart has done anything wrong. It hurt to hear Andreas accuse them of future crimes they wouldn't dream of committing. Like Quinn said, he was projecting his own soiled conscience onto everyone else.

Aphrodite's rough, warm tongue licks the skin of her forearm. After a while, the cat peers up at her, eyes narrowed. Zoe wonders if she can taste the Coco de Mer body lotion she put on after her shower this morning. A gift from Sofia.

'She's got loads of free toiletry samples from hotels and spas,' Zoe tells the cat. 'If they don't get used, they'll go to waste.'

When she put the body lotion on, it sank into her skin like liquid silk. Rich and decadent. Aphrodite resumes licking it from Zoe's arm. Her seal of approval?

As Zoe finishes her coffee, she marvels at how quickly human beings can adapt to loss. It's still strange not to see Andreas around the place, but life does move on. Yesterday Mel fixed an issue with the swimming pool filter and Joe and Carl built a new wooden container for the compost. Jobs Andreas would have dealt with.

The past does not exist. Zoe can't say that's true in the case of Andreas, but even Quinn has slowly returned to form over the past few days. Her foot appears to have healed and she is now feeding her hens every morning. Mel goes with her, of course. Mel goes everywhere with her. A sullen, burgundy shadow.

Zoe is still surprised Mel didn't tell Detective Louca about Sofia's offer when he questioned them. Why? In the police Mel had to take orders from higher-ranked officers, but Zoe doesn't think blind obedience is the reason. She saw how ashamed Mel looked when Quinn reprimanded her for her cynicism. Mel wants Quinn's approval, possibly even her love. Either that or she's trying to gather evidence to back up her suspicions.

Last night at dinner, Mel nodded along when Quinn told them all to take a wider spiritual perspective on recent events. Only in the fullness of time would Spirit reveal to them the reason for their sad loss. The universe was working to deliver all they'd asked for and now, more than ever, they had to believe in miracles.

Part of Zoe can't help believing whatever Quinn believes, but another part of her keeps asking the same question over and over. *What if she's wrong?*

Aphrodite's warm body grows tense in Zoe's arms. She follows the cat's gaze and glimpses Dmitri stealthily covering the ground between the olive grove and the polytunnel.

He vanishes from view. Will he go straight back to the house or walk through the orchard? When the dry grass crackles behind her, she opens her notebook, picks up her pen and pretends to be lost in thought.

'Good morning,' he says.

'Oh.' She feigns surprise. A stagey jolt in her chair, one hand across her chest. 'I was miles away.'

A smile twitches at the corners of his mouth. Aphrodite jumps from Zoe's lap and darts away into the orchard. One of the straps of Zoe's dress falls off her shoulder and she's pleased to see Dmitri glance at her exposed collarbone. His eyes flick down to her lotus flower tattoo and linger on it just long enough to make the skin beneath the black petals quiver. She remembers the thrill of sitting beside him in the Land Rover on the way to the restaurant. The anticipation of some accidental touch. Not that he touched her, not once, but the thought of it kept her aroused for the whole journey.

'Keeping an eye on everything?' she says.

'I make sure everything is safe.'

'Are we in danger?'

He shrugs. 'People, they seem to die here.'

She looks at his neat, strong hands. Even though she's sure Andreas died of natural causes, she's also sure Dmitri could have killed him if he'd wanted to. Fear shivers through her, mixed with a hot, dirty arousal at the thought of those hands holding her throat in a loose grip. 'Maybe you should all leave if it's so dangerous?'

'Maybe you should accept Sofia's offer so we can go.'

'I thought it was your job to protect Sofia?'

'This I do.'

'She's a vulnerable young woman,' Zoe says. 'You should advise her to give up on such a dangerous scheme.'

'Vulnerable.' Dmitri makes a sound that is half-snort, half-laugh. 'Sofia is the boss. She is always the boss.'

True. Sofia is running her own life and Zoe admires that. She certainly didn't look vulnerable yesterday, sitting out by the pool reading and sipping on champagne.

'I think you could be a boss,' Dmitri says.

Heat floods into Zoe's cheeks. 'Me?'

'If you are strong enough to take your chances.'

'Hi there.'

Zoe turns to see Carl hurrying towards her.

'Hey, beautiful,' he says when he reaches her. He bends down to kiss her upturned lips and at the same time pulls the strap of her dress back onto her shoulder.

Dmitri dips his head in a bow, a gesture Zoe reads as sarcastic. Then he turns and walks away through the orchard.

Carl watches him go. 'That guy's really got the hots for you.'

'The hots? That's so eighties.'

'Fuck off.' Carl sits opposite her. 'He does though.'

'Are you jealous?'

A beat of silence. Zoe isn't sure what she wants him to say.

'Love isn't possessive,' he says, in that calm, measured voice he uses when repeating one of Quinn's sayings.

She didn't want to hear him say that. Dmitri, she thinks, looks like a man who knows how to possess a woman.

'You didn't say goodbye earlier,' Carl says. 'I didn't know you'd gone out.'

'I did say goodbye. You just didn't notice.'

'Sorry.' He taps the table with his fingertips. 'Got a bit caught up.'

The sight of him scribbling away each morning fills her with a complicated blend of emotions. Happiness at seeing him in the flow again, connected to the creative activity that once brought him so much joy. Jealousy, for the very same reasons. She can't help thinking about the offer she had from Lizzie, her agent, when she was in Ibiza, not long before they came to Cyprus. At that time, reality TV was taking off, and Lizzie, who only the year before had told Zoe her career was over, offered her the chance to take part in a celebrity reality show set in a haunted castle in Scotland.

When she told Carl and Quinn about it, they said it sounded like a soulless freak show and that work like that was beneath her. She knew they were right. Selling her soul to the reality TV circuit would only make her more of a laughing stock. Yet many 'stars' of similar shows have rekindled their flagging careers. She could have ended up in musicals again. Or hosted a TV show. She might have been invited to perform at summer festivals for the nostalgic. Fields full of drunk, off-the-leash parents bopping away to the one song they knew her for.

'You're working on a novel, aren't you?' she says.

Carl nods. 'I think it might be quite good.'

'That's amazing.' Nerves buzz in Zoe's fingertips. 'What's it about?'

'It's the Cyprus novel I always wanted to write.' Carl is animated, his face lit up by his idea. 'Three different eras of Cypriot history. One story is going to be based on Andreas. The stuff about the Turkish invasion. It will be like a tribute to him.'

'That's beautiful.'

'The main theme is revenge.' A wasp darts at his ear. He bats it away. 'Once I realised that, the whole novel opened up to me.'

An Instagram moment. Carl sitting here at the table, working on a vintage typewriter, a cat curled at his feet.

Hubby hard at work on next novel. He runs regular writing workshops here at Pure Heart. #hubbyatwork #writerinthehouse

'What if I get ill again?' he says.

'Ill?'

'Burnt out. A slave to my ego. Like I was before I stopped writing.' He looks so vulnerable and childlike. Zoe kneels by his chair and rests her hands on his knees.

'Connecting to your creativity is a good thing,' she says.

'Really?'

Is this how it feels to be Quinn? To have others come to you for advice. Zoe can't remember a time Carl didn't need Quinn to guide him through life. Zoe always thought this was normal. After all, she did the same. Now it seems right that she, his wife, should know what's best for him.

'It sounds like you're in touch with an authentic creativity,' she says. 'The way you were when you wrote your first novel.'

'Yes.' He nods enthusiastically. 'That's exactly how it feels.'

'I don't see how that can be harmful.'

'I'm not even thinking about the end result,' he says. 'I'm just loving the process.'

'Ego doesn't even come into it.'

'Exactly. Even though it's pretty good stuff.'

'You're reconnecting with your true calling.'

'You really think so?'

She stares solemnly at him. 'I do.'

She does, and if he has found his calling, his way to shine, then maybe it's time she found hers. 'You'll need to do a lot of research.'

'Loads. Maybe this is why I was meant to come to Cyprus all along. To write this book.' He hesitates. 'It could take a long time, this kind of project.'

'Yes, we'd need to be here.'

They sit in silence. Birdsong swells around them. At the base of the nearest apricot tree, wasps crawl over a pile of rotting fruit.

'Do you think Sofia's still serious about the money?' she says.

'Surely not? Not after everything that's happened.'

'It's hard to tell.'

'It doesn't matter. We'd never accept it.'

'God, no.' Zoe gathers her hair in her hands. Smooths it over one shoulder. 'But there might be another way.'

48

Insight Investigators: Background Report

Melanie Harris (Mel): A contact of mine at SOCU told me to get in touch with Detective Sergeant James Kerrigan. Kerrigan, she said, would have a few things to say about DI Melanie Harris.

I contacted Kerrigan and, after I assured him everything he said would be off the record, he agreed to come for a drink with me.

Kerrigan was a junior colleague of Mel's. He worked closely with her for three years and respected her, but he became suspicious when a raid she co-ordinated on a shipment of heroin belonging to an Albanian gang turned out to be based on false intelligence. He said that rang alarm bells with him. Mel always had good intel and was a skilled handler of informants. During the preparation for a second raid connected to the same gang, he overheard her on the phone to one of her informants, a small-time dealer. She was giving him details of the raid.

Kerrigan told me this happens sometimes. Officers might do favours for one criminal in return for valuable intelligence on another. He said when you're in the thick of it like Mel was, when you're trying to make a difference, it's hard to see where the line is. He said sometimes people do the wrong thing for the right reason but that day, listening to Mel on the phone, he knew she'd crossed the line. Despite his conflicting loyalties, he reported her to their supervisor. Corruption is corruption after all.

He was told Mel's case would be referred to the anti-corruption unit and that a thorough internal investigation would take place. That never happened. Two days after he reported Mel, she resigned. He suspected his bosses didn't want the bad publicity. Racism, misogyny and corruption cases were being filed against male officers every day, and the top brass were doing their best to restore the public's dwindling faith in the Met. They didn't need Melanie Harris tarnishing the reputation of women officers.

Harris got lucky, Kerrigan said. In the end, the top brass want results but they don't want to know how you get them and they expect you not to get caught.

I wanted to know why Mel would risk her career by getting involved in corruption. That's what niggled at me. Why? That's when I decided to probe a bit deeper.

49

ZOE

2018

'My point is, we need to do something,' Zoe says, 'and we need to do it soon.'

She is standing at the centre of the cramped living room she shares with Carl. He nods his agreement from their scruffy armchair. Holly and Joe, sitting next to each other on the sofa, both look anxiously at her. Zoe suggested this impromptu community meeting as she, Carl, Holly and Joe returned to the house after helping to assemble a new sweat lodge in the olive grove. Sofia surprised them this morning with a delivery of willow sticks, organic cotton blankets and a set of volcanic stones sourced from Sicily. Quinn thought building the new structure together would be a positive bonding activity.

As Zoe secured a thick blanket to the willow frame, she knew she'd never go in a sweat lodge again after what happened to Andreas. The others must have felt the same because everyone except Mel declined Quinn's invitation to join her in the lodge for an inaugural session. As soon as Zoe realised the four of them could be alone, she invited Holly and Joe back to her room.

'What are you suggesting?' Joe glances at the door. 'You're making it sound ominous.'

'Hear her out,' Carl says. 'She's trying to find a solution for all of us.'

'I think Sofia's serious about her offer,' Zoe says. 'I know Quinn thinks she isn't, but I disagree.'

'But surely Andreas' death put everything into perspective?' Holly says. 'Sofia's been so upset about it?'

'Has she?' says Zoe. 'This morning I saw her lying by the pool reading *Crime and Punishment*.'

'What's not to love about the great Russian writers?' Carl says.

'This isn't a joke, Carl.' Holly's dark blue eyes gleam with the threat of tears.

'Sweetheart.' Joe takes one of her callused hands in his meaty one. 'Let's hear what Zoe's got to say.'

'Thank you, Joe.' Zoe, her kimono wafting around her black leggings and vest top, sinks to the floor and kneels on the faded Turkish rug at the centre of the room. She checks the chopstick pins Sofia gave her are still holding her messy bun in place. She likes her new style. She intends to experiment more often.

Everyone is looking at her. Waiting for her performance to begin. She lets the moment stretch out. When she opens her mouth to speak, a knock at the door interrupts her. She and Carl exchange guilty glances. Joe and Holly press closer together on the sofa.

'Come in,' Zoe says. There's no law against the four of them having a chat together. They could be talking about anything.

When the door opens, Zoe is not surprised to see Mel standing there.

'I had a feeling something was going on.' Mel steps into the room and closes the door behind her. Her face is flushed and shiny with sweat.

'Where's Quinn?' Carl asks.

'She's settling in for a long session in the sweat lodge. I told her I needed to go for a rest.' Mel folds her arms across her chest. 'What are you up to?'

Zoe sighs. No point in lying. They need Mel on side to make this work. 'I wanted to run an idea by everyone.'

'But not by me?' Mel says.

'You chose to do the sweat lodge with Quinn.'

'I didn't realise there was another choice.'

'We would have filled you in afterwards,' Carl says.

'I'm sure,' Mel says. 'What about Quinn? Would she have been invited?'

Zoe takes a deep breath. 'I didn't want her to be here.'

Mel frowns. 'Why not?'

'There are things we need to decide.'

Shock steals across Mel's face.

'No, not that,' Joe says.

'Not that,' echoes Holly.

'Jesus, Mel.' Carl shakes his head. 'This is Pure Heart. We're all trying to be our best selves here.'

'Quinn won't like my idea,' Zoe explains, 'so I wanted to share it with you all first.'

'Fine.' Mel leans against the door. 'Let's hear it.'

'Okay.' Zoe clears her throat. 'As you know, after Charles died, I suggested we apply for a commercial licence and turn this place into a spiritual retreat for paying guests. I still think we could make this idea work and create both a sustainable lifestyle for ourselves and a really beautiful experience for anyone who comes to stay here.'

Mel brings her hands together in a slow clap. 'Thought your pitch out, haven't you?'

'At least she's trying to do something positive.' Carl leans forward in his chair. 'Better than accusing innocent people of things they haven't done.'

'Aye, let her finish,' Joe says.

'Let's ask Sofia to invest in Pure Heart,' Zoe suggests. 'For a fraction of what she's offered us, we could get this place up and running. We could dedicate it to Eva. Make it a tribute to her.'

'I think it's a lovely idea,' Holly says.

'Sofia offered us money to kill Quinn,' Mel reminds them. 'How is this proposal going to satisfy her? What does she get out of it?'

'Sofia wants Quinn to be punished for what she did,' Zoe says, 'but I don't think she wants her dead.'

'What kind of punishment?' Joe asks warily.

'I don't know exactly.' Zoe places her palms on her knees. 'Quinn could step down as leader. Or... or maybe she'd have to leave us.'

'You want to kick her out?' Mel says.

'I don't want to,' Zoe says, 'but we need to offer Sofia something.'

'Something in return for her money, you mean?' Mel says.

'None of us condone Sofia's way of dealing with this,' Zoe says, 'but nor can we condone what Quinn did in the past. She lied to us about Eva.'

'She did what she thought was best,' Mel says.

Carl runs a hand through his silver hair. 'We're trying to be pragmatic. We can't keep this place going without money.'

'Why not set the place up without Sofia's money?' Mel says. 'Get a licence but start small. While it's getting off the ground, I'm sure we can find other ways to earn income.'

Shock flashes across Carl's face. 'Get jobs?'

Mel shrugs. 'Why not?'

'You want to take part in that bullshit capitalist society again?' Carl says. 'The way we live here is supposed to mean something. We're supposed to be different.'

'Quinn wouldn't get a job and you know it,' Zoe says. 'She won't embrace change.'

'She might,' says Mel, 'if she realises there's no other option.'

'You really believe that?' Joe asks.

Mel doesn't reply.

'I know you love this place, Mel,' Zoe says. 'It's your home.'

'It's Quinn's home too,' Mel points out. 'I can't imagine this place without her.'

'The good of the community comes before individual desires,' Zoe says.

The third of Pure Heart's rules. Zoe never realised how important it was, but now it makes sense. Why should Quinn be more important than Pure Heart's future? They can't sacrifice their community for one of Quinn's unrealistic dreams. 'We have to modernise,' she insists. 'Quinn's attitude is holding us back.'

'Spiritual tourism?' Holly says. 'Is that really what we're about?'

'What's wrong with sharing what we have?' Zoe says. 'Sharing all the things we've learned.' She rolls her eyes. 'I mean how much more bloody work can we do on ourselves?'

'I'm only just getting started,' Mel says. 'Quinn says discovering your true self is a life's work.'

'We'd still have plenty of time for our own development,' Zoe says.

'Maybe being with others will bring new energy to what we do here,' Joe says.

Zoe nods at him, grateful for the support.

'Sofia won't go for it,' Mel says. 'She's on a mission.'

'We have to try,' Carl says.

'Let's take a vote.' Zoe glances round the room. 'Everyone in favour of giving my proposal a shot?'

She raises her hand. Carl does the same. After a moment's hesitation, Holly and Joe follow. Only Mel refuses to join in, arms still folded across her chest.

'You're deluding yourselves,' she says. 'All of you.'

50

QUINN

2018

It's 11.30 p.m. Quinn is in the courtyard, perched on the stone bench that surrounds the firepit. The fire is unlit; she doesn't want to draw attention to herself. She wants to stay outdoors, in peace, until the midnight curfew. A jasmine-scented breeze caresses her scalp. Cicadas sing their noisy lullaby. The lights in Joe and Holly's room are off. Early to bed, early to rise. There's a light on in Zoe and Carl's room; night owls both of them. A dim glow also comes from Mel and Sofia's windows.

Quinn turns her back on the Pure Heart building, but she can feel the Furies behind her. Watching. Waiting.

Earlier that evening, she crawled out of the sweat lodge, dizzy and dehydrated after an intense ceremony, and made her way back to her room. After drinking several mugs of cold water and having a brief, cold shower, she collapsed into bed and passed out until just before eleven.

She kicks off the orange Crocs and places her feet on the cool flag-stones. Her injured foot has healed well, but she doesn't feel ready to walk barefoot again. With everything that's going on right now, she can't risk another accident. She tilts her head back and lets her gaze roam the inky black, star-strewn sky as she sifts through her experiences in the sweat lodge. She hoped the others would join her so they could collectively purge their recent troubles, but they weren't ready. Not everyone can confront their grief. More than once since Andreas' death, she has made eye contact with a member of the Pure Heart family, only to have them look away. She must be patient. Loss affects people in different ways.

As the heat of the sweat lodge built around her, she spoke to Andreas and thanked him for trying to protect her, misguided as his efforts were. When they packed up his meagre possessions from his room, Quinn kept the large evil eye that hung above his bed. It now hangs above hers. She still wears the evil eye bracelet he gave her too. Only as a memento of him. Not because she thinks she needs protection.

After speaking to Andreas, Quinn sank into the heat and as sweat leaked from her pores, her voice filled the sweat lodge with one of her favourite Navajo chants. It wasn't long before a memory of Tom Quinn came to her. So vivid. As if she had travelled back in time. She was wearing a long white dress, and was kneeling by Thomas Quinn's bare legs. He was telling her she was special. He asked her to place her hands on his gooseflesh thighs and to imagine a diamond white light entering the top of her head and passing through her into his body. When she closed her eyes and did as he asked, a searing heat spread from the crown of her head, down her neck, along her arms and finally into her hands.

Then she was in the memory, not as a child, but as she is now, and she opened her eyes and asked Tom Quinn what she should do about Sofia. She was being called upon to do something, but she didn't know what. He cupped her chin in his hand and told her to wait for a sign. She would know when it came, he said. The sign would be clear. Unmistakable.

After that, she intended to stay in the sweat lodge all night seeking this sign, but the smoky air pressed heavy on her chest and for the first time ever she began to find the heat claustrophobic. She kept picturing herself in the yurt doing trust games with the others. Lying blindfolded with their hands on her chest.

A tiny grey kitten in search of attention butts its bony head against her shin, bringing her back to the present. 'Hello, Gaia,' she says. She thinks this one is Gaia. It's hard to keep track of them all. She wonders where

Aphrodite is tonight. She hasn't seen her since coming back from the sweat lodge.

Gaia jumps up onto the stone bench and over the other side. When Quinn turns to pick her up, she sees Sofia silhouetted in her bedroom window. She is cradling a cat in her arms and for a moment, Quinn thinks it is Aphrodite. Then Sofia turns and the light catches the cat's fur. Much to Quinn's relief, it is one of the old black and grey tabbies.

Sofia looks briefly in her direction before closing the shutters over her window.

Surely, Quinn thinks, it must be obvious to Sofia that when circumstances get difficult, the Pure Heart family always sticks together. On the day they found Andreas' body, it would have been easy to get swept up in Mel's fear, but Quinn is glad she didn't because once again her community proved itself. They didn't need to tell Detective Louca about Sofia's offer because they had no intention of acting on it. She felt proud of everyone. The strength of a community can be measured by the secrets it keeps.

She hears a low moaning noise and, glancing around her, traces it to Carl and Zoe's open window. A tender sadness pulses through her. She thinks of herself and Blake entwined in her bed, lost in each other, the noise of their pleasure saturating her room and penetrating the house and courtyard. She doubts anyone will coax such sounds from her again.

The moaning morphs into grunts from Carl and gasps from Zoe. A primitive harmony.

'Oh, fuck,' cries Zoe.

The harmony grows louder and, in Quinn's ears, distorts from something natural and joyful to something animalistic and sinister.

She turns away from the building but can't escape the noise. She feels her home closing in around her, the Furies breathing down her neck.

A hand on her shoulder. She lets out a strangled scream.

'It's me.' Mel crouches beside her. 'It's only me.'

'Sorry,' Quinn gasps. 'I'm sorry.'

'We need to talk.' Mel glances at the windows surrounding them. 'Can we go to your room?'

'Can it wait?' Quinn asks. 'I'm a little tired.'

'No,' Mel says. 'It can't.'

51

QUINN

2018

'A vote?' Quinn folds the shutters over her living room window. 'Against me?'

Her temples throb with tension. Her throat is tight and dry.

'Not exactly.' Mel is sitting in Quinn's armchair, thumb of one hand massaging the palm of another. In a low voice, she explains again what happened at the community meeting that afternoon. A meeting Quinn neither organised nor was invited to.

'They want Sofia to invest in Pure Heart as a business, but they want me to leave?' Quinn says.

Mel's cheeks flush. 'They think you're not open to the idea of us becoming a commercial retreat. Or that you're not the best person to lead that kind of project.'

'I wouldn't want to lead that kind of project.' Quinn paces the room in bare feet. 'Millennials and Gen Zs moaning about their issues with no serious intention of fixing them. Can you imagine?'

Mel hesitates. 'It's not an ideal solution, but it's better than—'

'Better than what? My family are not going to kill me.'

Mel gets up from her chair. 'I'll make us some tea.'

'Is that what you think?' Pressure builds in Quinn's chest again. 'I can't deal with any more of this negativity.'

Mel goes over to the table, flicks on the kettle and starts fussing with mugs and the jar of mountain tea. Aphrodite, in residence on top of the desk, watches as Quinn takes several deep breaths. Her Pure Heart family won't harm her – she knows that. In fact, making this proposal to Sofia is sending a clear signal they don't intend to. However, they're also taking advantage of the situation to secure their own financial future. Since when did anyone at Pure Heart worry about money? How often has she spoken of abundance being a manifestation of universal energy, a pure force they can connect with at will and draw to them?

She knows this is just another challenge from the universe, but she's only human and she can't help feeling hurt after all she's done for her fellow community members. How often has she held the space so they can share their deepest hurts and darkest secrets? What would any of them be without her? 'Pure Heart was my idea,' she says. 'My dream. My vision.'

'Here.' Mel holds out a steaming mug of tea. 'Drink this.'

Quinn waves away the tea and resumes pacing. 'Sofia's in emotional turmoil. A living hell. We're supposed to be freeing her from darkness.'

'Sofia needs an exorcism not an investment opportunity.' Mel puts Quinn's tea back on the table.

'What did you say to them all?'

'They know I don't support what they're doing.'

'They're not as strong as us. We're different, you and I.'

'Really?' Mel sits on the armchair, hands clasped around her mug. 'I'm not so sure?'

'Of course.' Quinn crouches in front of her and tries to look deep into her impenetrable eyes. 'You've endured so much but you've had the courage to rebuild your life and heal yourself. You're a unique person.'

Mel reaches out and touches Quinn's cheek, her hand warm and clammy from the mug. 'Thanks. I need to hear that sometimes.'

Quinn springs up, hurries over to her desk and pulls open the right-hand drawer. 'I had a vision of my first guru in the sweat lodge,' she said.

'From the commune?'

'Yes.' She removes a large brown envelope from the drawer. As she does so, she sees her passport beneath it. She last used it to attend her father's funeral five years ago, so it's still in date.

From inside the envelope, she takes out a collection of photographs. A mixture of Polaroids and developed photographs. Quinn ceased taking pictures a long time ago, preferring to live in the moment and content to let the others record special occasions at Pure Heart. She takes the pictures over to Mel and kneels beside the chair. 'This is Tom Quinn.' She shows Mel a Polaroid of the small, wiry man in his white robe. Silver hair down to his shoulders and a flowing beard. 'He introduced me to my healing powers. He said I'd meet others like me during my life and it would be my duty to show them who they really are.'

'Do you mean me?' Mel's voice wavers. 'Am I one of those people?'

'There's a rare innocence about you, despite all you've been through.'

'I wouldn't call myself innocent.'

The photographs slip from Quinn's grasp and spill onto the rug.

'Who's that?' Mel asks, plucking a picture from the messy heap.

Quinn takes the photograph from her. In it, she and Blake are sitting on the steps of the yurt. His bony arms are wrapped around her, and they are beaming with happiness.

'That's your ex, isn't it?' Mel says. 'The one who left you.'

'It was time for him to move on,' Quinn says. 'I didn't own him.'

'Must have hurt though?'

Quinn searches for the right quotation. Something from one of the spiritual traditions about ego and possession and the true nature of love but all she can think of is the shock of finding his room empty. The terrible few months that followed where she moved through life like a zombie, overwhelmed by the base emotions of anger and jealousy and grief. 'Yes,' she says, sliding the photograph into the middle of the pile and returning them all to the envelope. 'It did.'

'Has there been anyone else since then?'

'No.' After Blake left, Quinn knew she couldn't share that intimate part of herself again. Damaged men always came into her life, and she always tried to fix them. Gave away a lot of herself to do so. She didn't realise Blake had taken so much from her until he left. She couldn't face going through it again and, as she'd learned, wounded hearts take longer to heal as you get older.

Mel takes Quinn's wrist and turns her arm over, exposing the soft flesh on the underside. Confused, Quinn remains motionless while Mel strokes her skin. Is she trying to give her some energy healing? When she looks at Mel, she finds herself hypnotised by those icy blue eyes.

'I've given up on men,' Mel says. 'They're more trouble than they're worth.'

Quinn realises Mel's touch is a sensual one. It is not unpleasant, but it is unwanted. She pulls her arm away.

'Sorry,' Mel says. 'I thought—'

'It's fine.' Quinn resists the temptation to rub away the energetic imprint of Mel's touch. 'I just... after Blake, I decided to channel my sexual energy into my spiritual practice.'

'But you told me everything's connected.' Frustration creeps into Mel's voice. 'Body, mind and spirit. You said intimacy can connect us to our souls.'

'The connection you and I have is so much higher than that,' Quinn says.

Mel's expression hardens and her eyes flash with anger.

Quinn rests her hands on Mel's thighs. 'We're facing a difficult situation here, and I can't get through it alone. I need you by my side.'

A shy smile transforms Mel's face. 'I'm here for you.'

A buzzing sound interrupts them. It seems to be coming from Mel.

'Shit.' Mel reaches into the pocket of her burgundy yoga pants and pulls out a small mobile phone.

'You have a phone?' Quinn says.

'It's the one I had when I arrived here.' Mel switches it off and puts it back in her pocket. 'My mum likes to text me now and again.'

'Oh.'

'I know you don't approve of phones, but I don't want her to worry about me.'

'It's fine.' Quinn wonders why Mel wouldn't just use the landline.

'Rose, my grandmother, had a stroke. She's in hospital.'

Panic squeezes Quinn's chest. 'Do you need to go home and see her?'

'I wouldn't leave you. Especially not now.' Mel sighs. 'Please don't tell the others about the phone. Dmitri might confiscate it.'

'He wouldn't do that, I'm sure.'

'Please, Quinn. I don't want anyone knowing my family's business.'

'Of course. I won't say a word.'

'Thanks. Let's just deal with what's going on here.'

'Okay.' Quinn's knees crack as she gets to her feet. 'We need perspective. We need to be logical.' The community prayed for abundance and, out of the blue, Sofia appeared. That was no coincidence. They can't give up now. Quinn has seen traces of the real Sofia. Warm-hearted and generous. Only last week she donated thousands of euros to Andreas' favourite political party in his name.

Quinn fetches her Tarot cards from the bookcase. She hasn't used them since Andreas died but she feels that now is the time.

'What are you doing?' Mel asks as Quinn sits on the rug by her feet.

'We need guidance.'

Quinn tenderly unfolds the tie-dye fabric that swaddles the cards. The material is a fragment of a sarong once worn by Tom Quinn. She shuffles the cards, soothed by their familiar weight and by the memory of them in Tom's rough, chapped hands. She spreads them out on the rug and lets her hands hover above them. She waits to be guided to the card she needs to see at this moment.

Nothing.

Then she realises. 'You need to choose,' she tells Mel.

'Me?'

'Yes.' Even though Quinn believes that the Death card she kept selecting signifies rebirth for Sofia and the community and not Andreas' death, the cards might be picking up some fragment of doubt from her.

'I'm not sure I should,' Mel says.

'Please. The cards are asking for you.' Quinn gives Mel a reassuring smile. 'Just ask them what we must do to save our community.'

'Okay.' Looking gratified but awkward, Mel joins Quinn on the floor. 'Can I shuffle them again?'

Quinn nods. Mel sweeps up the cards and subjects them to an expert shuffle like a croupier in a casino. A rapt expression on her face Quinn has never seen before.

Mel's hands, fast-moving and agile, spread the cards out on the rug in a neat, curved formation. Then her right hand hovers over them.

'Think about the question,' Quinn says. 'Go wherever the cards draw you.'

After a few seconds, Mel swoops in and pulls out a card. When she flips it over, Quinn is confronted by a picture of a multi-coloured wheel.

'The Gambler,' Mel says, reading out the description below the wheel. She clears her throat. 'I can't believe it.'

'It's good,' Quinn says. 'It's a good omen.'

'Really?'

'Yes. The Gambler or Wheel of Fortune card signals a change in luck.'

'But luck can be good or bad.'

Mel's right of course. The Gambler can also represent bad luck and negative external forces, but Quinn has a good feeling about this card. This could be the sign Tom Quinn spoke of in her vision. 'It's a sign things are about to change for the better,' she says. 'Luck is on our side, and we should take our chances.'

'I'm not sure anything connected with gambling is a good sign.'

'It is because *you* picked it. You understand honour and loyalty. Like me, you want what's best for this community.'

A shadow passes across Mel's face. 'There's something I need to tell you.'

'What?' Mel's intense stare is making Quinn uneasy.

Mel hesitates. 'We could run away. Just me and you.'

'What?'

'I might come into some money soon.'

'From your grandmother?'

'We could start a new life somewhere. You don't have to stay here and put yourself in danger.'

'I'm not in any danger and I could never leave Pure Heart.' Quinn takes the Tarot card from Mel and stares at the colourful wheel. 'Our luck is about to change. Trust me.'

52

Insight Investigators: Background Report

Melanie Harris (Mel): At the same time as I was looking into the corruption charges against Mel, I was also investigating her family. I got a break when her younger brother, Chris, a stockbroker in London, agreed to talk to me over the phone. I told him I was an old friend of Mel's keen to contact her again.

Our conversation started with a warning from him. He told me getting in touch with Mel wasn't a good idea. He said she was bad news and that no one in the family spoke to her any more. He said the only family member who ever liked her was Rose, her maternal grand-mother, but Rose was long dead.

53

ZOE

2018

'I will get Sofia for you,' Grigor says. 'One moment.'

When the kitchen door closes on Grigor's bulky frame, a tense silence descends upon the dining table. Zoe lays her hands on her thighs to stop them trembling. This is good, she tells herself. Better they face these difficult facts now and get everything out in the open.

Carl places a reassuring arm around her shoulder. Joe, sitting opposite her, is gazing into his mug of coffee. Holly, beside him, is scraping dirt from beneath her fingernails. Quinn sits at the head of the table as always, Aphrodite on her lap, both of them giving off a calm defiance. Zoe can feel Quinn's eyes on her. Probing. Trying to get beneath her skin. She tells herself she has everything under control, but her erratic pulse betrays her. She stares at the unfinished bowl of Greek yoghurt and home-made granola in front of her. The breakfast Quinn interrupted when she swept in. Righteous and superior, but Zoe detected fury simmering beneath her orange pyjamas.

Zoe planned to share the community's proposal with Sofia later this morning, but Quinn hijacked the situation and insisted they do it now. An attempt to regain control, Zoe thinks. She isn't surprised Mel told their leader about the plan. Mel sits beside Quinn now, hands clasped on the table, her cold eyes expressing her disapproval.

Zoe is annoyed to find herself feeling disloyal. She can't help remembering the times Quinn has held her and let her scream and cry and empty herself of the past. When she does look up, she is dismayed to find not anger in Quinn's eyes but disappointment. As if Zoe is a child who can't possibly grasp the complexities of the situation.

A loud pinging noise fills the room. Joe jumps up and crosses over to one of the large industrial ovens. He opens the door and pulls out a rack containing two round loaves of sourdough. The homely smell of freshly baked bread fills the kitchen, at odds with the fraught atmosphere. Zoe has a moment of longing for the past. For the time before Sofia when this room was a comfy haven, filled with love and laughter and the certainty they were living the good life.

She steels herself. Her solution to the problem is a good one. She will be the one to deliver the community into a sustainable future and give Sofia some kind of closure. That's all Sofia wants – she's sure of it. Then they can all move on.

What Quinn would move on to and where she would go Zoe can't imagine.

'Good morning.' Sofia sweeps into the kitchen in her white pyjamas. 'I believe I've been summoned?'

Grigor follows her into the room and shuts the door behind him.

'Is this it?' Sofia says. 'Are you ready to do it?'

'Zoe has a proposition for you,' Quinn says.

Zoe flinches as all eyes turn to her. No need to feel afraid. This is her idea. She doesn't need Quinn's permission to speak. 'Yes, we have a proposal for you.'

'*We* doesn't include me and Quinn,' Mel says. 'Just for the record.'

'A proposal. Intriguing.' Sofia sits at the opposite end of the table to Quinn. 'I'd love an espresso,' she says to Grigor. He nods and strolls over to the coffee machine. Zoe waits until he's finished tapping the spent grinds out of the sump before she speaks.

'We think we've come up with a solution that would suit everyone,' she says, avoiding Quinn's gaze. She explains her idea to Sofia, including her solution for dealing with Quinn. Sofia listens intently and nods, distracted only when Grigor hands her a coffee.

'A spiritual retreat in memory of my mother,' Sofia says. 'What do you think, Grigor? Can you see the lost and the lonely flocking here?'

Grigor, leaning against one of the workstations, shrugs. 'People pay money for crazy things.'

Sofia smiles. 'It's his optimism I pay him for, you know.'

'Eva knew that this place, at its best, could be an example of how to live well in the world,' Zoe says. 'That's why we all came here and that's why we've stayed so long. We believe in this place. In what it once was and what it could be again.' She risks a glance at Quinn and finds her sitting bolt upright, her expression serene.

'Pure Heart was Quinn's idea,' Mel says. 'You can't just take it from her.'

'Good point,' Sofia says. 'You must be angry about this, Quinn? You're sitting there all Zen, but you must be seething inside?'

'I don't seethe,' Quinn says. 'I'm proud of Zoe for feeling able to claim her power, and I don't judge any of you for wanting an easy way out of this. It's difficult to tread the higher path. I'm sure you all think you've got the good of the community at heart, but—'

'We wouldn't need three million euros,' Zoe says to Sofia, trying to keep the conversation on point. 'If you invested half a million, that would get us started.'

'Two and a half million more for me to spend elsewhere,' Sofia says.

Zoe's heart lifts. 'Exactly.' This is going better than she'd hoped.

'And in return, Quinny here gets exiled?' Sofia says.

Carl nods. 'There would be a change of leadership, yes.'

'You'd kick her out,' Mel says. 'Just say what you mean.'

'Financially it makes sense,' Sofia says, 'but this isn't about money. Not for me anyway.' She sips her espresso. 'I want revenge and kicking Quinn out of here isn't enough.'

'At least you've stopped pretending it's justice you want,' Mel says.

'We also thought we could sign the house and land over to you,' Zoe says, 'as part of the deal.'

'Aye, but with the caveat that we get to stay here for the rest of our lives,' Joe adds.

'That's… that's very important to us,' Holly says, in a timid voice.

'Slight problem with that idea,' Sofia says. 'I already own Pure Heart.'

A cold knot forms at Zoe's core. A muffled ringing sound fills her ears, almost blocking out the shocked responses to Sofia's announcement.

'What?'

'What do you mean?'

'That's not possible.'

'What the fuck?'

'I'll do my best to make a long story short.' Sofia holds out her cup to Grigor, who takes it and returns to the coffee machine. 'When I first went to live with my grandparents, they never talked about my mother. My grandfather made it clear her choices had led to her demise and, for many years, it was as though she'd never existed. I became their focus. I became the daughter they'd lost.' She pauses to accept a fresh espresso from Grigor. 'At first all I wanted was to return to Pure Heart. To my home. I was alone and afraid, and I could feel the poison my mother always talked about flowing through my grandfather. Through everything he touched. But I also had questions about my mother's suicide. I remembered Andreas telling me Quinn was responsible for Eva's death, and I wanted to find out what he meant. But I was busy becoming the person I needed to be to inherit everything.'

A momentary glimpse of fragility appears in Sofia's eyes, soon replaced by a bitter hardness. 'Just before my grandfather died, he called me to his bedside to tell me about a project he'd been involved in for some time,' she says. 'An entertaining sideline, he called it. Not long after Eva's death, he bribed the financial adviser who dealt with Charles' affairs to slowly mess them up.'

'Michalis?' Quinn's face pales. 'He… he looked after Charles for years.'

'Yeah, not so much,' Sofia says. 'Michalis encouraged Charles to put his money into high-risk investments and once the losses started, Charles was more susceptible to investing in even dodgier schemes.'

'You ruined him,' Mel says. 'That's highly illegal. We could report you.'

'Detective Inspector Mel.' Sofia smiles. 'Always upholding the law. Always fighting the good fight. Charles was a reckless investor, or at least that's how it looks to the outside world. A gambler almost.'

'You exploited a vulnerable old man.' Quinn can't control the tremble in her voice.

'The more losses Charles made, the more he was willing to bet everything on a big win.' Sofia shoots Mel a knowing look. 'I'm sure you can well imagine.'

Zoe waits for Mel to respond, but the ex-policewoman sinks back into her chair, apparently done with her interrogation.

'With his resources, my grandfather could buy anything,' Sofia says. 'As can I and rest assured, unlike some people, I know how to cover my tracks.'

Zoe is torn between horror and admiration. 'I still don't understand how you came to own Pure Heart.'

Sofia drains the last of her second espresso. 'When Charles realised he couldn't service his debts, Michalis persuaded him to take a loan from a company called Prospect Holdings. The company was based in the British Virgin Islands, but Charles didn't know that. To guarantee the loan, Charles had to mortgage Pure Heart. He was so desperate for money he didn't even have a lawyer look over the paperwork he was signing. The small print made it clear that accepting the loan would result in the rights to the Pure Heart property being transferred to Prospect Holdings.'

'I'm guessing your grandfather owned Prospect Holdings?' Carl says.

Sofia nods. 'And now it belongs to me. Thanks to the British Virgin Islands' relaxed rules, my ownership can remain hidden. I have a nominee director acting on my behalf.'

Zoe marvels at the intrigue in Sofia's world. The drama.

'Sofia, we love you,' Quinn says, 'and this is still your home. Don't let your grandfather pass on his poison as well as his money. Don't let his desire for revenge taint your life. You're better than that.'

'Unlike you I have no illusions about who I really am,' Sofia says. 'Or what I'm capable of.'

'When Eva took her own life, she left all of us with questions,' Quinn says. 'Most of all you, but none of us could have done anything to change what happened.'

The cold knot at Zoe's core expands into her chest. She turns her head to look at Carl, but he doesn't meet her eyes.

'With money like mine I can buy answers,' Sofia says. 'I can buy closure.' She pushes back her chair and stands up. 'Here's my revised offer. Kill Quinn and I'll give you three million euros and sign the deeds of the property back over to you.'

'Their souls are not for sale,' Quinn says.

'I'd also like to add a condition,' Sofia says. 'You must use some of that money to turn this place into a spiritual retreat. Eva's Paradise perhaps? I'll leave the details up to you, but a tribute to her does seem fitting.'

'Sofia,' Holly says. 'Please. What do you honestly expect us to do?'

Sofia smiles. 'Whatever your consciences dictate.'

54

Insight Investigators: Background Report

Melanie Harris (Mel): I'll come back to Mel's brother later in the report, as what he had to say relates to what I discovered next about her corruption charges.

At the end of my drinking session with DS Kerrigan – who turned out to have a low tolerance for whisky – he told me that Mel was partial to a game of poker. He said it wasn't his scene, but he named another officer she played with. Detective Inspector Pete Manson, who apparently was a good friend of hers. They went through training together but ended up in different Organised Crime units.

Pete was happy to talk, once I'd made it worth his while. He said he and Mel both enjoyed an occasional game of poker and often went to casinos together. He claimed it was a stress release. He says he only played once a fortnight and only betted what he could afford to lose.

After a while, he noticed Mel was playing weekly and not just poker. She played blackjack too and sometimes even the slots. When he joked she might have a gambling problem, she got angry with him. That's when he realised her habit was out of control. After a long losing streak at poker, she finally admitted she'd blown 'a shitload of money'. Only problem was, he said, she was determined to win it back.

She told him a guy they played poker with regularly had wangled her an invite to a private game in a club in West London. You didn't need a huge stake to get in but the wins could be big. She offered to get Pete an invite too and, against his better judgement, he agreed. As soon as he got to the club, he regretted his decision. The place was full of shady characters. People he was sure they shouldn't be mixing with. Mel had got hold of five thousand pounds' stake money and was sure she was going to win big. She needed to.

She lost all of it early on. Pete was soon out of the game too. He expected them to leave together, but after he went out for a cigarette, he returned to find Mel back in the game. He said it was clear someone there had given her the money to keep playing. He didn't know who, but he had a bad feeling about it. Months later, when he heard about the allegations against her and found out she'd resigned, he wasn't at all surprised. He tried to contact her, but she didn't answer his calls. A friend of hers told him Mel had gone on holiday, but no one knew where.

Pete also had an interesting theory. The Albanian gang Mel tipped off about the drug raid were relative newcomers to London. Around the time of Mel's resignation, Pete was at a briefing for a sex trafficking case and saw a photograph of a man believed to be one of this gang's leaders. He recognised him immediately as one of the players at the private poker game that night. He thinks this guy gave Mel money, knowing she had no idea of his identity at that point. Accepting money from a criminal like that would be an instantly dismissible offence and Pete thinks this gave the gang a hold over Mel. She had no choice but to do favours for them. He doesn't have any proof, but he thinks, and I agree, that it's the most likely explanation.

He warned me not to do any digging on the Albanian guys. He said they were not to be messed with.

55

ZOE

2018

Zoe and Carl are naked in bed together. He sits cross-legged while she sits on his lap with her legs wrapped around him. She can feel him hard inside her. Their foreheads are pressed together, and each has a hand placed over the other's heart. The yab-yum position, an essential part of their Tantric practice.

When their foreheads part, Carl's eyes search hers. His pupils are enlarged with desire, but Zoe also sees fear and uncertainty in his gaze. She closes her eyes and shudders as if overcome by arousal. Anything to prevent him detecting her own muddled feelings.

It's almost midnight, but neither of them is ready to sleep. After Sofia rejected Zoe's proposal at breakfast this morning, the Pure Heart members retreated first to their rooms and then into the mundane daily chores that keep their community running. They didn't observe formal mealtimes, resorting to taking leftovers from the fridge back to their rooms. As if each of them needed space to make sense of this latest turn of events.

'Are you sure I articulated our plan properly?' Zoe slowly undulates her hips. 'Maybe Sofia didn't really get what I meant.'

'You were amazing,' Carl says, his voice husky with lust. 'Amazing.'

'Really?' Zoe isn't sure. Looking back, she hopes her old loyalty to Quinn didn't weaken her message. All day she's been fighting the urge to beg Quinn for forgiveness.

'Just be with me here and now,' Carl says. 'In this moment.'

She lets out a deep moan, but she isn't here with him, she's back at the kitchen table, listening to Sofia's revelations about owning Pure Heart. Now, as then, she is wrestling with conflicting reactions. Shock and acceptance of the inevitable. Of course, Sofia would have blocked every financial escape route.

'We need to cleanse ourselves of today.' The minuscule movements of Carl's hips send shivers of pleasure from Zoe's belly to her chest.

'So much drama.' The shivery pleasure spreads from her chest to her throat.

Carl takes slow, deliberate breaths. 'We need to connect with our higher selves.'

'Yes.' She wants to connect to her higher self. She really does. When Sofia repeated her offer, Zoe felt something light and pure and good slip out of her. She could almost see it drifting across the kitchen and slipping under the door. Was it her higher self, abandoning her?

Carl caresses her face. 'When I'm with you, I reach such an elevated spiritual state.'

A prickle of irritation. Carl often says their sex takes him to a spiritual high, and she used to think that was a compliment. A testament to their unique connection. Now she wonders if sex is just a way for him to escape his anxieties. Maybe she's nothing more than a battery he plugs into to renew himself. Maybe he'd feel this way about anyone.

'Breathe with me, beloved,' Carl says.

She tries to turn herself on by picturing Dmitri's strong hands on the Land Rover's steering wheel. She imagines those hands on her face, as Carl's are now. She imagines them gripping her hips, forcing her to fuck him hard and fast.

'What's wrong?' Carl says. 'This feels a bit off.'

'Sorry. I need a wee.'

Her husband looks wounded as she clambers off him. In the bathroom, she sits on the toilet even though she has no desire to go. She just needs some breathing space.

Out of nowhere comes an urge to ring her mother. For comfort? For guidance? The last time she called home it was a lunchtime and Faye Aldridge was drunk. *I've got some friends round for Prosecco on the lawn.* Zoe cringed to think of Faye and her bloated, alcoholic friends guzzling cheap Prosecco from Aldi in the pitifully small garden at the back of her mother's bungalow.

Remorse floods through her. Many times over the years, Quinn has been the mother figure Zoe wanted and needed. Could life at Pure Heart really continue without her?

She stays in the bathroom for almost five minutes. When she returns to the bedroom, the moment of intimacy has, as she hoped, passed. Carl is standing by the open window, smoking a roll-up.

'Sorry,' she says, getting back into bed. 'I'm a bit drained, that's all.'

'I get it.' Carl blows smoke into the night air. 'There's a lot to unpack right now.'

They lapse into silence. Through the open window comes the low gurgle of the swimming pool, the relentless cyclical song of cicadas and the two-note hoot of an owl, soft and melancholy.

'That's a Cyprus scops owl,' says Carl.

Zoe remembers the dead bird Andreas pulled out of the pool. A symbol of the birth of a new generation.

Carl rearranges the papers on his desk and dusts the cover of the large, leather-bound notebook Sofia gave him a few days ago. A shaft of silvery light highlights the first signs of wrinkling, sagging skin on his buttocks.

Zoe looks away.

'See anyone out there?' she asks.

Carl shakes his head. 'The shutters are closed in Quinn's room,' he says. 'Mel's too.'

Zoe has avoided Mel all day. She did go to Holly and Joe's room this afternoon but as she was about to knock on the door, she heard Holly sobbing and Joe's voice murmuring to her, soft and soothing.

'What are we going to do?' Carl pulls out the chair at his desk and sits down.

Sofia's offer hangs in the air between them. Zoe picks up the Chanel scarf Sofia gave her from her bedside table. She hasn't worn it, but she finds the silk enticing and likes to touch it. 'I really thought my idea would work.'

'It still might,' Carl says. 'Maybe Sofia thought she'd lose face if she agreed immediately, but she might go away and think about it.'

'Really? You think so?'

Carl shrugs. An image of Quinn's empty grave swoops into Zoe's mind. The gaping hole in the ground. Waiting.

'Should we leave?' she says.

'Leave?' Blue smoke trails from Carl's nostrils.

'What choice do we have?' Zoe knows her higher self would pack a rucksack right now and leave Pure Heart.

'Maybe you're right,' Carl says.

Zoe imagines the two of them trying to live an ordinary life. What if they got jobs in Limassol or Nicosia? Zoe could work in a shop in one of the big hotels. She could even sing in the bar. Cover versions of popular songs for tourists. Carl could... she wasn't sure what he could do but he'd find something. An honest living. An honest life. If there was nothing in Cyprus, they'd have to go back to the UK. She thinks of them sleeping in her mother's spare bedroom until they get themselves sorted. Despair washes over her.

'I won't let Sofia drive me out.' Carl's fingers drum on the cover of his new notebook.

Zoe thinks of the words written inside it. The novel Carl is desperate to complete. 'I'm not saying I want to leave, but what if—'

'We're not the people she thinks we are.'

'I know that.'

Out in the courtyard a burst of hissing and mewling. Cats scrapping.

'Leaving makes it look like we've got something to fear,' Carl says. 'As though we don't trust ourselves.'

'True.' Zoe wraps the scarf around her left wrist. It's offensive really, that Sofia thinks so little of them. 'So, we're staying?'

Carl returns to their bed and lies down beside her. 'I think we should,' he says. 'I think it's the right thing to do.'

56

Insight Investigators: Background Report

Melanie Harris (Mel): As I said earlier, Mel and her family don't appear to be close and I can see why. When I told Chris I'd heard a rumour about her gambling problem, he didn't hold back. I taped the call and this is an extract: *Mel's habit was way out of control. Seriously. She'd been at it for ages. She made a decent living so fuck knows how much she was losing at the casino. I heard there were private poker games too. The shit hit the fan when I found out she'd been borrowing money off our mum for a couple of years. Fifteen thousand pounds. Maybe more. Mum didn't have a huge amount stashed away, but Mel can be very persuasive. My dad and I were furious when we found that out. He's never liked her that much, to be honest. He tried. I watched him making an effort with her so many times, but she wasn't interested. In the end, he gave up on her. We all did.*

As far as family goes, it seems like Mel has nothing and no one to go back to the UK for.

57

QUINN

As another dawn rises on Pure Heart, Quinn finds herself standing in front of Charles' memorial plaque, Aphrodite at her feet. She didn't intend to come here. She was on her way to feed the hens, alone for the first time since her accident, when the urge to talk to Charles came over her and now here she is, in the clearing beyond the olive grove, staring at the black rectangular slab of granite with its silver lettering.

Charles Higham Jones
Beloved friend
Generous benefactor
See you in the next life.

Last night, she couldn't sleep. The day's events buzzed around her head despite hours of deep meditation. Waves of volcanic anger rose inside her whenever she thought of Zoe's plan to banish her and Sofia's revelation about owning Pure Heart. She told herself these feeling arose from her ego, and she mustn't be guided by them.

This morning, however, in the pinkish light the sun has sent ahead of itself, the anger ambushes her.

'You arrogant prick,' she says to the memorial stone. 'How could you do this to me? I've given everything to this place. Everything.'

She thinks of the months she spent in Ibiza getting Charles off heroin. Cleaning up his shit, mopping his fevered brow, policing him every second of every day until he could be trusted. Getting rid of his junkie hangers-on. Finding him a place he could live out the rest of his years sober and in peace.

'Why did I bother?' she asks him. 'Did you hear what they want to do to this place? Can you imagine it?' Quinn pictures the Pure Heart that Zoe wants to create. Hordes of young pseudo-goddesses floating around in expensive silk kaftans and dancing seductively in the moonlight in their designer yoga pants and bikini tops. The earnest young men worshipping them. The thought of it appals her, but at the same time she feels envious of this future she doesn't belong to.

'And that bloody Michalis,' she says, thinking of the innocuous, balding financial adviser who helped Sofia's grandfather ruin them. 'How could he?' He always seemed so trustworthy. As Charles got older, Michalis would come to Pure Heart to spare Charles a trip into Limassol, and Quinn always made him welcome. Even made him a special tincture for his eczema a few years ago. 'What a creep.'

Aphrodite watches her through narrowed eyes. *Is that a disapproving look on her face?*

'I'm just venting,' Quinn says. 'That's all.' She crouches down and holds out her arms, but Aphrodite backs away. 'Come on, my love.'

A rustling in the nearby bushes makes Quinn's heart race. She thinks of the coin snake, uncoiling itself and opening its cavernous mouth. She thinks of her own grave nearby in the clearing, another gaping mouth.

'Come here,' she says to Aphrodite.

The cat obeys. Quinn scoops her up, turns her back on the home-made graveyard and hurries away towards the olive grove.

* * *

Despite the throbbing in her right ankle and the orange Crocs making her clumsy, Quinn makes swift progress up the terraces. As she passes through the orchard, a sweet stink fills the air. Rotting apples and apricots lie beneath the trees. They should have been picked by now. Joe could be making jams and chutneys. Filling up the larder for winter as he always does. Instead, wasps crawl over the ruined skins of apricots and disappear into the rotting cores of apples.

An irritating whirring noise spoils the natural sounds of dawn. The black, four-legged drone soars overhead, undertaking one of its daily patrols. Quinn resists the urge to stick her fingers up at it. She thinks back to the infamous Battle of the Beanfield, when she was part of a convoy of New Age travellers attacked by police on their way to Stonehenge. She fought hard that day, only narrowly avoiding arrest. She thinks of the Poll Tax Riots and fleeing from illegal raves on the M40 with the police giving chase. All her life she has resisted infringements on her liberty. Now the outside world with its surveillance culture has followed her here to Pure Heart. All her life she has been on the move, looking for a way to screw the system. Until Sofia arrived, she thought she'd managed it.

She hurries towards the house. Grigor is sitting at the courtyard table. To avoid him, she shuns the main entrance and takes the passageway at the side of the building. The passageway leads to the car park. She crosses the car park and makes for the little-used side door that leads to the kitchen, passing through the utility room and the larder on the way. In the larder, a crate of Dom Perignon gleams ominously at her from the shelf. Is Sofia saving it for a celebration?

The side door to the kitchen is open but the mesh screen attached to it is shut. When Quinn pauses to remove her Crocs, she hears voices from the kitchen. Holly and Joe. She creeps closer to the door. Joe has her back to her, but she can see Holly.

'Please, hon,' Joe says. 'Have some more toast. You've hardly eaten anything.'

'I'm not hungry,' Holly says.

'You look gaunt.'

Quinn agrees with Joe. Holly's cheekbones are more sharply defined, and her collarbones have emerged from her previously fleshy body. Holly told Quinn that her teenage fixation on weight loss stemmed from a desire to escape her emotional pain. What is Holly trying to escape now?

'I'm just tired,' Holly says. 'I doubt any of us slept last night.'

'It's hard seeing you like this.'

'What do you expect? Sofia owns this place. She could kick us out at any time.'

'I don't think—'

'She could do anything she wants with the land.'

'It'll be fine, I promise you. We're not going anywhere.'

'That's what scares me.'

Quinn retreats to the larder and doubles over, hands on her knees. Why so dizzy? Anxiety is a tight clamp around her chest. Is she picking up Holly's emotions or experiencing her own? She takes several deep breaths. She needs to gather herself.

Our thoughts create our reality.

Yes, she thinks, remembering this crucial Pure Heart rule. She needs to control her thoughts. Otherwise, she could create a terrible reality for herself.

What to do next? What is the right move?

Mel's cool blue eyes swim into her mind. She sees Mel's lips moving.

Sofia needs an exorcism, not an investment opportunity.

Of course. At the time she dismissed Mel's words as sarcasm but now she sees them as a revelation. A sign of what she must do.

'You were right, Mel,' Quinn whispers. 'You were absolutely right.'

58

QUINN

2018

It is just after six-thirty in the evening as Quinn approaches the trees on the land beyond the terraces, Dmitri by her side. The sun is beginning to lose its bite and a light breeze tickles her neck. Through the thick trunks of the pine trees, she can see one of the monastery walls. She hasn't set foot inside the place since Eva's death, but both she and Sofia must face the past if this cleansing ritual is going to work.

After Quinn had her revelation this morning, she approached Sofia and invited her to take part in a shamanic ritual in the monastery to exorcise the trauma of Eva's death. She expected Sofia to refuse, at least initially, but to her surprise Sofia accepted straight away. Quinn suggested they conduct the ritual tomorrow, but Sofia insisted they do it this evening, before she could change her mind.

Quinn thinks of the others waiting for her back at the house. Zoe and Carl wished her good luck, but Quinn wasn't sure they meant it. Joe and Holly were sceptical of the plan and thought Sofia shouldn't return to the monastery. Mel took her aside and spoke to her earnestly in a low voice.

'You don't need to do this,' Mel said.

'I want to,' Quinn said. 'How's your grandmother doing?'

Mel stared at her blankly. 'My grandmother?'

'Rose. Is she still in hospital?'

'She's... she's fine. We need to focus, Quinn. I think I've found us a way out of this situation.'

'Spirit has shown me the path I must follow.'

Mel gripped her arm. 'You need to trust me.'

'And you need to trust me.'

Mel offered to accompany her to the monastery, but Quinn refused. Sofia wants it to be just the two of them, and Quinn must respect her wishes. Not even Aphrodite has been allowed to follow her down.

She has come prepared. The large Turkish carpet bag slung over her shoulder contains her Tibetan singing bowls and a flask of cacao. She is wearing her best orange dress and her ceremonial jewellery. The orange Crocs too, although she resents their rubbery presence.

The trees are close now. She swallows, her mouth suddenly dry. Dmitri turns to her.

'You are okay?' he says.

'Of course,' she replies.

When they enter the trees, the skin on the back of Quinn's neck prickles. Dappled emerald light surrounds her. They weave between the pines and cedars until Quinn sees the monastery ahead of them.

At the edge of the trees, Sofia sits on a blue and white picnic blanket. A gold belt cinches in the white maxi dress that covers her slender body. Her hair gleams. Her skin glows. 'Come,' she says. 'Join me.'

Her voice is soft and welcoming. No sign of the conflict between them. Dmitri hangs back in the trees as Quinn sits on the blanket opposite Sofia.

'Thank you for suggesting this,' Sofia says.

Quinn forces herself to look at the monastery. The small, single-storey building is more decrepit than she remembers. Bricks are missing in the white walls and the wooden roof has holes in it. Set above the wooden door is an arched recess containing a faded fresco of a robed figure with a halo. A saint, Quinn has always presumed although she has no idea which one. 'Shall we go inside?'

'Let's sit first.' Sofia has a small, stainless-steel cup in her hands. 'I'm having some mountain tea. Will you join me?'

Quinn thinks of the cacao in her flask. It took her a long time to prepare and is a vital part of the ritual. 'I'd love some tea,' she says, wanting to reward Sofia for contributing to the ceremony. After all, she is only here to be the guide for whatever transformation Sofia is ready for.

Sofia pours tea from a large thermos into a cup identical to her own.

'Thank you,' Quinn says when Sofia hands her the tea. It's delicious. She drains the cup and gratefully accepts Sofia's offer of another, ignoring the hunger pangs gripping her stomach. She hasn't eaten all day, hoping a fast will bring clarity to the evening's proceedings.

'What's in your bag?' Sofia asks.

'My singing bowls.' Quinn explains she thought their sound could cleanse the monastery and release any negative energy trapped in the building.

'Could you play before we go in?' Sofia says. 'I'd find that very relaxing.'

'Of course. That's a lovely idea.' Quinn puts her empty cup aside, unzips her bag and arranges the five singing bowls in front of her, smallest on the left, largest on the right. She picks up her wooden wand with its black suede tip, closes her eyes and takes a few deep breaths. A luscious calm spreads through her. She opens her eyes to see Sofia staring at her with a soft, curious expression.

Quinn taps the wand against the side of each bowl, bringing them to life until their warm, pure notes vibrate in the early evening air. As one ringing sound fades, she revives it again until the wand is gliding between all the bowls, their varying notes melting into a harmonious melody that travels through Quinn's hand into the rest of her body. Sofia has a rapturous smile on her face. This reception prompts Quinn to keep going and she is soon lost within the music.

She has no idea how much time has passed when the final note from the deepest bowl fades away. The sound bath seems to have put her into a trance. When she lays down the wand, she turns her hands over and examines the violet ring road of veins on the inside of her wrists. She can almost hear the blood trickling through them. She glances back towards the woods and sees Dmitri leaning against the trunk of a majestic pine, like a wood nymph in a waistcoat. Beyond him, the emerald-green light falling through the canopy shimmers. The trees whisper to one another and Quinn feels privileged to overhear their conversations.

'You were playing for nearly half an hour,' Sofia says.

'Really?' Quinn smiles. She surprises herself with her own powers sometimes.

'How are you feeling?'

'Good.' Extremely good. That sound healing must have been just what she needed. A soft blanket of peace wraps itself around her. 'Are you ready?' she asks Sofia.

Sofia's eyes flick towards the monastery. 'I think so.' She uncrosses her long legs and stands up, smoothing down the folds of her dress. 'No,' she says when Dmitri moves towards them. 'Wait outside.'

Quinn's knees crack when she stands. Loud as gunshots. She puts out a hand and her heart contracts when Sofia takes it, compliant as a child. 'Let's do this,' she says.

59

QUINN

2018

When Quinn pushes the door of the monastery, it gives way with a rotting sigh. Together, she and Sofia step into the cool gloom of the interior. A space roughly the same size as the Pure Heart kitchen. Light slants through the broken window on their right but most of the space is deep in shadow.

A rustling sound at the back of the room makes Quinn start. A snake, hiding here from the heat of the day? Her sensitised ears trick her into thinking she can hear it sliding over to them on its smooth, treacherous belly. Ridiculous, she tells herself. She must stay calm, for Sofia's sake. She is here to facilitate the girl's healing. To hold the space for her.

Sofia is trembling. The tiny vibrations of her hand travel into Quinn's.

'It's just a building; it can't hurt you,' Quinn says, although it feels as if the ancient stone walls are closing in on her. An illusion. A trick of the light, or lack of it.

Sofia releases her hand and wanders around the desolate space that must have once been a picturesque place of prayer. Along each wall are faded images of the Virgin Mary and cloaked Byzantine saints. The floorboards beneath their feet are decaying, spoiled by the rain that seeps in through the roof each winter. At the back of the room, in what may once have been the altar area, there are no floorboards, just hard, compacted earth.

Sofia stops where the wooden floor and the bare earth meet and lifts her eyes to the ceiling. The wooden beam Eva hanged herself from is no longer there. Andreas removed it after her death. It had no functional purpose; unlike the two supporting beams it was connected to.

The creak of the door becomes that beam creaking with the weight of Eva's body. That sound was one of the first things Quinn noticed that terrible day when she ran down here to find Eva dead and swinging.

She shakes the image away. *Stay calm. Hold the space.*

Sofia stoops to examine the wreath of dried wild roses laid by Holly.

'We never forgot her,' Quinn says. She will never forget the enigmatic tilt of Eva's snapped neck or her bulging eyes.

'I watched her walk down here that day.' Sofia's gaze returns to the ceiling. 'I was sitting at my desk, reading the book Charles gave me, and I watched her walk across the field and into the trees.'

Quinn shivers. She hears the rustling again. Something dark slithering closer.

'I got sleepy, so I had a nap,' Sofia says. 'When I woke and she wasn't in her room, I knew something was wrong. I should have come down sooner.'

'You mustn't blame yourself.' Is it forgiveness Sofia wants? Is that why she came to Pure Heart? 'You were just a child.'

'I don't blame myself.' Sofia fixes her with a chilling stare. 'Not at all.'

Above Quinn's head a sudden, startling movement. A blurry vision of wings. An angel? A demon?

'It's only a bird,' Sofia says.

Quinn looks up again and sees a large jay, squawking and flapping.

Sofia laughs. 'Poor Quinn. You must be feeling the effects now.'

'Effects?'

'The psilocybin. I put a large dose of it in your tea.'

'The tea? But you drank it too.'

'No. I poured some for myself before adding the drugs to the flask.'

Mushrooms. Quinn's heart mutates into the flapping jay and thrashes around in her chest. When Sofia opens the door and sets the jay free, her heart remains trapped.

'I had to find a way to make you face up to yourself,' Sofia says. 'You're never in the wrong, are you?'

'That's very irresponsible, Sofia.' Quinn's voice sounds fearful. 'You've no idea how my body or mind might respond to—'

'Unpleasant, is it?' Sofia asks. 'Someone messing with your body chemistry? With your mind? Drugs are powerful, aren't they?'

Quinn lays a hand on her chest and tries to soothe the little bird trapped inside it. 'I didn't give your mother drugs,' she says. 'I helped her stop taking them.'

'And the withdrawal symptoms messed with her brain chemistry. That's why she hanged herself.'

The floor buckles beneath Quinn's feet. Straightens. Buckles again. Mushrooms. She first took them when she was thirteen years old. In her youth she tried everything except heroin. Twenty years of smoking and snorting and sipping and altering her consciousness in whatever way she could. Looking for spiritual enlightenment not cheap thrills. Her last drug experience was an ayahuasca ceremony in the depths of the Peruvian rainforest. After that life-changing experience, she knew she no longer needed substances to connect with her Higher Self.

You know how to do this, she tells herself. *Do not go to the dark side. Do not let in the fear.* She is not in the ideal mindset for taking hallucinogenic substances, nor is this the ideal setting, but if she relaxes into it, the drug should bring her some kind of insight.

The fear, though. She's not a teenager or a young woman any more. What if her mind and her nervous system don't react well to the trip?

'I'm tired of feeling this way,' Sofia says. 'Grief never ends.'

'Eva wouldn't want you to feel this way.' Quinn believes this. If she can just crack Sofia's hard, cynical veneer and reach the lost soul inside, she can resolve this crazy situation.

'What was I like before it happened?' Sofia says.

'You were a beautiful child.' Quinn strains to see the plump, smiling, girl in the lean, embittered young woman before her, but not even the drugs help with that. 'Warm, kind.'

'Gentle?'

'Always.' Sofia often cared for Eva when she was having one of her bad days. Reading stories to her as Eva lay in bed. Feeding her spoonfuls of nourishing soup.

'You've suffered so much loss,' Quinn says. 'Your mother. Your father.'

'I feel nothing for my father.' Sofia bends down and picks up the wreath of dried roses. 'From what I heard, we were better off without him.'

Quinn stares at the wreath. Are the roses nodding at her? She shakes her head. Tries to centre herself. 'Losing a parent so young was another deeply traumatic experience. I doubt you've ever addressed it.'

Sofia sighs. 'Oh, Quinn. Haven't you realised yet? I've no desire to compete in the Olympiad of Victimhood. I know it's more fashionable than ever to share your deepest wounds with anyone willing to listen but I'm not playing.'

'We all need to heal our—'

'I actually get why you don't want this place to become a retreat. The people who will come here aren't on genuine spiritual quests. They want a quick fix for all their problems. An escape from their everyday lives.' Sofia tosses the wreath aside. 'But you don't need to worry about all that. You'll be dead.'

'I'm not going anywhere.'

'Everyone has a price,' Sofia says. 'I wish that wasn't true, but it is. Perhaps that's partly why I came back here, so I could see if there really are people in the world beyond the temptation of money.'

'That temptation is coming from you.' Quinn tries to swallow but her mouth is too dry. Has her tongue always been this thick? 'Eva would hate how materialistic you've become.'

'My mother had a price too.' Sofia reels round, her face blazing with anger. 'When she eloped with my father, her parents threatened to disinherit her. She said she didn't want the money, but she did. She was a spoilt princess. They offered her a generous allowance but only if she signed a legal document that gave them sole custody of me in the case of her death. She sold me out.'

'I... I didn't know.'

'No. Eva didn't tell anyone that.' Sofia looks up at where the missing beam once rested. 'She sold me out so she'd have enough money to party in Ibiza with a second-rate DJ.'

'She was young,' Quinn says. 'Your father was a bad influence.'

'She wasn't a saint, but how can I judge her? I sold my soul too. I could have escaped my grandparents when I was old enough. I could have made a different life for myself, but I chose not to. I became who they wanted me to be so I could get my hands on the money.'

'The money is your birthright. You can do what you like with it. Transform it into something amazing.'

'Give it to you, you mean?' Sofia laughs. 'The money itself isn't the buzz. It's the power it gives you. People really will do anything for it.'

Quinn feels a sudden urge to liberate her feet. She kicks off her Crocs and tiptoes over the damp, rotting floorboards until she reaches the bare earth in the altar area. She stands still and imagines roots shooting down from her feet into the earth. Deep as a tree. No one will uproot her. This thought steadies her. Then she realises they could cut her down or poison her or—

'I can feel her.' Sofia's arms shoot up in the air. 'My mother's here. She's with us.'

Is she? Quinn squints into the gloom but sees only Sofia swaying side to side, her eyes closed. 'Speak to her,' she says. 'Tell her anything. Speak from the heart.'

Sofia stops swaying and opens her eyes. Cruel peals of laughter echo around the monastery. 'She's not really here. I'm not a lunatic.'

Quinn dips to one side as if blown by a strong wind. She senses a splitting deep inside her, a crack through which a dark, suppressed memory escapes.

Two days before Eva hanged herself, Quinn was with her in her room.

'I do not feel right,' Eva said. 'Maybe I should take the medication again?'

'No,' Quinn said, determined to help Eva stick to her healing path. 'You have to stay strong.'

'I am having suicidal thoughts.' Desperation in Eva's haunted eyes. 'I want to kill myself.'

'You don't want to kill yourself,' Quinn said. 'Your thoughts are symbolic. You want to kill off the sick part of you. The part that's stopping you living your life.'

Now Quinn is back in the monastery with Sofia and her bare feet are sinking into the earth. The earth is sucking her down and she is lying on her back, and she hears the metallic ring of a spade striking stone. The spade glints above her and then all is darkness. She is buried deep in the earth and she scrabbles around and she feels bones. They are her bones, and she thinks: *this is what will happen to me, this is where I will end up. Here alone in the darkness.*

Bones, bones, bones.

60

HOLLY

2019

None of us knew what had happened at the monastery. Not until it was too late. By the time Quinn and Sofia came back from there, it was dark. Quinn looked tired and dazed, but we assumed the ritual had exhausted her. When she said she wanted to go to her room and rest, we respected her wishes.

Sofia said the ritual at the monastery was exactly what she needed, and she promised to tell us more the next day. I was surprised. I didn't think Quinn reminding her of that terrible day was a good idea. Everyone else assumed Quinn had made a breakthrough of some sort and that the grievances of the past had been forgiven.

When Joe and I went to bed that night, he was in an optimistic mood.

'I think Quinn's done it,' he said. 'I think we're going to be okay.'

I smiled, hiding the anxiety churning inside me.

When he turned out the light, I snuggled into him. I wondered if Sofia really had forgiven Quinn. If so, she was a better person than me. I still couldn't forgive my family for their reaction when I told them what Uncle Mike had done to me.

Mike, my father's youngest brother, was only ten years older than me.

He was good-looking and cool, an adventurous traveller with great music taste and an exciting, bohemian life. He was my favourite uncle, and he said I was his favourite niece. When, aged fifteen, I finally found the courage to tell my parents Mike had been sexually abusing me for the past two years, they refused to believe me.

'If this is true,' my father said, 'why did you let it go on so long?'

How could I have explained that then? Each time Mike forced himself on me, I struggled with a complex set of emotions. I didn't want to have sex with him, but I also wanted him to like me. Afterwards, he would hold me and tell me he loved me. He said no one would understand the special bond we had.

'You've always had a crush on Mike,' my mother said. 'This is all just a silly schoolgirl fantasy.'

Not long after that, I heard my father on the phone to Mike, telling him the version of reality I would have to comply with for years.

'Holly's a bit of a mess,' he said. 'She's got this ridiculous crush on you, and she's convinced herself the two of you are having a relationship.'

A month later, Mike went travelling to New Zealand. He met a woman in Auckland and married her and lives there still. My parents were always promising to visit him, but they never did.

After that first Spiritual Restructuring workshop with Quinn in San Antonio, I finally told Joe about my past. He was so tender and understanding. He told me none of it was my fault. and he promised to help me get over it. Every crisis we've faced together, he's always been the strong one. He always knows what to do.

Lying in bed with him after Quinn and Sofia's trip to the monastery, painful memories swirling around my head, I didn't expect to sleep. However, his warm solid presence lulled me into a false sense of security, and I soon lost consciousness.

I didn't know then that neither of us would get to sleep through until dawn.

61

QUINN

2018

Quinn crouches barefoot on the courtyard floor, her heart thrashing in her chest, her blood roaring in her ears like a waterfall. She glances up and sees her makeshift rope – two yoga belts tied together – still dangling from where she secured it to her window frame. Even though it only stretched as far as the top of Mel's window, she was able to let go and land catlike on the flagstones below.

She stands up and puts some weight on her right foot. A dull ache but the ankle is holding up well. She zips up her orange hooded top and checks her small backpack is still attached to her.

All good.

A loud gurgling from the pool. The cicadas' deafening song offends her sensitised ears. The effects of the mushroom trip are wearing off, but she needs to keep her wits about her.

It is almost 4.30 a.m. Still dark enough to give her some cover. She plans to go through the olive grove, to where she can access the land that borders Pure Heart and scramble up to meet the road to Kakopetria. She doesn't know exactly how far Dmitri's surveillance extends but by avoiding Pure Heart property, she hopes to make a clean getaway.

As she darts across the courtyard, a figure appears out of the gloom. She freezes, but it's only a blank-eyed goddess statue. Got to keep moving. Before taking the steps down to the orchard she glances back at her beloved home. The new solar lights are shining on the mural of the Furies. The three vengeful hags stare down at her.

'Ssssh,' she whispers, pressing an index finger against her lips.

She descends to the orchard where the stench of rotting fruit fills the night air. Her legs are shaking but she has to keep moving.

After hallucinating about her own burial, Quinn fled the monastery, hysterical. Dmitri caught her at the entrance to the woods and instructed her to lie on the picnic blanket until she calmed down.

Time folded in on itself. Melted into a gooey substance Quinn couldn't keep hold of. Then she found herself sitting in the armchair in her room with no recollection of how she got there. Aphrodite was nowhere to be seen, but Mel came to visit. She asked a lot of questions, but Quinn feigned exhaustion and asked her to leave.

When she reaches the far end of the orchard, Quinn picks her way down rough stone steps towards the olive grove. She stops to take her barefoot trainers out of her bag and put them on. Before zipping her bag shut again, she checks her passport is still inside. Yes, there it is, next to her wallet.

An owl hoots. The disapproving sound scares her, but she shrugs off her fear and keeps moving.

Sitting in her room earlier, she tried to be rational about what happened in the monastery. Sofia had spiked her tea with mushrooms, and she'd experienced a bad trip. Nothing more. As for the painful memory of Eva that wormed its way to the surface, it needed to be put into context. After Quinn told Eva her suicidal thoughts were only symbolic and that she really wanted to kill off the sick part of herself, Eva sat in silence for a long time.

'You are right, Quinn,' she said eventually. 'I want this dark part of me to disappear.'

'We'll get rid of it together,' Quinn said. 'I promise you.'

Eva grabbed Quinn's face with her hands. 'I do not want to hurt myself. I never want to leave Sofia.'

'I know. I believe you.'

Quinn did believe her. If she'd thought for a second Eva was serious about killing herself, she would have acted differently. She didn't think Eva would ever leave the daughter she loved so much.

Now, in the olive grove, Quinn stops for a moment, entranced by the gnarled branches of the trees. She shakes herself out of it. Spirit has spoken and shown her what to do and now she must act on that guidance.

Back in her room, as she was thinking of Eva, she heard a scratching sound at her door. She hesitated, unsure if the sound was real or another hallucination. When it persisted, she opened the door and found Aphrodite there. Only when the cat padded into the room did Quinn see the dead bird hanging from its mouth. A tiny tree creeper. Aphrodite dropped the offering on the rug and retreated to the sofa, licking her lips.

Quinn knelt beside the dead bird. Entrails spilled from the wound in its stomach. A pink, glistening pile. She peered closer, thinking about the Ancient Greek oracles who read the entrails of birds and animals in search of omens. What did this dead creature have to tell her? The winding, twisting intestines reminded her of something. A road, she decided. A twisting, mountainous road like the one to Kakopetria.

That's when she realised Spirit wanted her to leave Pure Heart.

At the edge of the olive grove, Quinn pauses by the side of her grave. The moon, not yet full, spills pale light into the black hole. For a second, she feels the earth pulling her down and down and down.

She has to leave. By staying here, she is putting temptation in the way of her Pure Heart family. They are good people, and they love her, but they're only human. They don't have her strength of faith. She will sacrifice the home she loves to save them from doing something they will regret.

She isn't frightened. Not in the least.

A rustling in a nearby burnet bush makes her jump. She crosses over a stile into the neighbouring field and begins to run.

62

ZOE

2018

Zoe's eyes open halfway into bright, painful light. What time is it? Has she slept in?

'What the fuck?' Carl stirs beside her. 'Why did you put the light on?'

The overhead light, rarely used, glares down at them.

Zoe opens her eyes fully and sees Dmitri standing at the foot of the bed. Is she having one of her fantasies?

'Get up,' Dmitri says.

'Why?' Zoe sits up, blinking. Definitely not a sex dream. 'What's going on?'

Mel appears behind him, pulling on a burgundy sweatshirt over a crumpled T-shirt. 'It's Quinn.'

Carl rubs his eyes. 'What's happening?'

'She's gone,' Mel says.

Joe and Holly appear in the hallway, bleary-eyed and semi-dressed in pyjama bottoms, hiking boots and hooded tops.

'I told you the monastery was cursed,' Holly says. 'They should never have gone in there.'

'She will not be far,' Dmitri says.

'Sofia gave her mushrooms,' Mel says.

'Psilocybin,' Dmitri says. 'Is very pure.'

Carl lets out a low whistle. 'Shit.'

'How much did Sofia give her?' Zoe asks.

Dmitri shrugs.

'God knows what state she's in,' Mel says.

'I will take the car,' Dmitri says. 'Find her on the road.'

'No.' Mel faces him, shoulders pulled back. 'We'll bring her home.'

63

QUINN

2018

Quinn scurries through what remains of the darkness. A strip of orange already glows on the horizon. There should be some traffic on the road by now. Her plan is to walk in the direction of Kakopetria and hitch a lift as soon as possible. If she can get to Nicosia, she could cross the border into the north of the island or go to the airport. An airport. The thought of it almost makes her turn back. All those people. All that world.

How long will it take for someone to notice she's gone?

Her right foot throbs. Her breath is tight in her chest. As she jogs uphill towards the edge of the neighbouring land, the home she loves is just beside her. The home she must leave. When she finally glimpses the road ahead, a tall, rickety fence stands in her way. She uses one of the rusting fence posts to haul herself up and over the obstacle, stumbling as she lands on the other side.

She bends over. Her thigh muscles are burning. Blood pounds in her ears. As soon as she catches her breath, she strides down the road towards the Pure Heart driveway. When she gets closer, she will step up into the forest so she doesn't appear on any cameras.

She hears voices. Ahead of her, on the road, she sees dancing globes of light. Torches? She darts into the trees. The voices and the lights move closer.

'Quinn?' Mel's voice.

'Where are you?' Joe says.

They have come to find her. She hears the concern in their voices, but she can't trust them. Not for her own sake but for theirs.

A torch beam dazzles her.

'There she is,' cries Zoe. 'Quinn, it's us.'

Panic grips her. She turns and flees into the forest.

* * *

She finds the path she knows so well. This time she is not taking a leisurely hike; this time she is on the run. She tells herself it's only her family behind her, nothing to fear, but instinct has taken over. Her primal self is in control.

She jumps fallen branches and zig-zags between the ancient pines and cedars. She has only the dim dawn light to guide her, but now and then the beams of her pursuers' torches bounce off the trees ahead.

Her chest is on fire. Her eyes blurry. Is she crying? The dawn chorus of the birds is a threatening conspiracy of noise. The jagged stones and clumps of rock beneath her feet keep throwing her off balance.

Not far now until the viewpoint. She is heading for a dead end, but she feels compelled to run towards the place she knows. Even if she wanted to turn back or change direction, the others would find her.

The cries of the Pure Heart family echo in the forest.

Quinn.

Slow down. You'll hurt yourself.

Quinn, you're wasted.

Let us help you.

She is into the canyon now, backpack bouncing against her body. Knees protesting as she scrambles over boulders and jumps the small stream. She doesn't look back. Doesn't need to. She can hear them gaining on her.

Out of the canyon and now comes the steep, narrow path that will lead her to a place of no escape. Gasping not breathing. Skin slippery with sweat. Sharp stabs of pain in her feet, ankles, knees and hips.

Only when she reaches the viewpoint does she register the sunrise spilling into the sky. A pink-orange layer close to the horizon and above it a wash of dazzling yellow. The sky overhead has segued from black to lilac, like a healing bruise. Mesmerised she watches as, millimetre by millimetre, the sun begins its ascent.

'Quinn.'

She turns to see Mel, red-faced, hands on the waist of her burgundy yoga pants.

'Thank God,' Mel says. 'You scared us.'

Carl appears next, Zoe close behind him. Then comes Holly, her breath ragged and noisy. It is a few minutes before Joe brings up the rear. He looks a mess, Quinn thinks. So out of condition. He really should take her advice and lose some weight.

She peers behind them. 'That's it? No Russian hounds?'

'No,' Mel says. 'Just us.'

'I'm surprised they let you come alone.' Quinn wipes sweat from her forehead. 'I suppose Grigor figured out I was gone?'

'Probably,' Joe says. 'Those guys don't miss much.'

'It was me,' Mel admits. 'I raised the alarm.'

'You?' Zoe says.

Quinn shivers. Mel? Why would Mel do that?

Mel steps closer to her. 'I couldn't sleep for worrying about you. I knew something was wrong when you came back from the monastery. I should have seen you were tripping.'

'That was nothing,' Quinn says. 'Teeny amount. A micro-dose.'

'Sofia spiked you,' Mel says.

'Knowing Sofia, it was probably good quality gear,' says Carl.

Holly glares at him. 'It was a reckless thing to do.'

'Aye, bang out of order,' Joe says.

'Not to mention illegal.' Mel's face is a mask of concern. 'I heard you moving about upstairs. I went to check on you, but you weren't there. When I saw your window was open, I realised you'd run off.'

'But why did you raise the alarm?' Quinn is standing with her back to the precipice and a stiff breeze is biting through her hooded top.

'I was scared for you,' Mel says. 'I knew we wouldn't get out of the house without setting off the alarm, so I had to tell Grigor and Dmitri. I'm glad I did because that's when I found out about the mushrooms.'

Quinn swivels her head and examines the dizzying drop below. 'Sofia thinks you're going to kill me.'

No one speaks. A piercing cry from above shatters the silence. Quinn lifts her gaze and is overjoyed to see her Bonelli's eagle, drifting on the currents, its white belly gilded with the light of the rising sun.

'That's just paranoia talking,' Mel says. 'The drugs are still in your system.'

Her eagle. Quinn smiles up at the beautiful bird. Her messenger from Spirit.

When she looks at Mel again, she sees both fear and love in her eyes and she knows Mel was only trying to protect her. Mel, her lucky charm. The one person she can trust.

'If you run,' Zoe says, 'Sofia might come after you.'

'She *will* come after you,' Mel says. 'The safest place for you is with us. Let us look after you until we figure this whole thing out.'

'Until it blows over,' Carl says.

A gust of wind pummels Quinn's chest. If she's not careful, *she* might blow over. A golden shaft of sunlight strikes her face, bringing with it a moment of clarity. She knows now why she is here in this place. At this moment.

She steps towards the edge of the precipice. 'Spirit has spoken. I know what I have to do.'

'Hey,' Mel says. 'Come away from there.'

She needs to test them. She needs to know if she is safe.

'I'm going to jump.' Quinn spreads her arms wide.

'No,' Holly cries.

'It's the only way to save you.' She gazes up at her eagle. So majestic and free. 'That's why I was leaving. I wanted to save you from temptation.'

'You don't need to leave,' Joe says.

'That isn't what we want,' says Carl.

Zoe stays silent.

'I'm going to kill myself now,' Quinn says, 'and save your souls.' She watches the eagle soar and dip. 'To spare you the agonising choice Sofia has given you, I am prepared to sacrifice myself.' She looks at the members of her family, their shocked expressions, the terror in their eyes. 'That's how much I love you.'

'Quinn.' Mel's voice is low and steady. 'Come away from the edge.'

'You can say you pushed me,' Quinn says. 'Sofia won't know, and she won't care. You'll still get the money.'

Stillness descends over the scene. The wind, calmer now, caresses Quinn's face. The sun is peering over the horizon, gifting golden light to the land below. She can almost hear the minds of her community working through the implications of her words. As the silence stretches out, she senses the abyss at her back. When she takes a step towards it, panic seizes her by the throat.

'No,' Holly says, 'please don't jump.' Joe reaches for her hand, but she shakes it off. 'Please, Quinn.'

'Come with us.' Mel reaches out a hand. 'You've nothing to fear.'

'We're honourable people,' Carl says.

'No one here wants you to die.' Mel steps forward and before Quinn can resist, she grabs hold of her shoulders and pulls her away from the edge.

Quinn's legs collapse beneath her, but Mel holds her up.

'I've got you,' Mel says.

The others crowd round, until they are one group embrace. They are hugging Quinn so tightly she can hardly breathe but it feels wonderful. She knows that together they have passed a test from the universe. Maybe it was only the drugs that made her blow everything out of proportion. She needs to come down from this trip and then they can all discuss how to move forward.

'You still believe in me, don't you?' she says, but the group's embrace smothers her words until she gives up and surrenders to it.

64

ZOE

2018

'Lock Quinn in her room?' Zoe says to Mel, who is sitting opposite her at the dining table. The same thought did cross her mind as she and the others escorted Quinn down the mountain trail and back to Pure Heart an hour ago, but she's surprised Mel of all people has suggested the measure.

'For her own safety.' Mel rubs her eyes with the heels of her hands. 'Who knows how long the drugs will stay in her system.'

Carl, sitting beside Zoe, interlaces his fingers and cracks his knuckles. 'We can't risk her hurting herself.'

'Do we even have keys to the rooms?' Zoe asks.

'I spoke to Dmitri,' Mel says. 'He's got a padlock and they're fitting it now.'

'That sounds sensible,' Carl says.

'I've insisted we'll keep the key,' Mel says. 'By we, I mean me.'

Zoe knows Mel doesn't trust them. Perhaps her raising the alarm and locking Quinn in is just her way of protecting Quinn from everyone else.

Holly traipses over to the table, bearing a tray of hot drinks. Joe is close behind with a plate of buttered toast.

'Cappuccino for you,' Holly says in a flat voice, placing a mug topped with frothy milk down in front of Mel.

'Since when do you drink coffee?' Zoe asks.

Mel glares at her. 'It's been a somewhat stressful morning.' Her first sip leaves a faint foam moustache on her upper lip. For some reason it makes Zoe want to giggle. Hysteria builds within her. She fears it might spill out, but Aphrodite saves her by jumping onto her lap.

'Hello, you.' Zoe scratches her beneath her chin. Seeing Quinn in such a bad state must have unnerved the poor creature.

Holly and Joe settle at the table. Zoe is shocked by how gaunt and distressed Holly looks. The drama of it all – chasing Quinn through the trees, the punishing climb to the viewpoint, that terrifying moment when it really looked like Quinn would jump.

If she had jumped, it would all be over now and none of them would have done anything wrong. Zoe knows this isn't totally true, but it feels good to tell herself that. 'She was out of her mind,' she says. 'All that stuff about sacrificing herself. She sounded nuts.'

'That's how much she loves this place,' Mel says. 'That's how much she believes.'

Zoe clears her throat. 'I don't feel safe around her any more. I haven't done for a while.'

'What's that supposed to mean?' Mel asks.

'At least I'm honest enough to admit it,' Zoe says.

'I think what Zoe means,' Carl says, 'is that Sofia being here has given us all an opportunity to reassess a few things.'

'Like your writing career?' Mel says.

'Enough.' Joe reaches for a piece of toast. 'We can't afford to fight amongst ourselves.' He bites into the toast with a loud crunch.

'How can you even think about eating at a time like this?' Holly says.

Joe swallows. 'One of us has to keep our strength up.'

The curtness of their exchange unsettles Zoe. Holly and Joe rarely bicker.

The door to the kitchen opens. Dmitri enters, Sofia close behind him, glowing and unruffled in her white yoga outfit.

'Dmitri filled me in on your mountain-top drama,' Sofia says. 'Quite the morning you've had.'

'This isn't a game,' Mel says. 'We were lucky to get to Quinn before she jumped.'

'Were you?' Sofia leans over Joe's shoulder and grabs a piece of toast. 'Wouldn't that have made life easier for you?' She bites off a chunk of the toast. 'This is so good,' she says, her mouth full. 'I thought all that only happened in movies. People on drugs thinking they can fly.' She stretches out both arms and spins round the kitchen, coming to rest against one of the workstations.

As far as Zoe can tell, Sofia feels no remorse for drugging Quinn.

'You should have pushed her when you had the chance.' Sofia pulls off another hunk of toast with her fingers.

'I could never do that,' Holly says.

'None of you were tempted to give her a little shove?' Sofia's high, tinkling laugh rings out in the kitchen. 'A tiny little shove?'

'No,' Mel says. 'We had the ideal circumstances, but we didn't do it. That should tell you all you need to know.'

Sofia rolls the bread between her fingers forming a greasy, doughy ball. 'Shame. One quick push and it would all have been over. Now you'll have to find another way.'

Mel pushes her coffee away. 'We're not going to—'

'Poor Quinn.' Sofia rolls the ball of dough back and forth. 'I don't blame her for freaking out in the monastery. I had nightmares last night and I wasn't even on any drugs.'

'You shouldn't have gone in there,' Holly says.

'I won't be going again,' Sofia tells her, 'and neither will anyone else. I've decided to have it pulled down.'

'What?' Zoe says.

'You can't do that,' declares Joe.

'No, you can't,' Holly says. 'It's a holy building.'

Sofia crushes the dough between her fingers. 'It's a ruin. No one will miss it.'

Holly's eyes widen. 'But—'

'I own this place; I can do what I want.' Sofia turns to Dmitri. 'Find me a company that will come and tear it down. As soon as possible.'

He nods and turns to leave, holding the kitchen door open for Sofia. She drops the ball of bread on the floor and giggles when, out of nowhere, a black kitten appears and pounces on it.

'I do have a life to get back to and a rather large company to run,' she says. 'My offer won't last forever.'

'Even if it did, we wouldn't accept it,' Mel says.

'I hope you're not waiting for a miracle to save you? Quinn's miracle days are over, I'm afraid.' Sofia strides across the kitchen and pauses in the doorway. 'I suggest you all think about what you want for this community and its future.' She smiles. 'And remember, time is running out.'

65

HOLLY

2019

Flight. That's why Quinn ran. A natural physiological response to danger. Or perceived danger, in this case. I hate to think of her running scared from us. We only wanted to bring her home. I still shudder when I recall her standing at the edge of the ravine, threatening to throw herself off. She was obviously out of her mind on mushrooms, but it seemed to me as if Eva's spirit had possessed her in the monastery and filled her head with suicidal thoughts.

I also don't doubt Quinn meant what she said about sacrificing herself for us. She would have done it if we'd let her. We were all terrified, watching her teeter on the precipice. Shocked into silence. I remember being the first to cry out, but I don't recall what I said. I only knew I couldn't be responsible for another death at Pure Heart.

Flight. When I went to Ibiza for that graduation holiday, I didn't even realise I was running away. I didn't understand I'd been running since I was thirteen years old.

I was still running when I came to Pure Heart. For a while I thought I'd escaped the past, but no matter how hard and how fast you run, it always catches up with you.

PART IV

66

QUINN

2018

Time is still fluid after her trip to the monastery, but Quinn is sure almost two days have passed since she tried to leave Pure Heart and she knows it is now late morning. The door is always locked, but she hasn't protested. She is tired, very tired and, despite the recent drama, often finds herself slipping into deep, dreamless sleep.

She isn't always alone. Aphrodite is let in from time to time, although she doesn't stay long. The others bring her trays of food; Joe has been preparing all her favourites. This morning she had apricots on top of her Greek yoghurt. Finely sliced and arranged in the shape of a fan. Local honey drizzled on top.

Mel comes most often, of course. Each time, she apologises for having to lock Quinn in. Each time she explains it's for Quinn's safety. *I couldn't bear anything to happen to you.* At some point, Quinn will ask them to let her out again, but she can understand how worried everyone is after what happened. They only want what's best for her.

During her last visit, Mel said Sofia is going to pull down the monastery. A crew are coming from Nicosia the day after tomorrow. Maybe something good did come from their visit to that sad ruin. Maybe Sofia is finally letting go of the past? Quinn hopes so. She is weary. Very weary.

She has a vague memory of Mel saying something important before she went to the monastery. Something about finding a way out of the situation. Mel hasn't mentioned anything since, so perhaps she imagined it.

Not that she needs a way out. After what happened on the mountain, she should surely feel safe? Her community members could have let her jump off the cliff and claimed their prize, but they didn't. Doesn't that prove she was right to test them? Doesn't that prove their hearts are pure?

The memory of her feet on the edge of the cliff gives her vertigo. She knows, theoretically, that death is a beginning not an end, and yet, when she threatened to throw herself into the ravine, she was terrified. She always thought she would face death with dignity, certain of reincarnation, but instead she wanted to cling to life with every atom of her physical body.

She remembers Tom Quinn preaching about the crucifixion of Christ. He often pointed out that the Lord's son wasn't thrilled about dying in agony on the cross. If even Jesus feared death, Quinn can't blame herself for being human.

Her window is open although the mesh screen is secured with a clasp and padlock. None of the usual sounds of her community can be heard. No one splashing in the pool. No meals being eaten in the courtyard. Now and then she hears doors slam shut. A distant babble of voices. Earlier she saw Joe and Holly off to work in the garden, clutching spades and hessian sacks.

She turns away from the window. Where is Aphrodite? She could do with her cat's warm body and satisfied purr. Not fair to keep her locked up in here though. Overcome by a rush of vulnerability, she clutches at the Pure Heart necklace Blake gave her. She's been wearing it since returning from the monastery. She wishes he was here to look after her. She felt safe in his arms, with his warm hands massaging her back. None of this would be happening if he were still here.

Anger uncoils inside her. She tries to breathe it out. It isn't fair to be angry at Blake for wanting his freedom. She knew from the start how complex he was.

She glances down at the bracelet on her right wrist. The one Andreas gave her with the evil eye charm. She can't help wishing he was here too.

Returning to her armchair, she tells herself to get a grip of her fears. This country is getting to her. This country with its history of conflict and division. The current situation of occupation. She thinks of all the stories Andreas told her about the 1974 invasion. Neighbour turning on neighbour. Hand-to-hand fighting in the streets. Andreas attacked and injured by his best friend. People you love can turn on you, he used to say.

No, she thinks. That will not happen to her. Not here. Not at Pure Heart.

67

ZOE

2018

Lunchtime. Zoe and Sofia are relaxing in wicker chairs on the wooden balcony of a junior suite in the Mill Hotel in Kakopetria. The two of them wear matching white cotton robes and are sipping on glasses of cold, crisp Cypriot white wine.

From her seat, Zoe has a stunning view of the mountains and pine forests in the distance and the village of Kakopetria below. A maze of narrow streets flanked with traditional stone cottages, all with terracotta tiled roofs and wooden balconies. The Mill Hotel, a large, timbered building dating from the seventeenth century, is raised up above the village and Zoe can also see what passes as the centre of town, a cluster of modern buildings and the main road winding past them.

The town is busy today. Day trippers negotiate the narrow, cobbled streets, snapping pictures of the houses. A steady stream of cars passes through the town and drivers compete for parking spaces in the centre.

Dmitri slides open the doors to the balcony. 'They will bring lunch in half an hour.'

'Thanks,' Sofia says.

Zoe feels Dmitri's eyes travel over her before he closes the balcony door again and sits on one of the suite's armchairs. What would happen if Sofia were to leave the two of them alone? She imagines herself walking up to Dmitri's chair, slipping off her robe and lowering herself onto him.

Sofia stretches out her long, tanned legs. 'It's so good to get away.'

'Yes.' Zoe takes another sip of wine. The alcohol is a welcome antidote to their recent stresses. In fact, sitting here, out in the 'real' world, it seems absurd to think that three days ago she was chasing Quinn up a mountain trail. Absurd to think Sofia spiked the community's leader with mushrooms and definitely absurd to think Sofia wants Quinn dead.

She inhales the clean mountain air. After the intensity of the past few days, she feels like a prisoner released. This morning, Sofia asked Zoe to accompany her on a trip out. She needed a pamper day and didn't want to go alone. Purely pleasure, Sofia assured her, nothing to do with what was going on in the community. Zoe doesn't believe that. Sofia always has an agenda.

Mel disapproved of the excursion. No surprise there. Carl, Joe and Holly thought it would be a good opportunity for Zoe to see where Sofia's head is at. Joe was keen for Zoe to find out if Sofia will really go ahead with demolishing the monastery tomorrow.

When they arrived at the Mill Hotel, Zoe found two beauticians from a five-star hotel in Limassol waiting for them. Sofia had them driven in for the morning and insisted Zoe join her for a massage, facial, manicure and pedicure.

Zoe can't help admiring her glossy red fingernails and toenails. Her shiny face feels clean and polished. Her body is still absorbing the fragrant massage oils. The whole morning reminded her of the preparation she had to do for TV appearances or music video shoots. So much fuss for just a few minutes of film. So much pressure to be flawless.

That was a lifetime ago. She's a different person now.

While Sofia flicks through a copy of *Vogue* she found in the hotel lobby, Zoe stares at the view before her. So many cars in town. She sees a Land Rover with tinted windows pull up near the bank and wonders for a moment if Grigor has come to fetch them. A man emerges from the front passenger side, dressed in a black suit. He is tall with bleached white hair and looks familiar. Zoe realises she saw him at Dionysus by the Sea that night. He was the bodyguard of the old Russian guy who talked to Sofia. Roman Timchenko. Perhaps he and his wife have taken a drive into the mountains to escape the August heat.

'So busy here.' Sofia lowers her magazine and peers into the crowded street below. 'A spiritual retreat in this area could attract a lot of people. The air, the connection to nature.'

'I thought today was just pleasure?'

'Everything is always business.' Sofia drains the last of her wine. 'Property prices in this area are going up again. More people want to spend time here.'

Sofia is right. The mountain villages have regained some of their former popularity in recent years.

'The renovations wouldn't need to be excessive,' Sofia says. 'A new swimming pool, maybe. Some daybeds in the orchard and the olive grove. There are so many chill places for people to hang out.'

Zoe pictures herself reclining on a daybed in the orchard during cherry blossom month.

#newideasblossoming #pureheart

'You'll need to get the accommodation sorted first,' Sofia says. 'Obviously, you'll have some rooms in the main building, but you'll need to put up some yurts or glamping pods. Once I've got rid of the monastery you could even build accommodation there.'

That answers Joe's question, Zoe thinks. Once Sofia makes her mind up about something, she follows through. 'You really think the retreat idea could work?'

'The cult of wellness is big business.' Sofia's fingertips touch her smooth, glowing cheeks. 'Bigger than religion these days. Everyone is desperate to be their best self and live the longest, healthiest life possible.'

'What's wrong with that?'

'It's an obsession and obsessions can be dangerous.' Sofia shrugs. 'But they can also be exploited.' She examines her pink, manicured nails. 'The super-rich won't come to you, Pure Heart's not sophisticated enough, but with the right advertising you could get rich people keen to experience simplicity and you'll definitely get lonely, stressed career types looking for somewhere to belong for a week or two.'

'You talk as though the retreat is inevitable?'

'As Quinn would say, believe and it will happen.' Sofia's lips press together in a tight smile. 'I suppose she thinks that only applies to the miracles she wants.'

'But we—'

'Obviously you'll have to get some proper qualifications,' Sofia says. 'Yoga, tantra, whatever, but that won't take long and think how much fun it would be. You could travel abroad to do courses, meet new people.'

Zoe has seen Tantra teacher training courses advertised all over the world.

#reclaimingmyinnergoddess #meetingthebestpeople

'I'm flattered you think I can do all this, but—'

'With my money you could do it all.'

'Your money isn't free. What you're asking us to do for it is... it's a lot.'

Sofia looks down at her hands. In the silence, Zoe hears the river below the hotel gushing over the limestone boulders in its path. When Sofia looks up, Zoe is surprised to see real fragility on her exquisite face.

'What am I doing?' Sofia says. 'Am I crazy?'

Zoe, confused, puts down her wine glass. 'What do you mean?'

'Maybe I am like my mother? It's crazy, isn't it? What I'm asking you to do?'

What the hell is happening? Is Sofia about to change her mind about everything? Zoe is reminded of Eva's dramatic mood swings. Has this whole plan of Sofia's just been a rich girl's whim? Could she be about to leave Pure Heart and take her offer with her?

A hollow sensation unfurls in Zoe's chest. She has reached the line, but does she dare cross it? 'What about justice?' she says eventually.

'Is it justice?' Sofia's voice is strained.

Another silence stretches between them. Zoe senses the importance of any words she might say, and the pressure makes her throat constrict. She should really agree with Sofia and persuade her to abandon her plan.

'Is it?' Sofia asks.

Zoe clears her throat. 'I understand why you feel the way you do,' she says. 'I understand why you need to make things right.'

She feels like she's in the grip of a strange, disturbing dream. One where she does scary and unsettling things but feels safe because she knows it is only a dream.

Sofia nods. 'Eva would be proud of me, wouldn't she?'

'Yes, I think she would.'

'Thank you.' Sofia gives her a grateful look. 'Yes. Money for justice. A fair transaction.'

If this was a dream, Zoe thinks, if this was a world without consequence, what would she say next? She shifts in her seat. 'Not everyone feels able to give you that justice.'

'You're talking about Mel?'

'She's not open to a change of leadership.'

'Still under Quinn's spell, is she?'

'Quinn believes in her. Trusts her.'

'Quinn believes in everyone. That's her superpower. She makes everyone feel special.'

Zoe can't argue with that. She knows what it's like to have Quinn look deep into your eyes and tell you how beautiful your soul is.

'That's why your retreat will be a success,' Sofia says. 'People say they want enlightenment but all they really want is for someone to tell them they're special.' She gets up from her chair. 'You don't have to worry about Mel. Trust me.' She reaches out a long, slender arm and taps on the balcony doors. When Dmitri opens them, she speaks to him in Russian. He disappears and soon returns clutching a printed A4 document in a clear plastic folder.

'For you.' He hands it to Zoe. When she takes it, his fingers brush against hers.

'Thank you.' An intense surge of heat between her legs makes her press her thighs together. She glances at the cover page of the document.

Background Report: Melanie Harris

'My investigator told me there's still more to come,' Sofia says. 'He's trying to trace Mel's ex-boyfriends, but this will give you plenty of ammunition for now.' She nods at the report. 'I think you'll find it an interesting read.'

68

ZOE

2018

Zoe arrives back from Kakopetria with Sofia in the late afternoon. She goes straight to her rooms, hoping to find Carl, but he and his notebook are gone.

She hides the report Sofia gave her under her mattress. She'll tell Carl about it first and then show it to Joe and Holly. Before heading out again, she admires her reflection in the full-length mirror in the bedroom. After a long and boozy lunch, a stylist from Limassol called Maria arrived at the suite, laden with bags of clothing Sofia had ordered. *Let the shops come to us.* Amazing what money can buy. Amongst the outfits were several Sofia had ordered with Zoe in mind. Zoe protested at the generosity, but in the end selected the dress she has on now. A black silk slip with thin straps. The luxurious fabric clings to Zoe's curves and reaches down to the silver Grecian sandals Sofia had ordered in her size. Before they left the hotel, Sofia applied glossy red lipstick to Zoe's lips. The same shade as her nail polish. Zoe hardly recognises herself.

She finds Carl in the orchard. He is sitting at the wrought-iron table, captivated by the story spilling forth from his pen onto the page. When she slides her arms around his neck, he lets out a startled cry and looks around him, as if confused to find himself in the real world.

His confusion intensifies as his eyes slide over her revamped appearance. 'Wow,' he says finally, confusion giving way to approval. 'Just... wow.' He beckons her to him for a kiss. He tastes of coffee and tobacco. 'That's quite the pamper day.'

She takes the seat opposite him. Pulls it closer to the table. 'It wasn't all pleasure.' She tells him about the report on Mel and gives him a summary of its contents.

Carl leans back in the chair and rests his head in his clasped hands. 'Detective Inspector Mel has been a naughty girl.'

'I haven't told Joe and Holly yet.'

'Mel will have to concede the moral high ground – that's for sure.'

If Mel really wanted to stop Sofia's plans, she could have reported the events at Pure Heart to the police at any time, but she hasn't. Zoe used to think that was out of respect for Quinn but now she knows Mel has plenty of reasons to want to stay in the community. 'Sofia gave the report to me because she thinks we can use it.'

Carl nods. 'I expect we can.'

In the quiet that grows between them, Zoe hears the greedy insistent buzz of the wasps crawling over the rotting apricots nearby. 'Sofia won't give up on this,' she says. She wonders if, without her encouragement at the hotel, Sofia might have given up. Or at least had serious doubts about what she was doing. 'She wants justice.'

'And, in the end, Quinn was sort of responsible for Eva's death.' Carl drums his fingers on the cover of his notebook. 'Eva was in withdrawal from those meds and that made her kill herself. There's no one else to blame.'

He gazes at the ground and Zoe knows he's thinking about the night before Eva's death. The two of them lying in bed, kissing and touching each other when a familiar knock at the door interrupted them. Tap tap tap. Eva outside, wanting to join them. Lately, her visits had been less about pleasure and more about comfort. Sometimes she cried while the two of them held her. That night, Carl looked at Zoe and shook his head.

'I can't handle Eva tonight,' he said.

Zoe nodded her agreement. 'Me neither.'

She felt relief when the tapping at the door stopped. Relief because no matter how much she enjoyed sex with Eva and no matter how much she told herself true love was not possessive, she couldn't stop jealousy writhing inside her when Eva guided Carl's head between her long and perfect legs.

'Hey.' Carl reaches for her hand across the table. 'You okay?'

'Yes.'

'There's no one else to blame.'

'I know,' she says. For months after Eva's death, she wondered if they could have provided enough comfort to get her through that next day. She'll never know, and this isn't the time to dwell on the past. The future is still undecided and the chance to take control of it could easily slip away. 'Sofia really thinks we could make this place a successful retreat.'

'We could. With you in charge.'

Zoe thinks about the dead bird in the pool and the snake. Portents of regeneration and rebirth. 'I think I could do a good job of it.'

'You would.'

'And you're going to write a brilliant novel. Even better than your first.'

'I think I just might. I certainly want to see how this story turns out.'

'So do I.'

His eyes lock onto hers. She spies a wolfish hunger in them.

'If we accept Sofia's offer, there won't be any turning back,' she says.

'I don't want to turn back. Do you?'

'No.'

Gazing into Carl's eyes, she feels a spark of heat low in her belly. The sense of deep connection she's been longing for. As if they are truly seeing each other for the very first time.

Even when the black, four-legged drone appears and hovers over them, its irritating buzz disrupting the early evening peace, they cannot take their eyes off each other.

'I bet that's Dmitri,' Carl says.

Zoe nods. 'Probably.'

'You think about fucking him, don't you?'

'Yes.'

Carl gets up from his chair and kneels in front of hers. 'That's very bad behaviour.'

'I know. Someone should punish me.'

She gasps as Carl yanks her dress up her thighs, revealing the black lace underwear Sofia insisted on giving her. 'Yes,' she says as he pulls the underwear aside and slides two fingers deep inside her. She tries to shift her hips, but his other hand reaches up and grips the base of her throat, pinning her in place.

'Punishment is exactly what you fucking deserve,' Carl says.

The drone hovers for a moment. The thought of Dmitri watching her brings Zoe to the brink of orgasm. When the drone darts away, her tortured scream of pleasure chases it into the approaching twilight.

69

QUINN

2018

Something is happening. For the past half an hour, Quinn has heard raised voices in the house. Grigor next door in his room speaking Russian on his phone. Doors slamming. She has watched from her window as first Mel and Carl and then Zoe and Sofia hurried across the courtyard and disappeared into the orchard below.

It is not yet 9 p.m. but stars already speckle the sky. The cicadas' song is as rhythmic and urgent as always. A gang of cats brawl below Quinn's window.

Is she alone in the house?

Aphrodite sits on the armchair, her front feet pressed prissily together. Quinn is sure there is suspicion in her cat's green eyes.

What is going on out there?

Such a quiet day until now. She took a shower this morning and changed into clean orange yoga pants and an orange T-shirt. At lunchtime she had a short visit from Mel, during which Quinn learned Sofia and Zoe had gone into Kakopetria that morning. A pamper day, Mel said, with sarcastic emphasis on the word *pamper*. The news unsettled Quinn. She once thought Zoe might be a good influence on Sofia, but now she's not so sure.

Is their trip out connected with all this commotion? Why is a dark dread rising up inside her?

A metallic clinking from the other side of her door. The rattle of keys.

'It is me.' Grigor pushes the door open. 'Come.'

'Where?' The dark dread curls around her heart. 'Where are you taking me?'

He hesitates. 'There is something you must see.'

* * *

The last place Quinn wants to go is the monastery. When Grigor revealed their destination, she protested, but he insisted she accompany him. The others are waiting and have something to show her.

As they cross the arid land towards the trees where the monastery hides, Quinn's hallucination comes back to her. Sinking into the earth. Meeting her own bones.

Her heart smashes against her ribs. She's having a flashback – that's all. She just has to ride it out.

A voice in her head whispers a warning. *They are going to do it now. This will be the place.*

That would be fitting, wouldn't it? Sofia would enjoy watching her die in the same place Eva did.

So dark in the trees, but as they approach the monastery, she sees light through one of the broken windows. Someone is sobbing. Voices rise in urgent conference.

'What's going on?' she asks Grigor.

'Is better you see.'

When he pushes open the monastery door, Quinn is confronted by a disorientating scene. Holly is slumped against the left-hand wall of the space, deep sobs rattling her whole body. Joe crouches beside her, a desolate look on his face. When they see Quinn come in, Holly crumples against her husband, as if avoiding Quinn's gaze.

At the far end of the monastery, where the bare earth marks what was once the altar space, is a strange tableau. Dmitri and Mel are holding two large, bright torches. Beams of light illuminate a shallow hole in the earth. Two discarded spades and several hessian sacks lie nearby, close to where Carl, Zoe and Sofia are standing in a tight, stunned cluster.

'What's going on?' Quinn says.

Mel lowers her torch. 'I'm afraid there's something you need to see.'

Something about Mel's tone, official but gentle, makes Quinn wary. The tone Mel might have used in her former police career to break bad news to someone.

Why does the monastery look like a crime scene? The lights, the heaped mounds of earth.

The dark dread returns. When Mel takes her elbow and steers her to where Dmitri is shining his light, Quinn wants to flee.

When she reaches the hole, she doesn't see anything at first. Dry soil, stones, dead and twisted roots.

Mel raises her torch and Quinn sees two long, white bones, covered with tattered shreds of denim. Leg bones. She squints. Now she sees a ribcage.

'A body?' she says. Is this what she saw during her mushroom trip? Not her bones but these bones. Not her body, but this dead body.

Have they discovered one of the Cypriot people who went missing during the invasion? Others have been found in this area. They should contact the Committee on Missing Persons.

A silver chain glints around the skeleton's neck. Quinn's hand reaches to her own necklace. The one Blake gave her.

She drops to her knees and scrapes away dirt until she can pull the necklace round and read the inscription on the pendant.

Αγνή καρδιά

'Blake?' She looks up at Mel. 'It's him, isn't it?'

'Yes.' Mel's torch now lights up the corpse's skull. Empty sockets, grinning jaw.

A howl escapes Quinn's lips. She lays her hands on her dead lover's chest, like she used to when he was alive, and she wanted to heal his wounded heart.

'I'm sorry,' Holly says.

Quinn's head snaps round. 'What for?'

'I see them on the drone coming down here.' Dmitri points at Holly and Joe. 'They have spades and bags. When they don't come back, I come here and find them digging.'

'We can explain,' Joe says.

Quinn springs to her feet. 'What did you do to him?'

'I'm going back to the house,' Sofia says, 'I can't bear to be here any more.' She nods at Grigor who moves towards the monastery door and opens it.

'We must postpone the demolition crew until we sort this,' Dmitri says.

Sofia nods her agreement. 'Don't worry,' she tells Holly. 'This doesn't have to go any further.'

She sweeps out of the door. Grigor follows. The door creaks shut behind him.

'Let's sit down.' Mel ushers Quinn away from the grave.

Shaking with shock, Quinn lets herself be led to the centre of the space. She drops to her knees. Waits for someone to speak.

'It was nine years ago,' Joe says. 'You'd gone back to the UK for your mother's funeral. Carl and Zoe were away camping up the west coast. There were a few others still here then, but they'd gone to Limassol for a carnival. Blake stayed behind.'

'It was just the three of us.' Holly sits up, wiping her face. Her eyes are red and swollen, her expression haunted. 'Let me tell it,' she says to Joe.

Quinn is shivering. Mel takes off her burgundy sweatshirt and drapes it over Quinn's shoulders.

'Blake had been acting strange around me,' Holly says. 'I never felt comfortable when I was on my own with him.'

'You weren't the only one,' Zoe says.

Carl nods his agreement. 'I loathed the guy.'

'I did try and tell you,' Holly says, 'but you didn't take me seriously.'

'We all told you we didn't like him,' Joe says to Quinn, 'a number of times.'

Quinn remembers their complaints. She knew Blake could rub people up the wrong way, but she urged the community to make allowances for him. His troubled past called for compassion.

'This is hard.' Holly rubs her eyes. 'The day it happened, I came down here to lay flowers for Eva. I didn't know Blake had followed me. He pretended he was just out walking and happened to see me come in here, but I knew he was lying.' Another sob chokes out of her. 'He made a pass at me and when I told him to back off, he... he got nasty. He... he—'

'He attacked her,' Joe says.

'He started tearing at my clothes,' Holly continues. 'He said he wanted to be inside me. He pushed me down on the ground.'

Quinn doesn't want to believe this story, but she's never known Holly to lie. 'Something came over me.' Holly's eyes, wild in the torchlight, roam around the monastery as if watching her past self in action. 'I was so full of rage. There was a rock on the ground. Near my hand. Like Spirit had placed it there.'

Quinn doesn't want to hear any more. She can imagine what happened next. Holly, her past trauma triggered by the attack. Acting on instinct. Doing everything she could to prevent the same thing happening again.

'I don't remember doing it,' Holly says. 'It's like I blacked out and then I was sitting on the floor next to him and I had blood on my hands.'

A surge of happiness overwhelms Quinn. Blake didn't leave her. He didn't abandon their love like she thought. Then comes a sharp drop in her guts. He didn't leave but he is dead. He is dead and he did betray her. In the worst way possible. 'He must have been in a very dark place,' she says.

'No.' Zoe steps forward. 'You don't get to excuse him.'

'Did you know?' Quinn asks her. She turns to Carl. 'Did you?'

'Neither of us knew,' Zoe says. 'We found out tonight, just like you.'

Dmitri bends down to examine Blake's remains. He reaches into the shallow grave and tilts the skull one way then the other.

'You shouldn't be doing that.' Quinn looks pleadingly at Mel. 'Isn't this a crime scene? He shouldn't be touching it.'

'I'm not sure you should rely on Mel to preserve evidence,' Zoe says.

'What happened to Holly was a crime,' Carl says.

'What would the police make of all this?' Joe asks Mel.

Mel sighs. 'Hard to say. You don't have any physical evidence of the assault on Holly. It wasn't reported at the time and even if it had been there was no penetration.'

Holly moans. 'He was going to. I know he was.'

'I don't doubt you,' Mel says. 'But anyone looking at that skull can see you hit him more than once. Long after he must have been unconscious. That makes it harder to plead self-defence. And then you hid the body.'

'That was my idea,' Joe says. 'I was trying to protect her.'

'It doesn't look good,' Mel says.

'We were going to move the body,' Joe explains. 'When Sofia said she was going to tear this place down, we thought it was the safest thing to do.'

Quinn thinks of the number of times Joe and Holly have pledged their loyalty to her and to Pure Heart since Sofia's arrival. *This is our home. We can never leave here.*

'I'm sorry, Quinn,' Holly says. 'I'm so very, very sorry.'

70

HOLLY

2019

Fight. A natural physiological response to danger. I didn't know I was capable of it until Blake attacked me. I'd never fought before – not against Uncle Mike and not with my parents when they told me I was lying. When Blake had me down on the ground and I heard him unzip his jeans, one clear thought swirled around in my mind. *Not this time. Not this time not this time not this time.*

Afterwards, I helped Joe bury him. It felt like the right thing to do. The only thing to do. Who can think clearly in a situation like that? Psychopaths maybe, but we were two ordinary people doing their best to deal with an extraordinary situation.

We tried to leave Pure Heart. After six weeks of us lying to the community and me suffering nightmares and anxiety attacks, we bought a cheap camper van and told everyone we were going to travel around the Greek islands for a month. We planned to just keep going. A life on the road. A life on the run for a crime yet to be discovered.

That was the problem. I hoped being away would stop me thinking about the attack and about Blake's decomposing corpse, but I became even more anxious. What if his body was discovered? What if Charles decided to sell off some of the land to a developer? So much could go wrong. In the end, we decided to return to Pure Heart where we could at least have some control over our fate.

As the months and years passed, we grew used to our situation. We had to give up our dream of starting a family. No way we could bring a child into our world after what we'd done. We made regular trips to the monastery to check our secret was still safe and to lay flowers both for Blake and Eva. Pure Heart was our home, but it also became my prison. I told myself that was what I deserved.

71

ZOE

2018

Less than an hour after Dmitri and Mel escorted Quinn from the monastery back to her room, the remaining Pure Heart members and Grigor are in the yurt. Flasks of coffee and mountain tea, a bottle of single-malt whisky and an assortment of cups and glasses are arranged on a fold-down table. As if the yurt is the centre of a police enquiry in some sleepy village.

'Talisker.' Grigor examines the label on the whisky bottle. 'Good stuff.'

'Do you want some?' Zoe asks.

Grigor shakes his head. 'I go back to the house.'

'You're leaving?' Carl says.

'You have much to discuss,' Grigor says. 'I will not set the alarm until you return to the house.'

'We're not choosing the next pope.' Mel stomps into the yurt. 'We'll be back soon. We just need some time to debrief. Recalibrate.'

'Whatever you say.' Grigor steps out into the darkness and closes the yurt door.

When Zoe volunteers to fetch drinks for everyone, Mel steps in to help her. Tea and whisky for Joe and Holly. Coffee for Carl. Zoe wonders if this is Mel in police mode. How many dead bodies did she see in her years on the force? Thanks to the report Sofia gave her, Zoe knows Mel's calm, professional exterior hides a woman with questionable ethics.

Zoe pours a coffee for herself. Mel does the same and, to Zoe's surprise, adds a splash of whisky to it.

'I could drink a bottle of whisky in one session back in the day,' says Carl with a sigh.

Zoe, who desperately wants a drop of whisky in her coffee, declines the bottle when it comes her way, not wanting Carl to feel left out. The warm mug is comforting in her hands. Grasping it tight, she joins the others on the floor. Out of habit they have formed a circle, the usual set-up for a community meeting.

'I don't want to go to prison,' Holly says. She is sitting between Joe's legs, his strong arms around her.

'You won't.' Joe kisses the top of her head. 'I won't let that happen.' When he picks up his glass of whisky, Zoe notices his hand is shaking.

Holly knocks back her shot of Talisker in one go.

Carl clears his throat. 'We heard what Mel said. If this does get reported to the police, they're unlikely to take Holly's side.'

Joe stares at each of them in turn. 'Who's going to report it?'

'You heard Sofia,' Zoe says quietly. 'She told Holly this matter doesn't need to go any further.'

Holly moans. 'Sofia will report it if we don't... if we won't—'

'If we don't accept her offer,' Mel says.

'Deep breaths, love,' Joe tells his wife. 'You need to stay calm.' He looks around the circle. 'I'm sorry we put everyone in this position. We thought by moving the body we could avoid this.'

It is still surreal to Zoe that these two people, the most stable and reliable in Pure Heart's history, killed a man and covered it up.

'Did no one ever come looking for Blake?' Mel asks. 'What about family or friends?'

'He grew up in care homes,' Joe replies. 'He never knew his dad, and he was estranged from his mum.'

'And he wasn't exactly good at making friends,' Carl says.

Mel nods slowly. 'A perfect victim.'

'If Quinn had listened when we complained about him none of this would have happened,' Joe says.

Silence greets his words. Zoe knows she and everyone else is thinking the same thing.

'She was obsessed with the guy.' Joe's broad face is flushed and animated. 'She was so busy shagging him she didn't give Eva the help she needed. No wonder Eva killed herself.'

'I don't think that's a fair connection,' Mel says.

'I think Joe's spot on,' says Zoe.

'What if Quinn tries to report his death?' Carl asks.

'How can she?' Mel says. 'She's locked in her room.'

'That was your idea,' Zoe points out.

Mel's face glows with righteous anger. 'To keep her safe from you.'

'Quinn wouldn't report me.' Holly hangs her head. 'She'll understand why it happened. That's what makes this even worse.'

The whisky passes around the circle again. This time Zoe takes a slug straight from the bottle.

'Holly and I can't leave here,' Joe says. 'Do you understand what I'm saying?'

'I didn't want this,' Holly says. 'Honestly.'

Joe gets to his feet. 'The good of the community comes before individual desires. That's one of our rules and Quinn broke it. She was so infatuated with Blake, she put him before the rest of us. She wasn't thinking about the community or what would be good for it.'

A cold fury saturates Joe's voice. Zoe has never seen him this angry. She knows he will do anything to protect his wife.

'Christ knows what Blake would have done to Holly that day,' he says. 'The guy was capable of anything.'

'I don't doubt that,' Carl says.

'It's time for us to put our community before the individual.' Joe looks around the circle. 'I say we accept Sofia's offer.'

A fluttering sensation in Zoe's chest. Joe, of all people, saying the words she thought she'd have to say herself.

'You do remember what that offer entails?' Mel says.

Joe nods. 'Yes. We have to kill Quinn.'

In the hush that follows his words, a creature of some kind scurries over the roof of the yurt.

'I'd do the same for any of you,' Joe says. 'You know that.'

Holly stares into her empty glass. 'I don't deserve this support. I killed a man.'

'And you've paid the price every day, I'm sure,' Zoe says.

'You've no idea,' says Joe.

'Must be a tough one to live with,' says Carl.

'And you think killing Quinn will be easy to live with?' Mel groans with frustration. 'You think you'll just carry on unaffected?'

'Some days it's almost impossible to live with what I've done,' Holly says. 'Other days it's like it never happened.'

Zoe crosses the circle and crouches in front of Holly. 'If we do what Joe says, we'll never have to leave. We can build over the monastery. Cover up everything.'

'Maybe this is all *moira*,' says Carl.

'Moira?' Mel frowns. 'Who's Moira?'

'Not the name,' Carl says. 'The Greek word, *moira*. It means fate.' He glances at Zoe. 'The ancient Greeks totally believed in fate. Maybe that's what's happening here. This chain of events was put in motion a long time ago. All of us are caught up in Quinn and Sofia's destinies. We're like a chorus in a Greek tragedy. Here to witness.'

'You don't just want to witness events,' Mel says, 'you want to kill Quinn.'

Joe strokes Holly's hair. 'No one *wants* to kill her.'

'What if Quinn was right?' Zoe says. 'What if Sofia coming here *is* the miracle we prayed for? Her offer might not look like the abundance we hoped for but what if there's a greater plan going on here? One we can't see clearly just now.'

She glances at Carl. His eyes shimmer with fear and admiration.

'Wouldn't that be convenient?' Mel says.

Holly wipes her nose with the back of her hand. 'Do you really think so, Zoe?'

'It's bullshit, Holly,' Mel says. 'Zoe and Carl want the money and you and Joe don't want to end up in jail. At least be honest.'

'Okay.' Zoe puts down her cup and springs to her feet. 'Let's all be honest.' She strolls across the room and retrieves Sofia's report from behind the wood burner where she left it earlier.

'What's that?' Mel says.

Zoe drops the report on the floor in front of Mel on her way back to her place in the circle. No one speaks. Mel's hands shake as she opens the report and skims the first page. The silence remains until Mel has flicked through every page and tossed the report on the floor again.

'Have you all seen this?' Mel's eyes glitter with a cold, hard fury.

Carl nods. 'Zoe showed it to me this afternoon.'

'Me and Holly looked at it before you came in,' Joe says.

Mel gets to her feet. At first, Zoe thinks she might storm out but instead she walks slowly around the circle. Her face is flushed. The veins in her neck are taut.

'I didn't share this to discredit you,' Zoe says. 'I just think we should all acknowledge the mistakes we've made.'

'Knowing you're not perfect makes you more human somehow,' Carl says.

'None of you can imagine the pressures of that job,' Mel says. 'The things I saw. The people I had to deal with.'

'You were unlucky,' Zoe says. 'You didn't intend to get involved with that gang.'

'Yeah, I bet you don't fuck with guys like that,' Carl says.

'When they found out I'd been busted, they wanted to make sure I wouldn't grass them up,' Mel says. 'I was lucky to get away with a beating. They could have killed me.'

'And you were in an abusive relationship at the time as well,' Holly says. 'That must have been tough?'

Mel buries her head in her hands. 'My relationship didn't help.'

'No wonder you wanted to hide out here with us,' Carl says.

'We won't hold your mistakes against you,' Joe promises. 'We're not like that.'

Mel drops her hands. 'What about Quinn's mistakes? Does she deserve to die for them?'

'That's different,' Zoe says. 'Eva was vulnerable, and Quinn failed her.'

'Quinn took advantage of all our vulnerabilities,' Carl says. 'All of us met Quinn when we were at our lowest. Including you, Mel.'

'She helped me,' Mel says. 'She saw something in me.'

'So do we,' Zoe says.

'Even after reading that report?'

'We love and accept the real you.' Zoe hopes she sounds sincere. 'Not the version of you that fits Quinn's narrative. Yes, she's good at making people feel special, but you've got to feel it for yourself.' All her life Zoe has relied on validation from other people but now, for the first time ever, she truly believes she is special. 'These circumstances are challenging, but they also offer a chance for real transformation and growth.'

'Quinn loves me. I know she does.' Mel continues her orbit around them, veering away then coming closer again. As if she wants to escape the circle's pull but can't quite find the strength.

'Do you want to go back to the life you had before?' Zoe asks.

'No,' Mel says, 'but that doesn't mean I'll kill to stay here.'

'What if this is all part of your spiritual path?' Zoe says.

'Even if Quinn was indirectly responsible for Eva's death,' Mel says, 'our sin in killing her would be much greater.'

'Quinn is dangerous,' Zoe says. 'Look at how careless she was with Eva's mental health. Look at the position she put poor Holly in.'

'Let's vote on it,' Carl suggests. 'All those in favour.'

Zoe's hand floats up into the air and stays there. Carl and Joe raise theirs in unison. Holly lifts her arm slowly, as if it is unbearably heavy.

Mel stops pacing and stands frozen at the periphery of the circle.

'Mel?' Zoe says.

'I joined the police because I thought I could help people,' Mel says. 'I thought I could make a difference, but I soon had my illusions shattered. When I came here, I thought I'd found somewhere pure at last. Somewhere I could learn to be good.'

'Are you with us?' Zoe says.

'Fuck.' Mel bolts for the door and darts out into the night. 'Fuck.'

72

QUINN

2018

Quinn sits alone on the faded rug in her living room. The door is locked. Over an hour has passed since Dmitri brought her back here. What is happening down at the monastery? What are the others doing?

She can't erase the image of Blake's bones from her mind. His ribcage picked clean by time and earthworms. She must have known he was there when she was tripping on mushrooms with Sofia. His bones were calling out to her. She saw them beneath the soil.

She is still swinging between elation at knowing he didn't leave her and despair he will never return.

And shame because of what he did to Holly.

She doesn't doubt Holly. She wishes she could. Holly and Blake – two damaged people in the wrong place at the wrong time. Quinn's mission to heal the needy has not come without consequences.

She wants to believe Blake momentarily lost himself. As did Holly.

Why didn't she see it coming?

For the first time since Sofia's arrival, despair takes over her. She is sure Joe and Holly will do whatever it takes to cover up Blake's death.

What should she do now?

Her Tarot cards sit on her desk, wrapped up in their purple velvet cloth. Her heart lifts when she remembers the Death card. Was the card warning her about Blake's death? Not Andreas' and not her own?

The now familiar rattle of the padlock being released.

'Who is it?' Quinn's pulse slows a little when she hears Mel's voice on the other side of the door.

Mel slips into the room. Before the door closes, Quinn peers out into the corridor, hoping to see Aphrodite's sleek, familiar form, but there is no sign of her feline companion.

A familiar smell drifts in with Mel. Mildew and sandalwood.

'You've been in the yurt?' Quinn says. 'Was there a meeting?'

'Yes.' Mel places a half-empty bottle of Talisker on the coffee table and two tumblers. 'For our nerves.'

Quinn insists she doesn't need alcohol but is secretly pleased when Mel ignores her and pours shots in both glasses.

'Here.' Mel hands her a glass. 'You've had a terrible shock.'

The detective inspector, dealing with a bereaved person. Dealing with the aftermath of a crime. Or was it an accident? Quinn still isn't sure.

She braves a sip of whisky. The amber liquid scalds the back of her throat and makes her cough. How many years since she had a drink?

Mel drains her glass and wipes her mouth with the back of her hand.

'Tell me about the meeting,' Quinn says. 'What did you discuss?'

Mel refills her glass. 'How to proceed.'

Quinn's second sip of whisky slides down easier than the first. 'How is Holly?'

'She's a mess.' Mel leans back in the armchair, her cold blue eyes searching Quinn's face. 'Is it true what they said? That they complained to you about Blake?'

'People were always complaining about one thing or another. When you're in charge you get used to it. You can't please everyone.'

'Sounds like everyone knew he was bad news apart from you.'

'No,' Quinn snaps. 'It wasn't like that.' She inhales deeply, tries to recover her composure. What could Mel possibly understand about running a community like Pure Heart? 'Sorry,' she says. 'I'm in shock.' She puts her whisky aside. 'The situation was complicated.'

'Sounds straightforward to me.'

Quinn has never seen Mel like this before. Distant and cold and critical. Fear snakes around her heart. 'They're going to accept the offer, aren't they?'

'There's too much at stake now. If Holly and Joe don't play ball, Sofia will report Blake's death. She pretty much said so.'

'After all I've done for them.'

'I'm not sure they've got a choice.'

'There's always a choice. They aren't strong like us. Sometimes I think you're the strongest of us all.'

Mel downs her second whisky. 'I'm not strong.'

'The other day you said something about finding a way out of this situation. What did you mean?'

Mel shakes her head. 'I'm as weak as the rest of them. Why would you want to be saved by me?'

Quinn kneels by the armchair and puts her hands on Mel's muscular thighs. 'Look at me.' When Mel turns her cool gaze on her, Quinn tries not to flinch. 'You're nothing like them. You're a pure and beautiful soul.'

Mel gives her a sad smile. 'I like the way I look in your eyes. That's why I chose to stay at Pure Heart.'

'The way you look to me is the way you really are.'

'You've no idea who I really am.'

'I've seen deep inside you. I've seen the wonderful—'

'No.' Mel brushes Quinn's hands away. 'You've got no idea.' She reaches for the whisky bottle. 'Sofia does though, and she told Zoe and now everybody knows.'

'What?' Quinn says. 'What do they know?'

'Do you really think I'm a good person?'

'Yes.'

'I want to trust you.'

'You can.'

Mel sighs. 'Okay. In the past, before I came here, I used to gamble.'

'Lots of people do.'

'No, this was bad.'

Quinn sits on the floor, arms wrapped around her knees as Mel talks about her past. The growing gambling addiction. Losing her savings. Borrowing money from her family.

The soft, compassionate expression on Quinn's face doesn't change but inside she is angry and confused. Why didn't her intuition pick this up? Mel has been lying to her all this time, but, as Quinn knows from experience, addicts are accomplished liars. It's normal for people to hide what they're ashamed of. She shouldn't hold that against Mel.

She listens without interrupting until Mel stops to top up her whisky. 'You had an addiction,' she says. 'It wasn't your fault.'

'At first it was just a way of decompressing from the job. I never meant for it to get out of hand.'

'I believe you.' Quinn's gaze returns to her desk and her bundle of Tarot cards. A memory rushes back to her, dispersing her confusion and filling her heart with a bright, white light. 'The Gambler,' she says.

'What?'

'The Tarot card. The one you picked out.'

'Oh. That.' Mel takes a slug of whisky. 'I think the universe was trying to warn you about me.'

'It was a good omen. You're the good luck I need.'

'My history should tell you I'm not the lucky type.'

'I'd bet on you any day.'

'I want to be honest with you. There's more you need to know.'

'You can tell me anything,' Quinn says, elated by the memory of the Tarot card and what she thinks it represents.

As the next stage of Mel's confession unfolds, this elation evaporates and Quinn finds herself taking a furtive sip of whisky. Bribery and corruption? Organised crime? The encouraging smile on her face is getting harder to maintain, but she doesn't want her mounting disappointment to show.

'So you see,' Mel says, when her story comes to an end. 'I'm not a good person.'

Quinn rises to her knees and places her hands on the arms of the chair. She must choose her next words carefully. 'To live in the light, we must embrace the darkness,' she says, quoting one of Pure Heart's rules.

'Healing is not about denying our shadow side. We have to integrate it into the light if we want to be whole.'

Mel's eyes fill with grateful tears. 'You're the only person I know who accepts me as I really am.'

Quinn may have found the right words, but when Mel leans in and kisses her, she recoils, her body betraying her true feelings.

'I knew it.' Mel sinks back in the chair. 'You find me repulsive.'

'No... I... you caught me by surprise.'

'You don't think I'm a good person.'

'Everyone makes mistakes. All that's in the past.'

'No, it's not. My past has come back, and it will affect what happens next.'

'We could run away together, just like you suggested,' Quinn says. 'Is that what you meant when you said you'd found a way out of this?'

'I've taken some big risks for you, and I was happy to because I loved you.' Mel shakes her head. 'I thought you loved me.'

'I do.' Quinn takes Mel's face in her hands and kisses her. Mel's tongue is unexpectedly soft and delicate, her breath smoky with whisky. Quinn lets herself be pulled onto Mel's lap and when Mel slips a hand beneath her orange T-shirt to seek out a breast, she doesn't resist.

'No.' Mel breaks away. 'You don't want to do this.'

'I do.' Quinn leans in for another kiss, but Mel turns her head.

'You don't want me,' she says. 'Not really.' When she pushes Quinn from her lap, Quinn loses her balance and falls from the chair. She lands on her wrist and cries out as a sharp pain shoots from her wrist up to her elbow.

'Shit. Are you okay?' Mel is on the floor beside her, helping her sit up.

'It's okay.' Quinn twists and flexes her wrist. 'I just landed badly on it.'

'This is what I do.' Mel's voice is laden with self-pity. She jumps to her feet and backs away from Quinn. 'I hurt people.'

'I'm fine.'

'Even as a kid, I had this really weird feeling. Like it was dangerous for people to be around me.'

'It was an accident.'

Mel chokes back a sob. 'That's what my ex used to say.'

Of course. Mel's abusive partner left her with such low self-esteem she can't help seeing herself as bad. Unlovable.

'What your ex did to you was wrong,' Quinn says. 'You're not to blame.'

'I am. It was my fault.'

'Victims often blame themselves. It's very common.'

Tears stain Mel's cheeks. Quinn hates seeing her look so hurt.

'Forget him, Mel,' she says. 'Let's talk about us.'

Mel retreats towards the door. 'I wish I was the person you want me to be.'

'You are.' Quinn swallows down a surge of panic as Mel unlocks the door.

'Or maybe I wish you didn't know who I really am.'

'Mel. Please.'

'It's too late,' Mel says. 'I can't stop what's going to happen.'

'I believe in you,' Quinn says, as the door shuts, and the padlock clicks into place. 'Really, I do.'

Insight Investigators: Background Report

Melanie Harris (Mel): The situation with Keith, the ex-boyfriend, is not a pretty story. These types of relationships never are. I thought it best not to initiate any direct contact with Keith, but a quick social media search led me to his older sister Jacqui's Facebook profile. Under an old photograph of Jacqui with Keith and Mel, someone had commented how happy Mel and Keith looked. Jacqui's reply: *He's happier now she's gone. Total psycho bitch.*

Jacqui, as it turns out, had no qualms about meeting me to discuss Mel. She wasn't even bothered when I told her someone had paid me to investigate Mel's background. She allowed me to record the conversation, hoping it might help someone else avoid Mel's clutches. Extracts of the conversation below:

I liked Mel at first. I was impressed by her job, and she was modest and funny and seemed like she really wanted to make the world a better place. Keith's a social worker with kids in care. He's a genuinely good, sensitive guy and at first, I thought she was perfect for him. She said she'd just come out of an abusive relationship, and she really appreciated how lovely Keith was. He talked about her all the time. How amazing she was. How special. How strong. 'The cult of Mel' I came to call it but, like I say, I fell for her act too at first. I even approved when Keith said she was moving in with him four months into the relationship.

Keith was usually a really chilled and happy guy, but after a while I noticed he was tense and withdrawn all the time. He was always tired too. Said he was having trouble sleeping. He was usually so sociable, but he wasn't seeing his friends as much. At first, he wouldn't admit anything was wrong, but we've always been close and eventually I got him to admit he was having problems with Mel. He said it was his fault for not understanding the pressure she was under at work.

When I saw them together, I could see how easily she manipulated him. He was always on eggshells around her. Once I overheard her berating him for something trivial he'd done wrong... mixing up the recycling or something... and she was so vicious. Another time I saw her talking about some guy at work she had a strong 'connection' with. Another officer she admired. I could tell from Keith's reaction she'd talked about him before and that it made Keith feel insecure. It's a thing, you know. Triangulation. Abusers like her do it to create competition in the relationship. Keep the other person keen for their attention.

To be honest there was so much stuff I'd be here all night if I told you everything. It started to get really bad when I found out he'd lent her money. He said it was to help her clear some credit card debts her last boyfriend left her with. Later I found out it was for her gambling debts. Then one day I went round to see him and found him in a total state. She'd hit him. He said it was an accident. They were arguing – his fault for not giving her the support she needed after a tough day at work – and he was standing in the wrong place when she lashed out. Seriously, that's what he said.

I insisted he tell her to leave, or I would. I was so relieved when he rang the next day and said she'd gone to stay with a friend. Two days later, I turned up at his flat and she was there. She had bruises all over her face and marks around her neck as if someone had tried to strangle her. For a minute I thought Keith had lost it and attacked her. Would I have blamed him?

When I asked if she was in trouble with some money lenders, she got really angry. Those cold eyes of hers... they really creeped me out. She said her injuries were work-related. Something about a gang targeting her and she'd had to resign for her own safety and to protect Keith. Like she was some kind of hero. I told her she was full of shit and to get the fuck out of my brother's house.

She told Keith she was going away for a few weeks' holiday, but he hasn't heard from her since. I'm glad. His head's still in pieces about it. There are times he still doubts his version of events and thinks it was all his fault. That's how these things go though, isn't it? The guilty one always pretends to be the victim.

74

ZOE

2018

'Sorry about the mess,' Quinn says. 'I've been doing some thinking.'

Zoe takes in Quinn's chaotic living room. Books scattered across the floor and piled up on the armchair. *The Yogi's Way, The Shamanic Heart, A Guide to Reincarnation.*

'Sometimes the hardest journey of all is to go within,' Quinn says. Dark pouches of skin sag beneath her bloodshot eyes. Her unshaven scalp bristles with tufts of silver hair. It is now mid-morning and Zoe wonders if Quinn has slept at all since they found Blake's body last night.

Yet despite her dishevelled appearance, Quinn is a point of tranquillity in the messy room. Her aura placid and unruffled. 'You've made your decision,' she says.

Zoe nods. Unlike Quinn, she intends to take full responsibility for her actions. 'Mel told you?'

'Yes.' Quinn's small, agile body sways.

'Maybe you should sit down?' Zoe says, concerned Quinn is about to fall over.

'That's very thoughtful of you, Zoe. Thank you.' Quinn removes a pile of books from her armchair and sits down as instructed. 'That's better.'

Quinn's calm manner is unnerving. Zoe is sure it's an act, and she wishes Quinn would drop it. This would all somehow be easier if Quinn was cowering before her.

'Have you told Sofia?' Quinn asks.

'Yes. This morning.' When Sofia joined them in the kitchen at break-fast time, Zoe announced their decision. She wasn't sure how Sofia would react. Would she gloat? Celebrate? Weep? Sofia greeted the news with a curt nod and, before leaving the room, told them they should do it soon.

'Was Mel there?' Quinn asks.

'Yes.'

'What did she say?'

'She said she would do what was best for the community.' Seeing Mel humbled didn't give Zoe as much pleasure as she'd imagined. In the kitchen this morning, Mel looked tired and sad and somewhat pathetic.

Quinn's face pales. 'I see.'

'I'm afraid Mel isn't who we thought she was. Sofia had a full back-ground check done on her. You can read it if you like?'

'She told me about her past. I know everything.'

'Really?' Mel couldn't have enjoyed that fall from grace.

'The past is the past. She's a changed person.'

Zoe suspects that's what Quinn needs to believe just now.

'Mel has honour in her soul,' Quinn says. 'She has no idea how special she is.'

Zoe fights off a surge of envy. 'Mel's no better or worse than the rest of us. And she won't save you.'

'That's up to the universe now. There's nothing I can do to influence events.'

Does she mean that? Zoe isn't sure.

'It won't be as easy as you think,' Quinn says.

Zoe swallows. They haven't decided yet how to do what Sofia is asking of them. Making the decision has been enough for now.

'Not that.' Quinn's green eyes narrow. 'I don't know what that part of it will be like. I'm talking about leading.'

'We haven't discussed a new leader,' Zoe says. 'It won't be that kind of hierarchy.'

'Pure Heart is a hierarchy? I thought we were a community?'

'*Your* community.'

'And soon it will be yours.' Quinn smiles. 'It's fine, Zoe. I always knew you'd step into your power one day. It's what I've always wanted for you.'

Quinn's benevolence is freaking Zoe out. Has she misjudged her? The fear must be there, beneath the mask of serenity. She wants to pull the mask off and see what Quinn is really feeling.

'That frightened girl you once were has vanished,' Quinn says.

Vanished? Zoe has a mask on too. She doesn't want the frightened girl that still exists inside her to make an appearance.

'When I die, you'll have to deal with the consequences on your own,' Quinn says. 'I won't be here to advise you.'

When I die. The reality of what they are about to do curls tight around Zoe's heart. She can no longer pretend this is a disturbing dream. It is time to wake up.

'I know you think I'm responsible for Eva's death and for what Blake did to Holly,' Quinn says, 'but all I'm guilty of is following my beliefs. You think I'm outdated, and my time is over, but one day someone will come for you. A younger woman who will point out your mistakes and judge you mercilessly for them.'

'I don't doubt it,' Zoe says, although she's given that possibility no thought.

'Now that I've had all night to think,' Quinn says, 'I think I've worked it out.'

'Worked what out?'

'I thought I'd misread the signs, but I haven't.' Quinn's eyes light up with a manic zeal. 'Not at all.'

'What do you mean?'

'We prayed for help and Sofia came to us. We hoped she would offer us financial abundance and she did.' Quinn is aglow with wonder at her own thoughts. 'But now I see she came here to offer us an abundance of growth and learning. To test us.'

'You're saying this is a test and we've failed it?' Zoe says.

'Perhaps I'm meant to die for you. If that's what Spirit wants, I'll do it willingly.'

Zoe's brain is spinning, trying to keep up with Quinn's latest take on reality. 'This is nothing to do with Spirit. Sofia wants justice for Eva's death.'

'If we truly are a soul family and we've reincarnated together over many lifetimes, then we chose this path for ourselves. We wanted this to happen.'

Zoe stares at Quinn. Does she really believe what she's saying? The woman's ability to reframe the narrative has always frustrated Zoe but perhaps in these circumstances it could be a blessing. She sees now that Quinn's serenity is a sign of her delusions, not her strength.

'If I must be sacrificed for you to grow then so be it.' Quinn presses her hands together in a prayer position. 'It's the only explanation I can think of.'

'I suppose the signs have led us here,' Zoe says gravely. 'No one understands these things more clearly than you.'

'I meant what I said up at the viewpoint. I love you so much I would die for you.'

Quinn's certainty is infectious, and Zoe's old conditioning creeps in. It's tempting to believe a version of events that would exonerate their actions and lead Quinn peacefully to her death.

'If I truly believe death to be a rebirth,' Quinn says, 'then it's time to put that belief into action. We'll make a ceremony of it. A fitting ritual.'

'Of course.' Zoe executes a solemn, ceremonial bow. 'We wouldn't have it any other way.'

75

HOLLY

2019

It sounds strange now, but as soon as the decision was made, we began dealing with the arrangements as though we were planning any other community event. We didn't discuss how we would do it, not straight away, but we did have practical matters to sort out. I suppose focusing on logistics prevented us from facing the reality of what we were about to do.

Ritual was everything at Pure Heart, so we weren't surprised Quinn wanted to make a ceremony of her death. We assured her that whatever we decided to do would be in keeping with community tradition. She did make one non-negotiable request. She wanted her ashes to be scattered at Pure Heart, in the grave she'd dug for herself. Sofia promised to pay for Quinn's body to be flown back to the UK for cremation and to ensure her ashes would be returned to us.

During her conversation with Zoe, Quinn suggested the ceremony should take place in two days' time when there would be a full moon to bring magic to the occasion.

When we discovered there was a summer storm forecast for that night, we considered postponing the event.

'No,' Mel said when we discussed it at the kitchen table. 'It has to be that night.'

'Why?' Zoe asked. 'What difference will it make?'

'That's the night Quinn wants,' Mel said. 'Also, if we leave it any longer, I might change my mind.'

I excused myself then. I ran to my bathroom and was violently sick. Afterwards, I sat on the bathroom floor, sweating. I told myself the ritual would be over soon and then we would be ready to meet the future, whatever it might bring.

76

QUINN

2018

It is almost time. The ceremony is due to start at 10 p.m., which means someone will come for Quinn soon. She examines herself in the mirror over the bathroom sink. For the first time in years, she wishes for a full-length mirror. She wants to see all of the body she is about to vacate. She has spent decades investigating the body-soul connection and shortly she will know what happens when they are separated.

Her head is freshly shaved. She is wearing her orange wrap-around dress and her ceremonial jewellery. She has asked for these trinkets to be buried with her ashes. She did ask if Blake's bones could be buried with her but that isn't allowed. He has been reburied deep in the earth beneath the monastery and will be concealed by the concrete foundations of whatever her community build after she's gone.

She drifts into her bedroom. The bed is neatly made. Will these rooms remain empty for long? What will happen to her possessions when she is gone? Does it matter? She has no attachment to them. No attachment to anything. She floats through to the living room. She feels detached from her body already. When did she last eat a proper meal? Grigor came in this morning to say Joe would cook anything she wanted for dinner, but she requested only dates and toasted almonds. She's only eaten a handful of these, washed down with a glass of water. She is cleansing her vessel. She has requested cacao as part of the ceremony and has been assured they will all drink a preparation of the highest quality.

The air streaming in through her living room window is charged and muggy. There is a summer storm forecast and this afternoon, when Grigor took her for a walk around the courtyard, Quinn saw clouds massing behind the mountains.

Panic seals her throat but she swallows it down. Whatever happens tonight, she will not give in to fear. If Spirit is giving her the ultimate test, she will not fail. Her willingness to submit to the community will be the greatest act of faith of her life.

That doesn't mean she's stopped believing in miracles. She spent most of yesterday lying on the floor, sending waves of loving energy to Mel in her room below. Not because she is refusing to accept her fate but because she cannot be entirely sure what Spirit intends until it happens. At sunrise this morning, she unwrapped her Tarot cards, shuffled them and allowed herself to pick one final card. Heart thudding, she turned it over to see a multi-coloured wheel.

The Gambler.

She remembered Mel's ambiguous words to Zoe. *I'll do what I think is best for the community.*

What if Mel thinks opposing the community is the best thing for it? There is still time. Still time for Mel to believe in the pure heart that beats within her.

Only Spirit can guide Mel now.

Below her, Mel's bedroom door slams shut. Quinn's heart pinballs around her chest. She waits. She imagines the sound of Mel's footsteps approaching and the rattle as the padlock is removed. She pictures Mel opening the door and beckoning her over. *Hurry*, she will say, her voice low and urgent. *I'm getting you out of here.*

She hears footsteps. When the knock at the door comes, she finds she is holding her breath.

When the door opens it is Grigor standing there, not Mel.

'It is time.' His tone is as neutral as always.

'What will you do when this is all over?' she says.

He shrugs. 'I will keep doing my job.'

How fortunate she has been in this lifetime not to have to sacrifice her conscience and her ethics for work. 'I don't hold anything against you, Grigor,' she says.

Outside a startling clap of thunder reverberates in the night sky.

Grigor nods. 'It is time.'

* * *

When Grigor ushers Quinn into the yurt, the first scent she inhales is burnt sage. Someone must have cleansed the space. A tremor passes through her. She tells herself to stay strong.

The yurt is set up as it would be for any night-time event or community meeting. Cushions in a circle on the floor with a small cup in front of each. Thick church candles everywhere, their flames glimmering.

Where are the other Pure Heart members?

Sofia appears before her in a flowing white dress and gold Grecian sandals, a flute of champagne in her hand. 'Quinny. So pleased you could join us.' The candlelight catches the diamonds in her ears and on her long, elegant fingers.

'Hello.' Quinn's voice trembles. She clears her throat. Even at this moment, she must lead. She must show them she is ready to die for the principles she has lived by. Her heart throbs. She suddenly feels trapped by the image she has created of herself.

Dmitri steps inside the yurt. 'They are ready.'

'Why don't you take your seat?' Sofia gestures to the cushion at the centre of the circle.

Quinn obeys Sofia and claims her allotted place. Through the open door comes Aphrodite, head held high. Quinn calls her name, but the cat ignores her and strolls over to the wood burner. There she lies down, her green eyes trained on the circle of cushions.

Dmitri hands Sofia a large thermos flask. After unscrewing the lid, Sofia makes solemn progress around the circle, filling each cup with a steaming brown liquid.

'Don't worry,' she says when she gets to Quinn, 'this stuff isn't spiked.'

Maybe, Quinn thinks as Sofia moves away, all this might be easier if it were. She still doesn't know what the community have in mind for her. She thought it better to stay ignorant until the moment arrives.

Another roll of thunder. A movement at the door catches her attention. One by one the members of her Pure Heart family enter the yurt, wearing outfits Quinn has never seen before. Identical white tunics, loose white cotton trousers and white masks. Masks like those worn by members of a Greek chorus. Wide eyes, open mouth. She'd like to think the costumes show her Pure Heart family has respected her request for ritual and will treat this ceremony with the utmost respect. Yet even though she can easily identify each person, the effect of the costumes is disorientating. Where are the faces of the people she knows so well? Masks not only conceal, they also liberate. Inhibitions can be shed. People can lose themselves.

The community members take their places in the circle. Sofia retreats to a chair near the wood burner, flanked by Grigor and Dmitri. Quinn can see both men have their guns strapped below their waistcoats. They can't intend to shoot her? They need to do something cleaner than that. Something that won't look suspicious.

A dead weight at the pit of her stomach.

Zoe sits directly across from her. Mel is on Quinn's right, at the periphery of her vision. Mel's masked face hangs towards the floor, but her posture is tense and upright.

The Gambler.

Zoe lifts her cup. 'Drink.'

All of them, Quinn included, lift their cups. The bitter liquid scalds her throat. Is this really the last time she will ever taste it?

'Quinn,' Sofia says, 'do you accept the judgement your community has passed on you?'

Quinn places the cup on the ground. Her family aren't judging her. They know she never intended anyone any harm, but they are weaker than her. Still, what good will it do to argue now? 'I do.'

'Members of Pure Heart,' Sofia says, 'do you commit willingly to what you are about to do?'

'We do,' they chorus. Mel's voice, lagging behind the others, is barely a whisper.

Quinn struggles for breath. As if all the air has been drained out of the yurt. She looks at Sofia and sees only Eva. Beautiful, broken Eva. Will Sofia's mother be waiting for her in the next life?

She mustn't think like this. She must be strong.

'I want you all to know I forgive you,' she says. 'And I want you to know I still believe in miracles. There is a meaning in this invisible to us at this moment.'

'Your community are betraying you for money,' Sofia says. 'Nothing more.'

Zoe gets to her feet. 'We are here tonight to honour Quinn and to guide her into the next phase of her existence.' She adjusts her mask. 'We are also here to honour one of Pure Heart's most important rules. "To live in the light, we must embrace the darkness".'

Quinn wonders how long Zoe has been rehearsing her speech for.

'We must be guided by this rule tonight,' Zoe says. 'We must face our shadow selves. We must look into the darkness so we can emerge into the light.'

The combination of Zoe's rehearsed speech and the theatrical masks make Quinn feel like she is in a play. As if what is about to happen will not be real and at the end of it, she will be very much alive.

'Fuck this.' Mel pulls off her mask. Her face is red and glistening with sweat, but her blue eyes are as glacial as ever. 'Not like this.'

A tense silence fills the yurt. Thunder rolls overhead. The remaining masked faces turn to one another and then to Zoe, seeking guidance.

'These masks symbolise the destruction of our egos,' Zoe says. 'They show us—'

'I'm not going to hide.' Mel looks at Quinn. 'I don't need to hide from myself.'

Quinn feels a dangerous rush of hope. Has Mel realised she no longer needs to hide from her pure and beautiful soul?

'We're going to play a game of trust.' Zoe moves into the circle, pulls something from her tunic pocket and drops it in front of Quinn.

A black silk blindfold.

'Put it on,' Zoe says.

Quinn sees now how this will play out. She can almost feel their hands pressing down on her chest. Will it be like drowning?

Sofia rises from her chair and walks closer to the circle. 'Don't worry, Quinny,' she says, 'I'm not taking part. I just want to make sure I've got a good view.'

Quinn picks up the blindfold and ties it around her head. She thinks of the time Blake put the blindfold on her one night and fucked her right here, on the floor of the yurt. Will he too be waiting for her on the other side? When she has dissolved into the pure white light of universal consciousness?

She hears a chair being dragged across the floor. She hears another roar of thunder, closer than the previous ones. Then the first patter of rain on the roof of the yurt.

When instructed to stand she obeys. Hands guide her onto the chair. The scents of sage and incense and human sweat mingle in her nostrils.

'When you're ready to fall, we will catch you,' Zoe says.

Quinn raises her arms and launches herself into the air. She is light. So very light. She wouldn't care if she fell to the ground but no, their arms are there to catch her. A woven net of limbs lowers her to the ground.

Their hands pressing down on her chest. The combined weight of her soul family, squeezing her out of herself. She summons her years of discipline and spiritual training. She must relax and allow herself to merge with Spirit. The moment of her passing will be peaceful and holy.

Her body has other ideas. While she is contemplating her radiant transition into the next world, she begins to thrash about. Her arms are pinned by her sides, but her legs kick out and she bucks against the weight crushing her chest. All she can think about is air. She wants to breathe. She wants to live. She has made a terrible mistake. Only an abyss awaits her and she has been wrong, so wrong. These people are bad people and she is dying for nothing. Nothing.

Then comes a peal of thunder, followed by a sound like a car backfiring. The hands lift from her chest and air floods her lungs.

Why is everyone screaming?

77

HOLLY

2019

It was in the middle of our ceremony that the terrible events of that night began. The police investigation and the media reports made the story of what happened into a linear, logical one but at the time it was chaos.

There was a storm that night. Thunder and heavy rain and, at the exact moment a streak of lightning split the sky, four figures dressed in black, their faces hidden by black balaclavas stormed into the yurt. Four members of the kidnapping gang, only we didn't know that then. We may have only had seconds to look at them before all hell broke loose but that was long enough for their dark costumes and concealed faces to terrify us.

Two of the gang opened fire on Grigor and Dmitri. The other two grabbed Sofia, who was too far away from her bodyguards for them to defend her. At the same time, they were yelling at us. *Stay down. Stay down.*

Some of us spotted the Russian accents. Some of us were too scared to notice such details. Mel showed no fear or shock when the attack started. I suppose that was her police training kicking in.

We lay on our stomachs, ears ringing with the sound of gunfire. We heard a terrible scream from Grigor. The two men who had grabbed Sofia hustled her out of the yurt. The other two backed towards the door but not fast enough. Mel had crawled on her belly to Grigor's dead body, snatched up his gun and fired. One of the kidnappers slumped to the ground. The other one fled.

It was several minutes before we dared to move. When we did, a shocking sight greeted us. Grigor dead. Red stains on his pristine white shirt. Dmitri wounded, blood seeping from his left arm.

'Is nothing,' he said, hauling himself to his feet.

It was only then we realised some of us had been caught in the cross-fire. Joe, groaning, clutching his right calf. Carl screaming, blood all over the front of his white tunic and his mask.

'Stay here,' Dmitri said as he ran out of the yurt.

'Where's Quinn?' someone asked.

That was when we looked around at the candlelit carnage.

That was when we realised she was missing.

78

QUINN

2018

The miracle she had almost lost faith in has happened. As Quinn runs barefoot past the polytunnel and heads for the orchard, she sends silent thanks to the universe. She would never have wished for a miracle involving so much violence, but she knows from experience that Spirit moves in mysterious ways.

Even in her dazed state, she understands Sofia has been kidnapped. Who has taken her? A business rival? An organised crime gang looking to make a fast buck?

Rain pelts down on her. Lightning illuminates the mountains and gives her a glimpse of Dmitri's lean body running through the trees.

It all happened so fast. *Stay down. Stay down.* Her body still in panic mode, Quinn ripped off her blindfold and sat up. Within seconds, Mel pulled her down onto the floor, out of harm's way. She tried to squeeze Mel's hand, but Mel was already on her way to get Grigor's gun.

When Mel shot one of the kidnappers, Quinn realised what was happening. Mel, her lucky charm, wanted her to escape. Was all this part of the plan Mel talked about? None of it made any sense but she knew this was her chance and she had to take it. She crawled to the door and set off into the night. As soon as she entered the olive grove, she saw a kidnapper up ahead and before long she heard someone gaining ground behind her. She ducked behind a gnarled tree and moments later, Dmitri ran past. She followed cautiously. When the clouds briefly parted, allowing the benevolent full moon to light the scene ahead, she saw Dmitri shoot the kidnapper and bring him to the ground. Two more shots and then Dmitri took off in search of Sofia.

What will happen to Sofia? Will they hurt her?

As Quinn runs through the orchard, the ground slippery underfoot, she realises Sofia's fate is nothing to do with her. She tried to help her, but the girl wouldn't listen. Everyone does have a price. How much will these kidnappers ask for Sofia?

Rotting fruit squelches between her toes. She tries to block out the scene in the yurt. Carl's white mask sprayed with blood. Joe writhing in agony. Grigor's lifeless body and the dead kidnapper she had to jump over when fleeing the yurt.

What will she do when she gets to the house? She imagines the kidnappers will make a getaway as soon as possible. How did they get in? They must have scrambled the code for the gate somehow. Or bulldozed through it? She could take the keys to the Hilux and drive away. No. Too risky.

When she reaches the courtyard, she hears gunshots. Instead of entering the house, she creeps along the passageway at the side of it. When she reaches the point where the passageway meets the car park, she crouches in the dark behind a large terracotta pot filled with lavender. Rain bounces off the tarmac and drums on the roof of the black transit van that sits in the middle of the car park, its engine running.

The security lights Sofia had installed flood the courtyard, revealing two bodies lying on the ground. One is a kidnapper, all in black, his head lolling to one side. The other is Sofia.

Is she dead?

Sofia's body moves, a strange jerking motion. Her wrists and ankles are bound, and she groans with the effort of trying to propel herself away from the dead body beside her.

Quinn backs away. Should she turn around and try to reach the neighbouring land like she did the night she ran away?

Another kidnapper leaps out from behind the van, runs across to Sofia and tries to haul her to her feet. Sofia wriggles and squirms in his grasp.

A shot rings out. The kidnapper slumps to the ground, taking Sofia with him.

Quinn's head whips round to see Dmitri emerge from behind one of the Land Rovers.

'Sofia,' he says.

The door on the driver's side of the van opens. A tall, lean man jumps out. Dmitri turns to him and shoots. The man ducks but his primal roar suggests the bodyguard's bullet has hit him. Dmitri aims again, but this time the kidnapper is too fast for him.

After the shot rings out, Dmitri stands still long enough for Quinn to see the bullet hole in the side of his neck.

Then he falls. Straight and hard, like a felled tree.

Sofia screams.

The last man standing rips off his balaclava and tosses it aside. Blood pours from a wound to his head, seeping into his bleached white hair. Quinn has the strangest feeling she's seen him somewhere before.

Ignoring his injury, the kidnapper strides over to Sofia. Rolling his dead comrade out of the way, he grabs hold of her wrists.

Quinn gets to her feet and turns, ready to flee back to the courtyard, but at that moment the moon sneaks from behind a thick bank of cloud and sheds silvery light on the dark passageway behind her. On Zoe, creeping closer, her soaked white tunic plastered to her skin. Her white mask gone.

Instinct makes Quinn back away. In her panic, she stumbles over the large terracotta pot and falls into the pool of shadow in front of it.

A light flicks on above her. A security light she didn't even know was there.

She freezes, spotlit.

The kidnapper's head snaps up. He drops Sofia, raises his gun and walks towards her. 'You,' he says. 'Don't fucking move.'

PART V

2019

79

ZOE

Zoe sits cross-legged at the centre of the new yurt with Quinn's Tibetan singing bowls in front of her. She circles the wand around the largest bowl, releasing a deep, mellow note. She will use the singing bowls to open and close her first Boundaries and Conscious Touch workshop. She can't believe that this afternoon, the third of September 2019, the first ten guests will be arriving at Pure Heart for a week-long Transformational Retreat.

It's nearly 6.30 a.m. In an hour, the community will enjoy an early breakfast together in the courtyard before they complete the last-minute preparations for their guests. Zoe gets up and walks around the space to check everything is in place. The new yurt is twice the size of the old one and the rose-gold light of sunrise pours through the glass that has replaced the canvas walls. A large ceiling fan made of cedar turns serenely overhead, the blades shaped like hearts. Thick church candles sit on the hearth of the new wood burner. A faint scent of rubber hangs in the air from the ten new yoga mats arranged in a circle.

Zoe's vision has come true. There have been many moments over the past year when she's doubted the project would come together, but now it's really happening. She has manifested her desire. All their courses are booked out for the next four months, as are the weeks they blocked off for accommodation-only visitors. Bookings are even starting to come in for the winter months. Zoe knows this uptake isn't just because of her marketing ideas. The old saying is true. No publicity is bad publicity.

Heiress to Belov fortune survives kidnap attempt.

Sofia Belova invests in the community that saved her.

Getting to this point hasn't been easy. In the aftermath of the kidnapping, the police had questions about the timing of it. Wasn't it coincidental that the kidnappers picked the very night the community was distracted with what the media initially called a 'cultish ritual'? Zoe explained numerous times to the police about Pure Heart's traditional rebirthing ceremony. Why else would they have an empty grave on the premises?

Journalists also speculated about the timing of the attack. Had a community member tipped off the kidnappers? Or had they set the whole thing up themselves to claim a hefty ransom?

When no evidence surfaced to prove these suspicions, the police and the media finally embraced the community's story of what happened. They hailed Quinn as heroic for fearlessly chasing the kidnappers as far as the car park, hoping to save Sofia.

Sofia. Her witness statement confirmed the community's version of events.

Sofia lying in the car park, hands and feet bound. Shaking and traumatised but she remembered everything. She saw Dmitri sacrifice his life in an effort to save her. She saw the last of the kidnappers shoot him dead. She saw Mel run out of the house just as the kidnapper shot Quinn in her pure, pure heart. She saw Mel raise Grigor's gun, take aim and put a bullet right between the kidnapper's eyes.

In the end, the Pure Heart members emerged as innocent victims and heroes. When they announced they were opening up as a retreat, spiritual travel websites wrote features about them and they soon had a respectable number of followers on Instagram. They got press coverage of their business venture not only from Cypriot and British newspapers but also the travel section of *Elle* magazine.

The Pure Heart community honours its dead by opening up to the public.

As Zoe gazes at the sprung wooden floor of the new yurt, she is transported back to that stormy, violent August night. She hears rain drumming on the roof of the old yurt. Thunderclaps that merge into gunshots. She sees rich red blood pooling around her feet.

'The past does not exist,' she says. Then she repeats the words, not just to bring her back into the present but also to appreciate the incredible acoustics in this new, untainted space.

She's looking forward to teaching in here. Amidst the hectic renovation schedule and the legal process of setting the community up as a business, she managed to complete the first stage of her training as a Tantric Facilitator and Intimacy Coach at a Tantric Academy in Faro, Portugal. She can't wait to advance her skills further. Finally, she is doing what she's meant to do. She's found her soul's calling, as Quinn would have said.

She looks around the circle of yoga mats and imagines her future students sitting there, faces glowing with joy after one of her sessions. 'Thank you all so much for sharing your beautiful energy with me today. I hope this has been a juicy, sensual and empowering experience for you.'

She's been rehearsing her workshop for weeks now. She already has her costume on. Loose black yoga pants, a cropped black vest and a jade green silk kimono. Her red hair sits on her shoulders in the neat bob she has always wanted and is held back from her face by the Chanel scarf Sofia gave her.

#livingthedream #tantricgoddess #pureheart

* * *

Zoe leaves the yurt and walks through the olive grove, past the Shepherd's Hut sauna that has replaced the sweat lodge. No one at Pure Heart feels a strong desire to conduct sweat lodge ceremonies any more.

On the next terrace, she passes the two new polytunnels where Holly now grows most of their food and, thanks to the updated irrigation system, even has surplus to supply to restaurants in Nicosia. Guests will help out with gardening duties and one day a week Joe and Holly bring refugees from the camp to help them out, an initiative that has brought the community a lot of positive press.

#weareallrefugees #globalcommunitiestogether

The hens are still valued community members. Mel tends to them every day and recently bought more to ensure they have enough eggs for all the guests.

In the orchard, Zoe pauses by her favourite table. Carl will be teaching his writing workshops here this week. *Therapeutic Journal Writing – The Journey Within*. She gazes at the terraces below and the land beyond them, which is now dotted with glamping pods. Through the trees in the distance, she glimpses the new accommodation building on the site of the demolished monastery. 'Eva's Paradise'. A simple two-storey wooden structure on top of a thick concrete foundation. The team of women they've employed from Kakopetria will clean it and deal with the laundry. No need for any of the Pure Heart members to set foot in there if they don't want to.

At least the land and the Pure Heart property belong to them again now. Signed over by Sofia at the conclusion of their business.

* * *

When Zoe reaches the courtyard, she finds Mel removing leaves from the surface of the pool with a skimmer. They decided not to replace the heart-shaped pool. It has a kitsch quality they would all miss and Zoe felt sure it would make a good Instagram shot for their guests.

'Morning,' she says.

Mel looks up and nods. 'All set?'

'Ready as I'll ever be.'

Mel lays the skimmer by the side of the pool and caresses her shorn scalp. 'Good.' She shaved her head not long after Quinn died but Zoe still hasn't got used to it. Mel has spent all summer barefoot too. At least she hasn't changed her burgundy colour scheme for orange. These days she seems to wear the same pair of loose cotton trousers and the same long-sleeved linen shirt.

'It's exciting, isn't it?' Zoe says.

Mel shrugs. 'It'll be different.'

Zoe tries to avoid being alone with Mel whenever possible. The silences between them are full of the unspoken. 'Look,' she says, spotting Joe emerging from the house with two serving dishes of what will no doubt be something delicious. 'Breakfast time.'

80

ZOE

Zoe claims her usual seat at the head of the table. The others always leave it empty for her. They've never officially voted her in as community leader but somehow, she slipped into the role. She's the one who chairs the community meetings. She's the one who has the final say on big decisions involving finance and the renovations.

Aphrodite saunters over to the table and jumps on Zoe's lap. They are rarely apart these days. Aphrodite sleeps at the foot of her bed and follows her everywhere.

From here Zoe has a view of the whole Pure Heart building. All the windows have new shutters and the exterior walls have been repainted a gleaming white. Everyone agreed painting over the Furies was a good idea.

Mel slips into the seat on Zoe's left. Carl arrives with Yasmin, the twenty-eight-year-old yoga teacher from San Diego who arrived last week and will stay with them until the end of the year to teach yoga and be part of the community. A leggy blonde with a vast wardrobe of skimpy yoga tops and tight leggings. No wonder Carl has been so keen to help her settle in.

They both carry trays laden with an assortment of cups and mugs.

'Hey, you guys,' Yasmin says. 'Coffee's up.' This morning's outfit is a silver halter-neck top teamed with red yoga pants. Her long hair is tied in a loose ponytail.

She and Carl place everyone's orders on the table. Zoe takes a grateful sip of her flat white.

Carl sits beside her. 'Hey, beloved.'

Zoe, aware of Yasmin sitting on the other side of her husband, plants a lingering kiss on his lips.

'Okay.' Joe appears with two serving bowls filled with creamy Greek yoghurt. 'That's your lot.'

Greek yoghurt and platters of sliced apricots and figs. Fresh sourdough bread and bowls of feta cheese. Homegrown tomatoes and cucumber.

'Round of applause for the chef,' Zoe says, and everyone joins in when she claps. Joe waves the praise away with one of his chunky hands, although his smile shows how much he appreciates having an audience for his skills.

'Where's Holly?' Mel asks.

'She's on her way.' A tightness in Joe's voice. 'She's just washing her hands.'

'She does that a lot,' Yasmin says. 'I guess she's always got her hands in the dirt, right?'

'Aye.' Joe touches the long, curved scar on his right calf. A memento of the night of the kidnapping.

When Holly appears a few minutes later, Zoe notices her red, chapped hands and the raw, ragged skin around her fingernails. These days Holly is often found at the kitchen sink, desperately trying to remove the soil from under her fingernails with a scrubbing brush. Zoe is pleased to see the warm kiss she gives Joe when she sits beside him. It's taken a while for them to settle into their new reality. To believe they really can stay at Pure Heart forever.

Zoe and the others are already reaching for the food when Yasmin suggests they should bless the meal first.

'It seems wrong not to,' she says. 'Right?'

Zoe is unimpressed by Yasmin's judgemental tone. She remembers Quinn warning her about the younger women who would one day declare her obsolete. 'I was just about to do that.' She takes a deep breath in then out. 'We thank Spirit for this incredible food, and for such beautiful company to enjoy it in.'

'May it nourish our minds, bodies and souls,' adds Yasmin. 'May it—'

'Let's eat.' Mel closes Yasmin down with quiet authority.

'Thanks,' Zoe whispers. It didn't take Mel long to slip into an unofficial policing role. She insists on vetting the people who book to come here in case they aren't the right fit for Pure Heart. She only conducts a basic investigation of each person's social media profiles but, as she says, they must take some precautions. They have no idea who they're letting into their home.

As irritating as Yasmin may prove to be, she survived Mel's scrutiny, and she was the only applicant who offered to come to Cyprus for a face-to-face interview. Her enthusiasm is undeniable and, Zoe has to admit, Yasmin will be a good asset for the Pure Heart brand.

Cutlery clinks and plates and bowls clatter as everyone digs into the delicious spread. Carl announces his agent is going to call him this morning with feedback on the latest edits of his novel.

'That's amazing,' Zoe says. 'Hopefully there won't be much more to do.'

Carl groans theatrically. 'There's always more to do.'

After six months of fevered writing, Carl produced a draft of what he calls his 'great Cyprus novel'. He sent it to Danny Jones, one of London's top literary agents who signed him within a week of receiving the manuscript. Since then, he and Danny have been working on rewrites ahead of sending the manuscript out to publishers. Danny seems certain the novel will sell, possibly even at auction.

Carl doesn't sleep much these days, but he assures Zoe it's because his head is so full of ideas for the book.

'It's super cool you're a writer,' Yasmin says. 'I so have to do one of your workshops while I'm here.'

Zoe smiles. She's sure Carl will be giving Yasmin more than just writing tips before her time here is up. Not that Zoe minds. Ever since she and Carl agreed to an open relationship, they've never been happier, and their sex life has never been better. When she looks at him now, she can see the talented, roguish man she first fell in love with. She has her fun too. On a recent training course in Faro, she met Davi, a beautiful Brazilian man in his twenties. They took part in an Authentic Touch and Conscious Boundaries workshop together, and she spent the rest of her time in Faro authentically and consciously fucking him.

'I visited Quinn's memorial stone yesterday,' Yasmin says. 'Such a beautiful spot for it under the cedar tree. That little clearing is so peaceful.'

Our beloved founder
With us always

Aphrodite stirs in Zoe's lap. Pricks up her ears. The chatter at the table fades away.

'Sorry,' Yasmin says. 'I didn't mean to—'

'It's nice you went,' Holly says. 'We want people to pay their respects to her.'

'Pure Heart was her idea,' says Carl.

Joe nods. 'None of us would be here without her.'

'It's so amazing what she did,' Yasmin says. 'Going after the kidnappers like that. You guys must be super proud of her?'

'We are.' Zoe can tell Yasmin is keen to gossip about that night, even though she's only hinted at the subject since she arrived.

'So, the police never officially charged anyone with the kidnapping attempt?' Yasmin asks. 'It was some Russian guy, right?'

'Roman Timchenko,' Mel says. 'Semi-retired Russian gangster.'

'I read there was a feud between him and Sofia's grandfather back in Russia,' Yasmin says. 'Like when they were super young.'

'That's the rumour,' Zoe says.

'Sofia was lucky you were there to save her,' Yasmin says to Mel. 'I mean, my God, who knows what could have happened.'

Mel tears a chunk of bread in two. 'I was in the right place at the right time.'

'And you were brave,' Holly says.

'Fearless,' adds Joe.

'I bet.' Yasmin spears a succulent fig with her fork. 'Did you even have time to be scared?' she asks Mel.

'It's not a night I like to remember,' Mel says.

Yasmin nods. 'Sure. God. I get it.'

She doesn't get it at all, thinks Zoe. Yasmin, like everyone apart from the remaining Pure Heart members and Sofia, only knows the official version of that night's events.

'Yasmin, try this outstanding feta,' Carl says. 'It's from a farm a few miles from here.'

As talk around the table turns to food and the menus for the week's retreat, Zoe lets herself drift back to the night of the kidnapping. To the yurt filled with screams and dead and injured bodies. Carl, not hurt at all, just sprayed with blood from Joe's wound. Zoe saw Quinn escape and watched Dmitri set off after the kidnappers. She too seized her moment to run into the driving rain, staying back long enough not to encounter the fighting ahead. In the olive grove she found the dead body of one of the kidnappers and, without thinking, took the gun from the holster strapped around his chest.

When she saw Quinn take the passageway at the side of the house, she followed her, unsure what she was going to do but certain Quinn must not get away.

She had her chance. Quinn at the far end of the passageway. Gunfire blasting away in the car park. Zoe raised her gun, but as soon as she aimed, she knew she couldn't do it. She didn't have it in her.

As she lowered the weapon, lightning split the sky overhead and there was Quinn, staring at her. Then darkness again, Quinn a retreating shadow. Another gunshot. Zoe crept closer and suddenly Quinn was illuminated in a pool of light. A man's voice called out.

Still in darkness, pressed against the wall of the passageway, Zoe had a clear view of the tall, blond man, pointing a gun at Quinn.

When the next gunshot came, she expected Quinn to fall, but instead the tall man collapsed to the ground. Zoe crept closer, and that's when she saw Mel approach the dead man's body.

'Mel,' Quinn said. 'I knew it. I knew you'd come.'

Mel crouched by the kidnapper's body and picked up his gun. 'It's okay,' Mel said. 'It's nearly over.' Kneeling, she held out a hand.

Quinn rushed over to take it but before she could get close, Mel lifted the kidnapper's gun and fired. One clean shot. She wiped her prints from the gun before placing it next to the kidnapper's body.

That's when Zoe emerged from the darkness.

Mel froze. They stared at one another, ignoring the bodies lying around them.

'I had to do it,' Mel said. 'Going home is not an option for me.'

'We're all in this together,' Zoe said.

'My past is too complicated. Too dangerous.'

'I understand.'

'I thought she loved me for who I really am.' Mel's eyes broke away from Zoe's and settled on Quinn's lifeless body. 'I'm a good person.'

'I know that,' Zoe said. 'We all do.'

Mel looked at her again and nodded. Without saying another word, the two of them hurried over to Sofia and began to untie her.

'Zoe?' Yasmin's sunny, grating accent drags Zoe out of the past and back to the breakfast table.

'What?' Zoe says.

'Is Sofia coming back this week to see the place?' Yasmin asks.

'She'd love to but she's really busy,' Zoe says. Sofia has made it clear she will never return to Pure Heart. Her business here is done. She got what she came for and she has honoured her side of the transaction.

'Aye, she's full on with the family business,' says Joe.

'And it might bring back difficult memories,' Holly adds.

'My God, right,' Yasmin says. 'So triggering.'

Carl's mouth twists into a wry smile. 'Unfortunate choice of word.'

'Sofia's just happy she could give something back to the community,' Joe says. 'She had a lot of happy times here with her mum.'

How easily they all say their lines, Zoe thinks. A year of talking to police and journalists and prospective customers has made lying feel like the truth. Most of the time.

The kidnapper would have killed Quinn anyway. She'd seen his face;

she could have identified him. That's what Mel said at the first community meeting they had after that night. Zoe and the others agreed with her. They also assured Mel that even though she'd pulled the trigger, they were all equally responsible for Quinn's death. It was a secret they would share as a community forever. A secret that showed their commitment to each other and to Pure Heart's future.

'At least the Timchenko guy's dead,' Yasmin says. 'Sofia must be super relieved about that.'

'Yes,' Mel says. 'I suppose she is.'

After Zoe and Mel untied Sofia in the car park, she staggered over to the body of Timchenko's bodyguard.

'You,' she said. She instructed Zoe and Mel not to call the police. Not yet. They helped her to her room where she made a call to her godfather, Egor. A long, frantic conversation in Russian ensued. Timchenko's name was mentioned more than once.

'Kinda weird how Timchenko died,' Yasmin says. 'A hit and run.'

Before the police and paramedics arrived at Pure Heart that night, Sofia, Zoe and Mel coached the others about what they needed to say and when. Sofia asked them not to mention recognising Timchenko's bodyguard. By the time the police identified him and made the connection to Timchenko, it was too late. Timchenko, who made sure he was out of Cyprus when the kidnapping occurred, was on a city break in Athens with his wife. While there, he was killed in a hit-and-run accident. Sofia never mentioned any involvement in his demise, and Zoe never dared to ask her about it.

Mel sips her mountain tea. 'Guys like him have a lot of enemies.'

'Or maybe it was just an accident,' Carl says. 'Athens is a busy city.'

'Maybe,' Yasmin says.

'You never get to the truth when people like him are involved,' Mel says.

After Timchenko's death, Sofia and everyone at Pure Heart told the police they remembered him introducing himself to them at Dionysus by the Sea. That was when he discovered Sofia was on the island, the police concluded. That's when he began to put his kidnapping plan together.

'That restaurant where you guys met Timchenko looks amazing,' Yasmin says. 'We should totally go there sometime.'

'I'll never go back there again,' says Holly.

Zoe was nervous about mentioning the restaurant to the police. What if the staff there told the police about the scene with Andreas? She needn't have worried. Sofia's people must have tied up that loose end. The restaurant staff confirmed Timchenko had been at the restaurant the same night as Sofia, but they said it had been a quiet evening. Nothing at all unusual about it.

'It's all over now,' Mel says. 'It's in the past.'

Mel was especially relieved when they found out Timchenko was dead. Zoe assumed she was worried about some kind of reprisal for killing one of the gangster's men.

'Well, I think you guys are amazing,' Yasmin says, 'and I think this place will be a huge success.'

'Thanks.' Zoe thinks so too. Only yesterday she found a dead bird in the orchard – a symbol of rebirth and regeneration. An omen of things to come. Even with Sofia's money they still need this place to succeed financially. If they do well this year and next that would give them a solid start. Zoe can't see any reason why that won't happen. Visitors are not going to stop coming to Cyprus any time soon.

'I need a photo of you guys on your big day.' Yasmin pulls out her phone from a pocket in her yoga pants and pushes back her chair. 'Let me get set up.'

As Yasmin strolls into the courtyard, Zoe picks up Aphrodite and holds her close to her chest. Mel leans towards her. Holly, Joe and Carl get up and arrange themselves around her chair. This picture will no doubt end up on Yasmin's Instagram page.

#thepureheartcrew

'Okay,' Yasmin says, 'nearly ready.'

Zoe watches one of the small brown sparrows take off from the table with a beak full of bread. It flies towards the house. For a moment, the light is such that Zoe can see the faded outline of the Furies beneath the clean white paint. Her memory brings them to life again. Their twisted snake hair. Their righteous anger. The fury that drives them to seek out every wrongdoer and inflict the appropriate punishment on them. She shivers.

'Okay, you guys,' Yasmin says. 'Let's do this.'

Zoe turns her face to the camera and smiles.

81

HOLLY

Fight, flight or freeze. Some days I experience all three of them. I wake with an urge to run away from Pure Heart, but then I remember what was sacrificed to keep this place going and I know I can never leave. Sometimes, this realisation makes me lash out at Joe and we fight, but he knows I don't mean what I say and we always make up. Later in the day, when I'm in the garden digging, I freeze, transfixed by the soil. Thinking of Blake's bones and Quinn's ashes.

On days like these, I recall the official version of our story and choose to believe it. When all of us believe it makes life so much easier. One group mind. One version of the truth.

Groupthink is a powerful thing. Studying history taught me that. In certain circumstances, ordinary people can do terrible things and afterwards, despite what they've done, they find a way to keep on living.

Here at Pure Heart, we tell ourselves something beautiful has risen from the ruins of tragedy. Together, we've created a place Quinn would be proud of. A place where we can share all the many gifts she gave us with others.

At Pure Heart, you can drop the mask you wear in everyday life. The mask you show to the world because you believe you won't be accepted or loved without it. Here you can be your most authentic self. Here, no one will judge you.

Here, with us, you will finally see how unique and special you really are.

82

Insight Investigators: Background Report

Conclusion: This concludes the report on the current and recently deceased members of the Pure Heart community. The separate report you requested on Sofia Belova is almost complete and will be with you shortly.

When we spoke on the phone, you said one of your journalists has infiltrated the community and will be investigating from the inside. Lucky, her being a yoga teacher as well as a journalist but who doesn't teach yoga these days!

Who knows if there's more to discover about the events at Pure Heart, but, like you, I can't help feeling the community members are hiding something. Call me cynical, but they're just a bit too smug. I can see why, from a true-crime angle, you want to do some digging. This is a story with all the right elements.

The kidnapping itself was genuine, but I have uncovered some interesting facts that make me think there could be more to it. I had another chat with DS James Kerrigan, the colleague of Mel's who reported her, and asked if he could find any connection between Mel and Timchenko. Turns out she arrested Timchenko twice during an investigation into one of the Russian crime syndicates. Timchenko was a foot soldier with no real power, but he had a chip on his shoulder about his failure to rise through the ranks and make serious money, and Mel hoped she might be able to turn him into an informant. She never succeeded and he was released each time without charge. However, she would certainly have recognised him that night in the Dionysus by the Sea restaurant. Coincidence maybe, but I think it's interesting. Could Mel have helped Timchenko set up the kidnapping and, if so, why?

What's more, Christy, my woman on the ground in Cyprus, got something juicy out of one of the restaurant's former waiters. A guy called Pavlos. Apparently, Andreas Constantinou, the handyman who died at Pure Heart, was arguing with members of the community that night and waving a broken bottle about. He tried to talk to Pavlos at one point. He was slurring his words, but Pavlos was sure he was shouting something about murder. In the end, one of Sofia's bodyguards had to restrain Andreas.

I also investigated the community's financial background. When in doubt, start with the money. Charles' money was handled by Evimería Assets, a wealth-management firm in Limassol. His financial adviser, Michalis Elia, retired last year at fifty and I don't think his current lifestyle – big villa, expensive cars, a yacht – is funded solely by a financial adviser's pension. Christy made inroads with a guy called Deniz, who still works at Evimería Assets. Luckily for us, he's not a Michalis fan. Christy chatted him up in a hotel bar, and it was easy to steer him onto the topic of Pure Heart and the kidnapping. Everyone's heard about it, and Deniz was happy to impress Christy by sharing some inside knowledge. According to him, Michalis said more than once that managing Charles' money was a joke as the old guy was almost broke. Whether that ties in with any of this, I don't know, but it's worth checking out.

And why did Sofia Belova want to go back to Pure Heart anyway? Her mother killed herself there. That must have messed with Sofia's head. That and growing up in such a weird place.

If you decide to expand the scope of your story to include the history of the Belov family and their business dealings, I suspect you'll find yourself up against it. I've been in this game a long time, and I couldn't make any headway.

Anyway, despite what the Pure Heart community thinks, the past *does* exist, and I hope you find a great story there. Remember, all you have to do is believe in miracles!

ACKNOWLEDGEMENTS

As always, huge thanks to my brilliant agent, Charlie Brotherstone, for his unwavering support and for making good things happen for me. Once again, the talented and dedicated team at Boldwood have been a joy to work with and I'm grateful for everything they do to connect my stories to readers. To my editor, Rachel Faulkner-Willcocks, sincere thanks for whipping *The Last Resort* into shape and for sage advice when I was lost in the woods.

To the wonderful crew at the Novelry, gratitude is once again due. I used the Novelry courses to guide me when I was writing this novel and the input from author and writing coach Amanda Reynolds was invaluable.

Cyprus is a stunning country with a fascinating and complex history, and I wish I could have provided more than just a glimpse of it. I'm indebted to the Cypriot research contacts who helped me with this story. Thanks to Christy Melinioti, creator of the To Hani Coliving Space near Limassol. When I visited Cyprus, Christy generously invited me to view her beautiful property, which gave me huge inspiration for aspects of my fictional setting. She also shared insights into the island's past and present and gave me plenty of plot ideas. As well as all this, she gave me some useful research contacts and kindly let me hassle her with various questions as I wrote the novel. I'd also like to thank Charalambia Constantinou. Charalambia, you've been amazing; thanks for all your detailed answers to my often ridiculous questions! Huge thanks must also go to Anastasia Schini Kakkoura for essential legal advice.

I'm blown away by the generosity and knowledge of everyone who helped me with research for *The Last Resort*. I couldn't have done it without their input. Stuart Gibbon for police procedural research and expert advice. Stewart Hay for police anecdotes and gambling tales! John Nichol for insights into the Metropolitan police. Dr Mark Flynn once again provided his psychological expertise. Thanks, Mark, for this and also for letting me steal one of the many witty phrases that fill your emails. Thanks to Dr Olga Oikonomidou for sharing her contacts, bringing me real mountain tea from her home in Greece and for paying me the immense compliment of finding time to read my books when she's not saving lives! Heartfelt thanks also to Dr Peter Copp, Valerie Muller and Karen Beveridge for steering me into calmer waters when necessary!

I want to thank my dad for his love and support and my sister Susan for the chats and the cheerleading when I needed it most. Liz, my oldest friend, thank you for being there for me in so many ways.

Susie and Mary... you are everything. Thank you both for the journey so far. Onwards!

The Last Resort was inspired by a play called The Visit by the German writer, Friedrich Dürrenmatt. Decades ago, when I was studying for my German A-Level, The Visit was one of the set texts. Written in 1956, this tragicomic morality tale has never ceased to be relevant. I loved it when I first read it and it has remained one of my favourite plays of all time. So, I reserve my final thanks for Friedrich Dürrenmatt. For his genius and for giving me the seed of the story that became this novel.

ABOUT THE AUTHOR

T.J. Emerson's debut psychological thriller was published by Legend Press and received brilliant reviews. Her short stories and features have been widely published in anthologies and magazines, and she works as a literary consultant and writing tutor. She lives in Scotland.

Sign up to T J Emerson's mailing list for news, competitions and updates on future books.

Visit T.J. Emerson's Website: www.traceyemerson.com

Follow T.J. Emerson on social media here:

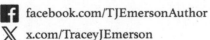

facebook.com/TJEmersonAuthor
x.com/TraceyJEmerson
instagram.com/tjemersonwrites

ALSO BY T. J. EMERSON

THE
Murder
LIST

**THE MURDER LIST IS A NEWSLETTER
DEDICATED TO SPINE-CHILLING FICTION
AND GRIPPING PAGE-TURNERS!**

**SIGN UP TO MAKE SURE YOU'RE ON OUR
HIT LIST FOR EXCLUSIVE DEALS, AUTHOR
CONTENT, AND COMPETITIONS.**

SIGN UP TO OUR
NEWSLETTER

BIT.LY/THEMURDERLISTNEWS

Boldwood

Boldwood Books is an award-winning fiction publishing company seeking out the best stories from around the world.

Find out more at www.boldwoodbooks.com

Join our reader community for brilliant books, competitions and offers!

**Follow us
@BoldwoodBooks
@TheBoldBookClub**

Sign up to our weekly deals newsletter

https://bit.ly/BoldwoodBNewsletter

Milton Keynes UK
Ingram Content Group UK Ltd.
UKHW042028070324
438958UK00002B/7

9 781805 490272